SEXUAL
Healing

Dear Reader:

What happens when two of the hottest and bestselling erotica authors team up? You get heat and more heat. The prolific Allison Hobbs and Cairo join forces with *Sexual Healing* for a fast-paced sexual journey of two lovers who by default end up on an unexpected romantic quest.

Diva Arabia Knight, who has a penchant for married men and uninhibited pleasure, lives as an advertising entrepreneur by day and a freak by night as she peruses sex clubs. Cruze Fontaine, a former street thug turned suit-and-tie, carries dark secrets while maintaining his bachelor lifestyle with a wild desire for variety. The two connect and find that it's more than passion between them as they fight the urges for a genuine relationship—something that has escaped them for years. Finally meeting their match, they become vulnerable and open each other's eyes to limitless possibilities. They both take pride in their self-control but temptation leads to more than physical yearnings, a fact that is frightening but satisfying like they've never known.

Get ready for the sizzling ride that's sure to be one of summer's steamiest reads.

As always, thanks for supporting myself and the Strebor Books family. We strive to bring you the most cutting-edge, out-of-the-box material on the market. You can find me on Facebook @AuthorZane or you can email me at zane@eroticanoir.com.

Blessings,

Zane

Publisher
Strebor Books
www.simonandschuster.com

ZANE PRESENTS

SEXUAL
Healing

ALLISON HOBBS
AND CAIRO

SBI

STREBOR BOOKS

NEW YORK LONDON TORONTO SYDNEY

Strebor Books
P.O. Box 6505
Largo, MD 20792
www.simonandschuster.com

ISBN 978-1-59309-672-4
ISBN 978-1-5011-1919-4 (ebook)
LCCN 2015957701

First Strebor Books trade paperback edition August 2016

Cover design: www.mariondesigns.com
Cover photograph: © Keith Saunders/Keith Saunders Photos

10 9 8 7 6 5 4 3 2 1

Manufactured in the United States of America

For information regarding special discounts for bulk purchases, please contact Simon & Schuster Special Sales at 1-866-506-1949

The Simon & Schuster Speakers Bureau can bring authors to your live event. For more information or to book an event, contact the Simon & Schuster Speakers Bureau at 1-866-248-3049 or visit our website at www.simonspeakers.com.

"There is a force in the universe that can join together
two vulnerable souls.
And, in love, two hearts can find healing. And beat as one…"
—ALLISON & CAIRO

One

Milk chocolate perfection, that's what she was…

Wet need stretched through her pussy in a slow-flowing river of heat as she stepped out of her Mercedes S600, handing her key fob to the tall, lanky, good-looking valet in his early twenties. Too young. But still worthy of a sly glance. Sure, she'd fuck him in a heartbeat had she'd been another type of woman, one smutty and unscrupulous. But he was just a horny boy in her eyes, one clearly mesmerized by her beauty. However, he wasn't worthy to sniff her panties or lick around her cunt, so…no thank you.

She needed someone old enough to know what to do with her and her never-ending curves. She needed a man who knew how to ride her body, and fuck her down into a mattress. She suspected the young valet would be a clumsy-fuck, at best.

Still, it was flattering. His ogling, that was.

A slight smile edged its way over her MAC-glossed lips as she caught his gaze sweeping over her body. Or maybe it was the back-less dress with the plunging neckline—red, silky…and very clingy—that had him seemingly flustered, and stuttering out a *hello*. What-ever the case, she found him adorable.

She slipped him a ten-dollar bill, then tucked her purse beneath her arm, and strutted toward her destination, her hips swaying, her ass bouncing, every which way. She felt her adrenaline surging through her veins as her strappy heels clicked over asphalt, then concrete, moving toward brick and mortar.

Sublime pussy.

That's what Arabia Knight knew she had.

Breath-taking.

Heart-stopping.

Toe-curling.

Sweet, sticky slices of wet heaven that melted over a hard cock like warm honey. There was no mistaking it. Her juicy cunt was the crème de la crème. And she had a scandalously long list of lovers *and* past stalkers to prove it.

And she had a few tricks between her smooth thighs that would drop a man to his knees, and have him eating out of the palms of her paraffin-soft hands. And she knew, the minute she slid down on his shaft, rolled her hips, and clamped her walls around his dick that he'd fall in love.

They always did.

Any time one of her many lovers cried out her name or sputtered out inaudible chants, she became keenly more aware, more empowered, more inspired. Each time her pussy spasmed, and she heard them call out to the heavens or whisper sweet nothings in her ear, she knew. Her pussy was some exclusive, platinum-plus-American-Express-Black-Card-type shit. She had to laugh to herself. Men never wanted to leave home without it. It was, what she liked to call it, that snap-trap pussy. Wet. Juicy. Steamy. Dick-clutching. Skin-sucking tight.

And, tonight, she was looking to snap her trap around something good, something dangerously thick. She was a woman on a mission, a woman on the prowl. She'd worn the dress and sexy heels for one purpose and one purpose only: to seduce.

Then get *fucked*.

She always wore red when she wanted to be wild, when she wanted to fulfill her wanton urges. Tonight was the night. She was a huntress, on the hunt. She knew the drill. All she had to do was use her womanly wiles to lure her prey to her. Then strike.

Luckily, she wasn't on a hunting expedition for another lover this evening, just a one-night stand. So there'd be no need for formalities. Not at this establishment. Just hot, naughty—*hopefully* dirty—sex.

Mmm, *yes*.

This was a sex club. Her secret rendezvous place to lose herself to temptation.

Sure she was *engaged* to…*three* different men.

And?

Monogamy had nothing to do with fulfilling her dark desires. She was a woman with insatiable needs. Needs her three lovers oftentimes fell short on fulfilling, which left her cunt weeping, aching, to be skewered by a long thick—

Her cell rang inside her crystal-studded purse, slicing into her salacious reverie.

She ignored it.

It rang again. Then buzzed that a message had been left.

She rolled her long-lashed eyes. Whoever it was could wait. Talking on the phone was the last thing on her mind. She was on a quest for some good hard, anonymous dick. And nothing was going to distract her from the quest at hand.

Her gaze honed in on the thick mahogany doors that led to the club's entrance and her clit pulsed. Fierce passion and seduction awaited her, and she couldn't wait to get bathed in its heat. The mere thought of being awash in pleasure excited her. She felt the fire roiling along the walls of her cunt, and her breath almost caught in her throat.

Her ten-thousand-dollar-a-year membership fee afforded her access to her share of freaky fun. Shamefully, it'd been months since she'd frequented the exclusive For Adults Only club. But, tonight, she'd make up for lost time. She wouldn't squander any opportunities. She'd be the naughtiest of them all.

Filthy and wild and indiscriminate.

Her nipples tightened as she stepped inside the marbled foyer and was greeted by a tall, chiseled, bare-chested hunk wearing a silken mask. She eyed the prominent bulge beneath his loincloth, imagining her hand reaching out and languorously stretching over its girth, then caressing it. She could tell, fully erect, it would be a deliciously long, thick dick.

She imagined herself holding his dick in her hand like an ice cream cone, licking at the tip, flicking her tongue over the pre-cum she imagined already gathering there, before swirling her hot tongue around the whole engorged head. *Damn him.* She felt herself on the verge of dropping to her knees and begging him for his cock.

As if reading her scandalous mind, he smiled, his gaze flickering over her swelling breasts. "Welcome, beautiful," he said in a deep timbre, his voice melting over her body like hot fudge, thick and rich. A fresh burst of heat shot through her cunt. She bit her lip. Then slid her hand into her clutch and handed him her gold membership card. Her gaze drifted from his eyes to his mouth, imagining her clitoris and nipples being sucked into its wet heat. She let her eyes linger on those sweet lips longer than she probably should have feeling her clit vibrate with want.

He caught a glimpse of her cleavage, again, before reaching for her card. Then he glanced at it, and she wondered what he did for a living. Perhaps he was a suit-and-tie guy by day, or…maybe a professional athlete. She quickly dismissed the thought. How he made his money really didn't matter. Whether or not he was a good fuck did.

Boldly, she allowed her gaze to roam his muscled body. She felt her body heating and wondered if her nipples could be seen through her dress. His smoldering brown eyes met hers as he handed back her card, and she felt her pussy rapidly warming to the possibility of fucking him.

He smiled again. "Enjoy."

"Oh, trust me," she said saucily, reaching out to touch him. "I plan—"

Before she could get the rest of her words out, or her hand on his cock, he surprisingly grabbed her by the arm and quickly spun her around, the heat of his muscular body pressed into hers, then— oh, God, yes…*mmm*—his growing erection nestled against her ass as he snaked his strong hands up under her arms and cupped her breasts. The sudden act caused her to drop her clutch, her membership card, and moan. She leaned her head back, surrendering to his touch, suddenly oblivious to the onlookers.

He moved against her, sliding the length of his now-hard dick up the crack of her ass. "I should fuck the shit out of you," he rasped near her ear, before biting into her neck.

God, yes.

It was a threat, but felt so, so promising.

She heard herself panting as his arm came around her torso, anchoring her to him as he cupped her right breast. She swallowed back a moan as he ran his right hand down over her hip, while his left hand kneaded her right breast, and then…*mmm, yes, yes, yes…* his right hand eased under her dress, up her bare thigh.

She purred low in the back of her throat, losing herself to his sizzling touch. She rocked into him now, grinding her ass deep into his crotch. She felt herself on the verge of an orgasm, especially when his thick fingers slipped into her panties, from the back, beneath her ass, and into her wet, sticky folds.

"Unh…mmmm, *yesss,*" she breathed—and then he used his other hand and flicked his thumb over her turgid nipple, peaked with lust, then pinched it over the flimsy fabric, making her whimper. And then—yes God—he slid two fingers up inside her as he teased her nipple. And, as he began thrusting those long, thick, dick-like fingers up in her, he nibbled on her neck, and she cried out.

He rasped near her ear. "You like me finger-fucking this wet pussy?"

"Mmm, yes. Uh, fuck me…"

"You want me to ram this dick in your ass, don't you?" Her pussy clenched around his fingers. She hadn't had anal in several years—well, not the kind that involved a man's dick fucking into it—but she was open to the possibility of having her ass fucked to shreds. "Oh, fuck yes!" she cried out, breathless now.

"You have a hot little cunt, baby." He rocked into her, then pinched her nipple again, while his fingers curled into her heat, stroking over her sweet spot.

Mmm, God—his dick felt so big and long and hard up against her ass. She wanted desperately to get on her knees and suck him into her mouth, taste him, savor him, swallow him whole.

Then take him deep in her ass.

But that wasn't his plan.

Teasing her, taunting her, toying with her desires, preparing her for what awaited her on the other side of the club's walls…those were his intentions.

Her breath came heavy, hot. She was on the edge of an orgasm. Within a few heated seconds, she would come. Oh, God—*yes!* She moved her pussy in rhythm to his fingers, greedily clutching them, wetting them; drenching them in her cunt's hungry need.

"Yes, yes, yes…"—she licked her lips—"*mmm*…fuck the back of my pussy," she breathed, rocking her hips with the sudden ache to have him inside her, his dick wedged deep between her folds.

She dug her nails into his arm in response to the sensations sizzling through her core. She didn't know him. Didn't know where his fingers had been—probably buried in tons of wet, horny cunts—before her. But that didn't matter. All that mattered was… right here, right now—his fingers plunging and probing her pussy, his cock raking over her ass.

White-hot bliss rolled through her body in heated waves, spilling out of her body, and splashing out onto his hand. "Ooh…ooh, ooh, ooh, ooh…oh God! Oh, fuck. Yes, yes, yes…!"

When the pleasure ebbed and she was finally able to stop moving, he pulled his fingers from her body, leaving her empty and wanting. This was a start. A very good one, but she needed something more. This was merely an appetizer that hadn't quite whet her appetite. It left her voraciously starved for more.

Catching her breath, she gathered her things from the floor, then turned to him as he slid his wet fingers into his mouth. He sucked them in deep, tasting her, then pulled out and licked his lips. "You're ready, baby," he told her with a wicked grin.

And ready she was.

"You owe me some of that big dick," she warned teasingly. "I'll be back for a taste."

He smiled at her. "It'll be here, baby. Waiting."

Too drunk with yearning, there was no need to pull her dress down over her hips. It would be off in a matter of moments. She simply glanced up as she stuffed her gold card back into her purse, then proceeded toward the threshold to decadence. Her cunt clenched, and she grew wetter, hotter, as she read the sign overhead.

PLEASURE AWAITS YOU…ENTER IF YOU DARE…

Two

The central air was on full blast inside the apartment, yet the place felt muggy and stifling. Sitting at his old friend, Moody's bedside, it was difficult for Cruze Fontaine to keep up his end of the conversation with his friend coughing and wheezing and struggling to choke out every word.

It had been thirteen months since Moody had narrowly escaped death. Caught in a hail of bullets, several had ripped through his chest and pierced both his lungs. Since then, his respiratory health had rapidly declined. And so had his finances.

Moody's wife, Ramona, interrupted the visit, telling Cruze it was time for her husband's oxygen therapy. Eager to escape the desolate environment, Cruze quickly rose to his feet. "It's time for me to bounce, man. We'll kick it again, soon."

"When?" Moody rasped.

"Soon, man. Real soon."

Cruze hadn't seen Moody since the fateful day of the shootout, and it wasn't likely he'd see him anytime soon. It wasn't easy witnessing his once-energetic friend lingering at death's door. But Cruze was grateful that Ramona had stuck it out with his boy. But it was obvious that being an around-the-clock caregiver had taken a toll on her. Ramona used to be one of the hottest and best-dressed chicks in Brownsville; now she looked haggard and drained.

Cruze cut an eye at her right arm, which was riddled with bullet wounds that zigzagged from her wrist to her forearm. Her pants covered the rest of the scars that trailed down her right thigh and leg. The bullet that shattered her ankle had left her walking with a limp.

Moody and Ramona had suffered tremendous losses in a single tragic day.

Within the narrow confines of the cluttered sickroom, Cruze squeezed past a set of oxygen tanks, a wheelchair, a portable commode, and other depressing medical equipment. When he reached the front door, he gave Ramona two bundles of cash, more than enough to cover household expenses for a while and afford them a few luxuries, as well.

"This should hold you and Moody for a while. Make sure you buy yourself something nice."

Ramona's eyes darted downward as if it embarrassed her to have to accept money from the man who used to be her husband's second-in-command. "Thanks, Cruze. This really helps."

Cruze nodded. "Take care of yourself, Ramona."

"You do the same," she replied.

Outside the building, Cruze threw up his hoodie and lowered his head. Security cameras were everywhere nowadays and he didn't want to end up on any of them—not in this neighborhood where he was very much a wanted man.

He took a deep breath, but the air he inhaled seemed as stale and oppressive as it had been inside Moody's apartment. It was the location—a section of Brooklyn where crime and concentrated poverty seemed to have suctioned out the oxygen. Crisp, cool air didn't travel to the 'hood. And like the flow of fresh air, Cruze also avoided his old stomping grounds.

Overly cautious, he'd parked near a deserted factory, about a quarter-mile from Moody's place. Walking swiftly along the uneven pavement, he appeared to look neither left nor right, yet his watchful eyes were carefully taking in his surroundings. On high alert, Cruze became keenly aware of the sound of footsteps that suddenly crept behind him.

He cursed at his stupidity for thinking he could slip in and out of Moody's crib without detection. No matter how much time had elapsed, his enemies were ever vigil. Hell, for all he knew, Ramona could have tipped someone off. In the world of crime, no one could be trusted.

Adrenaline flooded his system. He could take off running and risk a bullet in his ass or turn around and try to reason with the muthafucka who wouldn't let go of an old grudge. But Cruze knew better than to believe he could negotiate with a killer.

Surrendering to his fate, he slowed his stride, and he wasn't surprised when the footfalls behind him sped up. His luck had finally run out. Surprisingly, instead of fear, he felt an odd sense of relief. And acceptance.

The looming presence was directly behind him and Cruze braced himself for a bullet to the back of his dome.

"You know what it is, man, gimme your watch," the voice behind him demanded. "Give it up, and…and don't try nothing, either. Oh, yeah, reach in your pockets and gimme your money…and your phone, too."

I'll be goddamned. This isn't a hit…it's a fucking stick-up! Cruze almost laughed, but he was too infuriated to crack a smile. Quick as lightning, he pulled his piece and wheeled around and came face-to-face with a big bruiser who was almost as tall as Cruze, and as wide as he was tall. Chubby cheeks and a youthful face revealed an overgrown kid, seventeen or eighteen. Maybe younger.

The chubby-faced teen gawked at the gleaming Glock that was aimed in his face, and then his gaze drifted downward at the metal pipe in his own hand.

Cruze cocked the gun. With a simmering rage, he fixed hard eyes on the juvenile. "What's wrong with you, young nigga? You ain't got nothing better to do than try to rob hardworking muthafuckas, huh, fuck boy?"

In Cruze's darkened eyes, the would-be robber glimpsed a chained beast that was so angry and frightening; the youth couldn't help taking several steps backward. "Yo, man, I was only fuckin' with you. I ain't tryna rob nobody." Proving his harmlessness, he smiled dumbly and unfurled his fingers. The metal pipe, as ineffective as a water pistol, rolled out of his hand and clattered to the pavement.

In swift motions, Cruze grabbed the pipe and struck the teen in the kneecaps. The oversized boy pitched forward with a loud groan and then stumbled backward, hitting the ground with the force of a massive tree.

Cruze leapt on him. He pistol-whipped the boy unmercifully before pressing the gun against his forehead. "Your punk-ass is a few seconds from dying…was it worth it, stick-up boy?"

"Nah, it wasn't worth it. Don't kill me, Mister. Please. I'm sorry," the youth cried through bloodied lips.

Cruze fingered the trigger and then caught himself. *What the fuck am I doing? This fool ain't nothing but a dumb-ass kid.* He stood up, cursing as he returned the Glock to his waistband.

Looking down, Cruze noticed blood on his Air Yeezys. With renewed anger, he kicked the boy in the ribs. "That's for bleeding on my shit, bitch-ass fuck-boy!"

Leaving the bungling thief wallowing on the ground in pain, Cruze took off through the park. When he reached his nondescript rental car, he sparked a blunt before pulling off. As he merged into traffic, the calm that came over him quieted his pounding heart. But the violent altercation with the young punk had awakened something that weed couldn't appease. Feeling strangely energized by the murder he'd almost committed, Cruze made a sudden U-turn.

It was crucial that he got out of New York and returned to Philly, but the stirring in his groin was relentless, demanding that he make a pit stop, first. There was a long list of candidates to choose from, but Laila Stanley was the closest in proximity.

Head down to obscure his face, Cruze trotted up the steps of the Brooklyn brownstone and rang the bell. The door cracked open, and he flashed a smile that displayed the set of deep dimples that were sure to melt away any resentment Laila might have harbored against him.

"Hey, baby," he said in a low, sensual tone.

Eyes wide, Laila gasped, covering her mouth as if she'd seen a ghost. "Cruze? Oh, my God, Cruze!"

"Are you gonna invite me in?" he asked, looking over his shoulder.

Nodding, she moved aside, allowing him entry. Then, after closing and locking the door, she fell into his arms and buried her head in his chest. Clinging to him, she murmured his name over and over. Her slender body trembled and when she lifted her head, Cruze saw the tears that streaked her face.

"Aw, don't cry, Laila. Shh," he whispered, stroking her hair. "Come on, baby, don't cry."

"How could you?" she sobbed, looking up at him, her eyes filled with pain and relief. "Leaving all of a sudden, the way you did… you hurt me to my heart, Cruze."

Shit. He wasn't up for a bunch of damn tears. He felt like dipping on her crying ass, but the slow throb in his pants reminded him of why he was there in the first place. For some pussy.

"Shit got crazy," he said apologetically, "and I had to get ghost, but I never meant to hurt you." He wiped her tears and then brushed his lips against her cheek and her neck, then cupped her ass as he smoothly walked her backward down the hall toward her bedroom.

In her room, he stepped back from her and came out of his hoodie and pulled off his shirt. Sniffling, Laila cried harder. "It's been over a year, and not once did you ever try to contact me. How could you do me like that, Cruze?" She angrily pounded his chest with her fists.

Cruze caught her wrists, and held them tightly. "I didn't have a choice. I had to wait until the air cleared. But I'm here, now. I'm back."

"Are you here to stay?"

Cruze bit his bottom lip and nodded. "Yeah, baby." He hated to have to lie to her. Laila was a sweet girl and had been hopelessly in love with him for years. Although the feelings weren't mutual, she deserved better than being treated like a random ho, but with his dick on lump, he had no choice. He wanted to fuck.

Figuring he'd done enough talking, Cruze began to unzip his jeans.

Insulted, Laila scowled. "Really, Cruze? After all this time, you're still as disrespectful as ever—coming here thinking I'm supposed to just spread my legs and let you fuck me. I can't believe you! Without any explanation of where your ass has been, you come up in here and start stripping out of your clothes, expecting me to let you jump back into the pussy—with no questions asked. I'm not giving you shit until I know where the fuck you've been." Eyes narrowed, hand on hip—she waited.

Cruze reached for her. "Come on, babe, it's not like that. With my lifestyle…" He paused and shook his head. "You already know the kind of world I move in, and there's a lot of shit you don't need to know. I'm not deliberately being cold. Do you think I like keeping shit bottled up inside? I'd love to be able to come home to you and share my troubles, but right now, the less you know, the better off you are."

Cruze watched as a range of emotions crossed Laila's face. He was certain that his remark about coming home to her had given her hope and weakened her resolve. When her features finally relaxed, it was clear he'd successfully torn down the barriers she'd put up.

"The only thing I can tell you, Laila, is that I missed you so bad, it hurt," he added to speed up the process of getting some dick relief.

She swallowed as her anger subsided and her heart softened. "I missed you, too," she confessed. Her voice cracked and she seemed to be working herself up to more tears.

Oh, shit. Please don't start crying, again!

Horny as fuck, Cruze swallowed hard as his intense gaze roamed over her pert breasts and down to the crotch of her yoga pants where a pussy print was evident. Filled with raw yearning, he uttered a primal sound from deep in his throat. "Come on, baby. Take your clothes off for me. Let me see that pretty little body that I've been craving."

Laila's expression suddenly hardened and she stubbornly folded her arms across her chest. "You ain't right, Cruze. It's been more than a year—"

Yeah, okay. And? You already said that shit. He wasn't trying to repeat himself explaining why again. He moved closer, shutting her up by rubbing on her titties and whispering, "I've been having wet dreams about that pretty pussy of yours."

Laila gazed up at him and swallowed as heat swept through her. No man had ever had that effect on her, except for Cruze. Damn him! With a look of defeat mixed with sexual yearning, she began tearing off her clothes.

As Cruze finished undressing, he could feel Laila's eyes burning into him. Anticipation scorched through her veins. He was her only desire. And as angry as she was with him for abandoning her, she couldn't deny herself him. Standing at six-foot-four, his body was sculpted like a Nubian god, and Laila couldn't help running her hands over his bulging biceps and rippled abs. She'd missed the feel of his hard body.

"You 'bout to find out how much I missed you," Cruze warned, before licking his lips. He enveloped her inside his brawny arms and with his lips, he traced a moist path from her neck to her breasts, nibbling and sucking on her nipples, and coaxing desperate little moans from her.

His hand wandered downward, moving past her belly button and then stalling. A long finger made circles around her rigid clit, and then moved a little lower, caressing the seam of her pussy, where hot juices had gathered.

Cruze didn't tongue kiss or eat pussy because most bitches put their mouths on too many dicks and raw-fucked way too many different niggas. But he had no problem playing in a batch of hot pussy. One finger explored the pooling wetness between Laila's legs while his thumb orbited her juice-slickened clit.

"I love you so much, Cruze," Laila whimpered, her mouth hungrily seeking his. Cruze pulled away. "You know what I want, Laila... suck it for me, babe." He applied pressure to her shoulder with one hand and held the base of his hard, throbbing pole with the other.

Without hesitation, Laila sank to her knees and opened her mouth.

"Mmm," Cruze moaned as he slid the smooth head between her plump lips. "Suck it good," he coaxed. She pulled him in deeper, and the moment she applied suction to his hardened shaft, a fire erupted inside him and tiny sparks raced up his spine.

He could have easily lost control and released a hot load of cum right then and there, but he composed himself. With concentration, he was able to stroke in and out of her mouth, slowly and rhythmically.

"Damn, you suck a good dick, girl. That juicy mouth of yours drives me crazy." Cruze's dick glided along her tongue in a leisurely fashion, but when Laila puckered her lips around the middle of his shaft, tightening and releasing her hold like a quick-gripping pussy, Cruze's breathing intensified and he went wild, banging against her tonsils,

Laila deftly relaxed her throat muscles, allowing him to forcefit his lengthy cock down her tight windpipe. Realizing he was close to busting, he reluctantly pulled his burgeoning manhood out of Laila's neck and smeared his leaking pre-cum all over her mouth.

Looking confused, Laila licked the salty substance from her lips. "What's wrong? You used to love it when I sucked the first nut out of you."

"You can suck out the next one, all right? But right now, I gotta bust inside that hot pussy."

Laila stood up and Cruze roughly tossed her on the bed. Grunting with desire, he mounted her. Knocking her legs apart with his knee, he guided his swollen cock toward her creamy slit.

"Uh," he groaned as he pumped dick into her depths. Her satiny walls contracted around his thickness, possessively clutching at his manhood as if trying to keep him trapped inside her pussy, forever.

The lock-tight grip Laila had on his dick felt amazing. But he wouldn't last long if he didn't put up a fight. Grinding his hips into her hers, he took control, feeding her pussy slow, measured thrusts of rock-hard dick.

After a few moments, he increased the tempo, stroking in and out at a much faster pace. "Ooo, this pussy is so damn wet, I can tell you're ready for me to gut you. Are you ready, baby?"

"Yeah, I'm ready for you to gut-fuck me, bae," Laila replied breathlessly.

Cruze let out a groan as he pulled his dick out of her hot snatch. Coated with Laila's juices, his long, thick meat pulsed with readiness. He yanked Laila by her legs and pulled her into position. Stretching her flexible thighs wide apart, he situated himself in the V-shaped space. He looked down and saw that her dripping-wet cunt was gaped open invitingly.

Showing no mercy, Cruze rammed his dick in so deeply, his nuts slapped against Laila's ass. With every thick inch that he jammed into her gut, he'd pull out a little before pressing in more.

"Oh, God, I love this big dick. It's so good," Laila cried out in passion. "Can't nobody gut me like you do, Cruze. My pussy needs you, bae. Promise that you'll stay this time. Please, don't leave me, again."

"I'm not going anywhere," Cruze mumbled, steadily stroking.

In a euphoric zone where the only thing that mattered was the sensation of plowing through the heated slush that flowed from Laila's pink, hot gash, Cruze said whatever she wanted to hear. Sweating and straining, he pounded her pussy so hard, Laila curled her toes and her hands gripped the sheets. Driving in hard dick at a rapid speed, her head knocked repeatedly into the leather headboard.

"That's right, fuck my brains out, daddy. Tear me wide open. Goddamn, I love you, so damn much. You can't leave me no more, baby. *Mmm.* You gotta fuck me like this every night. Promise me… uhn…*please*," Laila pleaded as Cruze plunged deep inside her, fucking her in hard strokes, the head of his dick bumping up against the mouth of her cervix.

With every lunge inside her lush body, she grew slicker around his dick. Against her flesh, he rasped, "Come for me, baby. Let me feel your wet pussy melt all over my dick."

"Yes, yes, yes!" she screamed as she tightened her legs around Cruze's back. "Fuck me! *Mmm*, yes—God! Fuck me!"

Her nails dug into his back. Spiraling closer to nirvana, a spasm of delight gripped her pussy. She gasped, grabbing the sheets around her.

Then cried out his name as all the love and arousal she had for him flowed from her body.

Three

"Mmm, yes…goddamn you, *yesss!*" Arabia moaned over a sensual beat that poured out through the club's speakers. She was on her hands and knees, her ass cheeks pulled apart, her pussy splayed open. Behind her stood her six-foot-one anonymous lover, his face hidden behind a black spandex three-hole hood. A mask he wore for extra protection from anyone knowing his real identity despite the fact that every club member was not only interviewed vigorously, but also required to sign a nondisclosure agreement before being accepted into the adult playground.

Whatever.

She didn't care *who* or *what* he was out in the real world. Tonight, he was simply a random fuck. Tall. Dark. And sexy as hell—from the neck down, that was. She didn't care what he looked like behind that mask. Hell, a gorilla could have been hidden behind the latex for all she cared. All that mattered to her was the way his muscles rippled as he fucked into his lover's body, and the shrill cries of joy she emitted with each thrust.

It'd taken her nearly thirty minutes to find him. Up on the third floor. Fucking.

She'd stood back quietly, viewing intently for several moments as he rammed his dick—in rapid, piston-like strokes—in and out of the cunt of a pretty brown-skinned woman. He'd slammed his rock-hard cock into her body hard, *harder, harder,* again and again and again—each powerful stroke making the woman sob with exquisite pleasure.

Arabia had bit her lip, drunk in the sight of the two lovers, feeling her blood heat with desire. She could smell the woman's pussy as he sliced into her wetness. And mmm, it'd made her mouth water as she watched on with a wicked joy that made her own cunt tingle with need.

She wasn't a lesbian, but she'd wanted so desperately to snatch him out of his lover's sex and suck him into her mouth, licking his lover's cunt cream from his cock. Yes—oh God—yes. She wanted to taste *it*. Taste *her* on *him*.

Times like this—when carnal desire seeped through every part of her—was when she wanted to be unanchored and out of control. It was when she felt the freakiest, the dirtiest.

She stood there, watching, wanting—watering, for what seemed a long while before she'd boldly slipped out of her dress, allowing the garment to flutter to the floor. The club's music pulsed over her body as she stepped over her dress, and—in her panties and come-fuck-me heels—sauntered over to the couple, her gaze transfixed on the stretch of muscle covering her prey's back, his ass, the back of his thighs. Ropes of sweaty muscle tightening with his every thrust. His hips beat against Brown Skin's soft rounded ass, his dick pummeled and hammered deep inside her.

The Masked Man watched himself disappearing into his lover's hole, reemerging from each thrust wetter and wetter. Arabia licked her lips, feeling her veins flood with envy. She'd wanted what that bitch was getting.

She'd wanted a good hard dick down.

She'd felt the blood throbbing between her thighs as her gaze danced all over his body. Sweet heavenly Father, that beautiful ass of his. She'd wanted to bite into each cheek, inhale his musky scent, then chew into his flesh. Her pussy had flared at the thought. She'd trembled, her body hot and sizzling from a burning need to be stuffed with cock as she made her way over to them. She'd been so aroused, her nipples deliciously tight, her cunt aching. She hadn't cared if the two of them were a couple in real life, or not. She'd planned on stealing Miss Brown Skin's lover away from her, and having *her* way with him.

She'd slid out of her panties, then tossed them over to a tanned Italian who'd been eyeing her as he stroked his dick. He'd caught her panties—lacy and red—in midair, then brought them up to his nose and sniffed. She'd licked her lips, sliding a hand between her legs and brushing a delicate finger over the hood of her clitoris. Pleasure had splintered fiercely through her body until her clit swelled. She'd bitten back a low moan as she slowly slid two fingers inside the folds of her pussy. Her slit closed around her fingers as they lost themselves deep inside her arousal.

Her eyes fluttered, only for a brief moment, before she'd brought her fingers to her lips and sucked them into her warm mouth. Mmm. She licked her lips, then swallowed the saliva that had begun to gather in her jaws.

She hadn't minded the eyes that had watched her, hungry and wide, as she stalked closer, beginning to talk dirty over the music, telling Mr. Masked Man to fuck that pussy, telling him how badly she wanted him to fuck her, too, with his big, juicy dick.

And, she'd wasted no time reaching between him and his lover and grabbing him at the base of his wet, sheathed cock, fisting him, her hand hitting the back of Brown Skin's stretched sex. Each time he thrust forward, then pulled back, her hand glided along his shaft.

She licked over his sweaty skin, then rasped close to his encased ear, "Come fuck me. *My* pussy wants you more."

Finally aware of her presence, he'd turned his head toward her, still thrusting into his lover, and through the eye slits of his mask, she'd seen a flash of hot hunger. The mysteriousness of him wearing a latex hood had made him that more desirable. And she'd wanted him even more now that she was close enough to feel his raw, masculine heat.

Miss Brown Skin—her face flushed and jaws clenched—had glanced over her shoulder and shot Arabia a dirty look. *Who is this cock-blocking bitch? All these men up in here, why can't this thirsty bitch go find another dick to play with?* She'd thrown her ass back harder at Mr. Masked Man, reminding him of whose pussy he was still in. But it hadn't seemed to no longer matter as he slowly pulled out of her. Then, for good measure, he'd drawn back his hand and smacked her ass. Then, without another thought or second glance, was being snatched away by Arabia.

The nerve of that *bitch!*

Now here she was…

Naked.

On display.

Ass up, face down; the masked man's fingers grazing the soft brown flesh surrounding her cunt. She shook her ass. Made it clap back. And he still hadn't stuck his dick in and fucked her mercilessly. What the hell was he waiting for?

She glanced back over her shoulder. "Put your dick in me," she urged impatiently.

In response, he cupped and caressed her ass, then slapped it. Hard. Ooh, yes. He slapped it again. Harder. The sting cracked fiercely through her body until her clitoris swelled, threatening to burst open with pleasure.

Oh, he wanted to fuck her sexy ass, but not yet. His balls ached, his dick was long and hard and so goddam ready to explode. He wanted to be buried deep inside her. But he fought it. He wanted her to beg. Wanted her to cry out for it.

Arabia wiggled and bucked, demanding he fill her. In spite of her surging frustration, she'd gone unbelievably wet from the waiting. And now she wanted action. She didn't beg for dick, goddamn you; thank you very much. Not from any man.

Ever.

And she wouldn't start now. Especially not with this masked man. He reached underneath her to stroke her engorged nub. "Your ass, your pussy, is so fucking beautiful," he said huskily. "You want me to fuck you in it?"

She wasn't sure which hole he wanted. But she'd gladly give him either, or both. The choice was his. Just fuck her already.

"Yes," she hissed, lifting her head from the sofa, and glancing over her shoulder again. "Fuck me. *Now.*" She felt herself becoming agitated. This sweet torture wasn't what she wanted. She hadn't chosen him to toy with her cunt. She'd picked him to *fuck* her. Hard.

Yet this masked fucker wanted to tease her.

He pinched her clit again, and she gasped as wires of pleasure shot from her throbbing sex. "I'm gonna fuck you until your sweet pussy flutters and clenches around this big dick. Is that what you want, this dick to bust your guts up?"

Yes, yes, yes—Lord God, *yes!*

Promises, promises...

He slid his fingers through her wet folds, testing her arousal. She twisted restlessly, pushing back against his probing fingers, clutching them as he withdrew. Her patience was wearing thin. Her cunt was growing angrier by each finger stroke, his fingers grazing the back wall of her sex. Oh how she wished her pussy had teeth. She'd gnaw his fucking fingers off.

That would learn him.

And as she was ready to get up and dismiss him to seek out a more compliant, more willing, more aggressive lover, he was grasping his dick with one hand, rolling a condom down over the rigid column of flesh with the other hand, before spreading her, then positioning himself at the mouth of her pussy.

Then, then…mmm—thank God—she felt the thick head of his dick push against her, teasing her, testing her, then in one forceful thrust, he buried himself inside a burst of wetness, the plush walls of her vagina blanketing him, caressing his cock, wetting him.

"*Fuck*," he hissed. "This pussy tight. And wet." He pushed in deeper until his balls flattened between her ass and his thighs, and he felt her vibrating around him.

Arabia eagerly pumped her hips, fucking herself into him until he got with the program, wrapping an arm around her waist and pounding into her, opening her up. Moving faster and harder as she went slick around him; finally giving her what she'd come for, what she craved.

"Yes, yes, yes—*fuck* me! Give me that big black cock, mother-fucker! Oh, yes, yes…mmm, yessss…"

She ran her tongue over her upper lip, ecstasy sweeping through her. She rhythmically rocked her hips in greed to get more of him inside of her, her juices dripping down her thighs. Yes, God, yes. *This* was what her pussy needed. A pounding.

"Mmm, harder…harder." She reached in back of her and pulled her ass cheeks open wider. "Spit in my hole," she rasped, "and stick a finger in my ass while you fuck me."

The masked man groaned as he eased back and eyed her clenching asshole. Fuck a finger. He wanted to put his dick in it. But he obliged her, spitting down into her ass—once, twice, then shoving his middle finger in. Greeted by tight heat, his finger retreated, then sunk back in. In and out. In and out. His finger stirred her ass juices as his dick pumped into her pussy.

She gasped, and her cunt gripped him wildly. She couldn't deny it. His dick felt good inside her, real good. But it wasn't the kind of toe-curling, spine-tingling cock she'd hoped for. She needed a sex beast whose dick could make her whole body pulse nonstop, long after he'd been inside her with his tongue, fingers and dick, ravishing her cunt, fucking her to shreds.

She needed to feel herself swirling outside of herself, crying out in pleasure, the world blurring around her, lost in the white heat of passion.

Yes, Lord.

What she needed was a reformed thug-daddy who knew when to slam her up against a wall, rip her panties off, then choke the everlasting life out of her while he seesawed his roguish cock in and out of her, pillaging through her core, fucking her raw and swollen.

Dear God…

That was exactly what she wanted, no, *needed.* A man who'd pound her walls and fuck her guts inside out.

So far, she hadn't found him. No, no. On second thought, *he* hadn't found *her.*

All that had found her over the last two years were lazy, uninspiring lovers whose cocks teased her pussy, and left her starved and aching for something more the moment they'd flopped out of her.

Lazy fucks.

And now this masked man was in back of her…*fucking* her, but not really fucking *her.* Fucking him wasn't hot enough, wasn't dirty enough. It wasn't rough enough, rugged enough.

It was *just* enough.

Enough to stroke the ache in her cunt, enough to feed her craving, enough until the next time, until dirty need pierced her core.

He groaned. "Aaah, shit, yeah…mmm…I'ma tear this pussy up, baby. Uhhh, fuck…"

"Then tear it up," she urged huskily over her shoulder. "Stop all this silly shit and bang my pussy up." She lunged back against him, prodding him with more nasty talk, taking everything he had to give and, yet, craving more. "Feed my pussy that big dick. *Fuck* me. *Fuck* me. *Fuuuck. Meeeee!*" She grunted, and fiercely pumped her pelvis. Her walls squeezed him tightly, her orgasm coming around the width of him.

"Ah, shit, baby," he groaned as her asshole pulsed around his still probing finger. "Unh. Mmm. You about to make me nut."

"Pull your finger out of my ass," she demanded, "and stick it in my mouth. Then I want you to lick inside my asshole, then fuck me in it."

Damn, this bitch's nasty, he mused as he pulled his middle finger out and brought it to her lips, *but I ain't licking no ass.* She flicked her tongue over the tip of his finger, then parted her lips and slowly sucked it into her mouth—until she was knuckles deep, tasting her ass on it, then groaning as if she were sucking on a dick. The sensation made Masked Man's dick twitch inside of her.

She leaned forward more, stretching her arms so that she could clutch the side of the plush leather sofa. "Harder," she demanded. With raised hand, she reached behind her and smacked her own ass. "I watched you fucking that other bitch. Now give me the dick like you gave it to her. Fuck me like you hate me."

Masked Man didn't answer in words, but his hands dug into her hips, and he finally pounded her in rhythmic thrusts that made her nipples tighten.

"Yes. Mmm. Yes, yes…that's it. Get this pussy…" She rocked her hips, wanting more of him. Her pussy clutched his cock, tighter, wetter. "Give me that nut." His hips smacked against her ass, jostling her entire body. The pleasure escalated and she felt herself panting.

With each stroke, Masked Man relished in the magnificence of her cunt, its depths, its wetness, its silky walls; she was a good, freaky piece of ass, and he wanted to fuck her again.

"This…pussy…*unh*…so fucking *hot*," he muttered, teeth clenched.

Deeper, deeper.

Faster, harder.

His vision blurred. He could feel his release low in his balls, roiling through his belly, coiling through his body and then exploding from his cock, loud and hard. He began coming in endless streams, the semen flooding his condom. He closed his eyes and leaned over her, his heated body heaving. He thrust and grunted one last time as her walls clutched around him again, over and over and over.

She closed her eyes, pussy churning, hot need still clawing at her.

And came.

Four

Cruze couldn't get used to waking up in the morning to the sound of birds singing. Back in Brooklyn, his alarm clock had been the wail of fire trucks and police sirens, the rumble of trash trucks and city buses, and loud, indistinct voices. And now…

He was surrounded by tranquility and deafening silence. But it had been what he thought he needed—at first. Trying to stay off the grid, Cruze had bought a sprawling home in the suburbs of Philadelphia. The gated mansion was surrounded by a vast wooded area. He had sought privacy, but the endless peace and solitude had turned out to be too much of a good thing.

Many a night, after being jarred awake by the rustling sound of someone skulking around on his property, he'd grabbed his piece from the nightstand. Believing his enemies had finally located him, Cruze would rush down the stairs, gun in hand, prepared to blow a muthafucka's brains out.

Pulling back the drapes and squinting into the darkness, he sometimes found it comical that his "enemy" was nothing other than a deer munching on foliage or a family of raccoons scampering around the grounds of his palatial estate. Other times, when his sense of humor had abandoned him, he felt like shooting the shit out of the pesky creatures for fucking with his mindset.

It was the peacefulness of his location that had become bothersome and fueled his desire to buy a condo in downtown Philadelphia where he could fall asleep to the soundtrack of bustling activity and wake up to the ruckus of delivery vans, horn-honking taxis, screeching tires, and other familiar noises. The mansion, he decided, was too big for one person, and he now only spent time in that lavish environment when he wanted to remind himself how far a young cat from the streets had come.

Two maintenance workers from the Huntingdon Young People's Enrichment Center (HYPE) came out to Cruze's SUV with dollies and began unloading the trunk that was crammed with boxes of items that he was donating to the center.

HYPE was the vision of former NBA player, Bret Hollis, who used to play for the New York Nets. Through an online article, Cruze learned that Bret had been using his own capital to run the state-of-the-arts center that opened in North Philadelphia in 2012 with the goal of providing a safe haven for inner-city children. But after four years, money was running low, and Hollis was actively seeking outside funding. Looking for a way to give back, Cruze had hopped on the opportunity to do something good. Initially, he'd donated seven thousand dollars, and wanted to do even more, but couldn't risk drawing attention to himself by making huge donations. However, for the past few months, he had been doing whatever he could to help out and in the process had struck up a friendship with Bret Hollis.

After the trunk was cleared, Cruze strode into the building and passed a room where a group of teenage girls wearing leotards and Kente cloth headbands were dancing African-style to the beat of conga drums.

He hoped he didn't seem like a pervert by standing there and gawking at the dancers through the large window, but they were killing it, and Cruze was mesmerized. The rhythmical foot stomps, clapping, drumming, and shouting were all part of the powerful dance that felt like an unstoppable force was vibrating the floor beneath his feet.

When one of the girls caught his attention by winking and then plumping her lips together in a pouty kiss, he instantly backed away. Unwilling to participate in any inappropriate interactions with teenage jailbait, he quickly moved along.

He strolled to the gymnasium where the youth basketball team that consisted of seven- and eight-year-old boys was hard at practice. Cruze couldn't hold back a smile as he watched the little guys play. His mind wandered to a time when he used to shoot basketball from morning until night at a broken-glass-littered court where the hoop was nothing more than a rusted metal rim. He had dreamed of being another Bret Hollis or Marquan Naylor, but those dreams ended after he'd earned his first few stacks slinging drugs.

Shaking the memory, Cruze returned his attention to the practice area and couldn't take his eyes off a youngster named Barack, who consistently shot three-pointers. Neither Barack nor his teammates were aware that when they graced the court at their upcoming game on Friday, they'd all be rocking new uniforms with personalized jerseys, and also new pairs of Nikes—courtesy of Cruze.

He watched the boys for a while and then made his way along the corridor and quietly observed a group of kids who were in a classroom setting, diligently studying. Every child was using an iPad that Cruze had donated. It felt damn good to give back to the community, and he wanted to do even more to help steer the kids in the right direction. Hopefully, none of them would end up trying to commit a robbery using a metal pipe as a weapon like the punk whose kneecaps he'd shattered the other night. If his money could keep these young innocents away from the lure of the streets, then it was money well spent.

As Cruze turned away from the study center, he saw Bret Hollis approaching. Bret had been one of his basketball idols while growing up, and he still hadn't gotten used to the fact that they were kicking it now like equals.

"Hey, man," Bret said, giving Cruze dap. "The kids love those tablets so much, my staff has to search their backpacks every day to make sure they don't sneak them out of here."

"Why can't they take them home?" Cruze inquired. In addition to schoolwork, he had assumed the children would also be able to use the tablets for fun activities.

"You know how it goes, man. If an iPad leaves here, it won't come back. Big bro' will take over ownership and use it to watch porn. Big sis will snatch it up for her social media activities, and thieving Uncle Teddy will slip it out the crib and sell it for fifty bucks."

"Yeah, you're right," Cruze acknowledged. "By the way, I was checking out the youth basketball team, and they're good. That lil' dude Barack can handle a basketball—he has mad skills."

"Oh, yeah, Barack's the commander-in-chief," Bret said with laughter, and then his expression turned serious. "Barack won't be with us after Friday. Poor kid's mom has been sick. She's doing better now, but during her illness, she lost her job and now they're getting evicted. I believe they're moving in with her sister, or some family member who lives way out in East Jabip, somewhere."

"That's rough. Wherever they go, I hope the lil' dude finds an outlet for his talent like he has here," Cruze commented, though he doubted if Barack would find another opportunity to get the kind of support system that was provided at HYPE.

He checked his watch. "Yo, I gotta run. I only dropped by to deliver the uniforms and sneakers." Cruze wasn't actually in a rush, but he didn't want to overstay his welcome or act too Joe-familiar with Bret.

"I can't thank you enough for the contributions you've made," Bret said. "As you know, your donations are tax-deductible. Make sure you stop by the business office and pick up the tax forms on your way out."

Cruze nodded. "Will do."

Bret placed his hand on the door to the study center, and then turned and faced Cruze. "By the way, my wife and I are hosting a fund-raising dinner at the Ritz-Carlton Saturday night at seven. We'd love for you to attend as our guest."

Cruze smiled, feeling honored by the invitation. "Say no more. I'm there. Do I buy my ticket online or can I get it from your secretary?"

"You don't need a ticket; you're our guest."

"That's cool. Thanks. I'll see you there.'"

Bret went inside the study center to greet the kids and speak with the afterschool coordinator, and Cruze went on his way, breezing past the business office without stopping to pick up tax forms. Hiding behind several dummy companies, Cruze had cleaned up most of his dirty money since moving to Philadelphia. After years of slinging dope in the black community, he didn't feel the government owed him any tax breaks for giving back to the people who had been most harmed by the drug epidemic.

The door to the gymnasium burst open and Cruze had to jump out of the way as the throng of energetic boys stampeded out into the corridor. Their coach trailed behind them, yelling for them to quiet down.

On his way to the parking lot, Cruze sauntered toward the exit sign, but the bouncing sound of a lone basketball drew his attention. He backtracked, peeked through the circular glass pane on the door of the gym, and was surprised to see that Barack had remained behind and was still practicing. Still perfecting his shot.

That used to be me. A ball under my arm, arriving at the raggedy neighborhood court at six in the morning.

Though dressed for the occasion, Cruze hadn't planned on getting sweaty in his Alexander McQueen sweats, and he definitely hadn't intended on getting any kind of marks on his fresh pair of white and metallic gold, limited-edition Air Jordan 10 OVOs. But unable to resist showing the young homie what was what on the basketball court, he stepped inside the gym for a little one-on-one.

"Aw, you think you're nice, young buck, but I'ma show you something," Cruise threatened, wearing a deadly expression as he ran to the hoop and blocked Barack's shot.

"Oh, it's like that, old head!" Barack yelled as he enthusiastically chased the ball. "You got the height, but I got the speed and the moves, man!"

Cruze towered over the boy, guarding him, but Barack didn't seem worried. Dribbling behind his back and between his legs, he showed off his flashy moves.

"I'm watching you, little guy. I got you, I got you," Cruze cried out, quickly growing breathless as he played defensive, running and repeatedly reaching for the ball. Barack faked him out with a sudden spin move, and maneuvered his way behind the three-point line. Before Cruze could get to him, Barack had elevated in the air, shot the ball, and scored!

"Yo, I had you. I don't know how you got away from me, lil' man."

Barack laughed. "'Cause you slow, man. You can't rock with me. I'm on some next level ish," Barack bragged with a huge grin plastered on his face. Cruze couldn't get over the self-confidence and maturity of the trash-talking basketball prodigy. Those attributes would take him far if he didn't get tripped up by the risk factors associated with life in the 'hood.

Suddenly, the door pushed open, and a woman who looked to be in her early thirties entered the gym. She was rail-thin, wearing a turban, and clutching a thigh-length sweater around her frail body. With the same nutmeg-brown complexion as Barack and the exact mouth and nose, Cruze figured she had to be his mother.

"All your teammates left fifteen minutes ago. I'm standing outside waiting for you, while you're still in here playing ball. Boy, do you realize you made us miss the bus?"

"Sorry, Mom."

"Sorry don't cut it. Now, we have to wait forty-five minutes for the next one." With a weak smile, she shook her head as she glanced at Cruze.

"How you doing, ma'am? It's not your son's fault. I held him up and I apologize."

"Do you work here?" she asked.

"No, I'm a friend of Mr. Hollis's. My name is Cruze Fontaine." Cruze extended his hand.

"Nice meeting you, Cruze. I'm Barack's mom, Roxanne Cannon," she said, giving him a quick handshake. Turning away from Cruze and focusing on her son, who was still dribbling and shooting, she said, "Put that ball down, Barack, and go change into your street clothes. And hurry up! Since we have to sit around and wait for the next bus, I want you to go over to the study center and start your homework after you get dressed."

Bret had said that Barack's mom was doing better, but she looked sickly to Cruze. And with that turban on her head, she had the look of a chemotherapy patient. Maybe she was recovering, but the poor woman looked like she should be resting in bed instead of traveling on buses to pick up her kid from basketball practice.

"Uh, listen. I'm on my way out and I could give you and your son a ride," Cruze offered, feeling somewhat responsible for her missing the bus.

Roxanne raised a brow suspiciously as she eyed him. She shook her head. "No, thanks. We'll be all right."

"But I feel bad, and like I said, it's my fault." Cruze held up his hands. "Yo, I'm not a serial killer if that's what you're thinking. Mr. Hollis can vouch for me."

"I've seen you around here talking with Mr. Hollis…and you probably are a nice guy, but I try not to impose on people."

"It's not an imposition."

Cruze and Roxanne sat down on two folding chairs while Barack went to the locker room to change his clothes.

"Your son is very talented," Cruze said as Roxanne shifted in her seat and crossed her legs. "Making it into the NBA is never guaranteed, but his talent could get him a full ride to college if he sticks to it."

Roxanne bit her lip, a look of despair brimming in her eyes. "That's the thing. We're losing our place and have to move. I doubt if there're any youth organizations in the town we're moving to."

Cruze studied her for a moment as he carefully chose his words. "Do you want to move?" he asked.

She shook her head. "No, but I don't have a choice. I only have ten days before I get evicted."

Recalling how frequently he and his mom used to move around, Cruze regarded her thoughtfully, and then asked, "How much do you owe? I know it's not my business, but your son kind of reminds me of myself when I was his age. I wish I'd had a place like this to hone my skills. Maybe my life would have gone in a different direction."

Roxanne looked Cruze over, taking in his expensive-looking watch and leisure wear. "Looks like you made out all right to me."

He shrugged. "Yeah. I guess. But I know all about hardship. My mom was a single parent, who had to struggle to keep us afloat. I wish someone would have helped us out during some of the bad times." Cruze looked off in thought, recalling his tough childhood. "I realize I'm basically a stranger, but I want to help, if you'd let me. I promise you, no-strings attached. You won't owe me anything other than a yes."

Roxanne took a deep breath. "This is crazy."

"Life is crazy…and it can be harsh, too."

"Tell me about it," she mumbled, shaking her head.

"But sometimes, when you least expect it, you can find a little kindness in this cold world. So, um, how much do you need?"

Thinking, she sighed. She uncrossed her legs, and then bent forward and crossed her arms. Then she shook her head firmly. "No. I can't. Thanks, anyway, but it wouldn't be right."

"Why not?"

"Because I don't know you. And I'm *not* a ho."

Cruze laughed a little. "I'm not asking you to be." The idea of Roxanne turning tricks was unimaginable. It would take a really cold-hearted pimp to put such a fragile woman out on the track, and any scumbag-trick that paid for her services deserved to have his ass kicked.

"All I'm asking is for you to let me help you 'n' lil' man out," Cruze continued. "Nothing more. I promise. So, tell me. How much do you owe?"

She heaved a sigh, but relief was evident on her weary face. "I'm four months behind—I owe thirty-two hundred in back rent. Too much to ask of a total stranger."

"Nah, it's all good. It's not too much. I got you." Cruze stood up and jangled the keys in the pocket of his sweatpants. "I'll be right back, let me check the locker room, and see what's taking Barack so long."

Five

Runway ready and always fabulous, Arabia strode into the sleek Upper Eastside high-rise overlooking Central Park, where one of her fiancés, forty-eight-year-old Theodore Banks, took up part-time residence and rode the sleek private elevator up.

Married with three teenaged-children, he was an investment banker who owned one of the two sprawling penthouses up on the top floor that could have easily been featured in any of the luxury-home magazines. It reeked of power and wealth. Things Arabia believed every good man should embody.

She glanced down at the three-carat solitaire engagement ring she'd pulled from her safe and slipped on her ring finger earlier this morning. She reveled in its blinding brilliance as the elevator's lights shone down on it.

She smiled.

After all, she was worthy of nothing but the best. And she required it. Expected it. And, goddamn it…deserved it.

Why shouldn't she?

She was exquisitely stunning and, in her mind, a rare gem that should be coveted. No. Arabia wasn't a gold digger, unlike her mother, Claudia. But she loved a man who dug deep into his pockets, sharing his worth in gold—*and* diamonds, of course. The deeper he dug, the wetter her pussy became. Still, she never, ever, asked a man for anything. That would be in poor taste. And a woman of her caliber never stooped to such tactless methods. Asking a man. *Mmph. Please.* Not. She used creative coercion—okay, okay… she gently prompted a man when she had to—to get what she wanted out of him. But, truthfully, she rarely had to, though. The men in her life, more often than not, gave willingly.

Oh, don't be fooled by her sexual proclivities. Arabia wasn't a home wrecker. If anything, she was a peacekeeper. She fucked her lovers with purpose—to keep them happy, then send them home to their wives in a state of sweet bliss. She had no interest in disrupting a cheating man's life. She simply enjoyed sleeping with men who were sexually frustrated with their home situations, men who needed love and affection, and some stress-free pussy. Yes, she sought them out. Preyed on them. Those types tended to be more giving with their gifts and coins than any of her past so-called single lovers.

So all any married man was good for was trinkets and trips and, hopefully, some good hard dick. And if he couldn't keep a hard dick, a long tongue would do just fine. Truthfully—though she loved gifts, Arabia didn't really need the treasures men bestowed upon her. She simply loved being pampered and spoiled. So she expected the men in her life—married or not, to keep her *kept*.

Other than that, she didn't *need* a man for his money. She needed him for…?

Hmmm…wait. She'd have to think on that for a moment.

What did she really need him for, besides his hard dick and wet tongue?

Umm.

Well…

She didn't.

Men were simply a means to an end for her, period. They

couldn't be trusted. None of them; yet, she knew she couldn't *not* have them in her life. She loved the feel of a hard-bodied man, especially a successful one. She simply loved men who had it going on financially. And she loved them successful—shakers and movers. Hung men who hungered good pussy; that's what she loved most—powerful men who gave over their control—to her, losing themselves in heat and sex…in *her*.

She loved seducing her lovers.

Loved mind-fucking them.

Loved sucking their dicks deep into her mouth, then watching each one become powerless. Her need for control, at times, could be daunting; something that made some men—hell, *most* men; especially *black* men—uneasy.

Her mouth watered at the mere thought of it. Dick. Oh, God, how she loved it. Loved the way it felt, the way it tasted, the way it smelled—all manly and erotic. She loved sliding her pussy down on it, then using her walls to massage its shaft.

Mm, yes.

She felt her pussy clench at the thought of being stuffed with cock.

She had to admit. She was looking forward to seeing Theodore. It'd been almost three weeks since she'd last spent any quality time with him. And, today, she was eager to have his dick in her mouth, then inside her pussy. Sure he came fast every time he was bathed in her liquid fire, but she tried not to hold it against him. His saving grace was that his dick was deliciously thick, and always gave her pussy the best fifteen-minute pounding a woman could ever hope for in a quickie. And he was, surprisingly, always able to recover in minutes, ready for another round.

Still…

It was sometimes frustrating and unforgiveable for him to taunt her cunt like that. Coming quick. Leaving her pussy humming for more. That was, that was—well…it was simply downright obnoxious. Hell. She'd given him a vibrating cock ring for his birthday almost three months ago—something to help his staying power—and he had *yet* to wear the damn thing.

Mmph.

Men.

They could be so damn unappreciative.

She caught her reflection in the elevator's chromed interior, and smiled. She loved the image staring back at her. Perfection, that's all she saw.

At thirty-two, she still had the tight, firm body that most females half her age would kill for, or die trying to have. She couldn't blame them, though, for hating on her for being beautiful. Her traffic-stopping looks and body had been cause for more than enough slamming brakes and head-on and rear-end collisions by men trying to get a second glimpse at what sexy and fabulous looked like wrapped in one body.

Thanks to genetics and the help of yoga, kickboxing, and her morning five-mile run, she kept her perfect 34-22-38 body measurements tight and right. As far as she was concerned, being a top-shelf, sidepiece trophy required dedication and commitment. At all times.

It meant staying fit, fly, fabulous and…*always* fuckable.

Proudly, she was all four.

Still, she was nothing more than "on-call pussy" as her mother had so eloquently put it one night after one of their many heated phone conversations over her not being married *and* with kids—like her sisters. Her mother resented the fact that she'd wasted all of her good damn coins on her education only for her to end up stupid…*and* still single.

Claudia had been grooming her very early on how to snag a husband—not some damn married man. She hadn't spent hundreds of thousands of dollars on sending her to all those fancy-schmancy charm schools, and whisking her off to private schools as a child, before shipping her off to Spelman in Atlanta, so that she'd simply acquire a college degree and want to do something with it. No. Her degree was meant to be a showpiece, something to hang up on a wall. *Not* put to use. How damn ridiculous!

And Claudia hadn't demanded her youngest daughter pledge her beloved sorority, either—although she'd pledged herself as did her other daughters—so that she'd follow the principles of Sisterhood, Scholarship and Service to all Mankind. She expected it. But to her chagrin—once again, Arabia defied her and pledged a rival sorority just to get under her skin.

Simply put, her youngest was an ingrate. Everything Claudia set before Arabia was so that she'd land a Morehouse Man, a man of substance, a man with the right pedigree. As with her three older sisters marrying wealthy was all that Arabia should have ever aspired, nothing more, nothing less. Instead, the selfish little twit would rather slum around in stained sheets playing *wifey* to some *already* married man, being his nasty little cum dump.

Claudia was utterly appalled at her daughter's silliness. And, in so many words, she'd told her so. Why be a whore for many, when all she had to do was whore for one? What a stupid trick.

Her words had stung Arabia. They'd felt like a slap to her face when they'd rolled from her mother's lips. And, at times, she could still feel the sting. She had wanted to tell Claudia to kiss her plump ass. But she settled on disconnecting the call without so much as a goodbye.

How dare that gold-digging *bitch* judge her?

That's exactly what her man-eating mother was. A gold digger!

Arabia, along with her three sisters, had learned firsthand from their mother how to use what they *had* to *get* what they *wanted*. Claudia had used her Louisiana charm and striking beauty to seduce her way into each of her husbands' lives, starting with their father's. Bless his dead soul. She'd milked him for everything he had until she'd finally sucked him to his grave.

Three months after he died, the sheets hadn't even cooled and she was already in the arms of her next lover. They married two months later in a private ceremony in Maui. But that marriage only lasted for three years, before he suddenly collapsed to his death from a heart attack, leaving her all of his fortune.

Since then, Claudia had been running through husbands and rotating them like tires. She was now currently on husband number six.

Arabia shook away thoughts of her hateful mother, catching her reflection one last time. *Fuck her.* She was happy with the way her life was. Maybe it wasn't the most ideal situation, but she wasn't idealistic. She was a realist. And the reality for her was: she was living *her* life, *her* way and *fuck* anyone who didn't like it. Married man or not, Theordore was *still* a good catch for shacking up with. And his long bankroll, and his long, wet tongue kept Arabia inspired to keep him.

True. There'd never be any "I dos" or "happy-ever-after" being engaged to someone else's man. Being the sidepiece didn't come with any long-term rewards. But the short-term benefits were well worth all the empty promises and sweet nothings being whispered in her ear before, during *and* after a sweaty romp in the sheets.

And, when it came to playing her position, Arabia knew her place. And she was comfortable in her role. She was more than okay with letting Theodore and all the others *think* the pussy was theirs. Truth was, no man had claims to what she held between her thighs, except her.

And she suspected no man ever would.

Still, she loved giving them the illusion that they held permanent stake to the prize. So what if he, along with her two other current lovers, had put rings on it?

As far as she was concerned, she was still very much single. And always open to new possibilities. Did she love any of her current lovers? Absolutely not. Loving them would require her lying to herself. And that wasn't about to happen. So, hell no! There was no emotional investment where any of them were concerned. They were simply hard dicks, and financial benefactors. So, no, love wasn't on the blackboard for Arabia. Old-ass—well, maybe not *that* old. More like *seasoned*—wealthy men, horny and starved for attention, who, more often than not, felt unappreciated at home was the only thing on her menu, period.

She knew her pussy had the power to heal. To make a lonely, rich soul feel whole again. So why shouldn't she do her civic duty of mending their horny souls with a dose of good pussy?

She giggled to herself. *Ooh, this snap-trap keeps the dick on lock.* Oh no. She wasn't some mediocre two-pump bitch in the sack. Even though, two of her three lovers were. But what did she care?

She had—

The elevator doors opened, and, without further thought, Arabia stepped inside the tastefully decorated apartment. Tall and muscular—wearing a pair of silk lounge pants, Theodore greeted her with a smile before pulling her into his arms. She snuggled against his bare chest, and breathed him in. He smelled of Dial soap and masculinity all rolled into lots of dollar signs.

He pressed his lips to her hair and inhaled as he kissed her head. Her scent tantalized his senses. Theodore loved the way she always smelled, so soft and so sweet. He'd leave his nagging-ass wife in a heartbeat to be with Arabia if it weren't for his children, and the fact that his wife had him chained by the balls with the threat of taking him for everything he had if he ever tried to leave her. So, begrudgingly, he stayed. And cherished every moment he was able to sneak away on business to be with the woman he adored.

Arabia.

Theodore kissed the side of her temple, then along her cheek-bone, before brushing his lips over hers. He kissed her mouth, sliding his tongue in to taste her. Arabia felt herself going light-headed as he swallowed her breath. It was as if he was trying to suck out her soul, and she didn't know what to make of it. Theo-dore's kisses were always so gentle, so passionate. But this, this... this kiss felt so much different than all the others.

She'd kissed him more than a thousand times over the last two years, but she couldn't remember the tenderness in his kisses being this intense.

What the hell was going on here?

"I've missed you, baby," he said in a gruff voice, his erection pressing into her stomach. Arabia attempted to pull away from him, but he held her tighter, pressing himself into her, making his intentions clear. "My dick is so hard for you. I can't wait to make love to you." He smoothed a hand down the side of her hair, star-ing down at her. "I want to be buried so deep inside you that I feel your heartbeat on the tip of my dick."

Arabia blinked, surprised by his words, wondering what poetry book he'd borrowed the line from. She looked up at him through her lashes, feeling sensual pleasure slog through her veins. Sur-prised by her body's response to his touch, she couldn't wait much longer, either. She needed this. Needed to make him feel like he was the only man she desired, if only for the moment.

She caught his waist and eased up on the balls of her heels and covered his mouth with hers. He groaned into her mouth, gripping her ass and cupping her there as his tongue tangled with hers.

Ravenously, Arabia licked into his mouth, tasting him; a mixture of peppermint and wet heat that caused her cunt to clench, and her juices to seep into her laced thong.

Damn him.

She couldn't deny it. Theodore was extremely desirable and one hell of a sexy man. Which was why she had pursued him, preyed on him, until she was able to eventually break his resolve. Still, he hadn't wanted to cheat. He had been committed to his marriage, even though it was loveless and sexless, 'til death did them apart.

But…

Arabia reached between them and tugged at the drawstring of his pants. She seductively slid to her knees, dragging his pants down over his narrow hips with her.

Theodore's dick sprung out, its tip glistening with arousal. Arabia licked her lips, then flicked her tongue along its slit, before swirling her tongue over and around the crown of his cock.

And mmm, God—his precum tasted so sweet. She wrapped her delicate hand over his shaft and squeezed it gently in her fist, caressing it, before her tongue peeked out from between her sumptuous lips and swiped over the head of his dick.

"Shit, baby," he hissed, feeling every drop of his blood rushing straight to his now-painfully-hard cock. God, she hadn't even sucked him into her mouth—*yet*, and he was already about to come. "That feels so good."

She moaned and licked her lips. Then looked up at him through her lashes and licked him again and again, swiping the tip of her tongue along his piss slit, then wetly swirling it around his dick's bulbous head.

"Unh. Shit," he murmured as the moist flick of her tongue caused hot pleasure to ricochet through his body. He loved her wet, velvety mouth. She was such a good dick sucker.

Arabia leaned back a bit and took in the sight of his beautiful cock—arrow-straight, golden-brown, veiny, and thick—and prayed he wouldn't come until she had him wedged snugly down in her neck. She gripped it, again, and cupped his scrotum.

He grunted.

"You like that?" she asked all coy and vixen-like as she stroked him, her hand sliding up and down the length of him. She had to admit, she loved having power over his long dick.

"Fuck, yeah." She kissed the tip of his dick. Then licked it, again. "Suck it, baby. Put that big dick in your mouth." His hands delved into her hair as he tried to guide his cock into her mouth.

Arabia looked up at him, with raised brow. He had her all kinds of fucked up. *She* sucked dick when *she* wanted to, the way *she* wanted to. Not when someone told her to, or demanded her to. Instead, she licked over and around his balls while brushing the crest of his cock with her thumb. She wanted to extend her tongue out a little further and lick along the crack of his ass. But he'd never go for that. *Ugh*. She licked over his balls again.

A low moan slipped from his lips, letting her know that…mmm, she had him right where she'd wanted him. At her mercy. She was taunting him with her mouth and hands, and the shit was driving him mad, heat and sensation blistering through him.

Head back, neck arched, he shut his eyes, and bit into his lip. Arabia smiled as his fist tightened in her hair. *Yeah, snatch my scalp, motherfucker. Mmm.* The words never left her lips, but she'd thought it as her tongue cradled his cock, then slathered the underside of his shaft with her spit.

His leg shook, and he hissed in sizzling desire.

She drew her tongue up the length of him again—under it, over it, along the sides of it, leaving wet streaks of intense pleasure.

"Unh," he breathed as need spiked. He gritted his teeth. He

wanted…oh God, fuck, he wanted to come in her beautiful mouth. Badly. He didn't know how much longer he'd be able to hold out. It'd been weeks since he'd come. His balls were full with want, and need, for release.

He had to see her, watch her. He opened his eyes and looked down at her. "Aw, aw…unh, baby. Look up at me while you do that. Let me see you sucking this long dick."

She looked up at him and batted her lashes. "You wanna coat my throat with your sweet babies, don't you?"

Shit yeah. He couldn't get the words out fast enough before that sweet, velvet-slick mouth of hers opened, and she sucked him into her wet, silky mouth.

Her gaze locked onto his as she filled her mouth with his cock, taking him to the back of her throat, then easing out with a suction so strong that it almost took his breath away. *Fuck!* Theodore groaned out his pleasure and she sucked him more vigorously.

"Oh God, yes," he growled. "God, yeah, baby—suck me with them sweet, sexy lips." Arabia felt the throbbing in her mouth—he was about to release his warm man-milk. The thought moistened her panties. She was becoming deliciously wet. Her pussy clenched for some of him, the length of him; its own turn at milking his cock. She bobbed her head back and forth, his dick gliding in and out of neck, then mouth.

She wanted to suck him real slutty, wanted him to skull-fuck her, then throw her over the sofa and fuck her cunt deep. But she knew he'd never go for that. He was simply too damn gentlemanly.

Besides—

"Arabia," he whispered, her name nearly a groan. Need and desire fluttered madly in and out and around him as his pulse raced.

Lips and mouth and tongue.

Deep sucking.

Sweet licking.

And lots of wet heat.

He was already on the edge.

Just a few more sucks, a few more licks, and...

Clutching his chest, he growled out, his warm nut hitting the back of her throat.

Then collapsed to the floor.

Six

While Cruze dressed, grown folks' music played in the background—Erykah Badu and Andre 3000's collaboration of The Isley Brothers' "Hello." If ex-lovers could come together on a love song after years of conflict, Cruze figured he could get over his uneasiness about attending Bret Hollis's charity event.

Though he tried to keep it low-key most of the time, he realized he'd never get to the next level if he didn't start rubbing elbows with a different set of people. He only wished the dinner wasn't such a high-profile event with press in attendance.

Avoid cameras at all costs and everything'll be cool.

In the mirror, he observed his new persona, which was a drastic change from the Brooklyn thug who'd spent his entire adult life flipping kilos. As he studied his image, he ran his fingers over his fresh dark Caesar spinning with deep waves. On his suit-and-tie shit, Cruze cracked a smile, imagining himself kicking it with investment bankers and politicians instead of his usual crew of con artists, thieves, and killers.

One last glance at his reflection and he straightened his tie and then strolled out of the apartment.

Standing at the elevator, Cruze gave a head nod to a sophisticated African American couple who approached. The man, who looked to be in his mid-fifties, was dapper in a tuxedo and his female companion, who was several inches taller than he, looked about ten years younger. She was dazzling in a glittery black gown with a plunging neckline that displayed an exquisite set of tits. The spectacular diamonds that adorned her neck and her wrist shimmered beneath the light of the hallway chandelier.

On the sly, Cruze admired her lean body and the regal way she carried herself. Without meaning to, his eyes flitted to her ass, which was firm, plump, and round. She was a gorgeous well-preserved older woman, and she was obviously well cared for. Her entire look indicated that she was pampered and accustomed to the very best.

"Good evening, young man. You must be our new neighbor," said the man cheerfully. "We're the Hamiltons—across the hall from you in 2612. I'm Morris, and this is my wife, Valentina."

Cruze introduced himself and Morris shook his hand. Valentina's lips moved in an inaudible greeting, and then she quickly turned her head, barely glancing at Cruze. Embarrassed by his wife's rudeness, Morris held up his hands in an apologetic gesture.

Cruze instantly disliked Valentina. Beautiful or not, she was a stuck-up bitch that thought she was too good to be bothered with opening her mouth to extend a civil greeting. *Fuck her.* Although Cruze looked fly in a tailored, perfectly cut suit, Givenchy tie, and the five-thousand-dollar Hublot Classic Fusion watch that decorated his wrist, all Uppity-Ass saw was a young thug. She probably viewed his presence in the exclusive apartment building as a forewarning to a decline in property value.

Cruze's jaw twitched as he flicked imaginary lint from his lapel, then readjusted his tie. *Trick-ass broad can suck my fucking dick.*

When the elevator door slid open, Cruze gestured for the couple to enter first. Nose in the air, the bougie bitch glided inside as if being extended courtesies from commoners was her birthright.

Inside the elevator, Cruze stared straight ahead, refusing to make any small talk with the husband and definitely avoiding any eye contact with Uppity-Ass. But, pulled by the allure of the sensual fragrance she wore, it was a natural response to gaze in one of the mirrored panels of the elevator and steal a glance at her. As he stealthily checked her out, he quickly averted his gaze when he saw something that made him think his eyes were playing tricks on him.

The elevator continued its smooth descent, and right before it reached the lobby, Cruze shot her another surreptitious look. This time there was no mistaking that Valentina, while standing next to her oblivious husband, was licking her lips and giving him a seductive look. Even more shocking, her hand that was embellished with the big, glittery diamond ring was rubbing on her pussy in a slow, circular motion.

Before departing the elevator, Morris said cheerfully, "Have a wonderful evening, young man."

Valentina tossed Cruze a sly smile and said in a thick foreign accent, "Ciao, baby. Hope to see you soon."

The fuck?! Obviously, the stuck-up bitch was cray, but that accent of hers had his dick jumping in his pants and pulsing for release.

The charity dinner was a well-organized and classy event with over two-hundred guests filling the venue. Several of Hollis's old Nets teammates had come out to support him, and Cruze was honored to be seated next to Marquan Naylor. In his day, Marquan had been an electrifying and controversial player who had achieved popularity for injecting his hip-hop style into basketball. And he was equally infamous for his many skirmishes with the law.

Though Cruze was inwardly excited to be chitchatting with the great Marquan Naylor, he didn't let it show—at least not for the first half hour. But as he grew more comfortable, he let his feelings of idol worship slip out. "People probably tell you this all the time, but on some real shit, me and my friends used to rock your sneakers and your jerseys when we were kids."

"Oh, yeah? That's cool. Thanks, man." Marquan sort of chuckled and tossed back a long sip of tequila.

Cruze suddenly felt stupid. He'd made it seem like he and his boys were unique in wearing Marquan Naylor apparel, when actually the whole world rocked the former player's gear during the peak years of his career.

He was about to clarify his statement when an extremely tall white dude with a big belly and a head full of snow-white hair approached their table. Marquan stood up and embraced the man. "Dusty McDowell," Marquan greeted with a wide smile. "Good to see you, my dude."

The rivalry between Marquan and Dusty had been as heated as the rivalry between Magic Johnson and Larry Byrd, back in the day. Cameras began to flash as members of the press enthusiastically captured the moment.

As much as Cruze would have enjoyed having a bird's-eye view of the historic reunion of the two basketball titans, he couldn't risk being caught in any photographs. Pushing his plate back, Cruze vacated his seat and strode to the rear area where the bar was set up.

"Remy on the rocks," he told the bartender. With his back no longer facing the door, Cruze was able to keep an eye out for anyone who might have tried to come for him. Away from the flashing lights, Cruze relaxed in the cut and watched as Dusty and Marquan were joined in the photo op by Bret Hollis and two other former NBA players, whose faces were familiar, but whose names he couldn't recall.

Time could be cruel, Cruze thought, taking in Dusty's white hair and inflated gut. He glanced at the other two players and noticed that one walked with the assistance of a blinged-out cane, and the other had gone completely bald. Out of the group of former players, Marquan and Bret were the only two who still closely resembled the way they'd looked during their playing days. Good genes, he supposed.

"If it weren't for his height, I wouldn't have recognized Dusty McDowell," said a scholarly-looking, cinnamon-skinned woman who had sidled next to Cruze. Looking her over, he guessed her to be in her early to mid-twenties. She was petite, no more than five-four, give or take a few inches.

Her light-brown locs were styled in a braided bun, and her oversized, geek glasses were intended to downplay her looks. But she was clearly a cutie despite her subdued attire and understated makeup. She wore a plain black pantsuit and had opted for kitten heels instead of the five-inch stilettos that adorned the feet of most of the other women in attendance at the glitzy affair.

"We all gotta grow old one day," Cruze responded to her comment. "But cats like Dusty will be immortalized. He was a hella player in his day."

"True. They used to call him Dunkin' Dusty. The way he used to drive the ball down the court and then dunk on his opponents, he rightfully earned that nickname. But I'm not so sure he deserves his spot in the hall of fame."

Cruze tilted his head. "You know a lot about b-ball…for a girl."

"I'm a Harvard grad, and I know a lot about a many things," she countered with a smug smile. "Dunkin was the man, but Marquan Naylor was an exceptional player, and to be honest, I'm personally offended that the white boy was inducted into the hall of fame while Marquan is continually ignored by the committee. It's like they want to punish him forever for his controversial persona during his playing days."

Cruze nodded. "Yeah, Marquan used to be a rebel. He broke all the rules."

"But his youthful rebelliousness doesn't negate what he did for the sport," the woman said passionately. "The selection committee for the basketball hall of fame is an anonymous group. They don't have to explain or publicly defend their decisions. There's no transparency, and it's completely unfair." She exhaled in frustration and took a sip of her pastel-colored drink. "Marquan is a legend, and keeping him out of the hall of fame won't change his stats or the electrifying magic he brought to the game."

"Facts. Marquan has a place in history, no matter what," Cruze concurred.

"I'm Lourdes Dunning, by the way. I'm with *The Daily Grind*." Cruze wrinkled his brows.

"*The Daily Grind* is a hard-hitting news outlet," she explained.

"Never heard of it."

She pulled up the site on her phone and handed it to Cruze. He scanned the screen, noting that the lead story was something about Blac Chyna and Rob Kardashian. "Hard-hitting news, huh?" he said with a smirk and returned her phone. "I'm not really into the gossip blogs."

"We're a lot more than that. We cover politics, world news, sports…technology. But that's beside the point; I was hoping you could help me out."

"How so?"

"Well, I already interviewed Bret Hollis about his North Philly program and his dream to expand HYPE to other deprived areas in the city. But I'm hanging around, trying to get an exclusive with Marquan Naylor." She eyed Cruze intensely. "I noticed you and Marquan talking, and…"

Cruze held up his hands. "I can't help you. I don't know dude like that—I just met him."

"Damn," she muttered. "Okay, well, you had an opportunity to gauge his mood. In your opinion, do you think he'd be willing to talk to me tonight?"

"I have no idea. If you've followed his career, you know he detests the media and refuses to give interviews."

"Yeah, but maybe he's changed with maturity. Hell, the way he's been drinking nonstop, maybe he's twisted enough to spill his guts to me." She chugged down her drink and set the empty glass on the bar counter. "I'm going for it. Wish me luck."

Cruze watched with interest as Lourdes determinedly made her way across the room. Zooming in on her target, she speedily weaved in and out of the crowd. Her swift movements were impressive, and the kitten heels she was rocking suddenly made perfect sense.

Still, despite her tenacity, Cruze doubted if she'd get an interview with Marquan Naylor.

When the musical guest—a local rapper Cruze had never heard of—took the stage, Cruze ordered another drink and tuned out the noise emanating from the mic. Philly rappers couldn't touch New York talent. Diverting his attention to his immediate surroundings, he noticed that quite a few hot mamas had flocked to the bar.

During the next hour, he found himself surrounded by eye candy. Some struck up conversations and others sent him smoldering looks of lust. One chick, who was wearing the hell out of a very revealing, figure-hugging red dress with cut-out detail that showed off her ample boobs and midriff area, boldly sent him a drink. Her phone number was scrawled on the napkin. Out of all the women in close proximity, Skimpy Red Dress looked like the hottest piece of ass out of the bunch. He was about to go over and introduce himself when Lourdes suddenly came out of nowhere.

"I got it!" Grinning, she held up a small recorder. "It's all on tape."

"I didn't see you talking to him." Cruze looked over at the area where he'd last seen Marquan. "I thought he bounced when that corny rapper got on the mic."

"He did leave. In fact, we left together," she said proudly.

Cruze looked at Lourdes questioningly.

"Marquan and I sat in the back of the car while his driver took us on a tour of Center City. Marquan drank like a fish while I conducted the interview."

Cruze wasn't sure if he should be impressed by Lourdes's ambitiousness or if he should give her the side-eye for her unethical practices. "It seems a little unscrupulous to take advantage of an intoxicated man."

"No more unscrupulous than all the groupies Marquan took advantage of during his career."

"Hey, you can't blame the man for accepting what was given to him willingly," Cruze countered. Being a top lieutenant in the drug game was akin to being a rock star, and Cruze had enjoyed more than his fair share of groupie love.

"Let's not quibble over semantics. I'm in the mood to celebrate—care to join me?" Without waiting for an answer, Lourdes reached in her purse and took out a small envelope with a room number printed across the top and a key card inside. "Here you go. Meet me upstairs in ten minutes."

Cruze was pleasantly taken off guard. Lourdes had struck him as someone too tightly wound and too career-oriented to be interested in frivolous sex. She hadn't even bothered to ask him his name, which was cool with him.

He pocketed the key card and then shot a glance at Skimpy Red Dress, who sat on the other side of the bar. As she stared daggers at him, he tried to apologize with his eyes.

Though Skimpy Red Dress had body for days, she wasn't anything special—merely another empty-headed ho, looking for a sponsor. It wasn't every day that Cruze got the opportunity to heat up the sheets with a naughty-librarian type who was also a Harvard grad.

He'd expected to find Lourdes wearing something sheer and sexy…or better yet, he'd hoped to find her waiting in bed, butt-ass naked.

But she was fully dressed, sitting at the desk, hunched over her laptop with earphones on, listening to the tape player while her fingers clicked rapidly over the keyboard. Next to the laptop was a chilled glass of wine. She pulled off the earphones and swiveled around and faced him. "Give me a second while I transcribe some of the pertinent info from the interview and send it to my editor. There's beer in the fridge…and wine. Help yourself to whatever you'd like," she said with an offhand gesture.

Then she twirled back around and resumed typing.

Offended, Cruze wondered what this brainiac broad was on. She had to be smoking something if she thought he'd left the bar with all that wet pussy that was potentially primed and ready for a good fucking to come and sit in a room with his hands folded in his lap, while she worked on an assignment.

Oh, hell no. Him, a hotel room, and a piece of ass meant he was getting his dick sucked, sliding up into some guts, or both. He wasn't about to sit around watching some bitch dressed like a church secretary dictate some fucking notes. Nah, this four-eyed broad had him fucked up.

Cruze's jaw twitched. And a slight stirring in his groin made him push out a breath and curse under his breath. He was about to turn around and walk out the door, but for some unknown reason, his feet led him toward Lourdes. There was something about her nerdy ass that made him want to rip off her clothes and fuck her so deep that she would feel him fucking her soul. The thought sent blasts of heat straight to his balls.

Standing behind her, he reached down and pulled out the hair stick that anchored her locs, and watched as her hair unraveled and fell over her shoulders. When she didn't stop him, he boldly removed her glasses, and then eased off her jacket. He was pleasantly surprised that there was nothing beneath it except a bra.

Cruze grinned, pleased at the sight of the plumpness of her breasts, the lush inner curves rising from the cups of her lace bra. He licked his lips, then hooked his fingertips into both cups of her bra and yanked downward on the fabric, causing her breasts to tumble out. Fully bared, the tips of her dark nipples stiffened, ready for the flick of his thumbs over them.

She let out a little sound of protest, which he silenced by pinching her nipples, causing a moan to escape her lips, before picking up her drink and running the chilled rim along her neck and down to her collarbone.

Lourdes trembled as droplets of condensation ran down her left breast and pooled around her nipple, hardening the flesh. Wanting to gain better access, Cruze spun her chair around. With a pitiless smile on his face, he trailed the cold glass over her other breast, and he watched with interest as that nipple tightened into a beaded knot.

"Unh. Ooh. It's cold," Lourdes uttered, her eyes closed as she arched her back, welcoming the painfully sweet pleasure slowly tightening around her areola. She gripped the arms of her chair, sinking her nails into the leather. "Oh, God, yesss!"

"You ready for me to heat you up?" Cruze asked in a husky

voice that ignited visible shivers on the surface of her skin.

She nodded briskly.

"Stand up," he urged, the pupils in his eyes going liquid with lust.

With a stuttered gasp, she complied, standing up and awkwardly extricating herself from her pants, and then hurriedly peeling off her already wet thong. Bared to him, her body suddenly flushed with burning arousal. She gazed in his eyes expectantly, waiting for him to remove his clothes.

But Cruze didn't so much as loosen his tie. This chick had tried to play him like a chump, expecting him to wait around and twiddle his thumbs while she typed up some notes. She was on his time, now, and he'd give her every inch of his hard dick when he was good and damn ready.

"Yo, why you in such a rush." He dragged his gaze over her body, then licked his bottom lip. "Sometimes I like to just chill and sit back and watch."

Her eyes fluttered open. "Sit back and *watch* what?"

"Watch you make that pussy pop," he rasped, his voice so thick with lust that it made Lourdes's body shiver. Cruze's big, warm hands reached out and closed over her exposed breasts. He squeezed. Kneaded. Then ran the tips of his fingers across the beaded peaks, causing a slight high-pitched moan to echo from her throat.

Satisfied, he let go of her breasts, then nudged his head toward her bra that he'd pulled down, and that now dangled beneath her breasts. "Get rid of the bra."

She swallowed, hard. Then reached back and unhooked her bra, letting it float to the floor.

"Good girl. Now finger yourself for me."

She squirmed uncomfortably. "I don't know if I'm comfortable with that."

"You shouldn't be embarrassed to play in your pussy. Don't you want to get it hot and juicy for me?" He ran a hand over the front of his designer pants, bringing her gaze to the growing print beneath the fabric. "Let me see how wet you can get that pussy, and, tonight, this dick is all yours. All night."

Lourdes let out another soft moan. This fine-ass motherfucker had her juices trickling down her thighs already, and he hadn't even touched her there yet.

"C'mon, baby," he urged in a low, seductive tone. "Show me the inside of that pretty kitty. Open it up for me."

Swallowing back her inhibitions, she closed her eyes once again and took a deep breath as her hand ventured downward, past her taut stomach, and down to her waxed mound. Delicately, she spread the folds of her labia. Opening herself, she revealed her throbbing clit and the rosy, silken skin that was hidden within.

"Damn, baby," he muttered. "For a tiny chick, you got a plump pussy."

Her face flushed with a mixture of embarrassment and yearning. "I'm…uh, I'm ready for you," she stammered breathily.

"Nah, you're not ready—yet, baby. Your pussy can get a lot juicier than that. Stick your finger in it and stroke that fat clit."

She let out a groan, shaking her head. "I don't want—"

Cruze raised a brow. "What? You don't want this dick?"

She shook her head. "No. I mean, yes. I want it. Oh, how I want it."

Cruze smirked. "Then you're gonna have to earn it, baby. You got a lot of book smart, but you still have a lot to learn. C'mere 'n' let me show you something."

Lourdes took steps toward him and tilted her chin, offering him her lips, which he ignored. Still holding the wineglass, Cruze shoved it between her legs, then rolled the smooth, cold object against her hairless mound.

"Hump on the glass," he coaxed. "Slide your pussy all over it."

Her face flushed, but she obeyed the command. "It's cold," she complained as her body defied what she was thinking in her head—*hell, no!*—and she slowly grinded her quivering sex against the wineglass.

"Yeah, I bet it is cold. But it was also cold for you to invite me up here and then blow me off the way you did, fronting like you didn't ask me to come up here and get some of that sweet pussy."

She looked up at him sheepishly. "I wasn't trying to blow you off. It's just that—"

"Nah. Save the excuses, baby. You tried to play me. Now tell me you didn't invite me up here so I could fuck the shit out of you."

Oh, he was so very right. She had extended the invitation for a nightcap of hard fucking. But he frightened and excited her at the same time. She swallowed; every nerve in her body was aflame. She flushed again. It was a guilty flush, but also one that was telling.

"I'm sorry."

Cruze's lips curled into a sly grin, never dropping his gaze from hers. "Show me how sorry you are," he said, unbuckling his belt. "If your head game is tight, I'll warm that ass up for you."

"It's uh, it's tight," Lourdes assured him, looking both embarrassed and turned on at being treated like a slut.

"Word? Then get on your knees and let me test them skills."

With quivering hands, she helped him with his fly. She groped inside his briefs and caressed his thick erection before wrangling out the heavy club of pulsing flesh. All she could do was stare at his enormous dick, her breath held in anticipation. Her mouth watered for a taste of him.

"Oh, God, I want you," she murmured deeply as she sank to her knees and kissed the head, and then took him inside her mouth. She moaned as she felt his dick throbbing against her tongue. She cradled his heavy balls in her palm, sucking him deeply as she swirled her tongue. When she deepened the long, tight, suckling strokes, Cruze's breath came out in rasping pants. Hunched over, he gripped her shoulders, squeezing, and pressing his fingers into her skin.

Lourdes slid a hand in between her legs and began stimulating her clit in a slow, circular motion, sliding her fingers every so often over the slit of her pussy. Her mouth got wetter as Cruze's hot sighs wafted down over her, and his dick slid smoothly in and out of her mouth, the weight of his shaft gliding over her tongue. She slid two fingers into her aching cunt, then sucked him fiercely, greedily, like some feral animal, sucking him wild and sloppily. Soon Cruze began to fuck her mouth and she moaned frantically around his thick length, rocking her pelvis madly against her hand.

"Oh, shit," he growled out as jet streams of salty cum spurted into her mouth.

Lourdes swallowed and wiped the side of her mouth with the back of her hand. When she looked up and met his gaze, Cruze jerked his head toward the bed and loosened his tie. "You know what it is…face down, ass up, baby."

Seven

A heart attack...

Arabia still couldn't believe it. Even as the plane hit the tarmac, even as she drove herself to the graveyard, even as she slid out of her BMW rental, she'd still had trouble believing it—she didn't *want* to believe it.

She'd killed him.

Sucked the life right out of him.

And now Theodore was dead.

To think she'd been the cause of his heart stopping. Well, maybe not *the* cause. But she'd surely been a contributing factor. Why hadn't he told her he had a heart condition? If he had, she might not have swallowed his cock so mercilessly. She might have been a more thoughtful cocksucker taking whatever medical condition he had into consideration as she sucked him down into her throat.

But he hadn't told her.

And now he was taking a permanent dirt nap. *Snap*—just like that; he was *dead*. When he'd collapsed, she'd smirked—silently boasting on her oral skills, honestly thinking it was her wet, juicy jaws and masterful tongue game that had caused him to topple over and hit the floor. She'd kept sucking him until his nut had stopped spurting, hitting the back of her throat.

Oh how scandalous it had been for her to have to dial 9-1-1, and, then, for the paramedics to arrive on the scene to find her with her lipstick smeared and her lips still swollen from lust, and her sweet Teddy sprawled out on the carpeted floor with his sticky dick dribbling the slightest trace of cum from its slit, his lounge pants and underwear still draped around his ankles.

Oh what a dirty sight.

She'd been too distraught, too shocked, to—at least—fluff her hair and apply a fresh coat of lipstick to her greedy, dick-sucking lips.

The two male paramedics who'd arrived had grinned and eyed her lustfully as she recounted the events leading up to him collapsing. Before they'd entered the penthouse, she had wanted desperately to at least pull his pants up, to hide her dirty deed. But she was afraid it would appear…well, suspicious. So she'd left him there on the floor half-naked, his cock stained with her scarlet-red lipstick.

Oh what a harlot she was.

Embarrassed for herself, more so than him—hell, he was dead. God rest his soul—she had to be the one left to do the nasty "Walk of Shame" past the prying eyes of tenants, the police, and the *media*—for God's sake!

Now she had the gall—dressed in her black Versace dress and black gloves with her black clutch tucked under arm—to show her damn face *here*, stepping through fresh-cut grass—in her black seven-inch stilettos, flouncing her ass over toward his gravesite, holding a single red rose in her hand.

Did the heifer have no shame? Did she have no compassion for the grieving widow and his family? Out of courtesy, couldn't she have shown some decency and allowed them their moment of mourning without her trying to smear her sordid affair with the woman's husband in their grief-stricken faces?

Well, the prim and proper Mrs. Banks might have been his wife and the mother of his children. But the prudish bitch hadn't been giving him any pussy or sucking the skin off his dick. Arabia had been. So she deserved to be there to say her goodbyes. After all, she was, for the last three years, his mistress. And she'd been with him when he'd taken his last breath. So this was where she should be. Besides, she was engaged to the man, for Christ's sake! And she was grieving, too—goddamn it, thank you very much.

So they could all get over it. She'd come to pay her respects, then be on her merry way; back to her life in New York, and the hell out of this Texan heat. The sun's blaring rays were beating down on her, and burning her flesh through all that damn black she'd chosen to wear.

She took a deep breath, then pulled off her oversized sunglasses and sauntered up the red carpet that led to Theodore's casket. There were a bunch of beautiful floral arrangements around his casket. Arabia stepped up and looked inside.

For some reason, she felt a tear slide down her face as she leaned in and kissed his cheek ever so lightly, before laying the lone rose inside his casket.

Instantly, she felt the air around her go still. She felt the hot glares. Heard the hushed tones.

"Oh, no, she didn't."

"Who is that?"

"What is she doing here?"

Just as Arabia stepped back and turned on her heel to leave, she stood face-to-face with *her*. His wife.

Eyes ablaze with rage, the woman stood there and glared at her. Then dropped her icy stare at the Tiffany diamond on her ring finger. So *this* was whom her husband had found comfort and companionship in, this much younger, much more beautiful *whore*. She was sure the bitch had to be doing circus tricks with her tongue in order for Theodore to drape her in exquisite jewels. She reeked of hot sex and raw sensuality.

Her nose flared. She wanted to hate *this* hot-pussy bitch, wanted to claw her face and draw blood, but she couldn't. She was everything she once was. Alluring. Mesmerizing. And she had breasts and ass and a tiny waist to die for.

Sure, she'd known all about her husband's affairs, especially this one. It was her right, her duty, to know the goings-on with her husband, including who he was *fucking* and putting rings on. So she'd kept close tabs over the years.

All the others before Arabia had been flings. Quick fucks. But there was something about this one here that had opened her husband's nose wide and had him running back and forth to New York to see her every chance he could. He was happier. Not as argumentative. And always more relaxed every time he returned home from his trysts with this, this...enchantress.

From the beginning, she'd known *this* one was different from all the others. She had to be in order to keep her husband's interest for as long as she had.

Three fucking years!

Sure she'd allowed her husband's extramarital affairs as long as he respected her, and their marriage, by not flaunting his whores in her face.

And, over the years, he had not.

But he'd fallen in love.

With *this* one. And now the shameless bitch had the goddamn nerve to bring her ass *here*.

"Missus Banks," Arabia said, reaching for her hand. "I'm so sorry for your—"

Slap!

Arabia blinked, bringing her hand to her face.

"*Bitch*," the grieving wife hissed, her nose flaring. "How dare you *fuck* my husband, then show your face *here!* You filthy *slut!*"

Arabia quickly recovered from the shock, and the sting, still holding her face in her hand. "If it's any consolation," she calmly pushed out. "Teddy didn't suffer. He died with a smile on his face." She leaned in closer and whispered, "In fact, he collapsed doing what he loved most. Coming inside my—"

The grieving widow spat in Arabia's face, then attacked her, her fingernails raking her face and drawing blood. The last thing Arabia remembered—before the screams, before the fist, before the flowers were tossed about—was Theodore's casket toppling over and his body rolling out. And his distraught wife screaming, "You fucking man-stealing *whore!* I will kill you dead!"

"Why haven't I heard from you?"

Arabia held her icepack to the side of her face and winced, wondering why she answered the call. All she wanted was a hot bath and a night of quiet. She was physically exhausted, mentally drained… and sore from tussling around on the ground with Theodore's wife. She'd broken one of the heels on her thirteen hundred-dollar pumps and her designer dress was ruined, thanks to that bitch. Teddy's sons had to pull the two of them apart and pick their dead father's body up from off the ground. What a mess.

That hurt Arabia to her heart, her and his wife rolling around on the ground, fighting on top of his body. She knew for sure, she would be going to hell if she didn't atone for her transgressions. *I'll go see a priest first thing in the morning, and confess my sins.*

In the meantime, she was down a fiancé and needed to decide if she wanted a replacement, or to keep her man count at two—for now. Yeah, that was what she'd do. Just stick with the two she already had. Juggling three men was slowly becoming more of a challenge than it was worth. And there'd never be another Theodore. So to hell with it, she reasoned in her head.

"Well, hello to you, too, Mother," she replied sarcastically. "To what do I owe the pleasure of this call?" She glanced at the time. 10:46 p.m. "At *this* time of night?"

Claudia huffed. "I've been calling you for several days now. Why haven't you returned any of my calls?"

Arabia rolled her eyes. "I've been busy."

"Busy doing *what?*" her mother asked incredulously.

"With work, Mother. And minding *my* business."

"I beg *your* pardon. It could have been an emergency."

Arabia twisted her lips. "Well, was it?"

Claudia scoffed. "Well, no. But what if it *had* been?"

"Then I'm sure Maya, Alexis, or Tamara would have been blowing up my phone. And since none of them have, that says to me it wasn't." Arabia shifted her icepack to her other cheek. "But, anyway, now that we've cleared that up. What is it? Is everything all right? Has Kirk taken ill?" Have you murdered another husband is what she really wanted to ask her mother, but she knew that question wouldn't go over so well. She'd mentioned to her sisters on several occasions over the years that she believed their mother had killed at least two of her husbands for their money.

Her sisters thought her ridiculously silly for even thinking such a horrible thing. "She'd do no such thing!' they'd shouted in her defense. Yeah, okay. Arabia believed otherwise. In her gut, she believed that her mother had targeted those men for their money, then slowly manipulated them into leaving her everything, before killing them.

For all Arabia knew, she might have even murdered her own father. *That*, however, she kept to herself. Her sisters would stamp her certifiably crazy, for sure, if she ever told them that. But she knew what she'd seen that afternoon she walked into her parents' bedroom suite: Her mother standing at his bed; his IV tube in one hand, a syringe in the other. Ten-year-old Arabia saw her mother pushing something inside her father's tube, then—startled, Claudia dropped her hand, trying to hide the syringe when she saw her standing there wide-eyed, her jaw slack.

Nervously, Claudia shooed her daughter away. "Run along, Arabia. Your father needs his rest."

"But where's Miss Penny? Miss Penny always gives Daddy his medicines. Not you."

"She had to go out on an errand. Now go on. Go get ready for your piano lessons. You can visit with your father later."

Reluctantly, Arabia turned on her patent leather shoes and walked back out the room, not before glancing over her shoulder one last time, and witnessing her mother push whatever else was left in that syringe she'd hid in her hand into her father's tube.

Moments later, she heard Claudia wailing.

Her father was dead.

It hadn't been all in her head. Or had it? No, no, and no. It—

"No. Kirk hasn't taken *ill*," her mother spat, slicing into her reverie. "Why would you think such a thing?"

"Well, let's see. It seems like each of your husbands tend to mysteriously fall to their demise after around the second or third year of marriage. And…"

"Arabia Knight! What on heaven's earth are you trying to insinuate here?"

"Oh nothing," she replied snidely. "I've already said it. I'm simply pointing out an observation."

Claudia huffed. "Well, I don't appreciate your comments, or you trying to imply that I would have anything to do with any of my dearly departed husbands' deaths."

Arabia snorted. "Mmph. You said it. I didn't."

Claudia sucked in a breath. "You are so damn despicable. I've loved each and every one of my husbands. And, Kirk, thank God, is as strong as an ox. And as virile as a twenty-year-old."

Arabia let out a sarcastic laugh. "Mother, please. Despicable is, *you*. You run through men. You're nothing but a black widow spider, snaring men, then sucking the life out of them, before you run off to your next mark. You've never been with a twenty-year-old to know. The only men you've ever lured into your clutches have been old enough to be your father."

"Well, isn't that the pot calling the kettle black, when all you do is play the dumb mistress to men old enough to be *yours*. But that's beside the point. I've heard tales," she said, feeling herself becoming increasingly irritated by her daughter's indifference toward her.

Arabia feigned a yawn. "Look, Mother, I'm exhausted from my flight."

"Your flight from where?"

"Texas," she huffed. "So, unless there's something you need, I'd like to unwind for the night."

"And why were you in Texas?"

"Mother, I don't care to discuss my travel itinerary with you, because frankly…it's none of your business. So how may I help you? Please and thank you."

"Arabia Pauletta-Ann Knight, don't you dare dismiss me like I'm some common trash from off the streets! I am your mother." Arabia cringed. She hated her middle name, even though it'd been both of her deceased grandmothers' names combined. And she hated even more every time Claudia declared herself *her* mother as if she were able to ever forget that mishap.

"Yes, you are," Arabia said forlornly. "I'm reminded of that every time your name and number flashes across my caller ID."

Claudia's jaws clenched. "Arabia, what is going on with you? Can you for one moment have an ounce of decency and not be so damn obnoxiously rude?"

Arabia rolled her eyes to the ceiling. "I've already told you, *Mother*, that I'm tired from traveling. It's late. I've had a long, grueling day. So what is it you want? You already know I have no problem hanging up on you."

Heat flashed through Claudia. Arabia had been nothing but difficult since the day she was born. Always testing her, always challenging her, always pushing the envelope.

"Why you disrespectful *little bitch*," her mother hissed. "Your sisters would never think to talk to me in this manner."

"Maybe because you'd been a mother to them, which is more than I can say for me."

Claudia recoiled. Her pregnancy with Arabia had been an un-wanted surprise. She hadn't wanted any more children, and thought she was done with diapers and bottles. Sadly, she was already in her second trimester when she'd learned of the pregnancy. Still, had it been up to her, she would have terminated the pregnancy right there on the spot, but her husband Phillip wouldn't hear of it. He even threatened to divorce her. So grudgingly, she carried the baby to full-term. Seething. Resenting her unborn child.

And then came the postpartum depression that ate away at Claudia for almost two years. It had incapacitated her. Phillip had to hire a nanny to care for Arabia and her three sisters. Soon enough Claudia had to be hospitalized for her psychotic thoughts, for wanting to smother her infant daughter to death, for trying to drown her in her own bathwater.

"Why you, you ingrate!" Claudia snapped. "I provided you a good life. The very best of everything."

Arabia scowled. "And that's supposed to earn you a Mother of the Year award? No, Mother. You don't get accolades for *not* raising me, or for shipping me off the first chance you got. You didn't provide me *anything*. Daddy did. And after his death, *his* money—*not* yours—did. So let's be clear, *you* never wanted me, or have you forgotten that piece of truth."

"How dare you speak to me this way? I've done nothing but loved you..."

Arabia let out a harsh laugh. "Lady, bye. Get off your soapbox. You've *loathed* me from the moment you laid eyes on me. Admit it, Mother. For once in your pathetic life, admit that you hate me. That you've always hated me." Arabia felt her cheeks heat. "I'm a big girl, Mother. Trust me. I can handle what I've known all along. I just want to hear it from you. So say it. Let's finally get it out in the open. Tell me you hate me..."

Arabia hadn't even noticed she'd been crying until the line went dead.

Eight

His heart pounded in his ears and his body was soaked with sweat. Eyes wide and wild, he searched the darkness with extended arms and with both hands wrapped around his gun. His trigger finger worked frantically as he shot at any damn thing that moved. Out of ammo, he lowered his arms to reload, and then it hit him…

There was nothing to reload. His hands were empty.

Emitting a groan of anguish, Cruze clicked on the lamp and flinched when he saw his Glock on the nightstand, untouched and in the exact position he'd left it.

Another fuckin' nightmare.

And this one was more realistic than any of the others. It had been months since the last one, and he wished he knew what had triggered it. Was it the Rémy Martin he'd drunk at the charity dinner? That was a possibility since Remy wasn't his usual libation. He should have stuck with Henny.

Or maybe it was that greasy-ass Philly cheesesteak he'd eaten earlier in the day. That joint was piled sky-high with fried onions, loaded with three kinds of cheese, and was smothered with heaping portions of mayonnaise and ketchup. His system wasn't accustomed to eating that kind of shit. But then again, maybe it wasn't food or drink; maybe the nightmare was brought on by his own guilty conscience.

He was dead wrong for the way he'd mind-fucked that brainiac chick in her hotel room. That Harvard degree she was so proud of was of no use while he was up in her guts, knocking her organs around.

Cruze swung his legs off the bed and took his weed paraphernalia out of the nightstand drawer and began rolling a blunt. As he tucked, licked, and rolled the tobacco paper, he wondered if there was some kind of medication that would rid him of the nightmares.

He'd thought that giving back to the community would earn him some cosmic points and allow him to sleep like a baby. Yet, despite all the good deeds he'd done, he was still being fucked with during the night.

Weary and frustrated, he gripped his head. "This bullshit is sickening," he muttered aloud, as the gruesome images that had been haunting him for over a year began to flood his mind…

Blood was everywhere. Bodies were sprawled all over the house. Reliving the tragedy was overwhelming, and Cruze took another deep puff on the blunt before pulling up more ghoulish memories.

He saw himself stepping over eleven bodies downstairs. He'd found the twelfth victim upstairs—in bed. The only satisfaction he'd gotten that bloody night was when he'd taken out the two gunmen, adding to the body count. The shooters turned out to be members of the crew. Two greedy and disloyal muthafuckas that were in cahoots with a rival drug cartel.

As far as Cruze was concerned, it was all Moody's fault. The muthafucka let his ego bring the entire organization down. He refused to keep a low profile, always flaunting his shit. He shouldn't have allowed any niggas access to his fly crib out in Long Island, but Moody loved showing off his possessions, and smearing his success in muthafuckas' faces. He stayed throwing get-togethers and inviting members of the crew over.

On the night of the murders, Moody was celebrating his birthday and flashing the gift he'd bought for himself, a Cartier watch encrusted with more than twenty carats of diamonds.

Cruze wasn't supposed to be at the birthday bash. He'd been entrusted with a high-quality shipment and had gone out of town to transact business with a new client. But as he neared the meet-up spot, warning bells started going off in his head. He couldn't put his finger on it, but his instincts told him that something wasn't right with the new client who drove a flashy Lambo. Dude was probably with the Feds.

Moody, who'd been Cruze's mentor since he was eighteen years old, had told him long ago to always follow his gut. So, with a trunk filled with kilos, Cruze turned the car around. He was about to call Moody, but changed his mind, deciding it was best to discuss the situation face-to-face.

No one had expected Cruze to show up at Moody's doorstep that night. And no one...not even Moody, was aware that Cruze had a key to the crib. A key that he'd never used until that night of the murders.

Per Moody's orders, Cruze and the rest of the squad always parked several blocks away from the spot to prevent anyone from following them to the sacred place where he and his family rested their heads.

On foot, Cruze had become suspicious when he'd approached the front door. There was no music playing, no loud voices...only deadly silence.

Instead of ringing the bell, he pulled his piece from the small of his back and used his key to enter. He stifled a gasp when he stepped over the bullet-ridden body of his boy, Sameer, in the foyer. Blood splattered the walls, and as he inched along, the body count began to mount.

But it felt like all the breath left his body when he came upon Ramona lying facedown on the floor in the family room. He couldn't have screamed if he wanted to because his throat clenched shut and strangled his voice. With tears falling from his eyes, he turned her over and discovered that she'd been trying to shield her baby girl, Niyah.

Cruze doubted if he'd ever forget the sight of little Niyah's blood-soaked, princess-themed pajamas. Shocked and dazed, he stumbled like a drunk as he backed away from Ramona and Niyah. Losing his balance, he collided into the large entertainment center. The sound of the crash alerted the intruders who were in the basement where Moody kept his stash box. As footsteps pounded up the basement steps, Cruze's survival instincts kicked in. He quickly turned out the light and eased behind the entertainment center.

In the dark, he squinted and then recoiled in shock and disbelief when he made out the identities of the two gunmen—Khaliq and Steady Freddie—two of Moody's most trusted soldiers. Outraged, Cruze stepped out of the shadows and opened fire on their treacherous asses, watching them drop to the floor.

Stepping over more bodies, Cruze finally located Moody in the bathroom with his side bitch, Jayda. Both were slumped with their drawers around their ankles. Cruze wasn't surprised that Moody had invited one of his bitches to his little get-together. Moody had always enjoyed flirting with disaster, and it probably gave him a thrill to be able to convince Ramona that Jayda was nothing more than an ordinary worker, and then turn around and fuck the bitch right under his unsuspecting wife's nose.

When it came to getting pussy, Moody had never abided by any codes of conduct. He took what he wanted. Whenever. Wherever. And he didn't give a fuck who got hurt in the process.

Hopeful that Ramona and Moody's son, Chancellor, had slept through the massacre, and was okay, Cruze had crept up the stairs with his heart pounding in his chest. But as soon as he'd reached Chancellor's room, he could tell by how still he lay, that the boy— his godson—wasn't breathing.

"Chance?" he'd whispered, realizing that the eight-year-old kid who was tucked under his *Star Wars* comforter wouldn't answer. "Chance?" he repeated, while staring at the gaping bullethole in the center of his forehead.

Although Chancellor's death was the least bloody, to Cruze, it had been the most coldblooded. How could anyone press a gun up to the head of a sleeping child and pull the trigger?

Groaning and shaking his head, Cruze forced himself to return to the present.

He took several hard pulls on the blunt—holding the smoke in his lungs until it burned, trying to convince himself that if he increased his charitable acts, he'd find redemption, and the night-mares would mercifully stop.

"The kids today look up to rappers, ballers, and unfortunately, drug dealers. No one needs to know that you used drug money to invest in real estate. That's your business. All I care about is that you turned your life around and became legit and you're ready to be a positive role model to the young kids that I'm placing under your wing," Bret said, sitting behind his desk. "As their coach, you're going to have a huge impact on their lives, and I hope you won't take that responsibility lightly."

"I won't take it lightly," Cruze responded. It still hadn't fully sunk in that he was taking over Coach Sheridan's position. Coaching the youth basketball team was only temporary, until the coach fully recovered from the pulmonary embolisms that had suddenly landed him in the hospital.

He wasn't worried about his ability to coach basketball, but he'd be lying to himself if he said he wasn't a little nervous about his qualifications to be a positive role model. In the past, Cruze had taught the ropes to plenty of entry-level players of the dope game, but the lessons he'd taught corner boys were mostly about survival. Of course, he'd also pounded into their heads the dire consequences that would befall their asses if they fucked up his money. Taking on the kind of responsibility that Bret was referring to…ushering young lives into a future where they would hopefully become upstanding, law-abiding citizens was brand-new territory for him. Although he was both excited and nervous about taking on the responsibility, he had no doubt that he was up for the challenge.

"Teachers would love to get the kind of enthusiasm from students that you'll get from your players," Bret continued. "You see, kids enjoy being part of a team. And whether you like it or not, you have an obligation to set an example and teach them the right things in both basketball and life. When coaching kids that live in an environment that's loaded with risk factors, including drugs and violent crime, you have the daunting challenge of making them believe that they can grow into competent and productive members of society. "

"I got you. I can do it," Cruze said confidently.

After Bret finally finished his long lecture, Cruze left his office and headed for the gym. He spent the first half hour practicing form shooting drills as he tried to place faces with names. Some of the kids had the nerve to catch attitudes when he mispronounced their crazy-ass names.

By the end of practice, he had made sure each player knew his role and that the team had worked on refining their plays.

When Roxanne showed up to pick up Barack, it was on the tip of Cruze's tongue to offer her a ride, but he resisted, knowing it wouldn't look right if he showed favoritism toward one of his players.

"How you feeling, Roxanne?" Cruze asked.

She smiled weakly. "I'm okay…a little tired, but I'll be all right."

He didn't think she looked well at all. It should have been enough that the woman was forcing herself to work an eight-hour job, but to have to come clear across the city on public transportation to pick up her son seemed like too much of a strain. He'd learned from Roxanne that she'd battled ovarian cancer and was now in remission. Maybe if she didn't have to do so much, she'd pick up some weight and start to look a little healthier.

Even though Roxanne was only a couple years older than Cruze, there was something about her that reminded him of his mother. Back when he was Barack's age, all he could do was watch his mother struggle to put food on the table, and it used to make him feel so damn helpless.

When the boys went to the locker room to change, Cruze slid Roxanne a prepaid credit card. "Call Uber so you and Barack can get home quicker. In fact, I want you to use Uber to get around until we can get you some reliable transportation."

Her eyes widened and the corner of her mouth trembled. "Ohmygod! You're gonna make me cry."

He lifted one brow. "Why's that?"

Roxanne hunched her shoulders. "I guess I've been doing bad for so long, I've grown accustomed to struggling. All my life I've had to learn to get by with little to nothing. So, what I'm *not* used to is having someone looking out for me." She shook her head. "I don't get it. You've done so much for me and Barack already. From where I'm from, kindness doesn't come free. So please…make me understand what you're getting out of this, and why're you're being so nice to me."

Cruze ran a hand over his face. "It's hard to put into words. I really don't know how to express it," he said, swallowing back a knot of sorrow as he pictured his mother saying she wasn't hungry and offering him the last slice of bread. The average person had no idea what real poverty was like, but Cruze remembered all too well. Growing up dirt-poor and not always knowing when your next meal would come, or what it would be, had a way of carving a man's soul. Cruze had vowed to himself when he was old enough to sling packs that he'd never be broke. And above all, he'd sworn, he'd never, *ever*, be hungry again.

Roxanne gazed at Cruze through suspicious, narrowed eyes. "Nobody does something for nothing. What are you going to want from me when it's time to pay up?"

Cruze frowned. The last thing he wanted was for her to misunderstand his actions. "When it's time to pay up?" he repeated, shaking his head. "Nah, nah. You got it all wrong, ma. I'm not on it like that. Period. You owe me nothing. Everything I'm doing is from the heart." He put his fist to his chest, up over his heart.

She eyed him closely, curiosity and skepticism flashing in her eyes. "But *why?*"

Cruze inhaled deeply. A faraway look entered his eyes. "My mom was a dedicated mother, like you are. She always tried to make a way for us, even though life was beating her down. With so many trifling young mothers out there today, who don't give a shit about their kids, I have a soft spot for the rare ones who bust their asses trying to give their kids a decent life. Like I told you before, I don't want anything from you. Helping you out makes me feel better about myself…" He paused and held up his hands. "That's the only way I can explain it, and that's the honest truth."

Overwhelmed by emotion, Cruze swallowed and dropped his head as he collected himself. After a few moments, he lifted his gaze back to Roxanne. Although he could feel his eyes becoming a little glossy, Roxanne was blinking and trembling, visibly having a hard time holding back tears.

He gently placed a hand on her shoulder, and patted her reassuringly. "You're gonna be all right. I'm gonna make sure you're straight."

A glow of relief was evident in her eyes. "Thank you," she murmured. "Thank you for everything." Her voice cracked. "Excuse me, I don't want Barack to see me like this," she said and wiped at her eye with the back of her hand. And, before Cruze could say another word, she fled in the direction of the ladies' room, leaving him standing in the middle of the court, his heart filling with hope as he fought to hold back his own tears.

Nine

Cruze slid behind the wheel of his SUV and started his engine with thoughts of his mother on his mind. He missed her immensely. And after seeing the love Roxanne had in her eyes for her son, Barack, it made him now think of his life with his own mother. He'd do anything to have her back. Knowing she was looking down on him wasn't enough. He wanted so desperately to feel her arms wrapped around him, or to simply pick up the phone and call her, just to hear her voice.

Before putting his luxury truck in DRIVE, Cruze locked his doors, then took a few minutes to try to compose himself. He glanced into his rearview mirror and stared at his reflection. All he saw staring back at him was emptiness. Sadness. *"Don't nobody want you. Your own mother died and left you."*

Cruze shook the hurtful words from his mind. *Fuck that hating-ass foster care bitch!* He wasn't trying to go there. Not today. He'd left those memories behind him. Sighing, he laid his head back on the headrest and looked upward toward the roof as if he were looking up into the sky, through white puffy clouds, straight into heaven—where he knew his mother was.

"I love you, Ma," he muttered to himself.

Then closed his eyes, remembering…

"The doctor wants to keep me in the hospital overnight. I don't have the money to pay for a babysitter, so you'll have to look after yourself,

honey." Sherrell Fontaine grasped her son's shoulder, giving it a squeeze, as if trying to infuse her man-child with the confidence he'd need to get through the night.

Cruze, already a full head taller than his mother, gazed down at her uncertainly. "Why I gotta have a babysitter? I'm old enough to take care of myself. But why do you have to stay all night at the hospital?" His changing voice started out low, but midway through the question, it shot up to a high, squeaky pitch. He hated not being able to control his vocal range; it was so embarrassing.

Sherrell usually laughed and teased her only child whenever his voice made unpredictable sounds, but this time she didn't acknowledge it. "Because, sweetheart, the doctor wants to run some more tests and keep me overnight for observation," she explained in a somber tone, as she fought to hold back her emotions.

"And you'll be home in the morning?" Cruze asked hopefully. He had no fear of staying in the apartment alone for a day or two, but what he found unsettling was his mother's demeanor. She usually had a sense of humor about everything, but she was acting dead serious, and seemed somewhat nervous. Cruze watched with concern as her anxious fingers went from fiddling with the knot at the back of the bandana she wore around her head to fidgeting with the buttons on her coat. And there was something else—her eyes didn't look right. The whites weren't quite white, but were instead, an opaque shade of gray and her dark pupils were filled with worry.

Head tilted, Cruze looked at his mother skeptically. "Is everything okay, Ma? You can tell me."

Sherrell's eyes glanced to the floor, then back up to her son. "My doctor is, uh, he's trying to be cautious, I suppose," she stammered. "He wants to make sure all my levels are under control." Although her mouth curved upward, Cruze could sense the fear behind his mother's forced smile.

Cruze frowned. "But the doctor already operated—he cut out the cancer. And...and...you take those treatments to keep it from coming back. Right, Ma?" Cruze's gaze shifted from his mother's face to the bandana she wore to conceal the hair loss she'd suffered since starting chemotherapy.

Sherrell swallowed. "To be honest, honey, the chemo doesn't seem to be helping at all and that's part of the reason the doctor wants to run the tests. When he gets to the bottom of it, he'll be able to figure out the next course of action." She reached out and squeezed Cruze's hand. "I'll be okay after he makes some adjustments in my medication."

Cruze scrunched his brows together in thought. Something wasn't right. It seemed like his mother was hiding something, but he had no idea what.

Sherrell rustled his hair affectionately. "Hey, stop looking so sad. You don't have to worry about me, okay?"

Cruze nodded.

"And don't you give me any reason to worry about you while I'm in the hospital. Okay?"

"You don't have to worry. I won't get into any trouble," he said reassuringly.

Sherrell smiled her first real smile in days. "I know you're a good boy. But you like to hang out at the basketball court with your bad-behind friends, and I don't think that's a good idea when you don't have any adult supervision at home. I'll feel much better knowing you're safe and sound in the house with the door locked. Can you do that for me, baby?"

"Yeah, Ma," Cruze reluctantly agreed, giving a roving glance around the small apartment, taking in the darkened TV screen, the phone that had no dial tone, and the fridge that contained only a few slices of bologna and some hardened cheese. There wasn't even any bread to make a sandwich.

"I spoke to Miss Val about our situation. I told her how they cut off *my check and my stamps because I was too sick to keep my last appointment at the welfare office, and she was nice enough to help us out."* Sherrell reached inside her bag and retrieved a twenty-dollar packet of food stamps and handed it to Cruze. *"Mr. Woo takes stamps, so get yourself some Chinese food for dinner and pick up some milk and cereal for breakfast, and then come straight home. No hanging out on the streets...and no kids in the house. Do you hear me, boy?"*

"Yeah, I hear you," Cruze murmured, happily pocketing the food stamps and imagining filling his empty stomach with some chicken wings, General Tso's chicken, three egg rolls, and two cans of soda. He'd also throw in a couple of Little Debbie Honey Buns and a bag full of loose candy to grub on later.

"Miss Val said you can come up to her place to watch TV and use the phone if you want. But please be considerate. Don't tie up her phone for longer than a few minutes, Cruze."

"I won't," he muttered. He had no intention of sitting up in Miss Val's crib. He knew that the minute he got settled on the couch and started watching music videos on BET, Miss Val's bad twins would switch the channel to some kiddie crap. Maybe he'd make a quick stop to his boy Jerrell's house and see if he'd let him borrow some movies—maybe he'd also let Cruze hold his new Madden 2001 game and a controller. Both Cruze's controllers had broken a long time ago, and his mom didn't have the money to replace them.

While Cruze was plotting on how to keep from going stir crazy while sitting in a house with nothing to do, Sherrell's legs suddenly went wobbly, and she grabbed the back of the frayed easy chair.

Cruze quickly grabbed her and helped lower her into the chair. *"You all right, Ma?"*

Sherrell's face glistened with perspiration and she let out a long, shaky breath. *"Another dizzy spell. I had one at the Laundromat yesterday. I remember grabbing onto the dryer handle to keep from falling, but I* still ended up passed out on the floor." She looked up at Cruze guiltily, as if she wanted to apologize for being ill.

"I would have done the laundry for you if I knew you were feeling dizzy." Cruze's voice went up in pitch as fear clutched at his heart. His mother hadn't mentioned fainting at the Laundromat. She hadn't even asked him to help her put away the neatly folded laundry that she'd pushed home in a laundry cart.

She smiled warmly at Cruze. "Boy, you don't know the first thing about doing laundry. If I left it up to you, our clothes would be ruined with bleach stains." She briefly looked off in thought. "Maybe I need to teach you, though. You might have to start helping out around the house if the doctor decides I need to stay off my feet for a while."

"That's cool. I want to help out," he said, rubbing his mother's back comfortingly while wishing he were a grown man who was capable of taking all the burdens off of her.

Sherrell eyed her son and her heart warmed. He was her life. And she wanted nothing but the best for him. He was a good boy, and all she ever wanted for him was to have a good life. She wanted him to enjoy his childhood and not be burdened with duties that she felt were her own. "For the time being, your only responsibility is to focus on your school-work and to make sure you stay away from those street thugs you like to hang with. It would kill me if my son ended up on a corner selling drugs." She shook her head gravely.

"No way! That'll never happen 'cause I'ma future NBA star," he bragged, flashing a big grin.

The smile that touched his mother's lips never reached her eyes, and Cruze wondered if she doubted his basketball skills.

"I'm serious, Ma. I'ma get us out of the projects and into a big house as soon as I sign my first contract. We're gonna live somewhere with lots of trees and flowers. A pretty house; maybe even a mansion like the ones we see in movies and on TV."

Sherrell patted Cruze's hand. "Having dreams is a good thing, baby, but you also have to have a backup plan. So, don't neglect your studying, son. It's important."

"I won't," he said, but in his heart he didn't believe he needed a back-up plan. In his young mind, he believed that as long as he could dunk a basketball, a bright future was guaranteed. And soon enough, it would be his time to shine.

After school the next day, Cruze was surprised that his mother still wasn't home. He went upstairs to ask Miss Val if he could use her phone to call the hospital. The hospital receptionist put the call through, but when his mom didn't answer, she patched him through to the nurse's station on his mother's floor. The woman who picked up at the nurse's station told him his mother must be asleep. When Cruze asked if she knew when his mother was coming home, she told him she couldn't provide patient information to a minor or a non-relative.

Cruze put Miss Val on the phone, and she gave Cruze a wink when she told the nurse that she was Sherrell's sister. Cruze watched Miss Val's face intently as she inquired about his mother's condition. He got panicky when Miss Val dramatically pulled the phone away from her ear and started frowning and looking at the phone sideways as if the person on the other end had been speaking a foreign language.

"Why're y'all moving her to a hospice facility when she only went in to take some tests?" Miss Val inquired, astonished.

"Where're they moving my mom?" Cruze blurted, anxiously biting his bottom lip.

Miss Val held up a finger, quieting Cruze as she continued speaking to the nurse. "Well, her son needs to see her before she's transferred to that other place. He's thirteen...is that old enough to visit without an adult?" Miss Val listened for a while and then said in a somber tone, "Oh, all right, then."

Cruze was seized by panic. "What's going on, Miss Val? Why ain't my mom coming home? And why they moving her somewhere else?"

"The nurse said, um...To be honest, Cruze, she said she don't think your momma's gonna make it."

Uncomprehending, Cruze shook his head. "Okay, she might not make it home today, but what about tomorrow? Is she coming home then?" he asked in an urgent rush of words.

"Listen, hon. I don't know the whole story, so you're gonna have to get over to the hospital as soon as possible. That place they plan on moving her to is outside the county—it's pretty far away," Miss Val said with pity in her eyes. "I would go with you to the hospital if I could, but I got my hands filled with the twins. Do you have any money for the subway?"

Feeling dazed, Cruze shook his head. Miss Val went inside her purse and pulled out some wrinkled ones. "This is my last four dollars until I get my check next week. But here you go, take this money and go see your mother."

Heart pounding in his chest, Cruze hugged his neighbor, then said, "Thanks, Miss Val."

Thirty-five minutes later, a social worker was waiting for Cruze at the hospital. She introduced herself as Ms. Curry, then told him she would accompany him to his mother's room. She said she had to speak with him privately in her office after his visit was over. He nodded, and without waiting to be escorted, he moved his long legs briskly along the corridor. While the social worker trailed far behind, Cruze scanned each door in search of 1215, and when he reached his mother's room, he burst inside.

"Ma!" he cried out in alarm. Seeing all the medical apparatuses that cluttered the area near his mother's bed was disconcerting.

"Keep your voice down and be considerate of the other patient," the social worker quietly scolded as she entered the room.

The desolate hospital room was divided by a cloth curtain and it seemed that Sherrell had a private room until the sudden fit of coughing from the other side of the curtain made Cruze keenly aware of his mother's unseen roommate.

He looked down at his frail mother who seemed to have lost even more weight overnight. Her eyes were closed, as she lay deadly still, as if entombed beneath the covers. Cruze was jarred by not only her frailty, but also by the sight of her tiny, bare head. She looked so vulnerable without the bandana she always wore to conceal her hair loss.

"It's me, Ma. I'm here," Cruze said, watching for the rise and fall of her chest. Not sure if his mother was still breathing, Cruze bent down and shook her. "Ma! Wake up," he said in a frantic whisper, glancing over his shoulder at the social worker who lingered near the door.

Sherrell's eyelids fluttered open and in that moment, Cruze felt so euphoric, he could hardly restrain himself from gleefully jumping up and down on her bed as if it were a trampoline.

"Cruze," Sherrell whispered, bringing her shaky hand up and touching his face.

"Hi, Ma." Gazing at her, he smiled with relief. His mother was alive and everything was going to be all right. He told himself that from now on, he'd do the laundry, cook dinner, and clean the house so that his mother could stay off her feet and rest until she was completely healed. And since he was tall enough to pass for sixteen, he'd lie about his age and get a job to help pay the bills and take care of his mother.

"I'm trying to fight this, baby." Sherrell weakly raised both her fists and feebly attempted to mimic boxing.

"Fight, what?" In an instant, Cruze's feeling of euphoria was replaced with fear and dread.

"The cancer. The doctor said it's spreading all through my body, and that's why they have to send me to that hospice place. But I'm not giving up hope. I'll be back home before you know it." Sherrell winced and closed her eyes, again.

"What's wrong? Are you in pain?"

She coughed. "Yeah, I think it's time for more pain medication."

Ms. Curry cleared her throat. "Do you want me to get your nurse, Ms. Fontaine?" the social worker offered.

Grimacing in pain, Sherrell could barely nod her head.

"Yeah, she needs the nurse," Cruze interpreted.

When the social worker left the room, Sherrell took Cruze's hand. "The medication they've been giving me makes me groggy, so I have to speak my mind while I'm able to. Cruze, sweetheart, I'm gonna do everything in my power to come home to you, but it might take a while." She paused and began coughing uncontrollably.

Not knowing what to do to help, Cruze handed her a tissue from the box on the nightstand. After she collected herself, Sherrell continued. "Since I don't have any family to help take care of you, I don't have a choice but to let the social worker place you in foster care—only for a little while." Sherrell's voice broke and she used the tissue to dab at the tears that had gathered in the corners of her eyes.

"No, Ma! Please, don't let them do that! I can take care of myself. I'll get a job. And I'll get the cable turned back on so you can watch TV when you come back home."

"That's sweet, honey, but you're not old enough to get a job or take care yourself. Now, you have to promise me that you won't give Ms. Curry a hard time."

"I don't want to talk to that lady about nothing," Cruze barked stubbornly. In that moment, he hated being a kid. He wanted to demand that a doctor talk to him and explain what exactly was going on with his mom, and why she couldn't come home. He felt so helpless not being able to do anything for the woman who'd always worked so hard to take care of him.

"Cruze," Sherrell said in a weak voice, her face contorted as pain vibrated through her body. "Listen to me. Ms. Curry is going to help us until I can get back on my feet. Now, I need you to cooperate with her."

Sherrell was openly crying now and tears poured from her eyes. "Can you do that for me, honey? Please?"

"Yes," he reluctantly agreed. His Adam's apple bobbed up and down, his lips twitched, and his watery eyes bulged as he valiantly fought back tears.

"It's okay to cry, Cruze." Sherrell held out her arms and Cruze collapsed onto her chest, sobbing mournfully.

She stroked his hair. "It's only temporary, baby. We'll be together, again. Real soon."

"Okay, Mommy," Cruze blubbered, crying like a baby and reverting back to calling her Mommy like he did when he was a much younger child.

"Get all the tears out while you're here in this room with me because you're going to need to be stronger than ever after today. It's a rough world out there for young black men, and if you're going to survive, you have to learn how to control your emotions. Do you understand?"

Still crying, Cruze nodded.

"You're smart, well mannered, and the handsomest lil' dude in Brooklyn with those deep dimples in your cheeks." Sherrell smiled though her tears. She coughed again. "We might be from the projects, but the projects do not define you, sweetheart. You are bigger and greater than the 'hood. Don't ever forget that. You have all the qualities to make it in life, if you apply yourself. I want you to go to college, Cruze. Do you hear me?"

Cruze nodded, wiping his eyes with the back of his hands. "Yes. I hear you."

Sherrell swallowed. "I want you to do something worthwhile with your life—something that will help people, not hurt them. I didn't raise you to be a thug, or criminal." She closed her eyes momentarily, and took a deep breath. Slowly her lids fluttered open, and she locked her eyes on Cruze's wet gaze. "Don't let the streets get you, sweetheart. The worst thing you could ever do is to try to make a quick dollar by selling drugs.

You might feel tempted to make some fast money, but I want you to understand that slinging only leads to death or jail time. Now, promise me you won't ever try to take a shortcut by selling drugs."

"I promise," he whimpered.

"That's my good boy," Sherrell said, running her hand from the crown of his head down to his neck. "Ms. Curry promised to bring you to the hospice facility in a couple of days, sweetie. Until then, I want you to know that I love you with all my heart."

"I…love…you, too, Mom." Cruze was gasping and choking and crying so hard, he could hardly get the words out.

The nurse and the social worker entered the room and found Sherrell and Cruze clinging to each other—both crying. Ms. Curry had to physically wrench Cruze's arms from around his mother. When the nurse administered Sherrell's pain medication, she seemed to instantaneously fall into a deep sleep.

"It's time to go," Ms. Curry said when the patient behind the curtain went into a coughing fit that required the nurse's attention.

As he was being ushered toward the door, he cast one last glance over his shoulder, and felt heartened that his mother seemed to be resting peacefully.

That day, thirteen-year-old Cruze Fontaine had no idea that that would be the last time he'd ever see his mother alive.

Or hear her speak the words, "I love you," ever again.

Ten

A shrill sound woke a naked Arabia from a deliciously naughty dream. In the dream, hard bodies pressed into hers. Lips covered hers. Tongues licked at her clit. Hands squeezed her ass. Fingers curled around each breast as warm mouths suckled the tips. Her body arched, thighs parting beneath eager hips, thrusting inside her, deep…deeper.

She never begged—*ever*, but she couldn't stop begging. Couldn't stop saying the word, low and throaty. Please.

Please.

Please. Please, please, please…

Arabia's phone rang. And rang. Pussy clenching, her pulse raced. *No, no, nooo! Say it isn't so.* She was in the middle of being held down and fucked in all three holes by three dark-chocolate, six-foot-something hunks. Hard cock at the mouth of her pussy and at the rim of her asshole, the first two were about to stretch her open, while the third prepared to push his dick into her hungry, waiting mouth.

The dream had felt real, too real. So real that her nipples were tight, chocolate peaks of burning arousal. She'd experienced a threesome before. But having a truckload of hot, horny men fucking her was her most secret sexual desire. A fantasy she kept hidden in the darkest, most private parts of her mind. Multiple mouths. Multiple tongues. Multiple hands. Multiple cocks. All grabbing her, tasting her, devouring her—mmm, oh God yes—fucking her.

It made her skin flush. It made her…

Her phone rang again.

Now *this* shit.

Her salacious dream snatched away by some goddamn obnoxious ringing phone.

She cracked a bleary eye.

Almost instantly, Kelly Rowland's "Dirty Laundry" blared again. *Oh for the love of God!* She blinked. Slowly opening her other eye, she blinked again, her eyes adjusting painfully to the sliver of light slicing in through the slits of her blinds. She lifted her head just enough to check the clock. Four thirty in the morning—on a *Saturday*. Rude. Who the hell called at this ungodly hour?

She knew the answer without having to reach for her cell or glancing at the caller ID. But she groped at the nightstand, anyway, until her hand found her smartphone.

Irritated, she swallowed back the last bit of her dream.

What the hell?

She cursed herself for not turning off her ringer as she snatched her cell from off the nightstand. She frowned and rolled her eyes, glaring at the caller ID. It was her mother, of course. *Oh, she has got to be goddamn kidding me. Not today you won't.* She hit IGNORE. Then turned the ringer off. *You had better try back at a decent hour.*

She grabbed a pillow and buried her head beneath it. She was not in the mood for the likes of Miss Messy. She was exhausting, and it was simply too early in the morning for her shenanigans. There was nothing good that could possibly come from out of that woman's mouth at this time of the morning. Nothing.

It was bad enough that she'd confided in three sisters last week, over drinks, about Teddy's death and how she'd shown up at his funeral. She'd sworn them to secrecy as they sat and listened in utter disbelief, shaking their heads. The sisters thought it real nervy of her. Impolite. Inconsiderate.

"More like trifling, if you ask me," said her sister, Alexis. She was two years older than Arabia, living in Atlanta and married to a neurosurgeon. She was now six weeks' pregnant with their fourth child. "You need to stop acting so hard-up for somebody else's man, like you can't get a man of your own."

Arabia frowned. "Well, maybe I don't *want* a man of my own. Maybe I like sharing them. Fucking them, then sending them back. Maybe—"

Tamara, the second oldest, cut in and said, "Well, *maybe*, you need your ass beat again. You had no business showing up at that woman's husband's funeral like that. I would have done more than clawed your face up, boo. I would have sliced you good." She sucked her teeth. "I wish a bitch would."

Tamara lived in Denver with her husband, who played for the NFL, and their two children. Let her tell it, her man never cheated on her. But, as far as Arabia was concerned, he'd simply never gotten caught. He played for the NFL for fuck's sake! Pussy was being thrown at him like candy on Halloween. But, whatever! It wasn't her story to tell. So, maybe, he hadn't—nor ever would—cheated on Tamara.

Her sister Alexis shook her head. "Arabia, you need to really get a grip, girl. You're too damn beautiful to be settling for someone else's seconds."

Arabia sucked her teeth. "The only thing I've *settled* on is reaping the rewards of having a man *without* having to deal with all the bullshit that goes along with having a relationship with one."

Tamara grunted. "Sounds like somebody needs to be stretched out on someone's white couch. Issues, girl…you need counseling."

Arabia raised a brow. "Seems to me the only ones with *issues* about what I'm doing with *my* life is you three heifers. I don't have any issues with it. And I definitely don't need to be lying on some shrink's sofa, unless said shrink is packing eight or more inches of good hard dick."

"Ooh, lies," their sister, Maya, had chimed in. She lived between California and London, had two twin boys, and was married to an entertainment attorney.

The three sisters laughed.

"Whatever," Arabia huffed, giving them the finger. "What *you* three hoes need to do is stop being so damn judgmental all the time."

"Girl, bye," they'd said dismissively—at the same time. "No judgment here. We're simply stating a fact."

Arabia gave them a pointed stare. "And what *fact* is that?"

"That your ass is damn crazy," Tamara had stated.

"And mighty desperate," Alexis had added as she shook her head, "to think it's okay to screw another woman's husband. I don't care how good he looks, or how big his penis is, or how much money he has in the bank—a married man should be off limits, period."

"Well, he isn't," Arabia snapped. "So get over it."

"Now, now," Tamara said, wagging a finger at her. "Play nice, sweetie. We're only saying all of this because we love you. And we don't ever want to see you get hurt. There's nothing worse than a scorned woman; especially a married one. Believe that."

"Call me what you want," Arabia had said in her defense. "But I'm not the one stressed about what a man is or isn't doing when I'm not around him. It's all you married bitches running around, sniffing your men's drawers, hacking into his social media accounts, and going through his phones, trying to keep tabs on men you already *know* can't be trusted. See. I don't have that problem, boo. So who's really the crazy one in the room?" And for emphasis, she'd tilted her head and swept her gaze over each one of her sisters, waiting.

Alexis scowled. "And *that's* your justification for *why* you do what you do?"

"Yup," was all Arabia had said before she'd reached for her glass and took a deliberate sip.

"Y'all hearing this shit?" Alexis had countered, shaking her head. "Un-*fucking*-believable."

"Well believe it, boo. There are no misunderstandings when it comes to what I need, want. I'm not looking for love. I'm looking for gifts, trips, and some good hard dick. Every time I spread open my legs for a man who I *know* is already taken, I leave my conscience at the door. And apparently so does he, or else he wouldn't be creeping. Right or wrong?"

Tamara had expelled a breath. Her sister's reasoning and this conversation had been slowly draining her. She was done with it. Arabia was going to do whatever the hell Arabia wanted to do. This bitch was delusional. End of discussion.

They'd all blinked at her, then raised eyebrows and stared at her. *Bitch, are you serious?* they seemed to ask. Arabia stared back, defiant and daring.

"Well all right then," Maya finally had said, reaching for the bottle of coconut Ciroc. "It's time to pour it up. I've heard enough from this crazy ho for one damn night."

The four of them sat silently for what seemed like an eternity sipping on their respective cocktails, before Arabia's ringing phone had sliced into each woman's reverie.

It'd been one of her married men, of course.

Arabia sighed, shaking away thoughts of that night with her sisters. She had only wanted to share with them, *not* get talked at and lectured to. They could all lick her ass. She didn't care what anyone thought of her. But what bothered her most was how she carried herself at Theodore's gravesite. Underneath it all, she knew she'd been wrong for going there. And she was even more wrong for saying what she'd said to his grieving widow about having his dick in her mouth the day he died. How low of her. It was downright tasteless on her part. Then, as if that wasn't enough, to have the fight between the two of them go viral on social media was utterly embarrassing.

What had she been thinking?

Ghetto and Arabia didn't fit into the same sentence. And it didn't exist in the same space as she. She wouldn't dare mix or mingle with slum-dogs, or their little gutter rats. But, in the blink of an eye, what she'd done by showing up at that gravesite had spiraled into some ghetto-hot-trash brawl with a grieving widow and her family.

She wasn't one of those thirsty, weave-wearing, hoochie-coochie mommas from around the block they called *thots* these days. Nor was she some around-the-way, weed-smoking skank with the stretch marks on her titties and the rug burns on her back and knees to match, either.

No.

She prided herself on being a cultured ho. Classy. A ho with morals and standards. And, *yes*…very high expectations.

And that was exactly why she always preferred men who were cultivated. Polished. Educated. And well-traveled. Men who had large bankrolls and—*hopefully*, long, hard Magnum-sized cocks to go with all those zeros. And being a little—hell, no. Wait…a whole lot of—freaky in the sheets didn't hurt, either.

But that stunt she'd pulled in Texas—she shook her head as she replayed it in her head—had been downright *ghetto* and *trifling*. She cringed. *I would have slapped me, too.* Arabia touched the side of her face, then allowed her fingertips to brush over the scratches along her neck. Thank God they were only superficial marks, and there wouldn't be any permanent scarring.

She sighed, then shut her eyes and tried to will herself back to that place of hard dicks and heavenly bliss. She reached between her legs and touched her sweet spot. She was still swollen and wet from her late-night fuck, and juicier, now, from her early morning dream. She dipped her middle finger inside her, stroking herself there, imagining her cunt was filled with warm man cream—then pulling out with wet fingers and holding them to her mouth. She licked the tip, then sucked her whole finger into her mouth.

Mmm-hmm. Finger-licking good…

She moaned inwardly. *Pussy this good should be bottled and sold,* she mused as she stroked between her legs once more, again coming up with more wetness.

She smiled at the thought of having her sweet nectar readily available for the masses. If only there were truly a way she could bottle up her cunt juice, then sell it by the case. She'd surely be one rich bitch. Hell, she pondered, if lactating women could sell bottles of their breast milk across the globe, then why couldn't she sell her pussy juice?

Her creamy cunt cream was good for the soul.

She wasn't conceited by far. She didn't have to be. The truth lay in between the folds of her slick pussy lips. It was confirmed every time she spread open her long luscious thighs, and welcomed one of her lovers inside her warm, silky walls and heard their breaths hitch in the back of their throats and saw their eyeballs roll up in their heads as she allowed her muscles to milk the nut out of them.

Arabia was reminded of just how good she was every time she made love to one of her lover's cock with her mouth, lips, tongue, and hands, swallowing him whole until her neck was full, until his warm babies slid down into her tight, horny throat.

Right down to the last damn drop!

She rolled over on her side and stared at her *other* lover, Wellson Cambridge, while he snored beside her, like a hibernating bear. She'd managed to fuck him down into the mattress last night. And, now, look at him. Sprawled out on his back—naked in *her* bed, on *her* plush mattress, atop *her* 1800-thread-count Egyptian sheets, snoring and drooling like he didn't have a care in the world.

He'd flown in last night. "I miss you bad, baby. I need to see you," he'd told her the night prior to his flight. Like all the others, Wellson couldn't get enough of her wet pussy. And every chance he got—which was about three, maybe four, times a month to sneak off—he was on the first flight out of Scottsdale heading to New York for another dose of her hot juices.

Men like him—the cheating kind, were so…*predictable.*

Unhappy.

Sexually deprived.

Horny.

They'd say *and* do whatever they thought necessary, including a promise of marriage, to slide their dicks inside a warm, tight space. *Mmph.* Wellson was a damn fool if he thought she'd ever marry *him*, even if he had given her an engagement ring just two months ago.

Mmph.

Of course she took the ring. She always took the jewels. She wasn't born a fool. Still, Wellson could keep his baldheaded wife. And she'd keep giving him pussy as long as he kept her allowance coming, and showering her with gifts.

She glanced down at her diamond ring and marveled at the glittering gem.

Hell. She deserved it.

"A promise of what's to come, baby," he'd told her, before scooping her up in his arms, laying her on the bed, kneeling before her and spreading open her thighs, then sliding his tongue along the slit of her pussy until she melted all over his mouth and tongue.

For a man in his mid-fifties, sans the gray in his beard, he had a very youthful body and appearance thanks to his obsessive need to be in the gym and that God-awful dye and Murray's pomade he used in his short-cropped hair that spun around his head in thick ropes of waves.

Arabia had to admit. His deep waves were beautiful.

Still…

She reached over and turned on the lamp on her nightstand, then pulled the blanket back and stared at Wellson's six-foot frame. She gave him a disgusted look, taking in his flaccid dick. It lay limp like a long, brown noodle across his right hip. Her eyes flitted up to his head lying on her pillow. She cringed. He'd leave a nasty stain in her pillowcase, for sure.

She rolled her eyes.

How damn inconsiderate!

I need to start making him wrap his big-ass, greasy head in a plastic bag.

She sighed.

Another pillowcase ruined.

Wellson groaned and stretched, pulling Arabia from her thoughts. Aside from a muscled body, his meaty dick was an impressive nine inches when—with the help of Viagra—fully hard. And when it wasn't at its full potential, his long tongue worked wonders on her clit and all over her pussy lips. However, floppy dick or not, Wellson's tongue and six-figure salary made up for his occasional erectile disappointments.

She slid her fingers through her silky shoulder-length wrap, then gave him another long stare. Her hard gaze skimmed back down to his dick. She blinked, then a smile eased over her lips. His cock had come alive. He was rock-hard. And ready.

Never one to let a hard dick go to waste, Arabia contemplated taking it into her mouth and swallowing it whole. But there was something more pressing that had to be done first. So she eased her body up over his and grabbed the headboard with both hands.

"Rise 'n' shine, Sleepy Head," she prompted, shaking the bed. "Momma's got a treat for you."

Wellson slowly opened his eyes, blinked, and finally looked up at the sight before him. He groaned, then smiled. "Mmm. What a beautiful view, baby."

"Good morning to you, boo," she cooed. "Are you ready for your early morning feeding?"

No words were necessary. He lolled his tongue out as Arabia pulled open the swelling folds of her cunt, and slowly lowered herself onto his face. He grasped her waist. And then thrust his tongue inside her, his tongue fucking her swiftly, urgently. The frenzied licking drove her quickly toward an orgasm. He pulled her harder on to his mouth. He licked over her pussy, repeatedly, his tongue flat and firm; licking and licking and licking right over her juicy hole. Then came the sucking and slurping. He tasted her sweat heat and wanted more of it—all of it, so he opened her up with his mouth and lapped at every part of her outer and inner lips while she gasped and moaned on top of him. He captured her clit in his mouth and sucked on it. Then growled, and the vibrations sent shivers through her. Ooh, what a greedy pussy eater he was.

Her cunt juices pooled out of her and coated his lips and chin, and Wellson greedily drank her in. Dragging her nails over her headboard, Arabia looked down at him and decided not to let his dyed, greasy-ass hair irk her.

After all, it was only a pillowcase.

She threw her head back, and let out the softest sigh of pleasure. Then drowned him in her juices.

Seven

One of the conveniences of living in an upscale condo was the on-site fitness center. At five in the morning, Cruze had the facility to himself and he appreciated the privacy. Working on his chest and triceps, he started off with barbell bench presses. He wasn't motivated at first, but by the time he was midway into his routine, working on his second set of standing dumbbell flys, he'd finally gotten into a zone—a Zen-like-state where his mind was trouble free. For Cruze, working out was therapy. An outlet for all the toxic emotions that had been building up over the past year.

Pushing himself past his limit, he became so focused on the movement of the exercises, he didn't notice the gym door opening, or realize he wasn't alone until he heard the voices of a man and a woman.

A distinctive scent permeated the air, and without having to turn his head, he knew that the Hamiltons had entered the gym.

"Good morning, young fella," greeted Morris. "You're up bright and early."

"*Buongiorno*," Valentina said, speaking in Italian. Cruze had no idea what the bitch had said and didn't care. "Good morning," she interpreted, giving him a sly smile.

Valentina looked flawless early in the morning. Wearing fashionable workout gear and with her hair in a high bun that was accentuated with an intricately knotted leopard-print scarf, she looked like a model for women's athletic wear.

Cruze hadn't come to the gym to socialize, and so he offered the couple only a curt head nod and continued his grueling workout.

"Come along, dearest. We have less than an hour to get in our ten thousand steps," Morris said, looking down at the activity tracker on his wrist. Taking the hint that Cruze didn't want to be bothered, Morris ushered his wife toward the row of treadmills, leaving Cruze in peace.

He tried to get his momentum going again, but with the annoying couple chatting away as they fast-walked on the treadmill, he was having a hard time getting back into the zone. It wasn't solely their chatter that he found bothersome. Valentina's sensuous accent and the sexy perfume of hers was fucking with his concentration.

Irked by the intrusion, he gripped the set of dumbbells so hard his knuckles paled. Gritting his teeth and grunting, he completed the sets. When he finished working out with the dumbbells, he headed over to the chest pullover machine and positioned himself in the seat. Refusing to rest between repetitions, he switched to supersets, emitting loud grunts as he punished his body.

Seated with his eyes squeezed shut, he didn't see Valentina sidling up to him, but he smelled her, her floral scent tantalizing his senses and alerting him of her presence. He pushed himself harder, refused to open his eyes and give the perky-tit bitch the satisfaction of knowing she was disrupting his flow. However, every muscle and cell in his body reacted to her body heat and her bold intrusion of his personal space. Cruze's nostrils flared and his eyes snapped open just as Valentina eyed her husband, and then slyly dropped the towel that hung around her neck.

Cruze eyed her as she slowly, deliberately bent over—as if she were retrieving her towel—and slyly slithered her hand to his crotch, stroking him, and then brazenly gathering his balls in her hand.

Heat instantly blazed through his body. Reflexively, he smacked Valentina's hand away—but not before his dick had hardened into a piece of concrete.

Valentina licked her lips and lifted herself upward with her towel in hand, then sauntered back over toward her husband as if she hadn't just fondled his goddamn dick. Livid, Cruze snatched his towel from the back of the equipment, got up, and stormed toward the door.

"Have a good day," Morris called out cheerfully.

With his dick throbbing in his shorts, Cruze rushed out of the gym without as much as a backward glance at Morris or his out-of-control wife.

Back in his apartment, he headed straight for the shower to cool off and contemplate. His reaction to Valentina confused him. He'd never felt such conflicted emotions before. He couldn't stand the uppity bitch, yet he was fiercely attracted to her. And that nut-ass husband of hers…Cruze shook his head. Dude seemed clueless to the fact that his wife was shamelessly chasing dick right in his face.

Fuck both those assholes. If I expect to get a good, uninterrupted work-out, then I'll have to go to a public gym.

Standing beneath the rainfall showerhead enjoying the sensation of warm water cascading over his head and shoulders and running down his back, he lathered soap onto his rock-solid, cut forearms and biceps, while the scene from the gym flashed in his mind: Valentina making her desires crystal-clear as she ran her palm across his crotch and squeezed his nuts. He wasn't sure what kind of games she was playing, but he wasn't interested in getting caught up in any of her bullshit.

Obviously, the bitch was accustomed to getting what she wanted and the memory made him angry and horny at the same time. Cruze didn't understand how he could feel violated, and so turned on at the same time. It caused his dick to bob up and down in an attention-seeking manner. Breathing hard, he clamped a soapy hand around his lengthening cock, and began to pacify it with gentle strokes. With his long fingers closed around his shaft, he thrust upward, slowly pumping dick in and out, and letting his cock meat glide smoothly across his slippery palm.

His entire body throbbed as his hand twisted around the crown of his dick, collecting a gooey mixture of soap and pre-cum. His muscular thighs flexed and his balls clenched with need, but he didn't want to cum too quickly. Prolonging the pleasure, he gripped the base of his throbbing cock and held it tightly. Then, switching to a lazier pace, he slid his palm up and down his straining cock. Feeling the blood surging up his shaft, his hips jerked forward as he picked up speed, his cock jumping in his hand as he jerked eagerly, hungrily. Need clawed its way up from his balls. Ready for the rush of release, he groaned and violently drove his turgid flesh into his tightly closed fist, imagining it was that Italian bitch's cunt he was pounding. Fuck yeah—he'd fuck her until her ovaries shook loose, fuck her until she passed out.

In his head, he heard her begging him to fuck her. Heard her telling him how badly she needed his dick. Chest heaving, pleasure soared as he fucked his fist. His face twisted in a grimace. His heart knocked against his ribcage, he was almost there. Almost, almost...*unh, shit*—

The sound of the door chime interrupted him, mid-thrust.

Fuck! He ignored the chime and continued with quickened strokes that were angry and forceful, his rhythm and hold almost brutal.

The bell rang again, followed by frantic pounding.

Who da fuck?! Cruze brusquely turned off the water and yanked open the shower door. He snatched a towel off the rack and tied it around his waist. As he stalked to the living room with soap suds and water beads speckling his brawny chest, there was a clear imprint of his long, hard dick beneath the towel.

Looking through the peephole, a part of him wasn't surprised to see Valentina standing on the other side of the door. She stood there holding the handle of a large gift basket and wearing a trench coat and red fuck-me heels. *This arrogant, persistent bitch!*

He swung open the door, intending to curse Valentina out, but when her coat parted, revealing bare, cinnamon-colored thighs, Cruze's dick began to thump.

Noticing the anaconda that writhed agitatedly beneath the towel, Valentina blinked and moistened her lips. "Hello, darling. I come bearing gifts." She held up the basket, her coat splitting open wider.

His baser instincts taking over, Cruze was no longer able to remotely resemble a civilized man. "Yo, why you keep fuckin' with me?" he growled. Lapsing into caveman mode, he jerked her toward him forcibly—surprise and shock registering on her face.

"Oh, my," she uttered, the basket slipping from her grasp, and its contents spilling out and rolling in various directions across the floor. Not giving a damn about the gift basket, Cruze kicked it out of his way. Grabbing Valentina by the collar, he ripped off the coat, popping off buttons and revealing her radiant nakedness. As he pressed Valentina against the wall, he flung her coat to the other side of the room.

"I'm sick of your disrespectful ass! You keep tryna tempt a muhfucka," he growled. "Maybe if I fuck that pussy 'til it's raw, you'll get me out of your system and leave me the fuck alone!"

"Yes, I want you to fuck me until my pussy is raw and bleeding,"

Valentina cried out in unadulterated passion. The sound of her exotic voice affected Cruze like the slow-burning caress of a wet tongue flicking against his groin.

"Unh!" he groaned as a rush of desire swept through him with a dizzying force. He tried desperately to hold on to his sanity, but the dangerous beast inside was struggling to break free.

Infuriated by the effect she had on him, he grabbed her by the neck and choked her, uttering obscenities as he unknotted his towel and allowed it to drop to the floor.

Valentina's eyes instantly darted downward at his protruding hardness. "Oh, your cock is perfection—a large and a marvelous dark beauty."

"Shut the fuck up and open up your goddamn legs, bitch." Something wild and uninhibited that he could barely contain, raged within him and Cruze yanked her down to the rug on the floor and entered her roughly in one swift plunge, intending to inflict pain. But her hot pussy opened up welcomingly, accepting his thick, elongated cock with ease.

As he thrust inside her, he grunted like an animal. The primitive sounds he made were foreign to his own ears. Sweat and heat poured off of him. His blood surged hotly in his veins, and his dick stretched deeper and deeper, tunneling into the hot slickness between Valentina's velvety thighs.

This fucking bitch! Wet-ass pussy…

His dick was cocooned inside her tight, contracting walls, and Valentina ran her hands down his muscular back, and caressed his ripped arms. *"Mmm…*Oh God, yes! So g-good. *Mmm.* Fuck me, you magnificent stallion!"

"Yo, shut the fuck up!" Cruze growled, grabbing her legs and bending them back, holding them steady at the back of her knees, opening her wider to him as she grew wetter around him. Crazed with lust, Cruze fucked her like a wild beast, ravaging her cunt until it clutched wildly, weeping out in delight as the powerful, piston-like thrust sent heated chills through her body. Valentina clawed at the Persian rug, her eyes rolling wildly up in her head.

"Yeah, I see you ain't talking shit now, muhfucka," he hissed as he slammed into her so hard, her fake boobs bounced and jiggled. Eyes flaring open, Valentina's climax grew as her nails grasped at Cruze's sweat-slicked back, feeling the muscles flex; the rhythmic blows of his pelvis brushing relentlessly into her clit. Cruze grunted. "Sneaky-ass bitch! Is this what you wanted, huh? This hard-ass dick fucking the shit out of you?"

Valentina opened her mouth to speak, but no words came; just gurgling moans of pleasure. Her tongue knotted in the back of her throat. Valentina felt the ache inside her sizzle and spread like a wildfire. Oh God—yes! His dick was excruciatingly delicious; the exploding rush of pleasure caused her back to arch, and tears to spurt from her eyes. She'd never been fucked so damn good before, until now.

Cruze groaned. Sweat dripped from his face, slid down his chest, then dropped onto Valentina's bobbing breasts. He was getting there, and he let out a harsh moan as the familiar blast of heat ignited in his balls. He accelerated his strokes.

"Oh yes, oh yes, oh yes…give it to me," Valentina purred. "Fill me up with your seed; fill my pussy with your beautiful black babies." Her words struck a chord and Cruze exploded, bellowing in lust and anguish, his mind slipping from the present.

"Chancellor was yours," Ramona had tearfully confided after the children's double funeral.

Misunderstanding her meaning, Cruze had tried to comfort her by saying, "Yes, Chance was my little man. My godson will always be in my heart. Niyah, too."

"No, Cruze. I can't keep the secret any longer." She cupped his face and forced him to look into her eyes. "Chancellor was your son."

Still not believing what he'd heard, Cruze frowned, realization blooming in her words. "What? Chance was my what?"

Ramona swallowed, fresh tears filling her eyes. "Chance was your son, Cruze."

Cruze gazed at her wild-eyed and frantic. "And you never fuckin' told me?!"

Looking terrified, Ramona shook her head. Before she could say another word, Cruze wrapped both of his big hands around her throat, and shook her. "I should kill you, you fuckin' bitch! Why didn't you tell me that Chance was my son?" Frothing at the mouth, he tried to choke the life out of her.

"Ahh!" Valentina screamed. "Let me go! Get off of me! I'm not into that kind of kinky shit." Valentina gasped as she tried to break free of Cruze's vise-like grip. Desperate, she clawed his face and his hands.

Brought back to reality, Cruze suddenly released Valentina's throat. With confusion in his eyes, he looked at his hands as if they were unrecognizable weapons. He looked from his hands to Valentina's troubled face. "Get out," he said in a hoarse whisper.

"What?" Valentina asked.

"Get. Your. Shit. And. Get. The. Fuck. Out," he said, enunciating each word clearly. Valentina gave him an incredulous look. "What the fuck? I said fuckin' bounce, yo! Now!"

Shocked by the sudden change in his demeanor, Valentina gasped, brown eyes flashing up at him with a mixture of fury and hurt. How dare he speak to her in that manner! Impatiently, Cruze took three long strides and grabbed her arm with one hand and snatched up her coat with the other. Valentina tried to wrench her arm from his grip to no avail, cursing him in her native tongue as he hauled her to the door, opened it, and tossed her and her trench coat out into the hall. He slammed the door.

Then he sank down into a chair and closed his eyes—groaning in sorrow and regret, unable to stop the flashes of horrible memories: Ramona's devastating confession. That bloody night of carnage. The son he'd been denied, lying in bed with a bullethole between his eyes.

The dreadful scenes played over and over again like a sickening loop in his mind, causing his head to pound. Heart aching, Cruze threw his head back…

And cried out in agony.

Twelve

Thank God it's Friday!

Arabia couldn't wait to luxuriate. It'd been a long, grueling week of one meeting after another with account executives and her advertising firm's creative team by the time she slid into the cabin of her car, her body melting into the buttery-soft leather seat. She'd been given the Maybach as a gift from Theodore over a year ago, and had only driven it a few times. But since his death, she'd felt compelled to drive it more. She honestly missed him, sort of—in her own strange way.

A slight smile eased over her lips as her mind drifted back to the day he'd given her the extravagant luxury car. Christmas eve. That night, she'd almost collapsed from the shock of being led down to the parking garage with her eyes closed, then opening them to find herself standing in front of the three-hundred-something-thousand-dollar luxury car; a big red bow tied in front of its grille.

Clit pulsing—with key in hand, and a kiss on her lips, her cunt moistened at the imagery of having her legs up over his shoulders and her ass cheeks fucked down into the plush leather. Heat and desire and the excitement of having been given such an expensive gift surged through her body, causing her to reach for him, grabbing him by the nape of his neck and pulling him to her. A hand beneath her ass, he pulled her into him and their mouths met in a rush, a melding of lips, a burst of raw need; one moan after another.

Within moments, the two lovers were in the rear cabin—windows fogged, naked, lost in the throes of passion, christening the leather seats. She'd sucked his cock and given him some backseat pussy right there in the parking garage as a thank-you.

Arabia found herself warming at the memory.

Theodore's hard, veined dick flashed in her mind as she started her engine and it purred to life. He had always loved being swallowed—dick, balls, and every last drop of his nut. And he loved—oh God, yes, how he loved—snacking on her snatch.

Arabia gripped the steering wheel, a sly smile covering her lips, remembering the last time he'd slipped his tongue between her folds and inside her, finding her so warm, so wet. God—rest his soul—he'd surely be missed.

She caught her reflection in her rearview mirror just as she shifted the car into gear and sped off. She couldn't wait to get home. All she wanted to do was slip out of her heels and clothes, pour herself a glass of Chardonnay, then slink her body into a steamy bath and read a few pages from the novel she'd been reading. Some new author, Body of Work, had captured her with her raw writing style and Arabia wanted to get home to crack open her book to see what dirty little sexcapade would be going on next. Whoever the anonymous erotica author was, Arabia was convinced—she was a certified freak.

And she loved a nasty freak.

Too damn bad I don't have one of my own. She shook her head. Wellson had only scratched at the surface of her cunt's greedy need while he was in town. And she was thankful he'd manage to keep an erection, as needed, the two days they'd been together.

Well, in truth—she *knew* his dick would stay almost painfully hard, and he'd be able to fuck her nonstop. Unbeknownst to him, she'd taken L-arginine, Saw palmetto, Yohimbe, and some other male enhancement capsules and ground them in her blender, stirring the powdery substance in all of his drinks, starting with his morning glass of orange juice, then ending with his nightly tumbler of scotch. She'd even gone as far as purchasing a bottle of Oxy-Surge—some male enhancement serum she'd read about—and used it as a lube to give him a nice, slow hand job. His dick had swollen to a delicious erection. Powerful. And he'd piped her down like a horny twenty-year-old.

Still. It hadn't been enough. She'd asked him to choke her, and he'd cringed. She'd begged him to fuck her from the back and slide a finger in her ass, and he'd squawked at that. Sure he'd pounded her pussy, fucked her like a wild man, beat her pussy down like it'd stolen something from him, the entire two days they shared. But he'd still left more to be desired, more to be craved.

Nevertheless, Wellson had been shocked by the intensity of his erections. He hadn't complained. And she hadn't considered the consequences of mixing so many supplements together. But when his heart pounded in his chest and he'd broken out in a sweat, his vision blurring, his pulse racing erratically, Arabia feared the worst. That he was dying. Panic surged through her. Dear Lord. The last thing she wanted was another 9-1-1 call with another lover found naked *and* dead in her presence…from sex.

She definitely didn't need, or want, another body on her conscience, or another lover's funeral to attend. Then again—she shook her head—she wouldn't have gone. No. Not after what'd occurred the last time, when she'd shown up at Teddy's.

She cringed. *Crazy bitch.* She reached for the stereo system, and waited. Moments later, KEM's "You're On My Mind" oozed out of the speakers. She allowed his voice and the melody to take her there. *Yesss.* She snapped her fingers and bobbed her head as she zigzagged her way through the bustling city traffic.

"Yesssss, baby…I ain't too proud to beg," she sang aloud. She suddenly felt like dancing. Felt like swinging her hips, pussy popping, and booty shaking. She laughed at the thought. She hadn't been out dancing in a real club—*wow*—in years.

"Yesssss, dammit! Come get this loving…" She shook her hair, and found herself swirling her hips into the leather of her seat as she drove. Hell, maybe she should go out, let her hair down a little. Even snatch up some stray dick along the way. She could always go for a good fucking. She felt herself growing moist at the possibility. She reached between her legs and patted her kitty. "You ready for another feeding, boo?" she spoke to it as if *it* would speak back.

And it did. Clenching.

She chuckled. *It* wanted her to ride down on a cock like a porn star, stretching *it* in pleasure. And, maybe, she would. By the time Miguel's "How Many Drinks" started playing, she was seriously toying with the idea of *turning up* tonight. She blinked back the feeling of sleep coming down on her. Then stifled a yawn, and remembered what she really needed most—a quiet night at home with a good bottle of white wine, reading and relaxing. And, if her sexual urges overwhelmed her, then she'd open her toy chest—and fuck her own self to sleep.

She yawned again as she made her way to Tribeca—one of the most expensive ZIP codes in the downtown section of the city—to the cobblestone streets and the comforts of her spacious loft in a converted sugar warehouse. Some considered Tribeca the new Upper Eastside. But, for her, it was simply home. She'd been living in Manhattan ever since she'd graduated from Spelman, almost fifteen years ago. And she couldn't imagine her life anywhere else. Ever.

The music on her stereo faded and a call rang through. She

smiled, glancing at the name flashing across the screen. Eric. He was another one of her fiancés. Six-one, dark-skinned with a swimmer's build. She'd met the forty-eight-year-old architect in Chicago, while they both waited for a connecting flight to Kentucky. During their three-hour flight delay at O'Hare Airport, they'd talked and laughed. Then, over drinks at Chicago Cubs Bar & Grill—while they waited for their flight, he surprisingly confessed to being married, but wanting to spend time with her while they were both in Louisville, staying at the same hotel.

Feeling naughty, she'd bitten her lip and taken a moment to consider the invitation before she boldly leaned into his ear and whispered, "If I say yes, you'll have to spend most of your time inside this pussy."

Flashing a seductive grin, nothing more had to be said. The entire time in Kentucky, every moment of his free time was spent with *her*—fucking her. And he'd sexed her good—not great, but good enough for her pussy to stay wet, and for her to want to fuck him again, and again, and again.

Now, here they were, almost four years later, and—not only was she engaged to him, she was still fucking him knowing damn well he was *still* a married man.

She pressed a button on her steering wheel, and answered on the third ring. "Hey."

"Hey, baby," he said, his voice low and enticing.

"Hey yourself, sexy man," she cooed.

"I miss you, baby."

Arabia smiled. "I miss you, too." Although they texted and talked regularly, she hadn't seen him in over a month because of shit she really cared nothing about—his work, the kids, and his ailing wife. Still, she wasn't sure how much truth lied in her words. Did she really miss him? Not really. Hell, she rarely lusted him these days.

But he was good to her. And that's all that really mattered to her.

"I've been thinking about you all week," he said warmly.

"Mmm. Is that so?"

"Yeah. You're all that's been on my mind lately. I need you so bad, baby."

Oh, how sweet.

She moaned low in her throat. "*Mmm.* How bad do you need me?"

"Enough to want to spend the rest of my life making you happy. You're my whole world, baby."

Her smile widened. "Aww, baby, you say the most sweetest things." She couldn't bring herself to tell him he was *her* world too, because he wasn't. He was only a thin slice of it, a portion of her life that could be replaced at any given moment. "You mean so much to me," she offered instead. It was the best she could do.

"I know I do, baby, which is why I've finally made a decision."

"Oh?" Arabia said, curiosity spiking in her. "And what decision is that?"

"I'm leaving her."

Arabia almost lost control of the steering wheel, swerving into the other lane, not believing what she heard. "Excuse *me?*" she shrieked. "You're leaving *who?*"

There had to be some mistake. Her ears had to be playing some kind of nasty trick on her. She blinked, still not quite able to believe her ears. He couldn't possibly be leaving *her*—as in his *wife*. No, no. There had to be some other *her* he was referring to.

"Gwen. My wife," he said softly. "It's time."

She slammed on her brakes, almost running a red light. She blinked again. *What the hell kind of fuckery is going on here?* "Time for *what* exactly?" she asked, gripping the steering wheel tightly, so tight her hands were starting to go numb.

Over the last year-and-a-half, he'd been talking of *supposedly* leaving his wife of twenty years, saying he'd grown tired of her, that they'd grown apart. She was thirteen years his senior, and he felt like they were both traveling in different directions. But Arabia had heard that line before from all the others in her life over the years. Not that she had ever asked him, or anyone else, to leave his wife. After all, she wasn't like most sidepieces who eventually wanted more from the men they shared with their wives or girl-friends, whining and begging and nagging them to death for more than what he might be willing to give them. No, she was nothing like those silly bitches. She *knew* her position, and enjoyed being in her role as just that—the other woman.

Now this fucker was trying to throw a wrench her way. The gall of him! *Bastard!* She'd told him—hell, encouraged him—on more than one occasion when he'd first started talking of leaving his wife, to stay right where he was, where he belonged—with her old, tired, dry-pussy ass.

She'd told him in so many words that leaving the arthritic bitch was foolish. She wanted him to stay until she dropped dead, or at least until she succumbed to some tragic illness and became an invalid. At the rate her arthritis was eating at her bones, she was well on her way to becoming a cripple. All he needed to do was bide his time.

She'd never believed he'd really *leave* her. But—*now*, after hearing this shit, she guessed she was wrong. He'd been serious all along. She felt her stomach knot. What the hell was he leaving *her* for? He couldn't be that stupid to *think* or *believe* she'd ever trust his cheating ass. Could he? Most men didn't ever leave their homes; they only wanted something extra on the side.

What the hell was he trying to prove?

The horn of a silver Porsche blared in back of her, jolting her from her daze. "And why would you do that?" she snapped indignantly, speeding down the street.

"Damn, baby," he said, sounding disappointed. "I thought you'd be happy."

Well, goddamn it, I'm not!

"I am. I mean…this is a surprise."

"A nice one, I hope."

Arabia sighed. "Well no. I mean, yes. I mean I'm still trying to wrap my head around it. I can't believe what I'm hearing."

"Believe it, baby," he said, excitement coating his tone. "It's real. It's going to be you and me, finally."

She swallowed. "Oh," she said, trying to muster up some enthusiasm. But there was none. She couldn't even feign excitement. What the hell was she going to do with a full-time man? She sped through a yellow light. "When are you planning on leaving her?"

"I'm telling her tonight."

She gasped. "*Tonight?* Why so soon?"

"It hasn't been soon enough. Life is too short to stay in an unhappy marriage," he said, sounding like he was having an Oprah moment. "I want to spend what's left of my life loving the woman who has my heart—*you*, baby. I've already been looking at apartments for the time being. Once the ink is dried on the divorce papers, you and I will move in together. In the meantime, I figured we can start thinking about locations and looking for a house somewhere, since we're eventually going to be married."

She frowned, pulling into her building's parking garage. She liked the idea of being *engaged*—having a fiancé. *Not* being married. Not relocating. And definitely *not* having a cheating-ass husband.

"Now wait a minute," she said, shaking her head. "Slow down, tiger. Don't go doing anything hasty. You should really think this through."

"I have, baby. And my mind is made up. It's something I should have done sooner. I can't keep on living this way."

Well, I can. She frowned. "Don't you think *we* need to talk this through further, *first*, before you go making major decisions for me and *my* life?"

She felt heat rising in the center of her chest. She was seething. There was no way in hell she was letting *him*—or any other man— ever disrupt her life. She made and lived by her own rules.

"*Our* life," he corrected. "I'm doing this for us, baby. I'm flying in tomorrow morning so we can talk more about the future, our future," he said, his voice dipping an octave lower. "Besides, we need some quality time together. It's been too long. And I need some of that good loving."

Well, too goddamn bad. Arabia clenched her jaw. He wasn't getting shit from her—none of her delectable pussy or superb head. So, *ha!* He had another damn thing coming if he thought she was going to spread her thighs open for him. Not after hearing this news. Whatever juices might have been pooling in her cunt for him were now dried up, like the damn Sahara desert.

"Not this weekend," she said dryly.

"Huh? Why? I thought you'd be ready for some of this loving I've been saving up for you."

Arabia rolled her eyes. "I have other plans," she simply said. The lie rolled off her tongue quick, without thought. Truth was, she had nowhere to be. "And I won't be back until Sunday."

"Oh," he said, his tone tinged with disappointment. "Where are you going? I'll catch a flight there instead."

She shook her head. *Oh no the hell you won't.*

"Oh dammit. It's my sister calling in," she lied. "Let me take this."

"Oh, okay, baby. Call me when—"

She disconnected the call. Who the hell did he think he was, trying to make plans with her life? No man called the shots. Ever. She was her own woman, with her own mind—and her own damn life plan. And it didn't include *him* leaving his goddamn wife.

She climbed out of her car with a new purpose. Getting the hell out of town. She had no idea where she'd be going, but two things were for certain: she wasn't calling him back. And she wouldn't be anywhere near the city for the weekend, just in case he was crazy enough to show up at her door.

She'd be tucked away in some hotel, hopefully with her legs up…

Getting fucked.

Thirteen

Cruze gazed at his insane sneaker collection, trying to decide which pair to wear to tonight's game. Back in New York, his boys used to refer to him as a seasoned sneakerhead, but he didn't think of himself in that way. He didn't consider himself a sneaker collector, either. He viewed a collector as someone who invested in rare Air Jordans, Pigalle Lebrons, custom Air Force 1s, and other exclusive kicks, only to later trade them or jack up the price and sell them at sneaker conventions or on eBay. Cruze could never part with any of the sneakers he'd amassed over the years—not for any price.

Some collectors kept their sneakers inside their Jumpman boxes, untouched and only to be admired. But Cruze thought of his kicks as wearable art, and he definitely wore them. He sometimes wore two and three different pairs in the course of a day, depending on his mood. And he often bought doubles of his favorites, giving himself one pair to rock and one pair to stock—for later.

Of his over nine hundred pairs, he'd brought approximately a hundred pairs to the new condo. The rest were still showcased in his sneaker closet at the crib in the suburbs. The custom-made shelves at the house were backlit with a special wood that exemplified the sneakers. The shelving covered every inch of wall space and went from floor to ceiling. Despite his tall stature, Cruze had to climb a ladder to reach the sneaks on the top shelves of his collection.

Since taking over the youth basketball team, he'd made sure that his boys always looked fresh at the games, and looking fresh started with the Nike swoosh on their feet. Since he'd taken over coaching, he'd bought the members of the team three extra pairs of Nikes. The extras could be interchanged during school, recreation, and practice, but the first pair he'd bought to match uniforms were to be worn exclusively at their games. The team represented him and he couldn't have the boys wearing dogged kicks on or off the court.

Cruze's passion for sneakers began when he was a kid and got teased unmercifully for rocking cheap, no-name sneaks. "Hey, Cruze…what are *thooose?*" the other kids would taunt cruelly, pointing down at his feet.

He developed a sneaker obsession when he first started slinging, and back then he'd made it a point to buy himself a new pair of kicks every day. He even treated himself to the styles that were popular during his childhood, and that his mom couldn't afford to get him.

In recent years, he'd calmed down considerably with his sneaker purchases, only buying new pairs when something with a lot of hype came out, like the Drake-inspired Jordan 10 OVOs and the 12s as well as the "Dunk," a high-end sneaker designed for Nike by the creative director of Givenchy, Riccardo Tisci. Cruze had only recently copped the Dunks and added them to his vast collection. He was waiting for the right occasion to wear them.

As a coach, his focus couldn't be entirely on the boys' appearance. He also had to make sure they played exceptionally well. Especially tonight. There would be special guests in attendance at tonight's game that included Marquan Naylor and several other former NBA players who were big contributors to HYPE.

Tonight, Cruze's coaching skills would be scrutinized by the best of the best and he had to come through with a win. Needing to calm his nerves, he headed for his weed stash in the bedroom. He tugged on the handle of the drawer, and then suddenly changed his mind. Getting high prior to a sporting event violated the code of conduct expected of coaches. Even though no one would know that he'd smoked a blunt or two before the game and even though he doubted if weed would impair his judgment, he considered it grossly inappropriate to coach kids while lit.

But, he was super-amped and needed something to help him relax. His gaze landed on a candle that Valentina had included in the basket she'd brought over the other day. He wanted to give her back all her shit, but not wanting any more interactions with the nutty broad, he decided to keep the gifts.

Having heard that scented candles had a calming effect, Cruze picked up the Malin + Goetz candle and read the label: *Dark Rum with hints of plum and leather.* He opened the lid and inhaled the pleasant combination of scents, which were unquestionably masculine. Aromatherapy was supposed to be calming and he hoped the claim wasn't bullshit.

His nerves were becoming more rattled every minute, and if the candle didn't help him get into a peaceful state, then he'd have no choice but to spark up a blunt.

After lighting the candle, he sat in the bedroom chair, closed his eyes, and inhaled the rich fragrance. It was pleasant to simply be still and not think about being three steps ahead of the enemy.

In a relaxed state, he pictured his team beating the crap out of the opposing team from West Philly. In his mind's eye, he saw his star forward, Barack, leading the troops and dazzling the crowd by blasting off a series of three-pointers.

With his eyes closed and with the manly fragrance of the candle wafting through the air, his mind quieted down enough for him to be able to think clearly and come up with a defense strategy. He could clearly see his team playing their positions and clogging West Philly's path to the basket. He imagined numerous highlights of the game, and by the time he opened his eyes, he felt confident that his team would win by a landslide.

Crouched between Ramona's thighs, his lips glistening with her juices, Cruze lifted his head and asked, "Am I doing it right?"

Ramona brushed the top of his head. "You're getting a little better. But practice makes perfect." She grinned and pushed his face back between her thighs and grinded her pussy against his mouth. "More tongue, baby. You can't just lick around the clit area when you eat pussy. You gotta mix it up. Get a rhythm going between licking and sucking. And every now and then, you gotta bury that tongue as deep as you can up in the pussy hole. And wiggle it."

Seventeen-year-old Cruze came up for air again and looked at Ramona with a frown. "You want me to wiggle my tongue?"

She nodded. "You know, like a snake." Ramona sat up on her elbows and stuck out her tongue and demonstrated a wriggling movement.

"Oh, okay. I gotchu," Cruze said. Looking intense, he gripped her hips and yanked her toward him forcefully, causing her torso to collapse onto the pillows.

Ramona struggled upright and held out her hand. "Hold up, dude. You acting like you about to devour my ass. Should I be scared?"

Cruze cracked a smile. "Nah, you shouldn't be scared that I'ma hurt you, but you should be a little nervous about how I'ma make you feel." He stretched her legs further apart. "I'm getting tired of you complaining that I'm not doing it right, so I'm about to show you something." He winked at her and licked his lips.

"Somebody's talking shit. All right, big boy—show me."

"Yo, stop calling me that. I'm not a boy. I'ma grown-ass. And I'm your man."

Ramona burst out laughing. "When will you be eighteen?"

"Ain't shit funny, Ramona. I don't see you laughin' when I'm puttin' this dick in you. Anyway, I'll be eighteen in a couple more months."

Ramona rolled her eyes, then playfully waved him off. "Whatever, boy. How many more months 'til you'll be eighteen?"

"Around six," he said with a shrug.

She grinned, shaking her head. "Okay, well, when you turn eighteen ,you can legally be my man. Until then…you're still jailbait."

He shook his head, smirking. "But I bet this dick ain't jailbait. Is it?" He eased up on his knees and grabbed his hard dick, and shook it at her, then smacked it over her clit and her wet hole.

Ramona gazed at the size of his dick, and smirked, the answer to his question shining in her lust-filled eyes.

"A'ight then," he said smugly. "Just what I thought. Now stop talkin' that age shit. I might not be legal in your eyes, but I gotta license to eat pussy and fuck." Before giving her a chance to respond, Cruze was back between her legs, kissing her pussy.

Ramona moaned, flopping back on the bed.

Cruze clamped his hands on her thighs and then slid his tongue up and down slowly between her folds, provoking her to twist and writhe and coaxing a hot stream of moisture out of her. She inched closer to meet his caressing tongue. He lavished her pussy with long lingering tongue swirls. Then, he followed her explicit instructions and began alternating between licking deep into her hot hole with a wriggling tongue followed by suckling and teasing her sensitive clit with maddening tongue flicks. He kept building up the intensity until Ramona was desperately begging him to stop.

"First you said I wasn't doing it right, and now you want me stop," Cruze said tauntingly.

"Come on, that's enough, Cruze," she whined breathlessly. "Look at the time." She closed her legs as she pointed to the bedside clock. "You know you gotta be home by eleven, so stop playing and let's fuck."

"Nah, you always tryna call the shots. You wanted your box ate out and that's what I'm doing."

"Please, Cruze," Ramona pleaded. "Stop playing and put your dick inside me."

"Uh-uh. You was poppin' all that shit, now you actin' like a lil' girl and beggin' me to stop. Be quiet and let me eat this pussy. Then you can get all the dick you want."

Reluctantly consenting, she opened her legs for him, once again. This time, when Cruze tenderly slurped out her honeyed nectar, Ramona was taken to a screaming point of intensity. He burrowed his rippling and undulating tongue inside her until she was pitched over the edge. She grabbed a pillow, placed it over her face and screamed into it at the exact moment when a wrenching explosion jolted her into the infinite depths of an excruciatingly sweet climax.

As her body shook and convulsed, she reached for Cruze, pulling him on top of her.

Frantic with need, Cruze's dick was already leaking when he stuffed it inside her. Two minutes later, his breath came in deep, rasping pants and then his body jerked and was racked by spasms. He collapsed, his face buried between her breasts.

"I'm sorry, Mo," he muttered, using the pet name that he gave her.

Ramona rubbed his back briefly and then patted his shoulder. "It's okay, I know you can't last very long, that's why I gets mine first." She gently rustled his hair. "You have to go, Cruze," she whispered.

"Nah, man, I don't wanna leave, yet. Let me hit it again."

"Go home, big head. You can come back tomorrow," Ramona said with laughter, and playfully popped him on the head.

"Yeah, a'ight. I'll be back here tomorrow, and the day after that, and *the day after that, all up"—he grabbed her ass and cupped it—"in this."*

Ramona smiled and kissed him deeply. "That's my big boy."

"Nah, cut that shit out. I'm your fuckin' man."

She licked her lips. "You're right...you're all the man I need," she said, fondling his dick and pulling him back toward the bed.

When Cruze arrived at the center on Friday night, there were so many cars in the lot, he had to park around the corner. The place was so packed, Bret had to call in extra security.

The big crowd had arrived to see Marquan Naylor. The former all-star player had agreed to engage in some one-on-one playing with a few HYPE kids during the halftime festivities. He also was slotted to take selfies with the attendees, and sign basketballs for his fans. The press was in attendance and would be capturing promotional pictures of Marquan interacting with underprivileged kids. It was good promotion for HYPE and Bret Hollis had convinced Marquan that his participation would persuade the Hall of Fame committee to change their minds about inducting him.

Cruze hadn't expected the press to be involved with a kiddy basketball game, but Bret was going hard trying to get his organization noticed, and all Cruze could do was accept the media's presence and suck it up.

He had a big job to do and he wouldn't be able to function properly if he was consciously fending off and dodging cameras, and so he tuned out the media.

To his chagrin, his team played embarrassingly bad the first two quarters, and when halftime rolled around, he was livid as he herded them to the locker room. In the midst of pointing out everything the kids had done wrong, Marquan came in and gave them a pep talk. He told them that he was proud of their spirit, and sportsmanship, and that he expected to see them all playing in the NBA one day. After he pointed out what he noticed that each boy had done right, he opened the door to the locker room and allowed the kids' parents to come inside and take pictures of him posing with their sons.

When the team returned to the floor for the third quarter, they played as if a fire had been lit under them. Oddly, it hadn't been tough talk that got them motivated; it was Marquan's method of pointing out their strengths.

Cruze took notes for future games.

The fourth quarter was close, but Barack came through with an amazing string of three-pointers that put them ahead by five points by the end of the game.

The crowd erupted with a burst of cheers and joyful yells. The boys, grinning from ear-to-ear, high-fived each other.

Both Bret and Marquan approached Cruze, clapping their hands together. "Good game, man," Bret congratulated, patting Cruze on the back.

"After the first half, those kids got serious with defense and turn-arounds, and that Barack is a shooting lil' muhfucka," Marquan added, laughing. "Yo, Cruze, what are you up to tomorrow night?"

"Depends," Cruze responded.

"I'm hosting a party at Club Seduction and you're invited to join me in the VIP. Along with Bret and some of my other friends."

"Yeah, man. I'll stop through," Cruze said absently as his eyes roved around the gym, watching the happy expressions on the faces of his team. The boys were still soaking in the love from family and friends and Cruze felt a sense of accomplishment knowing he was making a difference in young lives.

"Yo, I'm co-hosting with this stripper bitch from L.A. who's like a social media goddess," Marquan continued. "The place is going to be bananas, and…"

As Marquan's voice droned on, Cruze tuned him out and retreated inside his mind, sending loving thoughts up to his mom, whom he knew was looking down on him and feeling pride now that he was finally doing something worthwhile with his life.

He smiled inside. *For you, Mom.*

Fourteen

Saturday morning, Cruze's eyes were glued to his tablet. The reporter had given a commendable play-by-play accounting of last night's nail-biting game. There was a poignant photo of Barack dunking on the opponent. The image was a testament of his hard work. The camera had managed to not only catch his amazing high-jump, but also captured droplets of perspiration that had been flung from his body and seemed temporarily suspended in midair.

The ref had allowed those lil' West Philly knuckleheads to get away with way too many violations during the first half, but Cruze's boys had miraculously pulled off a win, sparing him the embarrassment of losing in front of a full house of spectators, press, and vising sports icons like Marquan Naylor.

He decided to reward the team with pizza or dinner at Red Lobster after next Friday's game. Win or lose, as long as they continued to put their hearts into the game, he'd treat them to a special outing at least once a month. Most of his boys didn't get many opportunities to leave their neighborhoods, and even though a joint like Red Lobster wasn't a big deal to most people, the boys would enjoy it.

Wanting the kids to benefit from every possible opportunity, Cruze had been looking into a summer basketball camp that was located in the Poconos mountains. It was pretty expensive, and although only a few of the boys made good enough grades to qualify for a scholarship into the program, Cruze wanted the entire team to reap the benefits of mingling with kids in a more diverse setting. He'd have to have a talk with Bret and see if there was a way to get additional funding. If not, Cruze wasn't opposed to anonymously paying the fee for all the boys.

He'd never imagined that working with children would be so rewarding. But their moms, though. Many of the team mothers had wheedled Cruze's personal number from him under the pretense of wanting to be able to check on their sons when they traveled to away games. Some of the quietest, most polite moms were off-the-chain, undercover freaks.

Cruze laughed, thinking about some of the nasty text messages he'd been receiving from quite a few of the boys' mothers. Not to mention the wet pussy pics, naked asses, and bare titties that had started popping up on his phone. Some of the more sexually adventurous women had sent him videos of themselves cumming while playing in their pussies. A few sent videos of them sucking and fucking their boyfriends, husbands, or whomever.

One mom named Tanji was a tall and shapely chocolate chick. Every time Cruze saw her, her hair was fixed in an elaborate style with a different vibrant color. It was hot pink one day and neon green the next. Tanji had sent him several videos of her letting some short, muscular dude power-fuck her in the ass. Dude was bulked up like he was straight out of prison. In each video, he rammed the shit out of that bitch's asshole, and not once had Cruze seen him go anywhere near the pussy.

But the videos were hot, and Cruze had jacked off to Tanji's anal escapades numerous times. He personally had no problem sliding his cock between a pair of fluffy ass cheeks, but he'd be damned if he'd devote every dick stroke to a booty hole. He needed to feel a juicy pussy with a good grip, clenching and strangling the shit out his thickness.

With the moms on the team keeping Cruze supplied with good, ol' homemade, authentic porn, he no longer had to visit the boring sex sites he used to frequent.

Still, the moms were starting to go overboard, and pretty soon he was going to have to check their asses and tell them they had to chill. Although many of them looked extremely fuckable, there wasn't a chance in hell that he would disrespect any team member by smashing his mom.

Returning his gaze to his iPad, Cruze went back to the article about his team's win. He was proud and pleased that the journalist had referred to Barack as a young basketball phenomenon and someone to watch.

As his eyes scanned downward, Cruze let out an audible groan. Damned if there wasn't a big-ass photo of him, Bret, and Marquan kicking it together on the court after the game. He'd clearly told those journalistic sons of bitches not to take any pictures of him. He'd told them to focus their camera lenses on the team, but one of those sneaky bastards had caught him in a candid shot and had also identified him beneath the picture with his full government name.

Goddamn! Cruze could only hope that the people who would like to put him six feet under didn't have the kind of idle time that allowed them to be trolling the Internet and perusing a Philadelphia African American newspaper. What were the odds of his enemies seeing that particular article? Slim to none, Cruze convinced himself.

But he was still pissed.

And in order to relieve his aggravation, he needed to get up into some intestines. Sadly, his fuck-buddy, Laila, was all the way in

New York. He had no problem driving there real quick, but it wouldn't be easy to get in and out like he needed to. Once Laila's clingy, needy ass had him behind closed doors, she'd do everything in her power to try to keep him there. *Let me fix you something to eat. You want a massage? Wanna watch a movie?* He didn't have time for any of that shit after he'd nutted real good. Besides having to duck killers, the other reason he couldn't linger in New York was that he had accepted Marquan's invitation to be his guest at Club Seduction.

So, dropping in on Laila for a quick fuck was out of the question.

It was fucked up that he'd burned all his bridges with the Philly chicks he'd smashed since relocating here. It wasn't that he was a bad guy. The problem was the way the women had all tried to pressure him into a committed relationship immediately after he'd gutted them for the first time.

Anxious and aggravated over his picture being in the paper, Cruze was horny enough to forget about his moral code and make a call to Take-It-Up-The-Ass Tanji—or one of the other moms on the team. But nah, as a coach, he couldn't fuck with any of the team moms. It wasn't fair to their sons.

He pondered the situation, and concluded that the most convenient piece of pussy available to him was his nutty neighbor across the hall. His dick was throbbing so bad, he was close to trekking over to the Hamiltons' apartment and banging on their door. If the dumb husband answered, Cruze would simply ask if he could speak to Valentina—alone. There was no doubt in his mind that the jackass would deliver his wife right into Cruze's horny clutches.

In the mood to pound Valentina's pussy until the bitch's eyes rolled into the back of her head, he gave his pulsing dick a gentle squeeze and massaged it a little. Then he advanced toward the door with his dick hard as a brick as he pictured grabbing that snobby slut by the hair and dragging her back to his place.

No sooner had he placed his hand on the knob when his phone pinged. He looked at the screen and smiled when he saw that a new video had come through from Tanji. He pressed play and was delighted to see Tanji, the prison dude, and a lil' shorty with long blue hair, naked on the screen.

A threesome! Shit, yeah! He unzipped his pants, took out his throbbing dick, and dropped into a chair. His sex drive was off the chain and had been that way since back in the day when Ramona had first turned his young ass out.

"I ain't no kid, so why you always playing?" Cruze's nostrils flared and his eyes flashed with anger.

"I don't know why you getting mad at me. I didn't put you on a curfew," Ramona said saucily.

"Fuck that curfew. I can come and go as I please."

Ramona ran a hand through her long hair, smoothing it into place. "Until you can support yourself, you have to follow Miss Beverly's rules."

"I can support myself. My boy got me a job lined up at Blockbuster, but I can't go in for the interview until his supervisor gets back from vacation."

"How much you gon' make working at Blockbuster?" Ramona asked with her lips twisted in disapproval.

"Minimum wage, but that's better than nothing."

"Umph," she grunted in disgust. "You gon' end up with next to nothing after they take the taxes out of that little bit of money. It wouldn't be me workin' at no Blockbuster. Boy, you need to do something that pays under the table."

"Like what?"

Ramona stared at him long and hard.

"What?" he repeated, holding out his hands.

"You need to get your butt out on the block like everybody else. If you want, I can help you get your first package."

"You talkin' about selling drugs?" Cruze scowled and looked at Ramona like she had sprouted an extra head.

"What? You too good to sell drugs?"

"It's not that, but…"

"But, what?"

"When my mom was on her deathbed, I promised her I would never sling drugs, and I can't go back on my word." Cruze wore a pained expression as he stared off in the distance.

Ramona let out a sigh. "Do you think your moms would expect you to keep that promise if she knew how hard it's been on you having to live in a bunch of different foster homes over the years?"

Feeling pressured, Cruze wiped sweat from his brow. "You don't understand, Mo. My mom didn't play when it came to her son selling drugs. And I can't break my promise…I just can't, man."

"I'm just saying…your mom ain't here to protect or provide for you. And your ass is too old to be rocking bobos and wearing secondhand clothes that don't fit your tall ass right."

Cruze winced as if he'd been slapped. "So, what you saying, you ashamed of the way I dress? Is that why you only sneak around with me after dark?"

"We have to sneak around because you're an underage ward of the state, and I'm a twenty-four-old woman. I'm not tryna do time for fucking around with you. So, you goddamn right I'ma keep it on the low 'til you're legitimate and living on your own." Ramona suddenly shot Cruze a curious look. "What happens after you turn eighteen? Do you get housing and a check or something to help you get on your feet?"

Cruze shrugged. "Nah, not really."

"So what do they do for you?"

"Nothing that I know of."

"That's crazy. So they just gon' put you out on the streets?"

He lifted his shoulders again.

"Boy, you crazy if you just sit back and wait for Miss Beverly to take back her house key."

Cruze smiled sheepishly. "I was hoping I could stay with you."

Ramona turned up the corner of her lip. "Fuck if I'm taking care of your big, grown ass."

"I'll be working by then."

"Right. Making minimum wage at Blockbuster—before taxes. I don't know how you gon' support yourself off that lil' bit of dough," she muttered bitterly.

Cruze let out a groan of distress. He jumped up and started putting on his pants. "Okay, fuck it. Instead of throwing slurs, why don't you just admit you don't want to be bothered with my broke ass. Tell me the truth, and I'll leave you alone."

Ramona patted the bed. "Sit down, Cruze."

"Nah, I'm good." He pulled his shirt over his head. "I'm waiting for you to tell me it's over." He narrowed his eyes at her. "Say it, Mo, and I promise you won't have to worry about me anymore."

Ramona rolled her eyes and sighed. "Cruze, it's not that I want to break up, but you need to understand that sometimes in life, we have to do things we don't want to do. Do you think I enjoy going to the strip club and letting niggas paw all over me? I hate it. But I do what I gotta do to pay the bills and survive."

Cruze furrowed his brows. "Whatchu mean by 'paw all over you'? I thought you danced on a stage and niggas threw money at you. You never mentioned that muhfuckas was rubbin' and touchin' on you."

"I do dance on stage for tips, but that's only part of my job. Sometimes I have to do a little extra."

"Extra like what? I know you ain't tricking, are you?"

She frowned. "Lil' nigga, please. I ain't trickin' shit. But a bitch got bills, so if a man wants a lap dance, then that's what I give him. It's when they start tryna feel all up on my titties and ass that I have a problem."

Visibly distressed, Cruze cursed and palmed his head. "Yo, word is bond. I'll fuckin' kill a muhfucka for putting his hands on my girl."

Ramona looked at Cruze intently and then eased off the bed. Naked, she paced over to him and looped her arms around his neck. "I've been dancing since I was eighteen. That's a long time to be waiting for someone to come along and take me out of the strip club. I only have one question to ask you, baby." She eased up on the balls of her feet and pressed a kiss against the corner of Cruze's mouth. Then eyed him intently. "Is that man going to be you?"

With a troubled expression, Cruze matched her stare, nodding his head. "Yeah, Mo, I got you. I'll do whatever I gotta do to get you the fuck up outta there. I mean that shit, girl. On e'rything."

Fifteen

Saturday night, Arabia stepped from the town car in front of Club Seduction—a trendy Philadelphia nightclub on Sansom Street, and for a moment she stood there at the curb taking in her surroundings, while allowing onlookers to take in *her*.

Swathed in red—the color of seduction and sin. The fabric of her slinky dress clung dangerously to her body, outlining every single curve and dip of her voluptuous five-nine frame, cinching at the waist, then flaring out. Its hem fell a few inches from her ass cheeks, showcasing her long, sultry legs while leaving very little to the imagination. Beneath it, she wore a red lace thong.

It was nights like this—nights of prowling—when she was most bold, daring. And it showed in her dress, in her walk. It oozed from her pores. It swirled around her. Heat and passion and animalistic need hummed through her body.

A sensual club beat pulsed, spilling out into the night air every time the door opened, as partygoers eager to get inside stood in a line that extended down the sidewalk and wrapped around almost two blocks. Arabia was damned if she'd be standing in *that*. She waited on nothing, or no one.

She hadn't known of the club until two hours ago, when she'd asked the six-foot, twenty-something-year-old man/child behind the Marriott's concierge desk for a list of clubs in the City of Brotherly Love. He'd eyed her slowly, before licking his lips, then ticking off a list of hotspots. Nothing had stuck out until he rattled off this one. Club Seduction. *Mmm*—yes. How apropos, considering she was feeling seductive tonight. And she wanted something hot and dirty.

Hell, after the bomb Eric had dropped on her yesterday—what an inconsiderate asshole—she really did need a night out to let her hair down and do a little finger popping, after all. Still, Philadelphia was the last place she expected to come for her great escape when she'd gassed up her Benz and driven the Interstate, heading out of the Big Apple.

Yet, here she was.

Maybe, if the night heated up, like she hoped, and someone caught her eye and made her pussy tingle, she'd bend over and pull her thong to the side. Maybe.

Her cell phone buzzed, and she fished it out of her clutch. It was from a blocked caller. She swiped a fingertip over the screen and answered. "Hello?"

"I've been trying to reach you all day," said the gruff voice on the other end. "We need to talk, baby."

Arabia frowned. "Eric, I told you I'd be out of town. And why are you calling me from a blocked number?"

"Where are you?" he asked, ignoring her question. He had been trying to reach her all day and she hadn't answered any of his calls, or replied to any of his text messages. But, surprisingly, she answered a blocked call. He had to wonder had she been avoiding him.

Irritation scorched her veins. "Away," she said impatiently.

"Yeah, I know all that. Where?"

"Why, Eric? I told you I'd be with my sisters."

He scoffed. "No actually you didn't. And you never called me back after you ended our call. Nor did you respond to my text messages."

"I got sidetracked," she quickly said. Yeah, trying to get the hell out of town.

"Wel,l when will you be back?"

"Tuesday," she lied. She didn't need to have her weekend disrupted by his "I'm Leaving My Wife" news.

Eric snorted. "Ugh. Tuesday, huh? Just yesterday you said you'd be back Sunday. Now it's Tuesday? Yeah, right."

Oops. She'd forgotten that she'd told him that. See. This was why she didn't lie. She could never keep up with its deceitful trail. Lying was too much damn work trying to remember every minuscule detail. She simply wasn't cut out for it.

"Well, what's the urgency, Eric?" she said sharply.

"There's no urgency. Last night I told Gwen about us."

She shook her head. Sadly, there had still been a part of her that had hoped he wouldn't have done so. "And why would you do that?"

He sighed. "We already discussed this. I told you I was telling her."

Held tilted, hand on hip, she scowled. "No *we* didn't discuss anything, Eric. I told you *we* should talk about it *before* you did such a silly thing."

"*Silly?*" he scoffed. "What's so silly about wanting to be with the woman I love?"

Arabia blinked. Love? The only thing this asshole loved was access to stress-free pussy. He didn't *love* her. Hell, he didn't even *know* her. Because had he known *her*, he would have known that she would never commit to a cheating-ass man. Ever.

"It's me and you now, baby," he said smoothly. "Now we can finally have the life we've dreamed of having."

Her stomach lurched. She'd already been down this road twice with two previous lovers, and she'd broken it off with the both of them right on the spot. Now it looked like she'd have to do the same thing again. End it. She paced the sidewalk. How dare he try to ruin her goddamn night with this shit!

Arabia shook her head in disbelief. "And what kind of life do you think we'd have now that you've left *Gwen*. And now that she knows there's another woman you're leaving her for, do you actually think this is going to unfold smoothly? No, boo-boo. She's going to make your life a living hell. Drag you for everything you're worth. Tell me, Eric. What kind of life is that, huh?"

"Baby, she can have the house, and half my pension if that'll make her feel better. As long as I have you—that's all I need, baby; I can rebuild. I don't care about any of that."

Well, I care about it. She sighed. This man was clueless. And there was simply no time like the present to be done with him. Her heart panged in her chest. This was so disappointing. And here she thought she'd be able to get at least another year or more with him.

She glanced down the sidewalk. "Look, Eric. I don't think this is going to work," she said bluntly.

"Excuse me?" he said, baffled. "You don't think *what* isn't going to work? *Us?*"

Arabia stopped pacing, and glanced at the line in front of her, then at the time. It was already going on eleven. She needed to get inside to get her drop and pop on before the place got too packed. Besides, she needed a damn drink, and a hard body to grind up on.

"Yes. Us."

"And why not? I left my wife to be with you."

"I didn't ask you to. You left her because that's what *you* wanted to do. You did that with no regard for what I might have wanted. I need me a man who is going to stay with his wife, not leave her. What kind of life do you think we'd really have with me *knowing* you cheated on her to be with me? Leaving her gives me no guarantees that you wouldn't turn around and cheat on me too. Sorry, boo. I've never been a woman to be cheated on. And I'm not about to sign up for that now. I don't need that kind of stress in my life."

"Say what? Are you *fucking* out of your mind!" he yelled in her ear. He was irate. "Bitch, I fucking gave up everything to be with you!" Arabia pulled the phone away from her ear, surprised by his sudden outburst. Eric was shouting so loud she envisioned his veins popping out of his neck. In all the time they'd been screwing, he'd never once raised his voice to her, let alone called her out her name. "Why didn't you open your fucking mouth and tell me this shit *before* I fucking told my wife about you?"

She pushed out a frustrated breath. "Well, had you *waited* like I told you to, you would have known. And we wouldn't be having this conversation right now."

"I don't believe this shit! You've just fucked up everything."

Arabia frowned. "No, Eric. *You* fucked up everything by leaving your damn wife. You had a good thing. And now you've lost it. Go crawl back to your baldheaded wife and tell her you made a mistake. Beg her forgiveness. I'm sure she'll take your lying, cheating ass back."

"You fucking bitch! Gold-digging whore!"

"I've been called worse. Have a good life, Eric."

"I want my fucking ring back," he spat.

Arabia laughed. "Good luck with that."

Stupid-ass men, she thought ending the call, then turning her cell off before tossing it back into her purse. She couldn't believe this. She'd gone from having three lovers to one in less than a few weeks. *Whatever*. Good bye. Good riddance.

At this moment, she had her sights on having a good damn night. Tomorrow she'd worry about whatever would come. But, for now, it was time to let her hair down, and—*hopefully*, her red thong.

Arabia brought her attention back to the front of the club. Just outside the doorway was a dark-skinned bouncer—tall, bald, and bulky—who stood in front of a roped-off area, dressed in all black and wearing an earpiece that keyed him into all the activity going on inside the club.

It didn't take long before he caught sight of her and clearly saw what everyone else did. A woman bold enough to take what she wanted. A woman able to get any man she wanted without saying a word. Her body and presence said it all.

He gave her a head nod, and motioned her to him.

Arabia smiled, then glanced down the sidewalk, her eyes slowly traveling down the length of the ridiculously long line. A mix of beautiful—and, well, not so beautiful—people waited to get inside. Some of the females were glammed up in their most sultry outfits, donned in good heels and jewels, and hair that probably cost a small fortune. Others—wearing pixie-cut and bobbed wigs, multi-colored weaves, and obnoxiously long ponytails—stood there in their clunky platform heels and peep-toe pumps, looking like they were waiting to audition for the circus in their cheetah, leopard, and other animal prints—from leggings and cat suits to skintight dresses, they simple looked a hot mess from Arabia's assessment.

Still, some of the women in the line were stunning. Some alone, probably on the prowl—like her, using the club as a hunting ground for some drunk, horny dick. Others were there with their arms securely looped through the arm of a date, or perhaps a lover. Territorially. Staking their claims to their men—or someone else's.

Yes, yes, yes. The *men.*

Handsome, buffed, hard-bodied men with either fresh-shaved faces or well-manicured beards with spinning waves, dreads, or low-top fades—all donned in expensive hard-bottomed shoes and designer digs. Gold and platinum chains hung from thick necks with diamond medallions sweeping across muscled chests.

There were also the ones in the suits and ties and Florsheim loafers and tie-ups, looking stiff and terribly out of place, there for the stray pussy that would probably cost them multiple rounds of drinks to even sniff.

And then there were the ones barely over twenty-one in their khaki pants and thin pullover V-necks and pierced ears, looking preppy and rich, out to get white-boy drunk with hopes of scoring some late-night pussy.

Arabia slid her tongue over her red-painted lips and tossed her hair. Dramatic she knew, but necessary. She hadn't even been out there for more than a second and she already felt the eyes on her. But it was okay. She welcomed the stares, as she always did; even the glares from the hating-ass, jealous hoes. They had cause to be alarmed.

The night air, cool and light, licked over her skin causing her nipples to tighten. The bouncer regarded her intently, his smoldering dark orbs raking over her, before fastening his gaze on her breasts, on the imprint of her nipples, on their puckered ridges, through her dress.

With the toss of her hair, Arabia tucked her clutch beneath her arm and sauntered toward him, one heeled foot in front of the other, her pelvis thrusting with each step. Subconsciously, the bouncer licked his lips and swept his gaze over her body again as she made her way to the door.

Eyes zoomed in on her, and those women at the front of the line sneered, practically gnashing their teeth, as the bouncer leaned in and whispered something in her ear before he reached down and unlatched the red velvet rope that was strung between two metal poles, welcoming her in.

"You hot, baby," the broad-shouldered bouncer said, his eyes appraising her in pure male appreciation as he motioned her by.

Arabia smiled. Yeah, them bitches still standing in that long-ass line didn't hold a candle to her kind of hotness, and they hated her for it.

Oh, yes. She was hot. Hot like fire. She was a woman who knew how to make a man's dick roar to life by just the lick of her lips, or the sway of her hips. A woman who tugged at a man's libido and inspired him to want to fuck her on the spot, fast and hard until he burned in wet heat and sin. And she knew it. She was a temptress on a mission. She was on the hunt for a scandalous night filled with dancing, hard dick, and dirty deeds.

So they had all better beware.

Because, tonight...somebody was going up in flames.

Sixteen

Young Dro's "Fuck Dat Bitch" blared through the speakers, and Arabia didn't understand a damn word being said— except for *fuck that bitch*. Ooh, she was so out of her element. She sighed. With a name like Club Seduction, she had expected the club's dance selections to be a bit sultrier, more tasteful. Not this ratchet shit. But so far that's all her ears were being assaulted by. She felt a headache slowly edging its way to the center of her forehead. Nevertheless, the song had a nice beat, and Arabia—despite pressure building in her head—found herself bouncing her ass and swaying her hips as she made her way through the club toward the bar, pondering how many drinks it would take before she settled into her surroundings and didn't look like she didn't belong.

Strobe lights flashed across the space. The bass thumped. Drinks flowed. And the mirrored bar stretched from one wall to another and was lit up with red lights.

Arabia eased her way through a group of loudmouthed twenty-something-year- olds, their pants riding low on their hips, each holding a bottle of Hennessy in their grips. She eyed them on the sly in all their flashy jewels and mouths filled with gold. They were young drug dealers, she surmised.

Every now and again, she hungered for some thug dick—for a hard fucking, but there was nothing a drug dealer could ever do for a woman like her. Dismissing their hungry stares, she leaned in over the bar—feeling the young men's gazes caressing the back of her thighs and the rim of her ass cheeks peeking from beneath the hem of her dress. She murmured her order to the bartender. He smiled at her, his eyes twinkling in appreciation at the beautiful sight before him. Arabia took him in, and smiled back. He was handsome, not overly fine, with chiseled features.

She slowly slid her tongue over her lips, causing the bartender's skin to heat. He winked at her, then began making her drink—Fireball and a splash of orange juice. Tonight wouldn't be a martini night, or one of her frou-frou girly drinks. No, she needed something with a little kick to it, but nothing that would have her staggering or knocked on her ass.

She cringed when the DJ played a Bobby Shmurda song. Nigga this, nigga that…she blinked. *What in the hell?* She wanted to clap her hands over her ears. She couldn't believe anyone on any sophisticated level would dare play this, let alone *ever* dance to it. But the dance floor was packed, and the crowd danced hard, chanting out the lyrics.

Arabia twisted her lips in disgust.

Girl, get over yourself! she scolded herself. *You're here hunting for dick, not to give out a damn music award.*

As she waited for the bartender to return with her drink, she glanced around the two-level club, and experienced a sudden awakening as Fetty Wap's "Trap Queen" eased out of the speakers. It all made sense to her now. That's what she was surrounded by. Trap Queens and Trap Keepers. But she'd stomach through the ratchetness even if it killed her. She had no intentions of being derailed—shitty music or not. She'd simply get her drink on, then make the dance floor her personal playground.

She looked up at the second floor of the club and realized she was down on the wrong level. All the beautiful people, the classy type, were up on the second floor. Not down here with the—

"On the house, baby," the bartender said over the music when he returned with her drink. Arabia brought her attention back to the bar. She smiled, and thanked him, then quickly pulled a twenty from her clutch and handed it to him as tip for his thoughtfulness.

He winked again and smiled a *thank you* of his own, before heading down the bar to attend to another customer. Arabia pulled her drink to her sumptuous lips and took a long hard swallow. Instantly, the cinnamon whiskey began to heat through her veins and she felt her body relaxing.

Mmm—yes.

It was exactly what she needed, a little jungle juice to loosen her hips. She took another sip, then licked at her lips. Drink in hand, she headed for her next destination. The second floor.

VIP was where she needed to be.

As soon as *she* came into view, Cruze blinked, then leaned forward in his seat overlooking the VIP section's dance floor, pushing the half-Asian, half-black female, with the pouty lips and perky tits— who'd been rambling on incessantly—off his lap, almost knocking her to the floor. The bitch wasn't talking about shit anyway. And he'd lost interest in the bubblehead the minute she'd opened her mouth. All she did was wrinkle the front of his thousand-dollar pants.

She hissed out a curse as she caught her balance, careful not to spill the drink in her hand. "Are you fucking *kidding* me?!" She shot him an icy glare. "Fucking asshole." Cruze shooed her away, never giving her a second glance. She was blocking his view.

She stomped off, pissed that he'd dismissed her. He simply shook his head.

Dumb bitch.

Cruze eased up in his seat, and locked his gaze on *her*, a slow fire burning in his eyes. First glance, and he knew she wasn't from the Philly area. It was in her attitude, in her body language. Hands down, he knew without a doubt, she had to be from somewhere up north.

The seductive sway of her hips had every motherfucker in VIP looking down onto the dance floor at her, transfixed on her every move. Even those dancing with other females seemed to struggle to keep their eyes off of her.

Three Fireballs in, and Arabia was feeling good to the point that the Philly-style Trap music being played no longer bothered her. She simply shimmied her body, swayed, and pumped her pelvis, dipped her knees, and—every so often, swung her hair.

Cruze watched as she shook her head, or waved a finger, at cats trying to get up on her. She'd spin out of their grasp, then back away, putting a hand up for them to keep their distance from her. He couldn't help but shake his head. She was a tease, but not in a slutty way, and he found himself being drawn to her, caught up in a drowning sensation of need that came from someplace he hadn't expected. He hadn't come to the club to pick up broads, or even take one home, for that matter. But, now, the idea didn't seem too far from a possibility. For the first time tonight, Cruze felt his body jump-starting and his dick coming to life.

He stood up as she slowly twirled around in a sensual circle. He leaned almost over the rail for a better view. *Fuck.* He could see the edges of her ass cheeks jiggling seductively, practically calling out to him. He pulled in his bottom lip.

Arabia's eyes shut, then fluttered open as she found herself getting lost in the music.

DJ Khaled's "Gold Slugs" played and Arabia threw her head

back and looked up through her lashes. Their eyes locked. And, instantly, she felt her body heat. His masculine face illuminated when the strobe lights flashed, hitting the defined angles of his model-fine face. She swallowed. Then blinked. Oh, yes—she'd found her mark for the night. Her lashes fluttered shut and, then, she slyly licked her lips.

The seductive gesture caused Cruze to swallow. Not many women had the ability to bring him to full arousal without ever touching his dick, first. But somehow this temptress had accomplished that in a matter of moments.

Meek Mill's "All Eyes On You" began playing and Arabia threw a hand in the air and rocked her hips, and rolled her belly as if she were a snake charmer, as if she knew all eyes were indeed on her. She pretended to be oblivious to the effect she was having on her captive audience on the floor around her, and in VIP.

"Yo, man," Marquan said, stepping up next to Cruze and tapping him on the arm. "You see that?"

Cruze simply nodded. Of course he *saw* her. How could he *not* see her?

For a moment, he imagined he was seeing things. But when he blinked again, it was clear that he wasn't dreaming or hallucinating.

"She bad as fuck," Marquan slurred, slicing into Cruze's visions of the sexy vixen being down on her knees, and him slipping the head of his dick between those pillow-soft lips of hers, then sliding his shaft into that plush-looking mouth of hers until he was hitting the back of her juicy throat. He found himself imagining him parting her thighs, and her being wet inside, very wet, and hot; her pussy a slick glove of tight heat.

A slow fission of heat slowly spiked in his spine. She thrust her pelvis, almost deliberately at him—or at least that was what he thought he saw, what he *wanted* to believe—and his body flooded with primal urges. She was hella sexy. And, yeah, he wanted to fuck her—he wanted to fuck her sexy-ass brains out.

Shit…what the fuck?

He was bugging. Hard.

He hadn't lusted after a broad in years. Not since his days of hugging the block, not since his first love—the woman who'd turned him out, and betrayed his trust, and—eventually, had broken his heart.

Not wanting to think about old shit—not tonight, not now, not ever—he drained his drink, and another appeared before him on a napkin. He tossed the waitress only a cursory glance, before fixing his gaze back to the dance floor.

The DJ eased on Bryson Tiller's "Don't" and Arabia rolled her hips and licked her lips again, her eyes catching his, and Cruze's dick twitched. He wanted some sloppy top. Yeah, a dick suck was exactly what he could use right about now.

Marquan tossed back the rest of his drink. "Man, I'd like to take her home and dig all up in that. I'd split her wide open," he boasted, waving over a scantily clad waitress, carrying a silver tray of an assortment of freshly poured drinks. He took a shot from the waitress, licked the salted rim, then tossed it back.

Cruze gave his inebriated basketball idol a side-eyed glance, shaking his head. *This drunken muhfucka! I wish he'd shut the fuck up.*

He sighed, then took a long sip from his own drink as he brought his attention back to the dance floor, back to *her*, so engrossed in watching—a mixture of fascination and lust swimming in his stare.

Where the hell did she come from? he wondered as he kept his gaze locked on her. She was fucking flawless. One of the baddest bitches he'd ever laid eyes on.

His gaze made a slow perusal from head to toe. The dress she had on was made for her, sexy and alluring. And those heels…

goddamn—those smoking hot "come fuck-me" heels had his mind spinning with salacious thoughts of having those long cocoa brown legs up over his broad shoulders, spread open in a V, while fucking her with nothing but those heels on. He'd grab the expensive red-bottomed heels like handlebars and give her the business until she melted her sweet chocolate all over every inch of him.

The decadent thrill made his dick stretch and pulse. He licked his lips as her breasts bounced, her succulent nipples taunting him through her dress. Arousal hummed low in his body, desire licking over his skin as he imagined what it would be like balls deep in all that ass of hers.

She had his dick pulsing for the last fifteen minutes, and his balls had become heavy, the head of his dick sensitive. And, then—fuck. She started singing along to Justine Skye's "I'm Yours" as if she were giving him his own private concert. She pointed to him, letting him know she was feeling him; that she was his; that he knew exactly what to do. And he did. He'd fuck her until she tapped out.

Arabia stuck her pointer finger in her mouth, pressed it to her lips, then slid it down over her neck to the center of her breasts, then motioned with her finger for him to come to her.

Fuck this. He needed—no, wanted—to see more, up close and personal.

Like he always made very clear, he wasn't weak for pussy. But he loved to fuck. And he had a thing for beautiful women. And if the pussy was good, then shit, that was even better. Still, he usually had control over his libido, but something about the way she moved had gotten his dick hard—the throb so deep it almost hurt, and had him wanting to indulge himself.

The DJ slipped on Rae Sremmurd's "No Type" and Arabia started rocking and bouncing her hips, feigning awareness of him coming for her, stalking toward her with a dangerous glint in his eyes. The look made her feel as if she were about to become the hunted, and the tables were about to somehow be turned. She'd provoked him. Piqued his curiosity. And now…he had to know who this sultry temptress was.

She eyed him as he descended the stairs that led to the dance floor. Her pulse raced as she thrust her pelvis at him. *Yes. Come get this pussy, boo.* She twirled her hips, her dress swaying this way and that way, the slightest hint of her ass cheeks peering dangerously out from beneath the hem, playing peek-a-boo with all those who dared to sneak a look.

Cruze's dick throbbed.

Arabia threw her hands up over her head and eyed him. Then, as he slowly made his way onto the dance floor and closed the distance between them, she turned her back to him. Made him invisible.

Amused by the act, Cruze's lips curled. *Yeah, she knows what the fuck she's doing.* K Camp's "1Hunnid" eased through the speakers as Arabia popped her fingers and swayed to the beat. Cruze didn't dance. Ever. He bopped. But something about this sexy-ass broad in the sexy red dress made him want to slide cross the floor and do the Superman, then follow it up with the Stanky Leg. But he refrained from making a fool out of himself.

Coolly, he eased up in back of her, his arm going around her waist. "Damn, baby, you sexy," he said in her ear, over the music.

Arabia spun out of his grasp and faced him. Her pussy clenched. Oh my God, yes. He was everything she'd hoped he'd be up close. Tall. Dark. Dreamy. And ever so fuckable! A lascivious look flashed over her face as she said, "And I'm in heat, boo." Then her gaze dropped to the front of his pants.

Cruze simply laughed, and Arabia could see the beginnings of fresh lust flickering in his eyes. "Oh word?"

She licked her lips. "I'm not here to talk, boo," she said saucily. *I'm here to get fucked.* "So either dance, or walk on by."

Without another word, she thrust her pelvis at him, then spun around and threw her ass back into him—making her intentions very clear.

"Goddamn," he hissed under his breath at how *fat* her ass was, at how soft it felt. He tightened his one-arm grip around her waist, then moved his hips into her. He grinned as she threw her ass up on him. Heat splintered through his groin, the crease of her cheeks fitting perfectly in the center of his crotch.

Yeah, fuck what you heard. He was taking this fine piece of ass home with him tonight, and dicking her down. Something came over him and he had the overpowering urge to run a hand up over her thigh, to touch her silken skin.

When his hand brushed up over her skin, then inched dangerously up her thigh and under her dress, Arabia closed her eyes, and grinned. *Yeah, boo, I knew you wanted this.* By the time "Comfortable" played, the two of them had become just that—comfortable. They danced like old lovers, as if they'd known each other's bodies forever. Cruze and Arabia slipped into a zone and got lost in the music, in the building heat between them, in each other's rhythm.

Shit. She felt good. Cruze loved the way her warm body felt against his. She had him rock-hard, the head of his dick swelling for release. And Arabia let out a moan over the music at the feel of his ever-growing cock up against her ass. She felt her body melding into his, a sweet ache building in the wells of her cunt, swelling her pussy lips.

She spun out of his grasp, and faced him, her arms up over her head, her eyes flickering with lust. She slid a leg between his legs, and grinded and humped her pussy—daring him to thrust back. Oh, yeah, she was bold as fuck to play with him.

She was playing with fire. Cruze was a grown-ass man, and if she didn't watch herself, he was about to fuck her until her cunt went up in flames. Oblivious to his thoughts, Arabia tossed her hair, then slid down his thigh, looking up at him through thick lashes. Cruze looked down at her, and grinned—the flash of his dimples causing her juices to seep into her thong.

Yeah, her fine ass is a real live freak-bitch, he thought, trying to contain the thick swell of his dick from busting through his underwear as Arabia boldly felt him up. Grabbed at the fabric of his pants. Then squeezed.

Oooh, he has a nice big dick—mmm, yes.

Cruze blinked, stunned, and was turned on, by her aggressiveness.

Oh, God, yes—she was going to give in to her baser needs. Her pussy was wet for him. She was going to take the dick. Ride it dirty. She swept her eyes around the dance floor. She didn't need his name, or telephone number. Only what hung between—what felt like—muscular thighs.

Cruze didn't know how much more of her seductive moves he'd be able to take before he lost it right here on the dance floor. He felt his seed surging up from his balls, through the length of his shaft. His breaths came quickly as they moved in sensual harmony to an August Alsina song. He glanced around the club's dance floor. He blinked. *Oh shit.* He hadn't realized how packed it had gotten, or that—little by little—he and Arabia had been pushed further back into the crowd.

He hadn't realized any of this until he felt his back pressed up against a wall of mirrors, and Arabia had spun around and reached for the fly of his pants, yanked his zipper down, then boldly raised her gaze, licked her sexy lips, and said, "Fuck me."

Caught up in the heat and his burning need for release, Cruze—all hot breath and slicked tongue, groaned at her words. Then pushed out, in a voice so thick with lust that it didn't sound like his, "Take it, baby. It's all yours…"

Seventeen

He woke up with thoughts of *her* heavy on his mind, and the first thing he did was reach for a blunt. Had last night really happened? Cruze wondered, filling his lungs with the potent vapor.

Fuck me!

Those two words had come from her mouth, dripping with lust as they oozed into Cruze's ears, provoking him to act the damn fool.

Pulling on the blunt, he closed his eyes and began reminiscing, and hearing her say that sexy shit, once again.

Fuck me!

Her voice had been soft and sensual, yet demanding and guttural at the same time, rendering him powerless to deny the brazen request.

From afar, he'd been watching her lovely silhouette. Enjoying the sway of her luscious hips as she danced solo while bathed in a rainbow of strobe lights. Her seductive movements had enflamed his loins, causing his dick to stretch out and grow rigid with a savage-like desire.

The mystery woman seemed to be caught up in her own sexiness and didn't require a dance partner to get her groove on. As if bewitched by her, Cruze had been transfixed and unable to look away as he observed the mocha-colored goddess undulating and gyrating in time with the music—moving that cute ass around in a provocative circle.

Not only did she seem to be lost in the music, but she also appeared to be self-aroused, turned on by her own sensuality. His eyes had zoomed in on her with laser focus, like being a voyeur using a telescope to spy on a woman who was masturbating in the privacy of her bedroom.

Tauntingly, she had thrust her pelvis at him as if daring him to come and get the pussy. At that point, Cruze's dick was so painfully swollen, it felt as if it were about to burst open if he didn't hurry up and jam it inside her.

The bitch was asking for it and she was gonna get it.

Entranced, he scrutinized her for a few more moments. Then, lured by the flick of her tongue against her lips, he could no longer control his urges and he found himself moving slowly toward the dance floor. Like a predator. With the singular intention of fucking the broad's pussy hard and mercilessly until her walls collapsed and her guts spilled out on the dance floor.

With his back against a mirror and with her round ass pressed against his groin, Cruze, usually a private person, had come completely out of character, whipping his dick out in a public venue, like a depraved savage.

Thinking back to last night, Cruze couldn't believe that while he was trying to pound the life out of her velvety-soft insides, other couples were all around him, dancing and oblivious to the fact that his thick cock was entrenched inside a batch of syrupy pussy that was so overheated, it was leaking hot slush that splattered and sizzled against his balls.

The loud club music drowned out their fuck sounds. Cruze emitted a grunt that sounded like a primal call, erupting from deep within his soul, and his fuck partner softly whimpered and moaned before releasing a siren's scream that went unnoticed as it blended perfectly with the blaring, manic music.

Sweat poured off Cruze, drenching his Givenchy shirt as he pounded the pussy, grunting and groaning like a wild heathen. The sexy bitch had not only taken the harsh dick-down, but had thrown the coochie right back at him, effortlessly gobbling up his thick shaft and bathing it in a gooey pool of nectar.

Mmm. The memory of that juicy pussy was starting to fuck with his libido, motivating his cock to harden and pulse beneath the bed covers.

Who was that sexy bitch and why hadn't he gotten her number? Clearly, she wasn't like the clingy Philly women who readily offered him a set of their house keys after the first fuck. Nah, that self-involved, pretty bitch didn't give a damn about romance; she was all about getting deep dick-strokes, and hadn't bothered to give out her name or number. And after she got what she wanted, she readjusted the hem of her dress and bounced.

Being left on the dance floor with his pants gaped open and his dick hanging out was a first for Cruze and he hoped nobody had seen the look of surprise on his face when that erotic, little ma-ma danced away from him. If he hadn't had to straighten up his pants and get his shit fixed inside his drawers, he might have run after her—to at least find out her name.

But, without giving Cruze a second thought, the enigmatic beauty wove through the crowd, still shaking her ass and swaying her hips in time with the beat, while Cruze lay slain up against the mirror, covered in perspiration and struggling to catch his breath.

Whoever she was, she'd completely captivated him. The way she'd reined him in and then controlled the situation, it was a good thing he didn't have any way to contact her. That pretty bitch possessed some bomb-ass pussy, and as good as it was, if he did bump into her again, he might fuck around and hand her the keys to both cribs and all three of his whips.

Nah, that'll never happen. I learned at a young age that bitches ain't shit. Cruze laughed bitterly, thinking back to how young and dumb he once was.

At the mall, Ramona had Cruze holding bags from about six different stores, and she still wasn't finished spending his money. But he didn't mind. He loved seeing his girl looking fly. Sitting on a bench outside Victoria's Secret, Cruze started getting antsy, thinking about the block and all the money other niggas was getting while he was fucking around at the mall.

But when Ramona came prancing out of the store with her cherry-red lip gloss, skintight jeans, and a crop top that revealed her belly-button ring, he forgot all about the block and asked her if she wanted to stop at the food court and get something to eat.

"No, boo. I'll order something when I get to the club."

At the mention of the strip club, Cruze's cheerful disposition instantly turned sour. Brooding, he turned around and began walking in the direction of the exit sign.

"What's wrong with you, Cruze?" Ramona called from behind. Wearing stilettos, she couldn't keep up with his long strides as he headed for the parking lot. "Cruze!"

Ramona kept yelling his name and Cruze kept walking faster with Ramona's shopping bags knocking together. Furious that no matter how much he spent on her, she still wouldn't stop shaking her ass at the strip club where all kinds of random niggas rubbed on her intimate body parts that should have been reserved for his touch, alone.

When he reached the red Pontiac that he'd helped her pay for, he leaned against the passenger's side, waiting for her to unlock the door.

Huffing and puffing, Ramona approached, hitting the keypad, but before Cruze opened his door, she threw the Victoria's Secret bag at him. "Here, *fuck you! Keep all the shit you paid for because I don't want it. Walking off and leaving me running after you like I'm some skeezer.*"

"*Fuck you, too, and fuck all this bullshit,*" he lashed out, flinging the armful of bags he'd been carrying onto the ground and then kicking the contents as they spilled out.

"*Cruze! Stop fucking up my new shit,*" Ramona cried, quickly dropping down to her knees, picking up her purchases, dusting them off, and then stuffing the bags in the trunk of her car. "*You need to do something about that temper of yours.*"

He scowled. "*And you need to quit that fucked-up job of yours.*"

"*I am gonna quit.*"

He raised a brow, skepticism etching over his face. "*When?*"

"*As soon as we get enough money saved to move out of that rat trap we live in.*"

He sighed. "*We're never gon' be able to save the way you like to spend money.*"

"*Look who's talking...the boy who buys a new pair of sneakers every day.*"

He leveled an evil look at her. "*I told you about calling me that shit. I ain't no damn boy.*"

She rolled her eyes dismissively. "*Well, the man who buys new Nikes every single day has a nerve complaining about what I spend money on.*"

"*One pair of sneaks a day don't compare to three and four, full-on shopping sprees every week.*"

"*And that's why I have to keep working,*" she said sassily.

"*But I thought you were off tonight. That's what you told me, yesterday.*"

"*I was, but my girl, Blue Diamond asked me to work her shift. Her little boy's in the hospital, and—*"

Cruze's gaze narrowed. "*And you ain't even bother to check with me and see if I had plans for us.*"

Ramona gave Cruze a sidelong glance and burst into laughter. "*Check with you? Boy, you better kiss my ass; you ain't nobody's father.*"

"Tell me to kiss your ass again, and you gon' be picking your lil' ass up off the ground."

"Damn, why you so touchy lately? No matter what I say, you catch an attitude."

"'Cause you be on that bullshit. Just watch your mouth and don't be disrespecting me, that's all I'm saying."

"Okay, Cruze. So…are we good?"

Cruze rolled his eyes and exhaled loudly. "You might be good, but I'm not."

"Why you still mad?"

"Why you think?"

"I think you sexy when you mad, babe," Ramona said, bunching up her lips and making a kissing gesture.

Unmoved, Cruze glared at her.

"Is the baby mad at Mommy?" she teased.

"Stop fucking with me, Mo," he cautioned, giving her a deadly look.

"Aw, come on, boo. Where they at?" she asked.

"Where the fuck is what at?"

"Them sexy dimples that pop out when my baby smiles at me."

Taken off guard, Cruze blushed and broke into a smile. Both mad and fiercely in love, he grabbed Ramona and kissed her. "I fuckin' love you so much, I hate you."

"I love you, too, you jealous-acting bitch."

"Watch your mouth."

Ramona shrugged. "Well, that's how you act, sometimes."

"You make me act that way," Cruze said, grabbing two handfuls of her hair and yanking her head forward.

"Ow, Cruze. That hurts."

"Good. I want it to hurt. Now, shut the fuck up," he said, and then kissed her again. As their tongues lashed together, violently, they both were well aware that the fire that had ignited between them could not be snuffed out by a mere kiss.

Ramona gazed at Cruze and brushed her fingertips against his rock-hard cock.

"*Damn, baby. My dick is bricked up,*" *Cruze grumbled, his face scrunched up as if in pain.*

"*You want me to give you some head in the car?*" *Ramona asked, caressing the hardened lump in his jeans.*

"*Nah, that ain't gon' work. I wanna fuck. You know how I get when you make me mad,*" *he explained, pushing down his throbbing dick.*

She nodded. "*Soon as we get home, okay?*"

"*I need some pussy now, Mo,*" *Cruze demanded.*

Ramona glanced around the parking lot nervously. "*A'ight, come on,*" *she said, opening the car door and climbing in the backseat.* "*But you gotta be quick.*"

"*I will,*" *he promised, undoing his belt.*

Fifteen minutes later, as Cruze and Ramona pulled out of the lot, a call came through from his boy, Sameer. He started to ignore it until he noticed that Sameer had called five times, already.

Cruze put him on speaker just to let Ramona know that it wasn't a chick blowing up his phone. "*Yo, whaddup?*"

"*Where you been at all day, man?*"

"*Out with my girl.*"

"*Umph. Somebody's nose is wide open.*"

"*Whatever. Wha'sup?*"

"*Yo, the big man came through the block today. He was looking for you.*"

"*For what? I'm all paid up. I don't owe Moody nothing.*"

"*It ain't about that. He said you and me is the only young niggas in our territory that got potential, so he invited us to some type of get-together at one of his cribs.*"

"*Whaaat?*" *Grinning, Cruze adjusted the passenger's seat and leaned back even further.*

"*Yeah, man. Moody got a couple cribs, so I don't know which one. It's*" on the low, so he ain't giving out no address. I don't give a fuck where it's at as long as we invited." Sameer let out a burst of the goofy laughter that he was known for. The way he laughed sounded so stupid that nobody could hear it without laughing, too.

Everybody except for Ramona, who couldn't stand Sameer. Rolling her eyes and popping gum, she navigated through traffic, waiting for Cruze to ask her what was wrong, but he was invested in the conversation with Sameer and wasn't paying her the least bit of attention.

"So how we gon' get there?" Cruze asked.

"They on some espionage shit, man."

"Whatchu mean?" Cruze asked, finally cutting an eye at Ramona and noticing that she seemed upset.

"Somebody gon' text me about the meet-up spot and then somebody gon' drive us to the crib. But check this…"

"What?"

"We gotta ride blindfolded." Sameer fell out laughing, again. The ridiculous sound reverberating inside the car.

"Damn, it's like that?" Cruze asked, laughing too.

Ramona stopped for a red light and slammed so hard on the brakes, Cruze toppled forward. When he looked at her, he couldn't understand why her arms were folded and her lips were poked out.

"Yo, I'ma hit you back, Sameer. What time should I be ready?"

"Ten o'clock, man."

"A'ight. Bet. See you then." Cruze hung up and gawked at Ramona. "What the fuck's your problem?"

"Oh, you think you gon' go to a big-time drug dealer's high-profile party while my ass is slaving at work. Hmph, I don't think so." She swiveled her neck and cracked the gum she was chewing even louder.

"Don't blame me. You're the one who wanted to work so bad tonight."

"I don't want to work bad enough to miss out on Moody's party. Blue Diamond better call some other fool because I'm rolling with you and your boy, Sameer."

"Do you know Moody?" Cruze asked, studying Ramona's face.

The light changed to green and she focused on traffic. "I know of *him*. A few of the girls at work be bragging about getting invitations to one of Moody's get-togethers. From what I've heard, his parties are everything: free flowing champagne, top-shelf liquor, all the coke in the world. They say his house is laid out like something featured on MTV Cribs."

Cruze gazed at Ramona intently. "Since when did you start caring about coke?"

She shrugged indifferently "I don't go overboard with it, but I snort every now and then. You know, only to get me through the night down at the club."

"That's news to me," Cruze said suspiciously.

Ramona waved at him dismissively. "Are you taking me to the party or not?"

"Nah, it's boys night; you need to take your ass on to work," Cruze said, grinning devilishly.

"Don't play with me," she said, laughing.

"A'ight, you can go."

"Thank you, baby." At the stop sign, she leaned in for a kiss. "Baby, I feel like pulling over and fucking you, again."

"That's okay. I'm good."

"You stay horny, so you know that's a lie."

Cruze chuckled. "I'm good. For real."

Ramona gave him a doubtful look.

"I'm good until we get home, and then I'ma tear that ass up."

"But I'm feeling some kind of way right now," Ramona said, pouting.

"I'ma take care of you," he said, lifting up and taking a lighter out of his pocket while reaching for the half-blunt in the ashtray.

"Baby, can't that wait?" Ramona asked.

"Why?"

"'Cause I'm so excited about going to Moody's party, I feel like I need to bust a nut real quick."

"You want some dick or you want me to suck on that pussy?"

"I'll cum quicker with tongue, babe. You can fuck me when we get home."

"A'ight," he said nonchalantly. "Pull over on one of those sidestreets, over there." Cruze barreled into the back of the car while Ramona took a detour off the main road.

As she parked, Cruze lay awkwardly with his torso on the backseat and his long legs, bent at the knees. "Hurry up and bring that ass back here and squat over my face."

"Hush, Cruze. You talkin' all dirty, you gon' make me cum on myself before I even park the car."

"You taught me to how to talk dirty, so don't complain about it."

"I know, I know," she said breathlessly as she quickly zigzagged into a parking spot. "But you don't understand how my pussy feels right now."

"Feed me a hot nut and make me understand," Cruze said, staring at her intently.

"But, babe, I don't want you to get upset with me."

"About what?"

"I didn't have any wipes or nothing to clean my pussy after we finished fucking."

Cruze looked at Ramona like she was out of her mind. "So? I love you, Mo. You're my girl. Do you think I give a fuck if your pussy is dripping with my nut? Shiiiit. It probably gives it more flavor. Now, get back here and let big Daddy take care of that thing," Cruze said, reaching for Ramona and then lowering her downward until she was straddling his face.

Eighteen

Almost a week later, and her sordid nightclub rendezvous with Mr. Tall, Dark and Deep-Dimpled still played in her mind. She'd had her share of wild sex, but fucking *him*—whoever he was—like that was way beyond her wildest expectations. It had been one of her greatest *fucks*. She couldn't decide if it was the anonymous sex that had made it so deliciously dirty. The swirling strobe lights and lighted flooring. Or that he was so damn fine. That night, she'd hoped he'd be daringly uninhibited enough to drop to the floor and tongue her to August Alsina singing about being ridden like a porn star, but he hadn't. And she had to remind herself that she hadn't been at that *type* of club. It was a dance club, not a sex club. Still, a girl could fantasize. Couldn't she?

Yes, Lord! And fantasize she'd done ever since that night. Oh what she wouldn't do for another fill of him, stuffing her full. Maybe next time she'd drop down and worship him like the chocolate Adonis he was and suck his dick.

Maybe.

Ooh. Arabia, your slutty ass is out of control, girl!

She covered her face in her hands, smiling and shaking her head. The aftershock of what she'd done that night still heating her flesh. His dick had been deliciously big—long and thick, but not ginormous. It'd been the perfect fit, with just the right amount of stretch and burn. Her pussy pulsed at the salacious memory. She could practically still feel him swelling inside her as she'd clutched him, sandwiching his dick between her slick walls and milking him to orgasm. Mm-hmm. *This snap trap pussy does it all the time.* She giggled.

He'd been succulent. Edible. Not just his lips, every part of him. And she would have eaten him alive had she not had to keep reminding herself of her surroundings.

Arabia ran a hand through her hair. Oh God—help her. What a shameless bitch, fucking him like that. What had gotten into her? She almost laughed. The answer was simple: she'd finally gotten a good damn fuck—hard and hungry; that's what had gotten into her—a good dose of dirty fucking. Thankfully, she'd held a gold wrapper in her clutch that night. *"Fuck me,"* she'd boldly told him, before she slyly slipped him the condom, then turned her back to him and blocked anyone's view of him as he sheathed his throbbing erection with the Magnum, his back pressed up against a wall of mirrors.

She hummed Rihanna's "Work" and subconsciously grinded and bounced her ass slowly down into the leather chair, remembering how she'd bent over and grabbed her left ankle as Mr. Deep Dimples pulled her thong to the side and slid inside; her ass clapping around his dick as she held her free hand up and snapped her fingers to the music, her pussy popping, her hips dipping, her body rocking into him.

Arabia pursed her lips, wondering if Mr. Deep Dimples would have fucked her raw that night had she not handed him a condom. *Ooh, I bet his scandalous ass would have tried it.* She shuddered at the thought. At least at the sex club she belonged to, she knew that everyone was tested—and retested—every three months. It was a mandatory requirement of everyone who wished to remain in good standing with the club. So she'd been known to fuck without a condom on those rare occasions when she felt slutty, and wanted to feel some random hunk's nut filling her up, then warmly oozing out of her quaking pussy.

But she'd never dare haphazardly go raw, sharing her bare pussy, with some *stranger*—no matter how sinfully sexy said stranger might be.

Shifting in her chair behind her desk, she licked her lips, then crossed her legs at her ankles as she picked up her ringing phone, shaking away the steamy remnants of her salacious night.

"Arabia Knight speaking." She cleared her throat, running a smooth hand over the top of her sleek mahogany desk. "How may I help you?"

"Well, beautiful lady," the thick, husky voice on the other end of the line said, "you may help me, first, by having dinner with me tonight. Then allowing me to make love to you."

Arabia's lips curled. "Oh, Wellson. You're so sweet."

"Yeah, but not as sweet as you, baby. I've missed you."

Arabia moaned, running a hand through her hair. "Mmm. It's nice to be missed."

"Yes, baby. It is. Junior misses you, too."

Junior was the pet name for his dick, the dick that acted on its own accord, holding a solid erection when it saw fit. What a waste of dick. Maybe he'd finally wear the cock ring she'd given him, she mused. Yeah, right. Wishful thinking.

Arabia looked up from her desk to find a doe-eyed Ashley Givens, one of the agency's six account executives, leaning against the doorway of her office. Ashley had been with the ad agency for a little over three years now, and so far—with her excellent organizational and communication skills—she'd proven herself a great asset.

And the fact that she had a great body and exuded sex appeal didn't hurt, either.

Arabia motioned her in with a hand, telling Wellson to give her one minute, then she put him on hold.

"What's up?" Arabia glanced at her long legs as she crossed the threshold and sauntered farther into her office.

"You got a sec?"

"Sure."

Ashley slunk her lean, toned body in one of the leather chairs positioned in front of Arabia's desk, then crossed her legs. "I'll make it quick. I just got off the phone with The Center in Philadelphia…"

"Oh?" Arabia placed her elbows up on her desk, clasping her hands together.

"And it's a go. I have a meeting with the Executive next Thursday at eleven to discuss how we can best help them market and advertise."

Arabia smiled. "Great news." And great it was. Her agency had come highly recommended, and they'd sought her services out to discuss their advertising needs. The Center, from what she'd gathered from her talks with Ashley, was a statewide phenomenon, but they were eager to take their vision to the next level and become a more nationally known organization. Landing this account meant a cool million dollars in advertising funds. And a great look for Ashley's professional career.

Ashley smiled, swiping her bang from her eye. "Yes it is. Hopefully, we'll be a good fit."

"Oh, we are," Arabia assured her. "Trust me. Remember, they sought us out." She glanced at the telephone line blinking. "Listen, let me finish up this call. We'll talk more later."

"Gotcha." Ashley stood, smoothing a hand down the front of her skirt and then made her way toward the door.

Arabia waited until she was gone, then resumed her call. "Ooh, I'm so sorry about that. Now back to you, sexy man. Where are you?" she asked, picking imaginary lint from her form-fitting skirt. She crossed her legs and swiveled in her chair, glancing over at the huge wall of glass overlooking Manhattan. "Here in the city?"

She hoped not. She hated when he popped up unannounced, expecting her to be readily available to him—engaged or not, she had a schedule to keep with her men. Especially when she wasn't hungry for him *or* Junior. But she did enjoy wining and dining out with him. And she loved the way Wellson slid his tongue between her puffy lips from her slit, then gently sucked her clitoris into his mouth, his tongue lightly fucking her, tasting her from the inside out.

Oh—*yes*, how she loved his thick manly tongue laving her pussy. So, maybe…

"I'm in Chicago for a meeting," he said, jolting her from her dirty thoughts, "but I can have a ticket at either Newark or LaGuardia Airport ticket counter waiting for you, if you cared to join me."

"Oh…" Her voice trailed off as her smartphone chimed, alerting her she had a new text message. "I don't know, Wellson," she said, reaching for her cell. "You know how I am about last-minute plans. I have nothing packed."

"You don't need to pack, baby," he said quickly. "Everything you need is…"

She opened her message from an unknown number. WE NEED TO FUCKING TALK! IVE GIVEN UP EVERYTHING 2 B W/U

She blinked. Reread the text. Then frowned. *What the hell?*

Lifting an eyebrow, she texted back: WHO IS THIS?

Silly question she knew, still she asked, hoping Eric wouldn't be *that* damn crazy sending her this foolishness, even if she had been avoiding his calls and text messages for the last week. And since he hadn't shown up at her condo as he'd threatened he would, she had thought he'd finally gotten his mind together and gotten over it.

Obviously not…

She sighed, wondering how she had missed the memo that he was borderline-nuts. Either she'd been too damn blinded by all the shiny trinkets he'd bestowed on her during the course of their relationship—and she was using that term *relationship* loosely, or he'd done a good job hiding it. Either way, after almost two years, she'd never imagine it would come down to *this*. She hated ugly breakups. Why couldn't people simply part responsibly?

Mere seconds later, another text came through—confirming what she feared. U REALLY FUCKED MY LIFE UP! U KNOW THAT RIGHT?

Oh for the love of God. Now he was being melodramatic. He chose to cheat. So what if she'd agreed to fuck him—the whole week in Kentucky? Was she to blame for his marital woes? Hell no. He didn't have to get caught up in a sordid affair with her. That was his choice.

Reluctantly, she replied. ERIC. I'M SORRY U FEEL THAT WAY. BUT DON'T BLAME ME. U DID THIS TO U. NOT ME. U SHOULD HAVE WAITED TO TALK 2 ME B/4 U TOOK IT UPON YOURSELF TO TELL UR WIFE U WERE LEAVING HER. THE WAY U SPOKE TO ME WAS UNACCEPTABLE. I'VE NEVER TALKED 2 U IN THAT MANNER. BUT I AM BETTER THAN THAT. SO I FORGIVE U. LET'S BE ADULT ABOUT THIS N MOVE ON. OK?

Seconds later, another text message came through. IM SORRY. I WAS PISSED. I WANNA SEE YOU. JUST 2 TALK, BABY

She blinked. Oh so now she was *baby*. Ha. Unequivocally—*hell no!* Not after the way he'd yelled and cursed her. She'd have to be crazier than him to agree to see him. She'd never tolerated any man disrespecting her, and she'd be damned if she'd start now.

SORRY. THAT'S NOT A GOOD IDEA

WHY NOT?

GO BACK TO YOUR WIFE, ERIC

WTF?! U DONT GET TO DISMISS ME! MEET W/ME ARABIA. DON'T MAKE ME DO SOMETHING CRAZY. I SWEAR I WILL

Arabia frowned.

She quickly typed: IS THAT A THREAT?

I WANNA SEE YOU. TAKE IT HOW YOU WANT IT

That *felt* like an ominous threat to her. He had lost his damn everlasting mind, trying to intimidate her like that. What the hell was wrong with him? Who the hell did his bipolar ass think he was? *Men*. Where the hell were they teaching this kind of shit? Breakups happened every day. So why was he all of a sudden having a damn psychotic moment with her telling him it was best that they part ways? He was acting like she was his damn property or something.

Boy, bye!

She blocked the number, then laid her phone face-down on her desk.

He could kiss her ass—left check, right cheek, and inside her whole asshole. He didn't own her, or her pussy—or any other part of her body. Didn't he know what she held between her thighs had only been on loan to him?

Mmph. Apparently not! Okay, so maybe she should have handled the situation a little better, been more diplomatic. Bruising a man's ego was never a good thing. This she knew. But would he be crazy enough to try to harm her?

She refused to believe he would. After all, he'd never shown her he had too much to lose. A career. There's no way he'd do anything crazy to ruin that. Would he?

No, no, no—of course not.

Then why the hell were her nerves suddenly rattled?

"Baby? You there?"

Arabia blinked. "Huh? What did you say?"

Wellson chuckled. "Did I lose you, baby? I was saying everything you need is already here, right with me."

She frowned; clearly she'd missed the entire conversation. "What's already where?" she asked. She shook her head, trying to drive out the nagging thoughts that slowly began to swirl around in her mind. Eric had threatened her.

"Clothes, baby. Me. You. Here in Chicago."

She swallowed. Pushed back the crazy idea that he'd ever go there. He was just being childish, letting emotions overrule him, speaking out of anger. Yeah, that was it.

She was not about to let him work her nerves. No, no. Absolutely not.

"Oh, okay," she agreed, deciding a quick getaway was exactly what the hell she needed. "Sounds good."

"Perfect, baby…"

"*I'll make your life a living hell!*" Arabia could practically hear him spewing those same texted words at her, slinging them like battery acid.

She shuddered.

"And when you get here," Wellson prattled on, "we can stop in Cartier to pick you out something special"—now *that* put a smile on her face—"then grab a bite to eat at Cité, before heading back to the hotel for a night of lovemaking. I'll have you back on the first flight in the morning, in time for work, baby."

Snap—just like that. She perked up. Did he say Cartier?

Arabia licked her lips at the idea of being draped in exquisite jewels. And the thought of wrapping her lips around a succulent dish of butter-poached lobster didn't sound half-bad, either. In fact, it made her mouth water. She enjoyed dining at Cité, with its spectacular 360-degree views from the seventieth floor, perched atop Lake Point Tower. Hmm. It'd been a while since she'd been to the Windy City. Dinner, drinks, a little light shopping along Michigan Avenue…and, *maybe*, some hard dick?

How could she resist?

She couldn't.

Suddenly, Eric's silly tantrum no longer mattered. She wasn't about to let him ruin her day, night, or the rest of her week. No, no. It was over. And he simply needed to get over it.

"So what do you say, baby?" Wellson asked, jarring her from her thoughts.

Arabia shook her head, still trying to push past the nagging feelings, the words he'd texted: *Don't make me do something crazy* still milling around in her mind.

She glanced at the time in the upper right-hand corner of her PC. 10:23 a.m. She didn't have anything on her calendar for today, and so far, the morning had been quiet. Hmm. She could slip out of the building in the next half hour or so, quickly head home to pack a light bag—or not, then have a car service deliver her to the airport.

"Book it," she said, easing up from her desk. "The sooner the better."

"That's my baby. I have a one o'clock flight already on hold for you," Wellson said smartly.

She forced a smile. "Mmm. Presumptuous, aren't we?"

Wellson chuckled. "No, baby. Hopeful. See you when you get here."

"Okay. See you soon," she said before the call ended.

Reaching for her cell, Arabia sat on the edge of her desk and reread Eric's text messages. She wasn't about to let him get inside her head with this nonsense. Opening the bottom drawer to her desk, she pulled out her purse, then locked her desk.

Another text.

Another unknown number.

All the blood drained from her face as she opened the message.

IM SERIOUS ARABIA IF I CAN'T HAVE U NOI WILL!

Nineteen

Since relocating to Philadelphia, Cruze had purchased so much residential and commercial property that it was like he was winning big-time at a game of Monopoly. He'd probably be a black Donald Trump with his own private jet and shit if he'd invested in real estate a long time ago. He shook his head thinking about all the years he'd risked his life and liberty moving kilos for Moody. He could blame his recklessness on not having a father in his life or a decent male role model, but ultimately, he had to take responsibility for having lived on the edge for so long. With the kind of money he made hustling, he could have gone legit a long time ago, but it wasn't until he was forced out of the game and was compelled to clean up dirty money that he finally learned to make the kind of moves that led to a secure future.

"This space was formerly a bowling alley, but if you knock out the walls with the lanes, it could be transformed into pretty much any kind of business," said Becky, beaming at Cruze with her fake saleswoman smile.

"Nah, I'm not knocking out shit. When I buy commercial property, I don't fuck around with remodeling; I sell everything as is," Cruze replied bluntly, sauntering through the vast space and wondering how quickly he'd be able to unload it.

Becky, whose real name escaped Cruze (but he was sure it was probably Amy, Gretchen, or Molly…or some shit like that), turned a rosy shade of pink after Cruze spoke his mind. And the leggy, brown-eyed blonde hadn't turned colors because the off-color language he'd used offended her. She was blushing because she was turned on. He could tell by the way she kept fussing with her hair. He could see the lust in her glassy eyes. He smelled it seeping from her pores. Felt it swirling all around the air between them.

But he wasn't feeling her. Not like that. It wasn't that he was prejudiced against white chicks. She could probably get it if she had plumper lips and a fatter ass. Unfortunately for Becky, Cruze couldn't stand the feeling of paper-thin lips stretched around his dick, giving him the unpleasant sensation of enduring a bunch of paper cuts. He might as well slide his dick over sandpaper than be subjected to that shit.

Another strike against her was that flat-as-a-pancake ass of hers. When he was fucking, he liked to hold onto a meaty plump ass that jiggled when he smacked it. Snow bunnies like Becky, with their hard, fake tits tended to have sharp protruding bones and long, skinny legs. There couldn't be anything pleasurable about fucking a mannequin, so Cruze ignored all the signals she sent his way.

"I'ma sleep on this and I'll give you an answer tomorrow," he said, heading for the door, without so much as a glance her way. He'd seen and heard enough.

Becky rushed behind him. "What if I knock ten thousand off the asking price?"

"Make it twenty and we have a deal," Cruze replied without breaking his stride.

"Uh, I'm not sure if the seller is willing to—"

Cruze came to a halt, turned around and scowled at Becky. "How long has this place been empty?"

"A little over a year, I think."

Cruze snorted. He wasn't *that* new to the game. He'd already done his homework and knew the space had been unoccupied for almost three years. "Well, tell the seller to enjoy holding on to this vacant building for another three to four years."

Busted, Becky's face turned a deeper shade of red. "I'll contact the seller with your offer," she said, averting her gaze.

"Yeah, you do that." With that he was out the door.

Outside, Cruze disarmed his Jaguar, a new toy that he'd only driven a few times. He gave Becky a head nod before climbing inside his sleek ride, leaving her flustered and wet. That bitch could suck a dick if she thought she'd ever be able to game him up off his paper.

Needing to open the engine up, he headed for I-95 and drove his Jag as hard as he'd driven his dick into the silky tight clutch of that mystery bitch's pussy that night in Club Seduction. Why couldn't he get her out of his mind? It was maddening the way he couldn't stop reliving that night. Couldn't stop seeing the exotic features of her gorgeous face or smelling all the notes of her expensive fragrance.

Frustrated and angry with himself for being haunted by the memory of a slut-ho who fucked random dudes in a public place, he accelerated to eighty-five and then quickly shot to a hundred.

Fuck, yeah! Cruze felt an adrenaline rush that gave him the sensation of being invincible and powerful as hell. Driving fast took some of the edge off, but as soon as he began to slow down, he lost his natural high and once again began to brood, wishing he could dip his dick into that bomb-ass pussy, just one more time.

Not wanting to seem like he was flaunting his extravagances in the faces of the low-income people he was trying to help, Cruze had intended to take the Jag back to his house in the suburbs and switch it out for his SUV. But Bret had asked him if he could speak to the parents of his team about the summer basketball camp in the Poconos and about the importance of keeping their grades up in order to be eligible for a scholarship.

He pulled into the small lot of HYPE and deliberately took up two parking spots. Fuck if he wanted his whip scratched or dented by somebody's banged-up hooptie. Fuck that.

As he armed the Jag, he noticed a G-Wagon parked in a space next to Bret's Lexus sedan. Cruze wondered who the whip belonged to. Needing to be cautious at all times, he walked to the back of the SUV to check out the plate. When he saw Pennsylvania tags, he felt relieved. In his mind, he had conjured up the idea that the New York thugs had sent a henchman in a suit and a nice ride to take care of him.

Lingering at the back of the G-Wagon, he noted that the whip was a rental. The visitor was probably someone associated with the NBA with deep pockets who had flown in to make a contribution in person.

Inside the center, Cruze wanted to meet with Bret and go over the spiel he'd prepared for the parents, but he wasn't surprised to find Bret's office door was closed. No doubt, he was meeting with the driver of the G-Wagon, who was most likely a big donor.

As he made his way to his own office, Cruze smiled, wondering what his old crew would think about his new position in life. Having a respectable office and keeping somewhat regular business hours was hard for him to believe. His old crew wouldn't think him capable of becoming a contributing member of society. In Cruze's mind, he could hear his longtime buddy, Sameer with that crazy laugh of his, jokingly accusing him of using the center and the kiddie basketball team as a cover-up for some kind of a scam.

Unfortunately, he'd never get to hear Sameer's silly laughter again.

Jolted back to the night of the murders, Cruze saw the sickening image of his old friend's bullet-ridden body laid out in a zigzag positon in Moody's foyer.

Rest in peace, Sameer.

Cruze wished he could smoke a blunt, but couldn't conduct HYPE business or coach the boys with red, squinty eyes and while moving in slow motion.

Thinking about Sameer led Cruze to that dark place in his mind where the memory of his son resided. Suddenly agitated, he hated that he had to address the parents while in such a fragile emotional state.

He had an hour to pull himself together, and he struggled to fill his mind with pleasant thoughts. Sadly, all he saw was images of Darth Vader and other *Star Wars* characters that embellished the comforter that was on Chancellor's bed that night.

Unable to shake the gloom that engulfed him, Cruze's shoulders slumped and he dropped his head in his hands. *Oh, Chance. My boy, my boy. I should have known you were mine, and I should have been there to protect you. I'm so sorry, son.*

At the sound of a soft knock on the door, Cruze abruptly straightened up and cleared his throat. "Come in," he said in a clear, even tone that gave no hint of the anguish that consumed him.

Expecting Bret, he couldn't have been more surprised when the door opened and Tanji sashayed into his office. This time, her hair was lavender and she was rocking hooker boots, a short denim jacket, and a pair of tights that showed off some serious camel toe. The imprint of her vulva instantly took Cruze's mind off his troubles, and had his mouth watering like crazy.

"Hey, Mr. Fontaine, I'm here for the meeting." There was musicality in Tanji's voice, and her words had a soft, lilting quality, like she was singing a sensual melody.

Cruze checked his watch. "Uh, the meeting doesn't start for another hour."

"I know, but I wanted to get here early and have a private meeting." The way the word *private* rolled off her tongue and slipped from her glossed lips held heat, promise, and possibility. And for a fleeting moment, Cruze envisioned his dick sliding in and out of her mouth, sinking into the depths of her throat.

He swallowed. *Nigga, you bugging*, he scolded himself. *You know you can't fuck with this bird-ass bitch.* "I don't think that's—"

Tanji tossed her weave hair over her shoulder. "Don't *think*, boo," she said sassily, licking her lips. "Just do…"

Cruz frowned, then shook his head. "Nah. I don't think you're hearing me. This isn't—"

"Why you keep avoiding me, Mr. Fontaine?" she questioned, cutting him off before he could reject her sexual advances.

Cruze raised a brow and stared at her thirsty-ass, trying to keep his dick in check. He sighed. "Listen, Tanji. It's not that I'm avoiding you, but under the circumstances, your behavior is inappropriate," he said, backing up and despising how much he sounded like a straight sucker. If he wasn't at the center, he'd bend this smutty broad over his desk and fuck that pussy until the skin peeled off.

But she had him in a vulnerable positon, and as she grew closer, he found that he couldn't tear his eyes away from the thick pussy print that was staring him in the face. A hot-in-the-ass bitch like Tanji probably stayed having a sloppy, wet pussy. A pussy that didn't possess a perfumed scent. Nah, Tanji had that 'hood pussy, which tended to be slightly rank with a strong pungency that defied soap and water.

And a man would be lying his ass off if he denied that a pussy that had a little stank on it, felt extra good. And just by looking at her, he knew this 'hood bitch had some good and stank pussy!

On the videos she'd sent him, Cruze had already seen how much dick she could take up the ass, but he had yet to see that fat pussy put in some work. He wondered if she had a snap trap like the mystery bitch.

Mmph! Merely thinking about the mystery broad had his dick lengthening and thickening, and Tanji's gleaming eyes didn't miss the subtle movement in the front of Cruze's pants.

Encouraged by what she assumed was an invitation, Tanji slithered over to him. "Stop frontin' like you don't want this pussy, Mr. Fontaine," she murmured.

Being a handsome dude and having been a heavy-hitter in the game, it wasn't unusual for innumerable women to come on to him. But never in his life had any woman referred to him as "Mr. Fontaine" while begging for dick...and the shit sounded erotic as fuck.

Mentally disabled by the rush of blood that surged through his loins, Cruze could hardly process what was happening as Tanji suddenly dropped to her knees. "After I suck the hell out of this dick, I bet you'll stop being so stingy with it, Mr. Fontaine." Her hand went up over the growing bulge in his pants. "Mmm, yes. I knew you had a big dick," she said huskily, looking up through a veil of double-pack lashes. She bit over the fabric. Nibbled where the head of his cock pressed and stretched in his pants.

Fuck it. I can't fight this. Out of his mind with lust, Cruze didn't answer, just groaned and unzipped his slacks to drag the heavy length of his dick out.

He knew what he was about to do was wrong. Still, he latched on to the idea of having his dick inside something wet. Hell. What could a quick dick suck hurt? He could bust in her mouth, and ease the brewing sexual tension that had been building up in his balls all morning. Then send her on her way with the taste of his nut stained on her tongue.

Tanji felt her pussy getting wet. Finally. It was about to happen. She was about to make Cruze her new boo. She licked her lips in heated anticipation waiting for her feeding. She wanted him. Wanted to taste him. Drink him in. Swallow him whole. *Yeah, bitches, Mr. Fontaine's fine-ass is about to be all mine!*

Before Cruze could get his dick out and into Tanji's already drooling mouth, there was the horrific, metallic sound of the knob turning, followed by two sharp raps on the door.

"Hey, Cruze. You got a sec? I want you to meet…"

Before he could yank Tanji up off her knees and zip his pants, the door opened followed by a woman's gasp.

"Oh shit," Cruze and Bret said simultaneously as Tanji sprang to her feet, and the woman—with the sultry eyes and luscious lips— standing beside Bret looked on with amazement.

Shit. Shit. Shit.

Twenty

Ooh, scandalous…

Arabia's breath hitched in her throat, and her knees almost went weak at the sight of *him*—the man who'd taken up space in her fantasies over the last two weeks—standing *there* with his zipper down and some ex-stripper-looking 'hood bitch down on her knees as she was being quickly ushered out of the room by the elbow. But not before she glanced over her shoulder and let her gaze travel down to where his erection pressed against his pants, of course.

"My apologies, Ms. Knight," a seemingly embarrassed Bret said as he shut Cruze's door and swiftly led her down the hall back to the comforts of his own office. He could only imagine what she thought, and that alone made his temper boil.

He'd had what he wanted to believe to be a very productive morning with Arabia. During their forty-five-minute meeting, she'd impressed him. Not only with her beauty, but with her impeccable credentials and portfolio of big-name clients whom she'd worked with. He thought they were on their way to a mutually agreeable collaborative partnership.

They'd agreed to meet again in another week or so after she'd gone back to her office in New York and consulted with her creative team on developing the right concept for his ad campaign.

And now this shit.

What the fuck had Cruze been thinking letting one of *his* youths' moms suck his dick in one of *his* offices, in *his* goddamn building? If that were the type of shit Cruze was into, then he would sorrowfully have to let him go. He wasn't running some downtown slurp shop. And he damned sure hadn't opened HYPE for it to be turned into some den of iniquity.

Bret sighed inwardly. Who the hell was he kidding? Cruze had become in such a short period of time an asset to HYPE. But he would have to learn better dick control, or be out on his ass. He didn't give a fuck how much money or supplies he donated. This was business. And he didn't want his organization's name tarnished by some horny-ass mofo.

"Sorry you had to see that…" he continued on, but Arabia's mind had already wandered off. Her feet were moving, but she was nowhere in the moment. She honestly couldn't feel her legs, nor the immaculately polished floor beneath her feet. But, in her mind's eye, she'd run back to the man with the zipper down, and hard dick.

Cruze?

Hmm. So that's who her mystery man was. Now she had a name to attach to the face the next time she slid her hands between her legs and fingered her pussy. His face, his body…the feel of his dick had already been stamped into her brain.

Now—*mmm*—the name would be, too.

Cruze.

Arabia suddenly felt hot and flustered and surprisingly wet. Beneath her fitted chocolate-brown skirt, her juices were slowly seeping into her panties. Beneath the pink blouse she'd chosen to wear, her nipples were as hard as pebbles as a dozen questions swirled around in her head.

Had he just finished getting his dick sucked?

Had that trick swallowed him?

Were they lovers?

Or was she some random gutter bitch he dragged in from off the streets?

Mmmph. It was obvious that Mr. Deep Dimples didn't have any exacting standards when it came to whom he allowed to suck his dick.

Oh what she wouldn't have done to have walked in and caught his dick already stuffed inside her filthy, dick-sucking mouth, instead of catching what could have been either the beginning or the ending of a deliciously dirty act.

She swallowed.

"I assure you, Ms. Knight," Bret prattled on, "what you just saw isn't what HYPE is about. In fact, it goes against the principles of what I've built the center on."

Arabia gave him a sideways glance, her breasts bouncing, her ass swaying back and forth as she walked in step with Bret's long-legged stride. *Hmm-mm, if you say so.* She cleared her voice and, with her cunt clutching, said, "Well, Mr. Hollis. I would surely hope not. I mean…" She paused, trying to shake the image from her head.

Him.

Here of all places.

She couldn't believe it.

And to think she was livid with Ashley for calling her late last night to tell her she wouldn't be able to meet with Mr. Hollis today because her beloved pit bull, Peaches, had taken ill and the furry critter had to be rushed to the vet.

"*Fuck* Peaches," Arabia had wanted to say when she'd heard the excuse given as to why she wasn't able to be on the Amtrak train to Philadelphia, and how *her* morning would have to be disrupted to conduct a meeting that *she* couldn't. Arabia had been seething.

How could Ashley choose her pet—that ugly bitch—over a prospective client?

But, now, she was glad she'd come instead. Arabia pursed her lips, making a mental note to take Ashley out to lunch sometime this week, and buy her doggy a bone—as a *thank you*, of course.

Had Ashley come instead—

"You were saying, Ms. Knight?" Bret questioned, slicing into her thoughts as he held open the door to his office, and motioned her inside. He shut the door behind them.

Arabia touched the column of her neck. "Well, I was saying. What your staff does behind closed doors is surely none of *my* business, but *if* what I walked in on a few moments ago is common practice of how your staff engages with members of the community, then I don't think my advertising agency is the right fit for you. I—"

"Ms. Knight," Bret cut in, stepping around her and moving to sit on the other side of his desk. "Under no instance do I condone what you've witnessed. Your agency is *exactly* what HYPE needs to get to the next level. Again, I apologize."

"Apology not necessary," Arabia said. *But another night with that sexy-ass motherfucker and his big, horny dick back there is.* "But after what I saw, I'm really not sure if this will work. Perhaps I can refer you to—"

"No, no. Absolutely not," he quickly said. "The only ad agency I'm interested in is yours. Period." Bret gestured toward a chair in front of his desk. "Please. Sit." He remained standing, sliding a hand into his pocket. He eyed Arabia as she sat, then followed suit. Arabia crossed her legs, clasping her hands over her knee. His gaze landed on her smooth legs, before he lifted his eyes to meet hers. He swallowed back a knot of building lust. Damn, she was one hot dish of sexy trouble. If he weren't a happily married man, he'd happily offer her a ride on his thickening cock. He pressed his legs shut, and cleared his throat. "Ms. Knight, I can guarantee what you saw will not happen again. Ever."

Arabia gave him a doubtful look. "Well, tell me, Mr. Hollis. How many times has something like this occurred? If we're talking about branding HYPE, then a sex scandal is the last thing you'll want to be entangled in when it comes time to solicit for donors. I should warn you, now." She tilted her head, and eyed him sharply. "If I decide that my agency will work with you on your marketing and ad campaigning, then you'll need to rein your staff in. I don't like surprises."

Well, um, not unless said surprise was attached to a deliciously dark, deep-dimpled man. Then surprise on.

"There'll be none," he assured her as he glanced at the embossed business card she'd left on his desk. "I will address this with—"

There was a knock on the door, and in walked the freak of the hour in the tall, dark flesh. "Can I come in?" he asked, peeking his head through the door.

The sound of his voice sent heated shivers through Arabia's body. She hadn't even bothered to glance over her shoulder in fear he'd see the desire that still lingered on her face. So she purposefully kept her back to him, as he welcomed himself into the office without an invitation.

Fuck. Bret shot him a scathing look, and Cruze felt himself recoil inside. Still, he met his stare boldly. Though he felt like shit—of all fucking days to let his dick get the best of him, it had to be *today*—he wasn't one to cower to any man. It was a mistake. One he'd never make again. Still, he hoped Bret wouldn't toss him out on his ass when it was all said and done. Hell, he wouldn't blame him if he did after what he'd been witness to, even if nothing had happened; the shit still looked suspect.

He could tell Bret was pissed—rightfully so. Shit, he was pissed himself. Fucking bitches! They were nothing but trouble. He needed a blunt. Bad.

"Ms. Knight," Bret said, trying to rein in the bite of temper in his voice. "I believe you've unofficially met HYPE's newest coach, and one of the enrichment center's most giving donors. Cruze Fontaine."

Cruze walked further into the room, and Arabia swallowed, then slowly stood to face *him*, her eyes sparkling with fascination. He let out his breath in a long exhale when she turned toward him. Motherfuck. She was finer than he'd remembered from *that* night. His mind was spinning so damn fast, reeling between embarrassment and an inexplicable desire to have her again. For a second he was back at the club—his hard shaft gliding in and out of her body, her wet pussy sliding back and forth over his dick.

Yes. She stood confident and poised, but inside, she was a trembling mess. She felt her fingers twitch with the desire to touch him, press her body into his, but she managed to find her professional footing and stepped forward with an outstretched hand, and an inviting smile.

"Arabia Knight," she introduced herself, keeping her gaze fixed on his.

Damn, her name was *Arabia*. It sounded sexy to him the way she'd said it. Exotic. And now he was standing here with the beginnings of fresh arousal pooling from the head of his dick. Why the fuck hadn't he pulled out his shirt? Or worn those burgundy boxer briefs he'd decided against at the last minute? Now he'd have to hope like hell she didn't notice the bulge slowly stretching down his leg.

He kept his expression casual, struggling to keep from licking his lips at the swell of her breasts, the slightest hint of smooth flesh peeking from her blouse. Pretty in pink she was. All conservative and demure and sophisticated and innocent-looking, not the hot, sultry temptress he'd just fucked weeks before. So fucking hot and wild.

He clasped her hand, his attention full on her face, and for a moment, Arabia thought for sure she'd drown in the pool of lust swimming in his eyes. "Cruze Fontaine." His deep voice was thick with heat. The subtle scent of his expensive cologne wafted up her nostrils, and Arabia felt the room spin as she breathed him in. "It's a pleasure to meet you," he added, trying to ignore the way the tiny hairs on his arms stood up, the result of the electricity now swirling between them. He wondered if she felt it, too.

For a moment, she said nothing, but Cruze saw the inquisitive gleam in her eyes, along with the way her head tilted and her succulent lips slightly parted, as if she were contemplating what to say or do next.

Oh, yes—she felt it. And she could tell in the way his pulse beat a tad too quickly in his neck, and in the way his dreamy eyes were dilated that he felt what she was feeling, too. She wasn't a fool. She'd felt that same spark—the sizzling heat—between them the moment they'd laid eyes on each other that night at the club. She'd felt it the moment she felt the distance between them close as he came to her, standing too close behind her, making her pussy quiver. He'd made her pussy wet long before he'd spoken a word to her.

She'd felt it surging through her the moment she'd felt his arm curl around her waist and he'd pulled her closer so he could feel her chest rising and falling, the curves of her back pressing against his body as the fat, juicy ass of hers fitted into his groin.

And—oh what a perfect fit it had been. Arabia swallowed back a thick lump of desire, pushing back the decadent memory.

"The pleasure's all mine," she finally offered all prim and proper and professional-like as he engulfed her delicate hand in his.

Bret cleared his throat, and Cruze took that as a sign that said *Nigga, fix this shit.*

"Listen," he said, still holding onto her hand. It was so soft and warm and he wondered how good it would feel wrapped around his dick. *Shit, nigga. Get a grip.* "I apologize for you walking in on that back there in my office. It was…"

"Sucking your dick," Arabia heard herself say in her head. But, instead, she gave him an amused look, sliding her hand from his. "Compromising," she said teasingly.

Cruze gave a sheepish grin, almost at a loss for words. He shifted his weight, not liking the way this sexy-ass woman was all of a sudden unnerving him. He was a smooth dude, a magnet for pussy, for fuck's sake. He turned broads out, not lose words or train of thought.

"She was, uh, well…" *Shit, shit, shit.*

"No need to explain," she said, letting him off the hook. She glanced at her diamond-encrusted watch, then over at Bret. "Mr. Hollis. I'd better get going. It was a pleasure." She reached for her designer briefcase tote lying on the chair.

Cruze frowned. Wait. Was she leaving so soon? Where the fuck was she going? He thought she'd wanted to ask him a few questions as well. He glanced over at Bret as he stood, and walked around his desk to extend his hand to Arabia.

"Thanks for coming down to discuss HYPE's goals," Bret said.

"My pleasure," she replied cordially. Then she smiled. "I'll be in touch." Arabia brought her attention to Cruze. "Mr. Fontaine—"

"Please. Call me Cruze," he said, flashing her a dimpled-smile. When his eyes once again reached hers, she had to choke back a gasp at the fire flickering in his pupils. Heat flashed through her, and she felt as if she'd melt right there on the spot if she didn't make a mad dash for the door and lock herself inside her rental. Not now.

Right now.

"Well, *Cruze*. Nice meeting you."

"Oh, let me walk you out," Bret offered.

"Oh, no. Please. Stay. I'll be fine. I'll leave the two of you alone… to *talk*," she said pointedly. And with that she was sauntering toward the door, her heart pounding so fast she could feel its beat in the pit of her pussy.

She managed to keep her back straight as she walked, feeling heat searing up the back of her body as Cruze kept his gaze on her, taking in the way her fitted skirt curved over her hips and grazed at her knees. Her plump ass was like two fluffy biscuits he found himself wanting to bite into. He swallowed. He wasn't one ever at a loss for words, but he found himself standing here frozen as a hot coil of desire twisted through him, making his balls ache.

Bret cleared his throat again, shooting another scathing look over at Cruze. Then this time, he mouthed through clenched teeth, "Fix this shit. *Now*."

Cruze gave him a knowing glance, then turned to catch her. But she was already gone, melted away from his view. He stepped out into the hallway and, as he came up behind her, he said, "Yo, *Arabia*."

A shiver raced up her spine as she peeked over her shoulder, her brown eyes glinting surprise. She stopped and looked up at him through long-lashed eyes as he approached her. He was right in front of her, so close she could feel the air between them thicken. The hunger on his face was unmistakable, and Arabia's breath caught in her chest.

"Yes?" she coolly replied.

"Forgive my forwardness. But have dinner with me tonight."

She tried to control her breathing. She stepped back from him, her back practically brushing against the bar of the huge glass door.

If he noticed her reaction, he didn't let on. She tilted her head, and he could see that she was toying with the idea. "And why would I do that?"

Cruze stepped in closer, closing the distance between them, making sure she saw the heat brimming in his eyes.

"It's simple," he said smoothly. "I'm all you've been thinking about." It wasn't a question. It was an assertion. He could smell her heated juices wafting from beneath her skirt, her sweet cunt taunting his senses.

Arabia blinked. This was utterly ridiculous lusting over a man this way. His gaze made fire pulse through her veins. But she had no damn intentions of giving him the satisfaction of knowing that. And—before she could open her mouth to deny the yearning between her legs, his mouth curved, revealing those delicious dimples.

"And you're delusional," she said, her gaze fixed on his.

He laughed. "So is that a yes?"

"Mr. Fontaine," she said as she pushed back on the door's handle. "It's a 'you're not ready for a woman like me.' Have a good day."

And leaving that little bit of mystery dangling between the two of them, she stepped out into the sun; her smile slow and easy and full of heated challenge.

Twenty-One

This chocolaty motherfucker sitting in front of her was an egotistical asshole, a smug son-of-a-bitch. *Sexy bastard!* It was evident in the way he spoke, the way he carried himself—his confidence bordering dangerously close to arrogance—that he was the kind of man who was used to getting what he wanted, when he wanted. She was sure *no* wasn't a word in his vocabulary. And clearly he wasn't the kind of man who had to look far for pussy. He was probably used to women falling for his *GQ* looks, that deep-dimpled smile of his, and his never-ending charm. Hell, she mused, he probably had a slew of wet-pussy hoes catcalling and mewling outside his door, trying to claw their way into his sheets.

So why the hell had she accepted his invitation to dinner?

Well…because deep down—even if she hadn't wanted to admit it, yet—she wanted to be clawing at his bed sheets as well. Hell, she'd hang upside down from a chandelier and do the damn Tootsie Roll if it meant having her cunt stretching and creaming all over his cock one more time. One more time—*yes*, that's all she needed.

That's all she required.

Her stomach tightened.

She wasn't sure why the idea of him giving a string of horny bitches his long, hard dick bothered her. It shouldn't. But it did. It made her envious. And she didn't like it one damn bit.

So Arabia reached for her drink, then sipped and eyed him from out of the corner of her eye. She licked moisture from her lips as she set her drink back on the table.

She'd opted for a seat next to him, instead of across from him because, at the time, she didn't think she'd have enough strength to get through a full meal having to look him in those dreamy eyes without creaming in her panties.

But—*holy hell*—sitting next to him was far worse than she imagined had she'd chosen to sit across from him. Breathing him in was too intense, too intoxicating, too dizzying. And it made it difficult for her to think straight.

This kind of shit never happened to her. Not Arabia Knight. Not the sultry queen of seduction. But this man...this tall, dark, and goddamn deliciously sinful hunk of man did something to her that she couldn't quite put into words—not yet at least.

And—*no*, she didn't like it one damn bit.

Cruze hid a smirk behind his napkin as he dabbed at his mouth. He had been eyeing her from his periphery since they'd arrived for dinner. She hadn't wanted to sit across from him, but to the right of him instead. He'd found it odd, but okay—whatever. Several times, she slid her pretty pink tongue over her top lip, then pulled her bottom lip in. She twirled a strand of her hair, and shifted in her seat. He didn't know why he found the simple act sexy, but he did.

And several times he had to discreetly slide a hand down into his lap and press the heel of his palm against his hard dick. Fuck dinner. Why hadn't he asked her for a night of fucking in the backseat of his whip instead?

His throbbing dick would have thanked him for it.

Arabia reached for her glass again, and took a long sip of her wine, before shifting in her seat to angle her body so that she was almost facing him.

Was she nervous?

Did *he* make her nervous?

Nah. Not after the way she threw that pussy at him. There was no way in hell she was uneasy about shit. So Cruze shook the notion from his head. Still, he couldn't believe that *she* was *here* in the flesh. The freaky broad who'd consumed his fantasies for the last few weeks. He wasn't pussy whipped by any means. Yet, here he was sitting beside this broad, lust simmering in his eyes, with a hard-ass dick. Eyeing her made his balls flood with need.

He pressed his legs together. *What the fuck is going on here?* He hadn't asked her out to fuck—well, maybe he did, but that was beside the point. The point was, if she offered him some pussy, he'd gladly beat her guts up again—no questions asked. Then send her stuck-up ass on her way.

Shit.

Who was he fooling?

What was supposed to satiate his sexual appetite that night had only made him hungrier; he wanted more. He wanted her to suck his dick, use a lot of spit. Then bend over and let him lose himself inside her heat again. Without words, she had spoken to a part of his soul that night. Had gripped and begged and clutched and opened to him like no other woman, which is why he wanted to have dinner with her tonight. He needed to get a handle on who this broad was. And figure out what was it about her that had him ready to fuck the shit out of her again, repeatedly and in excess.

He sighed inwardly as his cock thickened.

Shit.

"What is it about this broad?" he asked himself again.

Yeah, okay. There was definitely lust; lots of hot, greedy need. The throbbing in his loins was proof of that. Still, he was a man in control. Always. Of everything. And, yet, here he was feeling his restraint slowly slipping out of his grasp, wanting to give into his hard dick, and his sexual urges, like he'd almost done earlier in his office with Tanji.

Fuck.

It was bad enough that memories of he and Arabia's nasty encounter in the club was still playing inside his head as they ate. In his mind he kept seeing the sway of her hips, her smooth milk-chocolate thighs, that juicy ass and…

That lil' red dress!

He kept hearing her screaming with abandon over the sound of the music, the bass pouring out of the club's speakers, vibrating through their bodies as her cunt clutched him.

He kept feeling his dick buried inside her—and how tight and hot and wet her pussy had been while he'd fucked her, while they both plummeted over the edge. He'd fucked her hard. And she'd fucked him back harder. He'd fucked her fast. And she'd fucked him back faster. Wetly. Greedily. And they'd done this on a dance floor, surrounded by partygoers who had been none the wiser.

He groaned inwardly.

Everything about that night was etched in his brain. He'd done some wild shit in his life. But fucking a broad on a dance floor?

Nah, that was the first. *She* was the first.

She was bold. Nasty. And goddamn sexy as fuck!

Inadvertently, he licked his lips.

And Arabia almost swallowed her tongue watching the reddish tip of his tongue sexily glide over his top lip. A hot ache grew inside her as she imagined his tongue sliding over her pussy. She quickly cleared her throat, and shook the imagery from her mind. She had to get ahold of herself.

"So tell me, Mr. Fontaine," she decided to ask, pushing her half-eaten plate back and slicing into his salacious thoughts. "Do you make it a habit of screwing random women in your office?" she bluntly asked, surprised that she'd gone there with him.

The corners of Cruze's mouth quirked into a half-smile.

He raised his brow and eyed her, his left dimple flashing ever so sexy. "Well, Ms. Knight, how 'bout *you* tell me. Do *you* make it a habit of letting muhfuckas you don't know fuck you in dance clubs?" he countered coolly.

Oops. She hadn't expected that.

Touché.

Arabia smiled indulgently at him, matching his stare with one of her own, a glint of mischief in her eyes as she leaned into him. "Mr. Cruze Fontaine," she said huskily. "I *fuck* who I want. When I want. Where I want. And I *fucked* you because my pussy told me to."

Well damn.

Surprisingly turned on by her candor, Cruze laughed—not that he found her *funny*, but she was refreshing. And it was the first time in a long time that a woman had actually made him laugh; one that didn't feel forced. And, shockingly, he felt...*relaxed*. So relaxed in fact that he'd turned off his cell—something he never did.

For several long seconds, Cruze studied her, and everything about her was threatening to make him unravel. And he wasn't entirely sure he liked it. But, God, if he didn't want to fuck her pretty little mouth. He wanted to fuck it hard, so hard that his heavy balls would slap her chin. He'd fuck her so hard until he fucked all of her teeth loose. And then he'd keep fucking that sweet mouth until her gums went raw.

Shit.

That stunt Tanji had tried to pull down at the center earlier in the day still had him feeling some type of way. Disgusted; yet, still very horny for some wet head.

"Oh, word?" he said, rubbing his chin. "And what is that sweet kitty telling you to do now?"

A slow, flirty smile eased over Arabia's lips. "Right now it's warning me to seal up the gates, and flee for the hills."

Cruze couldn't help but laugh again, reaching for his drink. "Yeah, a'ight. That's what your mouth says," he teased back. "But I bet your body is saying something else." He licked his lips, then took a sip of his cognac. The rich, bold elixir warmed his chest. All he needed now was a blunt and some pussy, and his night would be complete.

Arabia shifted in her chair, pressing her legs shut. Could he smell her arousal? Could he feel the heated need radiating from her skin?

God, what a horny whore she was.

She cleared her throat. "Anyway," she continued, choosing to ignore his last remark. "I bet you were a momma's boy growing up." That came from out of nowhere, causing Cruze to cringe inwardly.

Growing up, he despised being called *that*. A momma's boy; even if he had been one. His friends would tease him because his mother kept such a tight leash on him, doing what she could to keep him close to home—where she could keep an eye on him. And he'd end up getting into fistfights with his peers over them calling him *that*.

He scowled. "Why you say that?"

She shrugged. "I don't know; just a feeling. Are the two of you close?"

Cruze shifted in his seat. A faraway gaze entered his eyes when he looked at Arabia, and she'd noticed it the minute she asked the question.

"Nah," he offered. "Not anymore."

Arabia gave him a questioning look.

And before he knew it, he told her, "She's dead. She died from cancer."

Arabia gasped, more startled by the ache in her chest than the news of his mother's death. She'd heard it in his voice, pain. And she wanted to comfort him. What the hell? "Oh, no. I'm so sorry," she said in a soothing tone that made Cruze's body relax some. "How old were you when she died?"

"Thirteen."

"What about your father?" she asked, genuinely interested in knowing more. "Are you close with him? Do you have any siblings or are you the only child?"

Cruze's body stiffened. And coldness crept into his gaze. See, now this broad was starting to do the most. Give a bitch an inch and she started wanting to write your whole damn biography. *What the fuck?* He had already told her more than he'd expected. He didn't really like talking about his personal life. It was private. Shit he kept locked in a tiny box in the back of his brain and in the bottom of his heart. Shit that wasn't any of her damn nosey-ass business, or anyone else's.

And this was why he didn't take bitches out. They asked too many damn questions. But *he* had asked her out. And there was something about the way she was looking at him—all wide-eyed and curious and…interested—that made him slightly uncomfortable.

Damn, muhfucka, relax. She's only tryna make conversation. Not investigate ya ass or set ya paranoid ass up. That's what muhfuckas do on a date, nigga. They talk. Have conversation.

Cruze leaned back in his chair, and blew out a sigh. "Nah. I'm an only child."

Arabia cocked her head to the side, studying him, a question in her eyes the moment he caught her gaze. The fact that he hadn't said anything about his father didn't go unnoticed, and she took that as her cue to leave it alone. She'd leave whatever deep, dark secrets he had for someone else to uncover.

"A'ight, so enough about me, Ms. Arabia Knight," Cruze said. "Your turn."

She shrugged. "Okay. Well, what would you like to know?"

"Are you the only child?"

She shook her head. "No. I have three sisters. They're all married with children. I'm the youngest."

Cruze nodded. "Oh, a'ight. So you don't have a man?"

"No," she said. Well, *technically*, she didn't have one—not one of her own, anyway. She had someone else's. But that bit of news wasn't anything for him to know. "And I'm not looking for one," she added a beat later.

Cruze smirked. Broads stayed talking that "I'm not looking for a man shit" until they got the dick-down, then they were begging to get wifed up.

"Oh a'ight," he said. "I heard that. So what's good with your parents? They still alive?" Her gaze went beyond his for a moment before she allowed it to flit back to his face.

"My dad died…"—*more like was murdered*—"when I was ten."

"Damn. Sorry to hear that."

Arabia smiled faintly. "Thanks." She took a breath and shook her head. "It crushed me when he passed," she said solemnly. She rarely ever spoke about her father, or his death. And suddenly out of nowhere, she felt tears glittering her eyes, and felt herself getting choked up. She reached for her wineglass and took a deep swallow.

"So you were a Daddy's girl, I bet," Cruze said.

Arabia nodded and smiled at the thought. "Yeah, I was. My father doted on me. He loved me to the core. And spoiled me rotten. My sisters always said I was his favorite." She smiled, remembering. "Whenever he looked at me, he made me feel as if I were the most beautiful girl in the world. I felt loved by him. I was special. And he made me feel it. Every waking moment." She took her linen napkin and dabbed along the corner of her eye where a damp trail of tears had formed. "Ooh, forgive me," she muttered. "I don't like to talk about it."

Cruze nodded knowingly. "I understand." And he did all too well. That pain she felt was the same pain he felt. Losing the most important person in your life. "What about ya moms?"

Arabia rolled her eyes. "Please. For a lack of having anything nice to say, let's just say she's living her life."

Cruze chuckled. "Oh, a'ight. I'll take that to mean the two of you don't get along?"

"To say the least," she said dryly. "But enough about her. I'm not trying to ruin my evening or the rest of my appetite talking about her." She took another sip of her drink, then eyed him. "I have another question that's completely off topic."

His gaze narrowed. "Umm. And what's that?"

"Well, I've been staring at your lips almost half the night," she said boldly. "They're beautiful, by the way."

Cruze blushed. "Thanks. So what's the question?"

"Do you eat pussy?" she bluntly asked, her voice above a whisper. She'd been dying to know all night. Had been conjuring up images of riding down on his face since they'd arrived at the restaurant. And now she needed to know.

Cruze threw his head back and laughed, more from the shock of her being so brazen than anything else. He was still chuckling when he made a face, shaking his head. "Nah, nah. I'm good on that."

Arabia blinked. "Well, do you *kiss?*"

Again, he shook his head. "Nah. Why?"

Arabia's eyes flashed with sympathy. *Poor thing*, she thought. *No wonder his spirit seems so damn heavy.* He needed some pussy on his tongue.

She shifted in her chair—crossing her legs at her ankles, her cunt clenching furiously at that knowing. Who the hell didn't eat pussy? And what kind of woman accepted it?

In her world, she could forgive a man for not kissing. But one who *didn't* put his face and tongue all up in that special place couldn't be. It was unforgiveable—an abominable act of sexual neglect. Cunnilingus was a requirement, period. If a man expected to have steady access to her pussy, he had better be ready to dance his tongue over her clit, then slide it into her slit.

Bottom line, she despised selfish lovers. So there was no reason for her to be sitting beside him toying with the idea of sliding off her chair, then slinking under the table and sucking his dick. Absolutely not.

Still, there was something about him that intrigued her.

And she had to admit. The dick had been...*good*. No. Damn good—thank you very much. That night at the club had been the kind of raunchy fucking she'd needed. He'd stamped *and* stretched her pussy inside out with every thick inch of his cock, from the tip to the base, to his heavy balls slapping the back of her slit. He'd served her up right. She licked her lips.

If she closed her eyes tight enough, she could still see him straining with pleasure as he slid in and out of her body, her cunt greedily sucking at his cock. The way he'd growled and lost control, fucking her hard and fast, his body convulsing violently with the force of his orgasm, biting into her shoulder like some wild beast, was still etched in the forefront of her memory.

Her mouth curved wickedly.

Mmm—sweet Jesus, *yes*—lewd decadence, that's what that night had been.

Arabia reached for her wineglass. And their eyes met. She took a sip of her wine, peering over the rim of her goblet at him. Little did she know, that night at the club was seared into his brain as well, but he had no intentions of letting her know that he couldn't stop thinking about that sweet, tight pussy; or that his dick was harder than steel at the thought of being trapped inside her wet, clutching sex again.

Her pussy ached. She was done with dinner and talk.

Arabia needed something hot and dirty, before she caught her train back to New York.

She reached for her purse. Pulled out a condom.

Then discreetly slid it over to Cruze as she leaned into his ear and whispered, "Meet me in the bathroom for dessert."

Twenty-Two

Cruze gazed at the condom. First a crowded dance floor and now she wanted to fuck in a public restroom. *This raunchy bitch!* Obviously, Arabia was accustomed to dumb niggas indulging her twisted desires, and Cruze resented being ordered to perform like a goddamn circus act. But he'd promised Bret he'd fix the situation and so he languidly rose from the chair.

Eyes narrowed, he moved toward the restroom. If Arabia wanted to treat him like some kind of disposable sex toy, then he had something for that ass. His spirit ominous and heavy, he wasn't surprised that his dick responded to his mood by growing more rigid with every step.

When he entered the bathroom, Arabia was gazing in the mirror, no doubt enjoying her impeccable image. In her reflection, he saw her expression change from smug self-assurance to a look of panic when she noticed his clenched jaw and felt the danger of his dark mood.

Before she could utter a word, Cruze snatched her by the wrist, trapping it inside his powerful grip.

"Let go! Why're you acting like an asshole," Arabia spat. She was helpless to wrench free as he forcibly tugged her toward a stall and then shoved her inside.

"Is this what you want?" Cruze growled, pressing her dainty hand against his turgid erection. "Huh, you want some dick?"

Arabia gasped sharply as his hard shaft pulsed hotly against her palm. She wasn't sure if she wanted to slap the shit out of Cruze or rip open his fly. What the hell was his problem? After receiving the freaky offer of unexpected pussy for dessert, the average man would have felt immensely grateful. But not this motherfucker. He came bursting into the bathroom, looking half-crazed and grabbing on her like an uncouth barbarian.

She thought about escaping the confines of the stall by kicking him in the nuts with her pointy-toed Giuseppes and then running. But when he unzipped his pants and whipped out a throbbing, dark chocolate hard-on that was so perfectly sculpted with a slight curve, bulbous head, and pulsing veins, she gave a sharp gasp and gawked at his dick in lustful admiration.

Arabia's mouth watered and her pussy clenched at the same time. Seduced into a hot, quivering mess, she was faced with the dilemma of whether she should suck or fuck the monstrously beautiful work of art.

With his big hand clamped around the base of his cock, Cruze aimed the engorged weapon at her and smirked. The slightest movement of his lips put those damned dimples on quick display, forcing Arabia to avert her gaze.

Oh, he was an insufferably arrogant man, and under ordinary circumstances, she would have told the pompous motherfucker to kiss the inside of her ass. Unfortunately, these weren't ordinary circumstances. Her pussy was acting up something terrible, spitting and twitching and having some sort of conniption fit.

The flimsy strip of crotch material that pressed against her pussy lips was doing an appallingly bad job of containing the hot juices that bubbled out of her overheated cunt. Her delicate, pretty little thong was completely saturated. Motivated purely by lust, she hitched up her skirt and tugged off her pussy-scented undergarment.

The bastard didn't deserve her and she was mad with herself for not being able to control her urges. Fuck it, though. After she got what she wanted, she'd never have to look at his self-satisfied expression or speak to his ignorant ass, ever again.

Holding her lace and silk thong in her hand, her eyes shot upward when out of the corner of her eyes, she noticed Cruze making a sudden movement. He released his dick, and she watched in awe as it flopped heavily up and down. He extended his hand toward her, and it took her brain a few moments to comprehend what he was doing. She was absolutely stunned and her pussy began to weep when he eased her thong from her hand and brought it up to his nose. With his eyes closed, he deeply inhaled her drawers, looking like he was in ecstasy. The imagery was so damn seductive, Arabia nearly came on herself.

A tiny sound of yearning escaped her lips and she pressed into him, her hand automatically closing around his meaty dick, and then stroking it to a steel-like rigidity.

"Mmm," Cruze groaned as he began thrusting into her soft palm. Focused on the sensation of flesh against flesh, he seized her by the hips, and the flimsy fabric slipped from his grasp, floating down to the floor.

Staring hot-eyed at her pussy, Cruze rubbed his finger against the seam of her cunt and then slid it between her slick folds. Arabia was drenched and his finger quickly became wet with her slippery fluid. As he penetrated, she began to gyrate on his finger. Cruze explored her pussy, his thick finger searching and probing until it settled on a mysterious spot that was cushiony soft and radiated heat. Her pussy muscles gripped his finger and her strokes on his dick became more intense.

Cruze noticed the bitch wasn't talking slick out of her mouth, now. The only sounds she was making were gasps and murmurs of pleasure. Those soft sounds were sexy as fuck, causing a streak of molten heat to flare through his painfully swollen shaft.

He withdrew his finger from her wet, clutching cunt and then eased his dick out of her hand. Turning her around, he yanked her skirt up higher. His breath came out in harsh rasps when his eyes settled on the plump mounds of her luscious, mocha ass. Ready to fuck every coherent thought out of her head, determined to punish the pussy until the bitch was rambling incomprehensibly, Cruze fumbled in his pocket, pulled out the condom, and ripped it open.

Legs splayed, her palms pressed against the tiled wall of the bathroom stall, Arabia was in a position of complete surrender as Cruze entered her from behind. She shuddered and gasped hoarsely as he eased in the head and then began to slowly insert inch after thick inch until his dick was submerged inside Arabia's cunt that felt like a hot swamp of wetness.

Her juicy pussy throbbed to the beat of her racing heart, clutching his dick possessively each time. She bucked backward forcing him to go deeper. He gritted his teeth and his face twisted with agonizing pleasure as her walls hugged his dick in a tight, velvety embrace. Struggling against her pussy clench, he braced his hands on her hips, desperately digging the pads of his fingers into her satiny smooth flesh. He slowly pulled his dick out halfway, and when Arabia groaned and writhed in protest, he quickly shoved it back inside her humid warmth.

The sensation of her soft skin and the scent of hot pussy were driving him insane, and he pumped harder and faster, as if striving to demolish her pussy. Locked in a pounding rhythm, Cruze told himself to slow down, but he couldn't. Arabia's cunt was too hot. Too juicy.

The way she was slamming her ass into his crotch, she obviously liked the hard fuck he was giving her. They were building a frantic momentum, moving together perfectly, and he became suddenly and inexplicably angry.

"This pussy," he rasped, steadily pumping. "It's so fuckin' good," he exclaimed as he rammed her as hard as he could. "You need to stop playin' with me, Arabia, and let me dig in this shit on a regular basis." He hadn't meant to speak the words out loud, and he was infuriated with himself for coming out of character and expressing any type of weakness.

Needing to lash out and cause her some pain for having the kind of pussy that he knew was going to once again disrupt his thoughts and fuck with his mental status, he grabbed a handful of her hair and yanked the shit out of it while continuously pumping dick into that juicy hole.

Arabia cried out and began wiggling her ass around frantically. Desiring to look in her eyes and see the pain he was inflicting, Cruze pulled his dick out. With her pussy left unoccupied, Arabia let out a cry of distress.

Cruze yanked her around, forcing her to face him. He snatched open her blouse, sending buttons flying and hitting the floor and scattering about, exposing her silk-and-lace-clad breasts. God— those sweet, mouthwatering tits. He wanted to see more. Wanted to cup them. Bite down on her nipples. He fucking wanted her— all of her.

Arabia gasped, shocked. *Ohmygod! Oh no this Barbarian mother-fucker didn't!* But she was too overcome with burning need to be stuffed again with Cruze's thickness to curse him for ruining her goddamn blouse. She wanted him back inside her—*now*.

"Mmm. Fuck me," she rasped, lifting up a leg and planting the sole of her stiletto on the toilet seat. "Stuff me with your cock." Panting and moaning, she reached out and helped guide his throbbing erection back inside her depths.

Arabia winced as she felt the cold tile against her back, but she was quickly warmed by Cruze's heated thrusts. Pleasure coursed through her system, but she wanted to feel it even more intensely. Oddly, when he'd pulled her hair and manhandled her, he provoked something inside her that was wild and unrestrained. Now she needed to feel the kind of pleasure that was mixed with a little pain.

With his knees bent and his body hunched over to meet her height, Cruze rammed the pussy, deep stroking as he clutched her shoulders. Arabia pinched her own nipples, and choked out a cry of pleasure.

Their eyes locked, and she softly whispered, "Choke me."

Cruze frowned, slowing his strokes. "Huh?" he asked, thinking he was hearing things.

"I want you to choke me," she rasped, panting.

Oh, shit! His dick stretched and tunneled deeper inside her. Obliging her dark desire, he clamped a large hand around her delicate neck. Feeling her pulse beating rapidly beneath his fingertips, he reacted like a possessed man, driving his dick in and out of her pussy, hard and fast.

"Oh, yes. That's how I like it," she moaned. "Mmm. Give me all that hard, pretty dick."

Listening to the shit this freaky bitch was saying and getting caught up in the sensation of feeding her hot, gripping snatch, Cruze squeezed her throat tighter, unaware that he was cutting off her air passage. When Arabia frantically clawed at his hand, he loosened his grip. "Sorry," he muttered hoarsely. "This fat pussy, though. Goddamn, Arabia. I'm feeling the shit outta you."

In that quick rush of words, Arabia heard a passionate, unguarded admission of something much more than lust. And she was relieved to know that this cocky bastard was no different than any of the other men who fell under her spell.

As his delicious-looking dick stroked her plush walls, she was startled by the intense pleasure that suddenly burst from the very core of her being. Flooded with waves of heat that pulsated through her system, every nerve ending in her body felt raw and exposed.

Cruze felt the tremors that shook Arabia's body. Fighting to last a little longer, he bared his teeth and let out a growl. Thrusting and pumping, he bit down on his lip as her powerful little pussy muscles clenched violently around his dick.

He couldn't take it. Her snug cunt was pure hot bliss. He was going down in flames. He couldn't think, could only feel. Oh, God, fuck. He fucked her harder. Harder. Faster. *Yeah baby, take this dick.* Unable to hold back, his body jerked and he gave a strangled roar as ropes of hot cum exploded into the condom. When his thudding heart finally calmed down, Cruze pulled Arabia into his arms and hugged her fiercely. He hadn't planned such a drastic show of affection, and was stunned by it, but he couldn't help himself.

As he held her, his hands, seeming to act on their own accord, stroked her hair.

Arabia closed her eyes, and inhaled him—all of him. Encircled by Cruze's muscular arms was as close to heaven as she had ever been before. She had her head buried in his chest while he ran his fingers through her hair, and it was such a blissful feeling—so warm and comforting—she could have easily dissolved into joyful tears.

But refusing to be lured into a false sense of security, she broke his hold on her. Wriggling free, she stepped away from him.

"That thong was handmade in Paris, and you owe me a new one," she said coolly, pulling her skirt down over her hips and glancing downward at the expensive fabric that was crumpled on the floor.

Cruze twisted his lips and blew her off with a hand gesture. "Ain't no thing. You got it," he replied, making sure to inject indifference into his tone. Dismissively, he turned his back to Arabia and concentrated on removing the used condom and then flushing it down the toilet.

Nose in the air, Arabia kicked the desecrated thong out of her path as she yanked open the door, and pranced out of the stall, her warm scent wafting up around them. Cruze groaned inwardly, wanting more of her. Grabbing tissue from the dispenser, he wiped his dick, pulled his pants up and zipped himself, then headed for the door.

Five minutes later, Cruze seemed to be engrossed in the music that poured from the speakers of his SUV, while Arabia stared aimlessly out the window.

Two of a kind, they both struggled to keep their guard up during the drive back to her car; trying desperately to re-erect walls that had somehow come tumbling down over dinner, leaving them both feeling exposed. Yet, neither hadn't ever felt this satiated.

Something was frighteningly different. A flushed condom and a pair of wet panties weren't the only things they'd left behind in that bathroom stall.

They'd both greedily taken a piece of the other. And, in the tangle of their minds, one thing stood out. *They wanted more.*

Twenty-Three

Arabia blinked.

Then blinked again.

No, no, no. She had to be seeing things.

Ghosts.

Impersonators.

Some*thing*.

Because there was no way in hell Eric would be standing in the lobby of her damn building. But he was. And he spotted her the minute she stepped through the glass doors, and was now stalking toward her, a scowl on his face.

Her heart dropped.

She thought to run out of the building and scream for help, but then quickly dismissed that absurd idea. She'd look straitjacket crazy making a mad dash out into the busy streets, hiking up the hem of her eleven-hundred-dollar dress and sprinting in her six-inch heels. No. There was no need to run. This was the safest place. Besides, he wasn't wielding a gun or brandishing an electric saw, so she didn't think she'd be in too much of danger.

Still, she slid her hand down in her purse and grabbed ahold of the canister of mace she kept tucked inside, just in case.

"E-eric," she stammered when he reached her. "W-what are you doing here?"

"You won't take my calls," he said in a deceptively mild tone, his narrowed gaze aimed at her. "And you insist on ignoring my texts. So you've left me no other recourse, Arabia."

Since the night she'd been forced to end their affair, he'd gone from calling her from restricted numbers to calling from phone numbers she wasn't familiar with when she'd stopped taking calls from blocked callers.

She didn't know if he was using prepaid cell phones, or changing his number using Google Talk. All she knew was, this shit was getting old.

She bared her teeth. "You have no business just showing up here, Eric."

"We need to talk."

Arabia huffed impatiently. "No, Eric. We have nothing to talk about. I told you it was best we end it, and then you took to calling me out of my name." She shook her head. "So, no, Eric. You've said all I needed to hear."

His eyes narrowed. "So you're willing to throw away everything we have together, is that it?"

Arabia frowned. "What is it that you *think* we have, Eric, huh?" she hissed. "What, a few nights of fucking every other month or so?"

"Bullshit," he snapped. "You can't honestly mean that."

"Then you're a bigger fool than I thought," she said, struggling to keep her voice calm and low. The last thing she wanted was a scene. "It's over, Eric. Period. Now, I'm asking you nicely to—"

He pulled Arabia into his arms and fused his mouth to hers, cutting off the rest of her words in a hot, breathless kiss that both shocked and enraged her.

Pulling back from him—*whap*, she slapped him with an open hand to the cheek, hard, causing everything in the lobby to go still, and wide-eyed glances to lock on to the couple.

Fire flashed in Eric's eyes, making Arabia instantly regret having done that. Yet, she stood her ground. "Leave, Eric," she warned, revulsion twisting her lips. "And don't come back. Or the next time I'll have you arrested."

She turned to leave him standing there.

His jaw twitched. He was becoming more pissed by the minute, and he was seething as he stared at her. He swore viciously under his breath. This fucking bitch! Since telling his wife that he was in love with someone else, he'd packed his things and was slowly moving them out of the marital home he shared with her. He hadn't wanted to hurt her, but his words of wanting out of their marriage had hit her hard, shocking her to her core. And she'd cried and sobbed, and threatened to leave him penniless by the time she was done with him.

At the time, it hadn't mattered. The only thing that mattered was that he'd spend the rest of his life building a life with Arabia, the woman that made his heart skip a beat.

And now this ungrateful bitch was standing here telling him that she wanted nothing else to do with him, after he'd given up everything. He felt like taking his bare hands and wringing her goddamn neck.

But there'd be witnesses, and surveillance footage pinning him to her murder. He couldn't risk that. So, he decided to let this lecherous bitch have a pass for slapping him.

And still his heart ached in his chest.

He hadn't considered this—her wanting to bail on him.

He couldn't fathom her with someone else, some other motherfucker's hands cupping her fat ass. He couldn't imagine her giving her sweet pussy to some other motherfucker, coming all over his mouth the way she'd always come in his; his dick possessing her body.

The thought alone was maddening.

"You can't fucking end it, Arabia," he snapped, grabbing her by the arm, his grip cutting into her circulation. "And think I'm supposed to be okay with it."

She whirled in shock, staring at him like he'd lost the rest of his mind. "I just did," she said acidly, yanking her arm back. "So leave now, or so help me God, you'll be dragged out of here in handcuffs, Eric. I promise you."

Eric's eyes narrowed as fury washed over his features. His nose flared. His jaw clenched. His expression was murderous. Arabia's glance skittered down to his hand that was closed tightly into a fist. OhmyfuckingGod! He was going to hit her.

"You can't fucking do this to me, Arabia! To us!" he yelled, spittle flying out of his mouth. Arabia felt her knees buckle now that he was speaking loudly enough for the entire lobby to hear. So she did the only thing she could to disarm him. She quickly yanked out her can of mace and began spraying wildly in his face.

"Ahhh, shit!" he screamed, his hands flying up to his face. He coughed and gagged. "You fucking ass-licking bitch! Dick-sucking whore!" And she sprayed him again for good measure.

He tried to lunge at her, stumbling.

But then to her surprise—and relief—two bulky security guards materialized in a matter of seconds, charging out of nowhere to intervene, roughly snatching Eric up and tossing him like a rag doll back and forth between the two of them, before dragging him toward the door, and tossing him out on his ass.

The doorman rushed to her side. "Asshole," he muttered. "I knew something was off with him the moment he walked inside here." He shook his head, bringing his attention to Arabia. "Are you okay?" he asked in a gentle tone.

She nodded. "Yes, yes. I'm fine. Thanks."

But the truth was, she wasn't fine. She was utterly embarrassed. Eric had come to her place of residence and caused a scene. She would have never thought he would turn out to be so goddamn messy. She was beside herself with disgust.

She grabbed her aching arm. Great. He'd bruised her. Bastard.

"Would you like for me to call the police?" he asked, walking her to the elevators.

She groaned inwardly. Oh God no. The police were the last thing she wanted called, even though she had threatened to call them herself. Still, the last thing she needed was the police showing up at her building for a domestic violence dispute.

"No, no. It was just a silly misunderstanding," she quickly asserted. But Arabia didn't miss the quick lift of the doorman's one eyebrow as if to say *yeah—right*.

Arabia shot him an icy look—a warning to mind his goddamn manners, as she pulled out her key card and inserted it. The doors to the elevator slid shut in his face, and Arabia fell back against the paneled wall, shaking.

"Can you believe that shit?" Arabia hissed, pacing the carpeted living room floor as she spoke to her sister, Maya, over the phone. "That crazy bastard showed up here, then had the nerve to put his hands on me."

Maya gasped. "Girl, I can't. You mean to tell me he *hit* you?"

She huffed. "No, Maya. He *grabbed* me."

"That's still bad. What did you do after he grabbed you?"

Arabia grunted. "Mmph. What you think I did? I maced him up real good, then watched as security tossed his crazy ass out of the building." She took a deep breath. "I still can't believe he showed up here and embarrassed me like that. The goddam nerve of him! And now I have this nasty-ass bruise on my arm, thanks to him."

"Ohmygod, girl. I can't believe what I'm hearing. Did you call the police?"

Arabia's eyes flew open. "Hell no. And have my neighbors gawking at me, and whispering shit behind my back about me? I don't think so."

"But what if he comes back again, and tries to hurt you, Arabia?" Maya asked, alarm ringing in her voice. "You should at least file a report against him."

Arabia sighed. "I guess. But I don't think he'd be crazy enough to show his face here again. Not after what happened. Eric might be acting crazy right now, but he isn't stupid."

"I hope you're right," Maya said, not sounding the least bit convinced. God she hoped Arabia was right about this Eric guy, but he sounded like he had a few screws loose.

Arabia shuddered. "Maya, you should have seen the look in his eye. If looks could kill, I know I'd be dead right on the spot. And why is his leaving his wife my fault? I didn't ask him to. I tried to encourage him to stay with her ass. What the hell do I want with a cheating man?"

Maya sighed, shaking her head. She loved Arabia, but she felt her younger sister was reckless when it came to men—married men, that was. And she feared something like this—or worse, would eventually happen. She wondered if Arabia even remembered the drama she'd experienced her junior year at Spelman. Marcus, if Maya remembered correctly, was his name. He was almost nine years older than Arabia, and very married. But when Arabia tried to break it off with him—after only four months, he became obsessed with her to the point that he'd stalked her, showing up at campus and camping out outside the gates of the condominium she shared with one other girl.

Arabia had to file an order of protection. But that hadn't stopped him from walking up on campus one spring afternoon, and snatching her by the back of her hair and beating her in front of her peers. She ended up being rushed to the hospital with a mild concussion, a broken eye socket, and three cracked ribs.

He'd tried to beat her half-to-death.

Luckily, a group of fraternity brothers intervened and held him down until the police arrived. He'd been charged with aggravated assault and violation of a protection order, then, eventually, sentenced to four years in prison. If Maya wasn't mistaken, that order of protection was still in place. Still, she had hoped, along with her two other sisters, that that dreadful experience would have been Arabia's wakeup call, but obviously not.

"Look, Arabia," Maya said evenly. "You've had a good run with these married men. Maybe it's time for you to leave them alone. Besides, extravagant trips and jewelry, what are you really getting out of it? You can't possibly be happy with—"

"I am happy," Arabia snapped, cutting her sister off. She didn't need this shit right now. She hadn't called her to be chastised. She needed a moment of compassion from Maya; for her to simply let her vent; not get all goddamn Mother Teresa on her. "I have a fabulous career. I own my own home. I have money in the bank. And I live my life on my own terms. What more could I possibly want?"

"Arabia, no one is discounting the fact that you've done well for yourself, and I am proud of you. We all are. But, at the end of the day, all of your success means nothing when you have no one to share it with."

Arabia blinked. "What do you mean, I have no one to share it with? I have *you*, and two other sisters when you get on my nerves."

Maya chuckled, shaking her head. "Of course you have me, girl—*even* when I get on your nerves. But that's not what I'm talking about. And you know it. I mean you have no one special in your life to share those things with. Don't you want love?"

Love?

Oh God, that word sounded so damn dirty.

She wasn't about to let that filthy thing get ahold of her heart, infecting her with its toxic lies and mystical promises of a happily-ever-after—that she knew didn't exist. No, no, love was not about to have her somewhere wringing her hands at night stressing over a man, or twisting her edges out worrying about what some man was or wasn't doing when she wasn't around. She learned a long time ago that a hard dick had no conscience, so she'd be damned if she'd spend her energy worrying over whose sheets it was staining up. No. She wasn't about to babysit no damn dick, monitoring it. No, no, no. She wasn't built for that type of life. Them silly bitches chasing behind a cheating man could have that craziness.

Arabia was fine with her life *exactly* the way it was.

As far as she was concerned, love was pain. And she was allergic to both.

"No, thank you," she simply replied. "The only thing I will ever love is the idea of being stress free."

Maya huffed. "Whatever. I'm not saying jump out and fall in love with the first man who waves *hello*. All I'm saying is, be open to the idea."

Arabia cringed. The only thing she was opened to was…

"Goddamn, Arabia. I'm feeling the shit outta you…"

Arabia's pulse quickened. His name momentarily escaped her. It was at the tip of her tongue, dammit. But everything else about him was stamped into her memory. Heat splintered through her pussy, and she felt herself growing wet. Oh God, what was happening to her?

She could feel the way her body had opened to the length of him, clutching the width of him, welcoming his thrusts.

Ooh, she was such a naughty bitch, fucking *him* in that bathroom stall like that. The sordid act had been deliciously dirty. He'd fucked her wickedly. The memory alone sent her teetering practically on the brink of an orgasm.

God, what was his name again?

Her breath hitched.

Cruze.

Yes, yes. Cruze Fontaine. *Mmm*—God, yes.

"You need to stop playin' with me, Arabia, and let me dig in this shit on a regular basis."

She shook her head.

Had he meant that? No, of course not. Men were notorious for saying shit they didn't mean in the heat of the moment. So there was absolutely no way that self-serving bastard—with his fine, chocolaty self—meant...

"If you'd stop putting up walls," Maya continued, snatching her from her reverie, "you might be pleasantly surprised at how good it can feel to be in a relationship with a man of *your* own."

Arabia blinked.

Hmm. A man of her own? That concept was foreign to her. A man of her own hadn't ever figured into Arabia's life plan, or her goals. She'd been too preoccupied with her career and fucking other women's men to entertain thoughts of a relationship—particularly a *monogamous* one with anyone.

"No thank you," Arabia said. "I have no time for that."

Maya frowned on the other end of the phone. "Well, then make time. I'm sure there are a ton of good-looking, single men out there who would love to date you, Arabia. In fact, now that I'm thinking of it, I have someone I know would be a perfect match for you. And he's—"

"Um, hold up, boo. Let me stop you right there," Arabia warned. "I am not some lonely charity case who needs you to play match-maker for her."

"No one said you were. All I'm saying is, maybe it's time you broadened your horizons some. And I have just the man to help you do that. He's a corporate attorney, making six-figures. He's single. No kids. Owns several homes. And…"

"Does he have a big dick?" Arabia heard herself asking. But settled for, "What's wrong with him? Why is he still single if he's such a good catch? What, is he a paraplegic?"

Maya laughed. "Girl, no. That man is fine. And I do mean *fine*, in every sense of the word, with all of his limbs."

Arabia grunted. *"Mmph.* He sounds too good to be true if you ask me."

"Girl, stop. And you don't think you're deserving of something good? You could be a great catch too if you weren't so damn obsessed with married men."

Arabia finally stopped pacing, and crawled up on her chaise lounge. "I beg your pardon? I'm not *obsessed* with them. I simply find them convenient."

Maya chortled. "Ha! Girl. Lies. You find them as an *excuse* to not allow yourself the chance at real love. Tell me, Arabia. What are you really afraid of?"

Arabia blinked at the question, stunned.

"I don't know," she whispered. *Myself.*

"Bullshit, Arabia," Maya blurted. "I know why you do it. And so do you. So say it."

Arabia sighed. God she hated her sister for being the only one to pull her secrets out of her with such ease. "Okay, Maya. Damn. Maybe I'm scared that if I opened myself up to someone and fell for them, that I'd fall apart and wouldn't know how to pick myself up, or put myself back together again. Maybe I don't know how to let myself be vulnerable."

She nearly choked on those words. She hated to admit it. Hated putting it out there like that. But it was her truth.

Arabia was afraid of love.

Twenty-Four

The drive to New Jersey before the sun had come up was oddly comforting. At four-fifteen in the morning, there were hardly any motorists on the road and Cruze felt like he owned the highway. The dark sky was beginning to streak with reddish-yellow colors, and it was eerily beautiful.

Like Arabia.

She was weird as fuck with her freaky self, but so eerily beautiful with that luscious mouth that seldom smiled, and her dark-brown eyes that were filled with mystery. When Cruze had looked deeply into those illuminous orbs of hers, he'd felt like he was sinking into an ocean of pain and despair. In her eyes, he'd seen his own tortured spirit revealed. He sensed that like him, Arabia was engaged in an inner war and was terrified of showing even a hint of vulnerability.

He didn't know her story, but was certain that she had one. Everyone did. As far as he could tell, no one made it through this life without experiencing their fair share of unbearable grief. Cruze swallowed, thinking about the loss of his mother. She'd been so young. So brave, trying to raise him on her own. She'd never told him who his father was and had always dodged the question by saying it didn't matter as long as he had her.

But it turned out that he didn't have her. He ended up trying to make it in the world, all alone. As twisted as it was, he now realized that he'd been looking for something that resembled a mother's love in Ramona. What a laugh. Ramona had exploited his naiveté and had abused the pure love he had for her in the cruelest way. He didn't need a shrink to tell him that he was damaged goods.

And so was Arabia. He could feel it. Maybe that was why he was so attracted to her. Couldn't get her off his mind. He thought back to their bathroom encounter and his dick thumped and enlivened, but it instantly went limp when he recalled grabbing her thong and sniffing it like some kind of sick-o. *What the fuck was that shit about?* He had surprised himself with that blatant show of perversion. It made him cringe to even imagine what Arabia must have thought of him.

With her repeated warped behavior, she had a lot of nerve thinking that Cruze had issues. Sniffing a thong was mild compared to the way she liked to get down. Grabbing the first nigga with a swinging dick and serving him up juicy pussy in the midst of a huge crowd was straight bananas. Although bathroom sex was freaky, too, at least it was somewhat private. The way Arabia had lured him into the freak zone at Club Seduction was proof that she had a loose screw or two.

But he had to admit that he liked her kind of crazy.

He had fucked more bitches than he could ever count, and in every position of the Kama Sutra, yet he couldn't stop thinking about Arabia's tight pussy and the way she'd spread her legs for him with her high-heeled shoe planted on the toilet seat. Both times they'd smashed had been the most erotic adventures of his life. If he'd had the foresight to pick her thong off the floor and stick it in his pocket, he'd be sniffing that hot pussy fragrance right now while he was driving.

With a sigh of regret, he exited the interstate highway and followed the GPS directions to the dock.

Dressed in bummy sweats, hoodie, and dogged boots, Cruze joined two middle-aged white dudes and one Asian who were prepping for a long day of fishing, tinkering with tackle boxes and busily setting up their rods. He glanced at the hats they wore, taking notice of the colors: tan, brown, and a dingy off-white.

Cruze held a duffle bag in one hand and the other hand was stuffed in his pocket as he discreetly tried to determine if one of their caps was possibly a dull yellow.

The guy he'd contacted over the phone had said he could be identified by his yellow cap, but none of the fishermen's hats were any shade of yellow.

The men returned Cruze's curious glance with cold, unwelcoming looks. Carrying no fishing equipment, Cruze stood out. It must have been unnerving to have a tall black guy hanging around on the dock in the pitch-black darkness. They probably thought he was planning to rob them.

Cruze let out a snort of disgust. Their old, broke asses didn't have shit he wanted. To put their minds at ease, he took down his hood and moved several yards away from them, meandering in the direction of the darkened bait shop.

He looked around impatiently. Where the hell was the guy in the yellow cap? Trying to occupy his time, Cruze pulled out his phone and was pleased to see a message from his real estate broker, informing him that one of his properties had sold. Flipping houses was so much easier than flipping kilos, but a part of him missed the danger.

He studied the screen on the phone, reading the details of the sale. After he returned the phone to his pocket, he resumed craning his neck, checking out a new group of retirees that moseyed onto the pier. No yellow hats. He was beginning to grow antsy and wished there was a number he could call to find out when the dude was planning on getting there, but the guy used burner phones that he changed regularly.

Cruze checked the time. Thirty minutes had elapsed since his arrival. That was a lot of time considering the nature of the business he was there to conduct.

Maybe he was on the wrong pier.

The lights inside the darkened bait shop suddenly flickered on and all the fishermen began moving toward the dinky little shack like it was Mecca. Cruze slowly maneuvered toward the shop, as well, but not because he wanted to buy bait. Through the window, he could see that the guy behind the counter had on a bright yellow hat.

Up close, Cruze could tell by dude's complexion and features that he was Italian. But he'd been expecting a much younger guy.

Nah, this dude couldn't have been the dude Cruze had spoken with—not with those bent shoulders, worn, leathery face, full set of clicking false teeth, and a wide gratuitous smile that he bestowed upon each customer.

Cruze's guy would have to have a steady hand and be quick on his feet. Cruze had expected to meet up with a terrifyingly malicious contract killer, not some smiley-faced senior citizen who made a living selling worms and fish guts and shit. He should have known better than to take someone seriously who advertised on Craigslist. Disgusted, he whirled around, prepared to drive back to Philly.

"Is anyone looking for snake bait?" asked the gravelly-voiced man behind the counter.

Recognizing the voice, Cruze stopped in his tracks and glanced over his shoulder. The customers standing in line shook their heads. None were looking for snake bait. The old guy settled his gaze on Cruze and Cruze detected a glint in his eyes.

If you want to kill a snake, you chop it off at the head, the killer had said over the phone when Cruze confided the dilemma he was in with an unforgiving drug gang. He'd learned that the top dog, Big Crockett, had been recently locked up, but would most likely get out in thirty days or less. Cruze was prepared to pay someone to go after the second-in-command and the rest of the organization while Big Crockett was incarcerated. He wanted the whole crew dead so he could stop looking over his shoulder and start living his life to the fullest. He'd take care of Big Crockett personally when he was back out on the streets, disoriented and hastily trying to reorganize.

Over the phone, the hit man had suggested that Cruze take down Crockett first, and he'd seemed confident that he could accomplish it while Crockett was behind bars. He'd demanded a hefty fee for his services, and Cruze was willing to pay it—to someone who could get the job done. Judging by the old man's slow movements, it seemed like his arthritis was killing him. With his gnarled, crooked fingers, he could barely bag up the worms without winching. There was no way such a feeble person could orchestrate a prison killing of a high-profile drug kingpin. The guy's glory days were long over.

After the customers thinned out, the man in the yellow hat asked, "Did you bring the money?"

"Man, who da fuck you kidding? How you gon' get to Crockett when it takes you forever to press the buttons on the damn cash register?"

"Don't worry about my capabilities. I get the job done," the man replied knowingly. "Been running this joint for over forty years and none of my customers have ever asked for a refund." He winked again and Cruze read between the lines. The bait shop was a front for a more sinister business.

"Okay, look, old man, I'ma give you half down like you requested, but don't try to fuck me over or you'll find this little shack you running, burnt down to the ground."

"Be careful with the threats, *moulinyan*," the old man said with his mouth twisted viciously. Then he quickly displayed a huge smile.

The old dude had called Cruze a nigger in Italian and had followed the insult with a ready smile. But the menace that lurked beneath his broad grin hadn't gone undetected by Cruze. He was dealing with an old-school mobster, the kind of man who killed without flinching and never lost any sleep.

And though Cruze had his share of bodies, unlike the Italian, he didn't sleep well at night.

Still…fuck the old bastard's credentials. He was gon' be introduced to some new-school learning if he called Cruze a moolie, again. Moolie, *moulinyan*, whatever. They meant the same thing. Moolie was the short version of *moulinyan*, the slur Italians used for black people.

Begrudgingly, Cruze handed over the duffle bag that was stuffed with crisp bills and sauntered out of the bait shop.

The team took up three tables at Red Lobster. The boys were excitedly looking over the menu when Tanji and the woman Cruze recognized from one of Tanji's sex tapes slinked in, uninvited. Both were dressed inappropriately for a kiddie event, showing cleavage and midriff and looking whorish. Earlier that night at the game, Cruze had noticed them both jumping out of their seats and twerking in celebration every time one of the boys scored a point.

Just ratchet!

Now they were ogling Cruze while pretending to peruse the menu. Licking their glossy red lips, they sent him salacious promises of double-dick-sucking pleasure. Tanji was determined to give

Cruze some head and he was just as adamant that he wasn't going to give her the chance. She had caught him during a weak moment in his office and it bothered him immensely that he'd disappointed Bret.

"Y'all boys were on fire tonight!" Tanji exclaimed and then passed her phone around showing the footage she'd filmed. Her friend passed her phone around, too, and the boys excitedly watched the highlights of the game.

Cameras had been flashing all night, and having the moms there snapping pictures and handling the filming hadn't thrown Cruze off his mark the way the media cameras had done at previous games. It was a relief to coach without the pressure of Bret and Marquan scrutinizing his coaching methods. Those two icons always felt the need to give Cruze pointers and took it upon themselves to give pep talks to the boys. Cruze felt he'd never be a good coach if he didn't learn by his own mistakes.

After winning with a fourteen-point lead, Cruze felt the boys deserved to be indulged, and he allowed them to order anything they wanted, including all the dessert they could handle. After they filed out of the restaurant and were lined up to get back on the bus, Tanji's son complained of a tummy ache, and Cruze pulled him out of line. He told Tanji it was best if she drove her son straight home instead of driving behind the bus as she'd intended.

Cruze figured Tanji was going to try to pawn her kid off on one of the other moms who were waiting at the center for the boys to return from Red Lobster. After her son was out of her hair, Tanji and her girlfriend would try to worm their way to his office for a threesome that Tanji would no doubt try to sneak and film.

Outmaneuvered by Cruze, Tanji took her frustration out on her kid, yanking him by the arm and fussing at him for being greedy and eating too much dessert.

Despite being presented with the opportunity to penetrate two hot mouths, Cruze's dick was oddly uninterested. It didn't respond to Tanji's or her friend's plump tits and fat ass. There was only one ass on his mind…Arabia's. And he had no idea when their paths would cross again.

"Congrats on the win Friday night," Bret said, sitting at his desk. "That Barack is starting to look more and more like he has Kobe Bryant potential."

"Yeah, and Breon did a helluva job, too. All the boys pulled their weight," Cruze responded. He still didn't consider himself one of Bret's peers, and he found it difficult to kick it with him casually. Being in his office was like being in the principal's office, and he shifted in his seat, waiting for Bret to get to the reason he'd asked to speak with him.

"Cruze, I realize you have good intentions, but don't you think the luxury bus you rented for Friday's game was a bit excessive?"

I knew it. Here we go…

"That raggedy yellow school bus you got us riding around in is an embarrassment and an inconvenience. Personally, I couldn't go to another game in that cramped-up rat trap. That bus was a necessity—it's a quality of life issue for me."

Bret chuckled. "Having a bus equipped with Wi-Fi, video screens, and leather seats is a necessity?"

"Damn right, man. I need those roomy, reclining seats to stretch out my long legs. I'm getting sick of arriving at games with my legs cramped and hurting. I don't like being in pain while I'm coaching. And the boys need the video screens for recreational purposes during the ride. I bet you won't see white kids in the suburbs riding to their games in outdated school buses with no perks, so why should my boys?"

"My only concern about your extravagances toward the youth league is the message you're sending the teenage players. The older kids are being outshined by a group of little knuckleheads and they're starting to feel some kind of way about it."

"I'm not the teen coach and they're not my problem, man," Cruze retorted, leaning forward.

"All the kids here are your problem, Cruze. You can't enrich the lives of a select few and treat the rest like second-class citizens."

Cruze pondered Bret's statement for a moment. "Let me ask you something. Outside of HYPE, do you and your wife donate to any other charities?"

"Of course. Martina is passionate about supporting the National Breast Cancer Foundation."

"Why breast cancer as opposed to…prostate cancer?" Cruze asked.

"Her mom is a breast cancer survivor." Bret wrinkled his brows. "Where're you going with this, Cruze?"

"I was a young ragamuffin playing b-ball on glass-littered courts with metal hoops and I'm passionate about giving the young kids I'm coaching a better experience than I had. They're my pet project. You're the head of this organization, Bret, and if you want the teen league to rock new sneakers, if you want them to wear fly uniforms, and travel in style, then I suggest you and their coach get some funding that's specifically earmarked for that cause."

"Coach McKinney is not into fund raising. He's doing enough by coaching the teens free of charge."

"Oh, well," Cruze said, hunching up his shoulders. "Stop trying to make your problems mine, Bret. If you want the teens to look fly, then that's on you."

It felt good speaking his mind, and with nothing more to say, Cruze stood up. Hovering over Bret's desk, an impressive-looking business card with embossed, gold foil lettering caught his eye.

He made out the name of Arabia's agency and his heart took a quick dive. The card represented her flair perfectly and for a fleeting moment, he was tempted to zoom in on the glittery card and memorize the phone number. But that was stalker behavior. The bitch knew where to find him the next time she was in the mood for more raunchy, public sex.

There was a sudden burst of rowdy noise out in the hallway and Bret rushed out the office to go investigate. Cruze was about to follow, but had a better idea. The moment Bret left, Cruze grabbed a Post-It and jotted down Arabia's personal number that was listed beneath her office number.

He jammed the sticky note in his pocket and joined Bret out in the corridor where a fight had broken out. Cruze gripped up one of the troublemakers by the scruff of his neck and Bret grabbed the other.

With both Bret and Cruze towering over the boys, wearing menacing expressions and threatening to take them somewhere private and jack them up if they didn't calm the fuck down, the two brawlers eagerly called a truce and shook hands.

Later that evening, relaxing in bed and smoking a blunt while the TV kept him company, Cruze bolted upright when he heard a breaking news story. Anthony Crockett aka Big Crockett had been murdered behind bars. The anchorman reported that investigators had no suspects in custody at this time as it appeared to be an inside job.

Well, I'll be damned. That old Italian bastard came through!

Cruze felt a mixture of profound joy and overwhelming grief at the same time. The killing had only just begun, and there would be a lot of bloodshed on the streets of New York. Innocent people that were at the wrong place at the wrong time would probably end up as collateral damage. And no matter how many bodies he'd accumulated over the years, Cruze still couldn't make peace with the man he'd become. And tonight, he wouldn't rest easily.

He hated being alone right now. He needed his dick sucked and wanted to pump into some hot pussy in the worst way. Tanji was probably available. If he let her, she'd come running with her mouth wide open, happy to swallow several splashing loads of hot cum.

But he didn't want that horny bitch knowing where he lived, nor sucking his dick. And he wasn't in the mood for the funky pussy she was offering. He thought of Arabia's sweet-smelling drawers and his dick swelled up so big, it felt like it was about to pop.

He got out of bed and took the jeans he had on earlier out of the hamper. He rifled through the pockets, and fished out the yellow Post-It. Although when it came to women, rejection was never something he had to face; they willingly came when he called. But, for some strange reason, when it came to Arabia, something about her made him so terrified of being rejected. His heart knocked in his chest as he picked up the phone and quickly pressed the ten numbers imprinted on the card.

Fuck pride. Fuck acting like a stalker. He needed Arabia, and no matter how wishy-washy the broad acted, he knew in his heart that she needed him, too.

The phone rang four times before she picked up.

"Hello?" she answered in her hot, silky voice.

"What's good, Arabia? It's Cruze."

He heard the surprise in her voice. "Oh. Cruze. Isn't this… Wait. How did you get my number?"

"I have my resources," he answered coolly.

"Mmhmm," she purred. "I bet you do. So now that you've found me, to what do I owe the pleasure of this call?"

"I was hoping we could link up…" *I need some pussy.* He paused. "Uh, tonight."

He took a deep breath and closed his eyes. He was expecting her to say something slick, before cursing him out.

Instead, a deadly silence ticked between them, and he felt the hammer of rejection about to come slamming down on his plans, when she sliced into the quiet and breathed out, "I'll come to you."

Cruze hadn't realized he'd been holding his breath until that very moment. A slow grin eased over his lips. "Cool," he said, before giving her his address, then telling her he'd see her when she arrived.

"And Cruze?" she said, low and husky.

"Yeah, what's up?"

"I hope you're not planning on getting any sleep."

With that said, she was gone. The line disconnected.

And Cruze felt his dick stretching, along with an unexpected smile.

Twenty-Five

Candles flickered, their flames dancing seductively across the walls, as Arabia's heated breath cascaded over Cruze's dick, and she parted her lips, stretching wide to accommodate the girth of him. She whimpered around the long, rigid column of flesh, and pleasure pulsed through him.

Oh how she loved sucking dick by candlelight. There was something sensual about flames flickering, something soothing, something sexy and wild. And Arabia felt wild—wild for fire, wild for cock, wild for delicious sin.

She breathed through her nostrils as Cruze tangled his fingers into her hair and palmed her head with his hands. Slowly, he thrust in and out of her mouth. Her mouth was hot and silky and so very wet. She peeked up at him underneath her lashes to see his face etched in ecstasy. She decided to allow him to take her mouth. Give him control—something she rarely did when it came to fellatio. But she'd give it, only for a moment.

Mmm.

His grip on her head tightened and his hips moved fluidly in and out, his dick sliding over her tongue again and again and again. His thrusts deepened. Then he started fucking her mouth as if he was fucking her pussy, and she hadn't choked or gagged. Yeah, this broad was a pro.

Arabia blinked, her eyes brimming with tears. *Oh hell no!* He was trying to gut her throat, smash out her tonsils, beat up her uvula. She reached up and grabbed his hands, prying them from her head, then smacking them down.

She shot him a telling look, one that warned him to keep off her damn head, and out of her hair, then sucked him back into her mouth.

Cruze frowned. *What the fuck?*

He wasn't accustomed to having his hands slapped away, or some pushy-ass broad trying to be in control. He wasn't used to a female being so aggressive and commanding in the sheets. But, Arabia took the dick, sucked it, like she owned it.

He clenched his fists at his sides. Fuck it. If she wanted to control how she gave him head, then have at it. She could suck him until her jaws locked for all he cared.

Unh, shit…

Her tongue and mouth moved synchronously over his dick. Cruze shut his eyes, and allowed himself to get swept up in the heat. He hadn't expected to be laid up with her *again*. It'd been two weeks since he'd seen her last—the night after their pseudo-dinner date, the night she so boldly invited him into a bathroom stall of a busy restaurant for *dessert*. And, damn, that had probably been the best dessert he'd had in his life. The memory alone hardened his dick.

She was wild as hell. And—*yes*—a sexy-ass freak.

Still, he hadn't wanted to see her again. Truth was, all she was good for was a good fuck. And he'd fucked her good—damn good—twice already. A third time wasn't usually his thing; although Laila had been one of those rare exceptions where he'd pushed up into her guts regularly; more out of convenience than anything else. Still, they'd been fuck buddies up until the night he fled New York. Other than her, giving out the dick had to be rationed. Or smashing out some broad more than twice would end with dire consequences. Like some bitch unraveling and stalking him.

Nah, he wasn't built for the bullshit. After all the shit he'd been through, he was good on that. He'd learned a long time ago that broads usually started feigning for the dick after the first night of him fucking the shit out of them. By the second round, they were already planning a wedding, trying to chain a muhfucka down. And *if* they got the dick a third time, they officially became straitjacket crazy right after about the fifth stroke.

With that in mind, Cruze wasn't sure how stable, or *unstable*, Arabia was. And he wasn't interested in finding out what level of nutty she was on. He planned on shutting this—whatever *this* was—down, before shit got hectic, right after he got his nut. Truth was, he thrived off of variety. And loved an assortment of pussy at his beck and call. All he wanted was some occasional companionship, good pussy, good head—a different face, a different hole. Nothing more.

Bitches couldn't be trusted for anything else.

But he couldn't deny it. There was something about *her* that had him…*shit*… she had him bugging.

And he didn't like it, not one damn bit.

Cruze always prided himself on having self-control—over pussy, over drugs, over alcohol, over anything that would become a distraction in his life. Distractions could get a muhfucka killed. So he learned to do everything, except stacking paper, in moderation. He never wanted any of it to become his kryptonite.

He'd already experienced that shit once with Ramona. Being all fucked up over some broad. That shit was crippling. No way in hell he was about to go there again. Bomb-ass head game or not, it wasn't going to happen.

Period.

So what was it about *her* that had him stretched out on his bed, naked, with his dick disappearing in and out of her mouth, and him wanting more of *her?*

Shit. Damn if he knew.

And that bothered the hell out of him. There was definitely chemistry between them, he'd admitted to himself before he'd called her—sexual chemistry that thickened the air, and made him lightheaded and almost swallow his tongue.

Wait, then again…maybe it wasn't *that*—the carnal attraction—that had his head spinning. Maybe it was the fact that Arabia suddenly did some kind of trick with her tongue that sent chills reeling through his body.

Her fingertips skittered along the trail of hair that led from his navel to his magnificent dark-chocolate cock, lightly brushing over his skin—while licking under his balls, unexpectedly making him moan and shiver. She bounced them up on her tongue, curling and swirling the wet organ over and around his swelling sac, savoring the taste of him—the manly flavor of his skin, the hint of musk, his maleness on her tongue. So delicious.

Arabia moaned, her tongue and lips sliding up the side of his dick. She licked over the two thick veins that roped over the top of his shaft, and cupped his heavy balls. Every inch of him felt like heated steel. Arabia stroked the length of him once…twice…thrice, grazing the head of his dick with her thumb.

Cruze grunted, and her lashes fluttered before her gaze eased upward and his dark eyes flew open and met hers.

"Get on your knees. I want some pussy."

Her body tingled, her clit and nipples swollen and aroused. His dark tone; the commanding look on his face, made her shiver, slightly. But not enough to take heed to his order, or his want. She simply flicked her tongue over the slit of his dick, swiping at the pre-cum drizzling out of its tip, before her tongue teased the sensitive spot just under his crown.

Groaning, Cruze tried to pull free from her tongue. His balls tightened as his need spiked. He had enough of her tongue teasing. He wanted to sink deep into her silken heat.

"Yo, c'mon. I wanna fuck."

Too bad. She slid her lips up and down, up and down, her mouth growing wetter as she made him wetter and wetter, sucking him in a slow, heated rhythm that was making him feel crazed with pleasure.

He didn't like—*uhn...ah*—feeling out of control like this.

His teeth clenched. "Aah...yo, stop. Hold up. Wait, wait..."

There was no waiting with Arabia; there was no holding back. She did what she wanted, how she wanted. And then his dick was between those heavenly breasts of hers, sliding wetly, hotly—as she cupped them in her hands and pressed the soft flesh around his throbbing shaft. Her breasts blanketed his cock in slippery heat, her tongue lolling out every so often and flicking over the head, capturing his heated arousal. Ah, damn—fuck yes. The shit was maddening.

No, he wasn't wild about giving up his control. She had him rushing toward the edge of nirvana. And he wasn't ready...not yet. He liked to control how and when he came. But Arabia was relentless.

Damn her greedy-ass...unh. Shit...

Instead of stopping, her tongue cradled his dick, and then she took him to the back of her throat—all of him. Cruze nearly lost his mind. He rocked his hips, gliding his shaft over her tongue. *Oh shit! She 'bout to make me nut!*

In less than twenty seconds, she was bringing him dangerously closer to the edge. Forgetting her warning, once again, he fisted his hands in her hair as desire swelled. He didn't want to come in her mouth. He wanted to nut in that pussy. Yeah, that's where he needed his dick to be. Deep.

"Yo, stop," he growled, trying to pull her off his dick. "Hold up, hold up. You about to…make…me…nut…"

Oh well. Come for me, boo. Arabia was in her own zone, on a mission. And had no intentions of giving him pussy. Not today. Yes, she'd made the almost two-hour trek down the turnpike to Philly for another round of his aggressive dick. But, now, she'd changed her mind. No pussy for him. Still, she felt conflicted. She didn't know what the hell she was doing *here* between his legs, her jaws stretched with his cock when his selfish ass had, yet, to lick her, kiss her— *nothing.* It was obvious he didn't eat pussy, lick ass, kiss, or indulge in any other foreplay. Arabia wondered if he even knew the purpose of a woman's clit. Or where to find her G-spot, or what the hell foreplay was.

"*Unh,* shit…let me fuck you."

If her mouth hadn't been full with cock, she would have sucked her teeth. Apparently, somewhere in the middle of all those bed sheets he'd helped a slew of hoes soil over the years, someone had failed terribly at teaching him the art of seduction and making a woman's toes curl. Sure he fucked like a wild bull, but he seemed to lack the wherewithal to know his way around a woman's body. All big dick, and no lovemaking skills made for a lousy-ass lay.

He'd never turn a woman like her out. Ever. But, luckily, she had no interest in teaching him, or telling him. He was simply a *fuck*, a deep pounding of turgid flesh inside her hungry walls. Nothing else mattered. But he'd only be fucking *her* if—and when—*she* wanted to be fucked.

Honestly, any other man and she would have already tired by now. He obviously thought having a big dick was good enough. Well, maybe it was for those other bitches he fucked. But, Arabia, wasn't the type of woman who could ever be okay with some man simply pounding in and out of her pussy regularly without so much as a tongue swipe over her clit, her slickened pussy lips, or along her slit.

He wasn't freaky enough; that was the bottom line.

Then why the hell was she naked in his bed?

She hated admitting, even to herself, that she'd come to the realization that Cruze was unlike any other man she'd ever known, and she wasn't sure what to do with that.

Except—for now…keep sucking his dick.

"Oh, shit," he hissed, feeling his desire rising incredulously fast. He looked down at her through lust-filled eyes; watched her as, she meant for him to. The sight of her head rapidly bobbing between his legs, along with the wet-suck sounds her mouth made, had his skin prickling with heat.

Arabia looked up at him, a coy smile drifting across her mouth. "You like that?"

"Ah fuck, yeah. Suck that shit," he murmured, momentarily forgetting, only seconds ago, he'd tried stopping her so he could get inside her. He tried to palm her head again, and she slapped his hands away, before she pulled him from her mouth, then kissed and licked her way up his abdomen, dipping her tongue into his navel, pushing his knees farther apart with her shoulders. She climbed up over him, grinding and sliding her pussy up and down the length of his wet cock, slicking it with her juices.

Cruze tightly pressed his lips together to keep in a groan as her mouth enveloped his right nipple. She swirled her tongue over it, then lightly blew over it. Cool air escaping between her lips, turning his nipple hard.

"You like that?" she whispered, her lips grazing his throat.

He grunted his answer, cupping her ass and squeezing. "You gonna let me get in that pussy?"

Arabia ignored him, her tongue laving over his shoulder, then his chest, then—oh, fuck, yeah—her teeth grazed over his nipple, nibbling, sucking it into her mouth.

Cruze bit his bottom lip.

Neither of them had expected to *still* be in lust with the other, still wanting more of the other. But this shit had to end. It had to. For the both of them.

Arabia looked up at him through a veil of lashes, and seductively licked her lips. "I'm going to suck your soul out." *Then walk out of here and never look back.*

Her whisper rasped over his skin, his senses, even as she enveloped him, and he felt the back of her tight throat, her tongue swirling around him. Suddenly, pleasure seemed to saturate the room, filling the air around them as she laved the head of his dick with her wicked tongue, one palm at the base of his erection, the other holding his balls, lightly grazing over his sac with her fingernails.

Oh, shit…

She knew exactly what to do to take him there. Fast. Her lips dragged up and down his shaft again, and Cruze watched, relishing the view. He let out a deep sigh of approval as she took him all the way back inside the sweet heat of her lush mouth, inch by hard, pulsing inch. She had his breath coming hard and fast, so fast he felt the room spin. She was a beast.

"*Unh*," he groaned. "Aaah, that mouth…"

He wanted to keep shit between them light, no pressures. No expectations. No hard feelings. No more ongoing encounters; just this one last time. But Arabia's wet mouth was slowly making a liar out of him. He wasn't trying to get caught up. He knew a broad like her would disrupt shit in his life. But—*fuck*, he was loving the way she gave him head, kissing and licking, then swallowing him whole, taking him to the back of her throat, before extending her tongue and lapping at the center of his balls.

There was an art to sucking a dick. And somewhere, somehow, she had perfected it. A part of him silently wondered how many dicks she'd had sucked down into her neck over the years; how many muhfuckas' nuts she'd let coat the back of her throat. Then there was that part of him that didn't care. He wasn't about to make her his girl. So she could suck as many muhfuckas as she wanted. It was her mouth, her business.

Arabia's tongue swirled around his balls, making his toes curl once more.

"*Shit,*" he hissed, grabbing her head again, holding it steady as he slowly thrust his hips and fucked her mouth until her mouth grew wetter, hotter. She sucked him harder, grabbing his dick at the base, then fisting him up and down, from the base to her lips; her mouth locked on the head of his dick, her tongue doing figure-eights over and around it.

Cruze groaned as his climax neared.

Goddamn.

He closed his eyes, and made a guttural sound that escaped from his chest, losing himself to the sensation. He felt his nut surging up from his balls, and he wasn't ready to bust. Fuck no. He wanted to revel in it. But Arabia was making it difficult for him to hold out.

"Aah, shit…*mmm*, fuck…"

She glanced up, saw his head thrown back, his abdomen muscles rippling with strained pleasure, and she smiled around his shaft. She pulled back, then with wet-sucking noises, nursed the head of his dick for several toe-curling moments, before popping Cruze's dick from her mouth. Determined, she planned on giving him the dick-suck of his life, the kind of sloppy head he'd never forget.

"Oh shit, oh shit…fuck, fuck, fuck…"

He'd had his share of mind-blowing head by some top-notch dick suckers in his life, but, thus far, none had compared to Arabia. She knew how to make love to his dick with her mouth, lips, tongue and hands. *Goddamn*. She sucked it like she loved it. Sucked it like she had a purpose. What the fuck was she trying to do to him?

She made his dick feel like it was the best dick she'd ever topped. And the shit was driving him wild. Her skills were addicting, the scent of her aroused cunt, intoxicating.

"Aaaaah, yeah. Suck that shit...*unh*..." His voice was almost an unrecognizable growl. Slyly, Arabia slid a wet finger along the center of his crack, then pressed it against his asshole. His dick jolted inside her mouth. And then a burst of liquid heat hit the back of her throat and quickly flooded her mouth.

Primal lust overtook him, and Cruze's whole body shook. He'd never come so hard, so fiercely, his entire life.

Arabia swallowed and gulped. And swallowed some more as he continued thrusting, grunting, and spurting. His creamy seeds bathed her tongue, the insides of her cheeks and the back of her clutching throat, filling her with the very essence of his tormented soul.

Slowly, she pulled him from her mouth, and lovingly bathed him with her tongue, licking his dick clean of his release, leaving him spent.

Twenty-Six

Pulse steadying, Cruze blinked through his lust-induced fog, wondering *what the hell* had just happened. Had this freaky broad pressed a finger to his ass? Had she tried to stick her finger in him? Or had he imagined it?

He closed his eyes, slowly rewinding his mind, the memory still fresh, the sensations all coming back to him.

Nah. He hadn't imagined that shit. It *did* happen. His jaw twitched. Lucky for her, she hadn't tried to push it in him, or he would have probably spazzed out and punched her dead in her forehead. He groaned inwardly. *Shit*. The fucked-up thing was, there was something about the sensation of her finger being *there* that had unexpectedly intensified his orgasm; made him explode in fierce waves of toe-curling pleasure.

Still, he frowned. That slick shit she pulled was disrespectful. He didn't play them ass games. He didn't know what type of freakshit she was into, but he wasn't down with it. So why hadn't he stopped her when he'd felt her finger go there?

He breathed in, then slowly exhaled, his hand languidly sliding to his groin. The answer was evident, the remnants still on his sticky dick. Because she'd been sucking his dick so damn good, that the shit had caught him off guard. He'd been too wrapped up in the moment, in the heat of it all—on the verge of busting, to shut it down. It was an unnerving sensation, one he wasn't sure he liked or not.

Still, he felt…violated.

Then to make matters worse, the stingy bitch hadn't let him get up in them guts.

So why hadn't he thrown her the hell out yet?

Why was she still in his bed?

And why was he lying here all up in his feelings?

He sighed inwardly. He knew the answer to that as well. She unnerved him and piqued his curiosity at the same time. His gut told him she was a problem. A headache. Hell, she was everything he'd spent his life avoiding. Yet there was something about her that aroused him. Arabia made him hot. There was no denying it, and that shit fucked with him.

Nevertheless, he was a man—a horny man that was. And he wanted some pussy. Nah. Pussy he could get anytime, anywhere. He wanted *her* pussy. Wanted to lose his dick in *her* rippling pussy. Wanted to fuck her one last time, before showing her kinky ass to the door.

Freak bitch.

Yeah, that's what he'd do. Fuck her deliriously.

Then toss her the hell—

Arabia rolled onto her side, and blinked. Cruze lay inches from her on his back, his eyes closed. He seemed to be in deep thought. She eyed him—her eyes still hooded with the unmistakable look of arousal. Her simmering gaze drifted down his chiseled frame, then fastened on the thick meaty slab of veined flesh shining in the glow of candlelight. She swallowed back the drool beginning to pool in her mouth. Then took in his face. He had beautiful chocolate, kissable lips. Yet, she had to remind herself that he didn't eat pussy, lick pussy, kiss pussy, or do anything else with that beautiful mouth of his.

Still, that didn't stop her from wanting to feel them pressed against the ones between her thighs. Oh, God, yes. Curiosity had her pussy aching for the feel of his tongue, caressing and soothing the slow throb still pulsing there.

But she'd leave here with her pussy angrily clutching before she allowed him the pleasure of being back inside it *without* his tongue in it, first. He'd have to take it because she damn sure wasn't offering it.

Still, she felt like climbing atop him and smothering him with her cunt, smearing it all over his lips, grinding her pussy into his mouth, forcing him to eat it up—lick it up. Then beat it up.

But that would be real smutty of her.

She sighed. *Bitch, what is going on with you? Why are you still lying here? Get your ass up. Get your things. And go.*

No. She wasn't ready to leave. Not yet. She felt like they still had unfinished business. Ugh. What business though?

She had no idea. All she knew was, there was something about this mysterious man that aroused her, piqued her curiosity. He unnerved her, intrigued her. Yet, looking at him, she surmised he was a womanizer. A player. Egotistical. Perhaps even a whore-monger.

Cruze inhaled. He felt her heated gaze on him, but he willed his eyes shut. He wasn't ready to look at her. Not after she'd put her finger in his ass. He knew if he did, he'd snap on her. And he didn't really want to do that. But why did he care about some random broad's feelings? If this were any other female, he would have blacked on the spot, tossing her out the front door.

But here he was. In his bed, sulking *and* feeling satiated—conflictingly at the same damn time—from only having his dick sucked, a first for him.

And here *she* was. *Still* in his bed, breathing in his air—naked. He could feel the heat radiating from her body. He inhaled, savoring her smell. Remembering how good her mouth and tongue had felt on his dick. Now he wanted to be reminded of how wet her pussy could get, how hot and tight it was.

He silently groaned. *Shit.* He had to get her out of here, out of his bed, out of his space, before he fucked around and…

Arabia couldn't fight it any longer. She had to touch him, feel his muscled flesh.

So she touched him.

Her warm hand pressed lightly over the hard wall of chest, and then—

Cruze's eyes flew open and he roughly grabbed her wrist. "Yo, what the fuck you doing?" he demanded in an icy tone. He hadn't meant to have so much bite to his voice, but—oh well. He didn't like being touched. He wasn't touchy-feely. And he didn't indulge in that cuddle shit, either. Besides, she'd already overstayed her welcome and he hadn't done shit about it, thus far.

Shock registered on Arabia's face. Before she could process what the holy hell he was doing with her wrist in his tight grasp, she yanked out of his grip, matching his glacial stare. "*Oww!* What the fuck is your problem?" she clipped, her eyes flashing wide. "How dare you try to break my damn wrist! I thought you were asleep."

Shit, shit, shit.

His stare softened. "My bad, for grabbing you like that," he said, more gently than before. "I wasn't tryna break your wrists, ma. Or frighten you."

She huffed. "Well, you could have fooled me. Grabbing on me like that."

"It was instinctive reflex; that's all."

Arabia rolled her eyes. "Whatever. I only wanted to feel your chest. *Not* maul you."

"No disrespect," he said apologetically. "It's not you. I'm just not beat for being touched. I don't know you like that."

She hurled herself out of his bed, yanking the bed sheet from off him and the bed, leaving him gloriously naked. *"Really?* You're not *beat* for being touched?" She let out a sardonic laugh. "Boy, bye! How convenient." She wrapped the sheet around her, her body heat and scent swooping up with her. "Mighty funny *you* didn't know me when *you* had your dick inside me that night in the club. And *you* didn't know me when *you* invited me out to dinner, sniffed my damn panties, then fucked me in that bathroom stall...."

Cruze bit his lip, the memory rushing back to him, causing his dick to stir.

"And you *still* don't know me," Arabia continued, stabbing a pointed finger in the air. "Yet, *you* called *me* to come here, and *you* didn't—Mister I Don't Know You Like That—seem to have a problem with *me* touching all over *you* while having your dick in my throat."

Cruze scowled. "Yo, hol' up. Don't come at me like that. *You* didn't have a problem throwing the pussy at me each time, either; or hopping your hot ass in your whip 'n' driving down here for this dick, either. Now did you?"

Arabia blinked. *Ooh, this cocky motherfucker!* "Yeah, I came for the dick." She tilted her head. "And *you* called for some more of this pussy. But we both see how that turned out." She slipped her feet back into her heels, then turned and faced him. "If you don't like anyone invading your personal space after they get you off, cool. Say that. But you don't go manhandling them."

Now Cruze felt like shit. And this thing—whatever it was, was starting to turn into an unnecessary beef. He wasn't built for a bunch of arguing, or back and forth, especially from some random pussy. She was acting like she was his girl and he wasn't feeling it.

Bottom line, he didn't play that touchy-feely shit after sex. Unless they were fucking, there was no need for any wandering hands on his body.

He sighed. Yeah, it was definitely time for her ass to bounce.

Fuck. Maybe he'd given her the wrong impression by letting her linger around after he'd popped his nut. But he hadn't wanted to be a total ass.

Still…

Looking at her smooth, silky thighs, his mind wandered lasciviously to the idea of having them wrapped around his waist and him pummeling his dick inside her juicy, wet cunt.

Cruze sat up in bed and eyed her as she began snatching up her bra. *Shit.* His gaze settled on her bouncy breasts and, and…those mouthwatering, thick, chocolate drop nipples. He had to fight the urge to hop up and throw her down on the bed and pop each succulent nipple into his mouth.

What the fuck is wrong with me?

Shit. He needed a blunt. Now.

She caught his gaze and slung the sheet at him, baring her sexiness in all its glory. He swallowed, reaching for the sheet and covering his growing erection.

"I'm not sure what type of women you're used to having in your bed," she continued as she fastened her bra, "but I'm *not*…"

She paused, but Cruze was still eyeing her, though his icy expression had already melted and had become replaced with bemusement, as though he didn't quite know what to make of her.

Truthfully, he didn't.

But the one thing he did know was, she was a freak who needed a hard dick in her life—to be fucked often. Hell, maybe, daily for all he knew. She was thirsty. Dick hungry. Greedy.

And it fucking turned him on.

Still, females like her were only good for a night of sucking dick and wild sex, nothing more. Hell, she'd sucked him off and swallowed his nut, licked around his balls, before finally licking her lips like she'd just finished eating a chocolate-dipped ice cream cone less than ten minutes ago. How many other muhfuckas' nuts had she gobbled up? Not that he judged, but he typically kept females like her strictly in the freak zone.

Still, his eyes went liquid with a strange mix of lust and heat, his dick pulsing to a level of hardness he couldn't comprehend. He grabbed the pillow she'd lain on and placed it over his now rock-hard dick.

He couldn't understand why he was so inexorably drawn to her. She was nothing more than a mere stranger. A random broad he'd fucked in a nightclub—no name exchanges, just music, body heat, and an unexplainable connection. Then he'd fucked her again—in a bathroom stall, no less.

Just the sight of her made his skin heat. But he wasn't about to let his dick or his desires cloud his judgment.

Cruze reached over and retrieved a half-smoked blunt lying in an ashtray on his nightstand. He opened the top drawer and pulled out a lighter.

"You're not what?" he pushed, trying his damnedest not to drool at the sight of her heart-shaped ass as she bent over to snatch up her lace panties.

"I'm not the one to be manhandled unless *I* want to be. And you grabbing me like that was uncalled for." She shimmied into her crotch-less panties.

He swallowed a thick knot of lust. "You're right. My bad." He lit the blunt, and inhaled, filling his lungs with weed smoke, trying to distract himself from looking at her, her ass, them hips. He shook his head, blowing a white billowy cloud of smoke up into the air.

Arabia glared. "Are you serious? You're going to smoke that nasty thing *now?*"

Cruze shrugged, taking another deep pull. "*Pssft.* My crib, ma."

Smug sonofabitch!

And to think she'd left her purse with her pepper spray in his living room. She'd do his eyes up real good, burn out his retinas for being so damn fine and cocky and goddamn desirable.

He kept his eyes on her as he held smoke in his lungs. The shit burned along with the ache in his groin.

Arabia rolled her eyes, quickly picking up her multi-print dress that had been tossed on the other side of the room. *Shit.* She held the dress up and shook it. Then cursed under her breath. Her dressed was a wrinkled mess. Now what?

There was no way she'd be caught dead walking the streets looking like some displaced vagrant.

"Do you have an iron?" she asked curtly. But the way he sat there all bare-chested and badass and cocky, made the pit of her pussy churn in desire.

Cruze smirked. *Fuck you 'n' ya wrinkled-ass dress…dick-teasing ass.* "Nah," he coolly said, eyes now half-lidded from the weed.

Arabia huffed, twisting her hair up in a bun. "Well, I need something to put on, if you don't mind."

Cruze raised a brow and stared at her. Oh sure. His closet was stuffed with bitches' clothes for days like this. Get real. *"Not my problem. You better put on that wrinkled shit 'n' take ya ass on,"* he heard himself saying in his head.

He inhaled more weed into his lungs. Eyed her as she paced around his room, her ass swaying in them skimpy-ass, lace panties. She felt his hot eyes on her, roaming all over her, his gaze searing over her skin.

Let her go, let her stay? Fuck her six ways to Sunday, or send her on her way?

Fuck it. The more he tried to suppress it, the more acutely aware he became of its presence, filling the air around them.

The heat.

The sexual chemistry.

"Yo, fuck all that," he said, low and husky, giving into to his animalistic need. He slung the pillow he'd had his hard dick pressed under off his lap, then pulled back the comforter. "Come back to bed."

Arabia blinked. Tilted her head. Then feigned indignation. "And why exactly would I want to do that after the way you tried to manhandle me?"

He reached over and extinguished what was left of his blunt in the ashtray, then climbed out of bed and stalked over to her, his dick hard and thick. "When I manhandle you, ma, you'll know it. So let's both stop playing this silly-ass game, and get down to what we both know we want."

Hand on her hip. "And what is it you *think* I want?"

"Some hard dick, and a good *fucking*." His eyes, the way he looked at her, promised just that.

Arabia's mouth went dry. Her pussy wet. Before she could process what he was doing, he pulled her roughly into his arms, and hurled her against his body. She tried to put her hands up to push him back, to keep him at bay, but as soon as she made contact with his chiseled chest, more heat, more fire, radiated through her entire body.

"Get your—"

The words were cut off with a gasp when Cruze hoisted her up over his shoulder. Stalked back over toward the bed. Then threw her down on it.

Arrogant. Cocky. Big-dicked bastard.

And then…mmm…oh God…the head of his dick was there, hovering ever so lightly over her clit, then sliding over her slit… oh, no God…yes…then nudging at her slick opening.

Every nerve ending in her body jolted, and she gasped again as his gaze burned into her as he said, "Now tell me you don't want this dick."

Twenty-Seven

She hadn't planned on seeing him again. Ever. She'd gotten what she'd wanted from him, so there was no further need to be in his presence again. But, several days later, when Cruze called out of the blue—his deep, sexy voice sliding over her senses *and* her skin, something inside of her tingled and she'd quickly forgotten her proclamation that she was officially staying away from his egotistical ass.

Oh, God, this was bad. *He* was bad.

But how the hell could something so bad feel oh so good?

Everything that looks good and feels good isn't always good for you.

She had to keep reminding herself of that.

Yet, here she sat.

Across from him at Miss Tootsie's in downtown Philly, a South Street multileveled restaurant bar and lounge that was praised for its golden fried chicken and gravy-smothered turkey chops. Neither of which Arabia ate. But she'd ordered the tilapia and a side of mac 'n' cheese that was flooded with butter and cheese and sinful goodness that she was afraid to eat it all for fear of becoming addicted. In just a few bites, she could already feel the pounds packing on to her hips and clogging her arteries. So she took tiny, dainty bites, then pushed the rest aside.

Cruze looked up from his plate and eyed her. "Is everything a'ight? How's your food?"

She stared down at her plate, realizing that the fish was half-eaten and she honestly had no recollection of eating what was gone.

"It's surprisingly really good," she said.

"See," he said. "Told you."

"Yes, you did. But it's still a bit too rich in cholesterol and calories for my blood."

The corner of his mouth lifted. "What, you watching your waist?"

"My waist, my hips, my ass…"

Cruze chuckled. "Well, how about this. You indulge yourself one day, and let me be the one to watch all that"—he leaned to the side, eyeing her hips—"for you. It'll be my pleasure. Because from where I'm sitting, I'm diggin' the view."

Arabia's cheeks heated, and she blushed. "I bet you say that to all the girls."

He shook his head. "Nah. Only to the ones I like."

She waved him on. "Uh-huh. And I bet you have a harem of women at your beck and call."

Cruze laughed. "Nah, nah. I'm not even on it like that."

She gave him the side-eye, and he laughed again.

"Nah, I'm dead-ass."

She playfully rolled her eyes at him. "Okay, Mr. Fontaine. What-ever you say."

He fixed his eyes on her. Damn, she was damn near flawless. "So, what's good with you? Why you single?"

She shifted in her seat, and reached for her drink. "Maybe I haven't found the right one to change that." Not that she'd been looking for the right *one*. She preferred Mr. Right Now. But sitting across from him, feeling the strong chemistry between them, she wondered if he could be the *one*.

She quickly shook the silly notion from her head. She mentally scolded herself. *Girl, you know damn well this fine motherfucker isn't your type.*

He wasn't old enough.

He wasn't married.

He wasn't refined.

He wasn't…

Her mental rambling was cut short when their server came back to their table, flouncing her ass and bouncing her breasts, grinning all up in Cruze's face. "Can I get you anything else?" she asked, staring at Cruze like he was the only one in the room. How dare she ignore her like she was some hot trash?

Rude bitch.

What if she was his woman? She wasn't. But—*shit*—that was besides the point. This *bitch* didn't know that. "No, *you* can't get *him* anything else," Arabia snapped, not hiding her irritation, giving the trick a hard stare.

The server slowly turned her attention to Arabia, tilting her head. "Then what would you like?" she asked with an attitude of her own.

Oh this tramp must really want me to put this six-inch heel in her forehead.

"I'd like for you to run along," Arabia said icily. "Come back when you're summoned." *Because right now, bitch, your tip is looking real slim.* Arabia flashed her a tight smile, then shooed her away from the table. "Please and thank you."

The server sneered and shot Arabia a dirty look, then stomped off, her ass bouncing and shaking hard and nasty.

Cruze shook his head, and laughed. "Damn, ma. Why you go in on her like that? She was only doing her job."

"No, she was only being messy. She saw me sitting here with you."

He flashed his dimples. "What, you jealous?"

She gave him an incredulous look. "*Jealous?* Boy, bye. Hardly. Like I said, she was being obnoxiously rude. And I didn't appreciate it. What if you were my man?"

He grinned. "Do you want me to be?"

Arabia gave him a blank look. "Be what?"

"Your man."

She swallowed. Suddenly, the room felt smaller, hotter. "You know what I mean. She came over here like you were all she saw. Flirting with you, like I wasn't even sitting here. That's very rude and disrespectful."

Cruze nodded. "True. But she didn't mean any harm by it."

She tilted her head and stared at him. Men. "Okay, whatever you say."

He grinned. "But you still didn't answer the question."

"What question?" she asked coyly.

"Yeah, a'ight. Don't play."

"Annnnnnway," she said, shifting the conversation in a completely different direction. "Is Philly where you're from? You sound like you're from New York somewhere."

He nodded. "Yeah. I am. Brooklyn."

Arabia smiled knowingly. "I thought so."

"And what about you? Where you from?"

She twirled a lock of her hair. "Originally from Jersey. Grew up in Bergen County."

"Oh, word? Where at?"

"Alpine," she said blandly.

"Oh, a'ight, a'ight. I see your work," Cruze said, impressed at hearing the mention of one of America's most expensive ZIP codes. "That's nothing but money out there. Your peoples must have some long paper to afford living out there."

Arabia shifted uncomfortably in her seat. She didn't like anyone knowing she'd lived a privileged life. They automatically assumed she was spoiled. Stuck-up.

Well, okay—she *was* spoiled. Still...

She shrugged. "I guess. I spent most of my school years at boarding schools."

"Damn. How was that?"

"Lonely," she wanted to say, but she settled for, "Different."

Two years after her father…died, she was shipped off to a school in Switzerland. Her mother had wanted her out of her hair once she'd remarried. Claimed she was sending her thousands of miles away to help broaden her horizons. The bitch was a liar. She'd shipped her across the Atlantic Ocean because she *hated* her. Period. Two years later, she was *allowed* to attend the Emma Willard School—an all-girls' private school in Troy, New York. Had it not been for her sisters begging their mother to bring Arabia back to the States, she'd have spent her entire time over in Europe isolated from her family.

Cruze regarded her thoughtfully. "And you went to college?"

Arabia nodded. "Yeah, Spelman. All of my sisters did, as did my mother, and grandmother. So…"

"It was your legacy," Cruze said.

"More like a curse," she muttered. Cruze gave her a questioning look, so she reluctantly went on. "It was hell having to stand in the shadows of my sisters, and be held to standards that only my mother got to approve of." She blew out a long breath. "I was expected to be a certain way. Pledge a certain sorority. Be groomed for the perfect mate."

"Damn. I can't imagine having that kind of pressure on me."

"I rebelled." She laughed. "I'm the black sheep of the family. The wild child."

He laughed. "I like you wild."

Arabia swallowed. "So how many baby mommas do you have?" she blurted out. It was a random question, one that felt more like an assumption, but she wanted the attention off of her.

Cruze scowled at her. "*What?* What makes you think I have *one;* let alone—multiple?"

Her eyebrows rose in curiosity, in question. "Do you?"

He shook his head. She was officially a fucking wet-dream killer. Ignorant-ass broads like her pissed him off assuming every young, black man was out in the streets slinging raw dick, making a bunch of babies. Yeah, he'd been reckless in his life over the years, and dumped his nut in his share of wet holes. But he wasn't looking for a baby momma, let alone multiple. He felt like checking her dumb ass. He decided to let her think whatever the fuck she wanted instead. He cleared his throat, and a silence stretched between them as he reached for the linen napkin in his lap and wiped his mouth, before he asked a question of his own: "How many baby daddies do *you* have?"

Arabia made a face. "Excuse *you?*"

He smirked. "You heard me. Since you're asking me how many BMs I have—straight up assuming I have kids to begin with, I asked you how many cats you've let seed you?"

She blinked. *Seed me? What the hell?* "I'll have you know," she said, indignation lacing her tone. "I don't get seeded, breeded, or anything else by a man. I'm allergic to raw sex."

He looked at her as if amused by her response. "So I take that to mean, you don't have a bunch of baby daddies?"

She shook her head. "Absolutely not." He smiled, and Arabia found herself helpless to stop from staring at his dimples. Damn him. "I don't do babies or baby daddies."

His eyebrow went up. "Oh, okay. Yet *you* assumed I would have multiple kids by a bunch of different women."

She swallowed, feeling regretfully silly for how she'd posed the question. "I apologize for assuming," she said earnestly. "I should have simply asked if you had any children."

He cocked his head to the side. Satisfaction gleamed in his eyes. "Yeah, you should have. But you're forgiven. This time." A slow smile worked over his mouth as he reached for his knife and fork, and said nothing more on the matter.

End of discussion.

Arabia shifted in her seat again. Then tilted her head to the side, and eyed him as he cut into his fried chicken breast. Oh how she wanted to reach over and slap his damn face. And yet there was an aura of mystery surrounding him that made her skin tingle with curiosity.

In that moment, she let out a breath—one she hadn't realized she'd been holding.

The rest of the evening, they finished their dinner making small talk, mostly talking about HYPE and how much he enjoyed working with the kids there, especially now that he was one of the basketball coaches there.

Arabia smiled. "That's great. Sounds like you really enjoy what you do."

Cruze nodded, and grinned. "Yeah, I definitely do. It's like those young cats give me a renewed sense of purpose. Many of them remind me of myself when I was their ages."

Arabia nodded. "So you played basketball in college?"

Cruze shifted in his seat. "Nah." He paused a moment, still staring intently in her eyes. "College wasn't a part of my life plan."

"Oh. Well, it looks like you've done well for yourself regardless."

Cruze smiled. "No doubt. Thanks."

"How old are you?" she wanted to know.

"Twenty-eight. And you?"

Arabia feigned insult. "Don't you know it's impolite to ask a woman her age?"

Cruze smirked. "Nah. I didn't know that." He shrugged. "So, what, you're like thirty?"

Arabia playfully rolled her eyes. "I'm thirty-two."

"Oh, a'ight. A cougar," he teased.

She laughed, feeling her skin heat.

Ooh, this man was dangerous.

And she'd eat him alive.

Twenty-Eight

2006

The thrill of gazing at the stacks of money that lined the dresser had started to wear off. In fact, Cruze was getting so irritated waiting for Ramona, he was about to call Sameer and get a ride to the strip club. But, nah, he couldn't make a sucka move like that. He'd never live it down if Sameer found out how bad Ramona was clowning him.

Lying on the bed, fully dressed with his hands clasped behind his head, he glared at the red digital numbers on the clock. It was four in the morning and Ramona wasn't picking up his calls. The last time she'd pulled this shit, she promised it wouldn't happen again, and like a fool, he believed her.

Obviously, their relationship wasn't anything but a game to her. Maybe it was time for him to pack his shit and roll out. Shit, the money he was planning to spend on an engagement ring for her and an upgrade on their apartment could be used to get his own spot, brand-new furniture, and a set of wheels. He wouldn't be able to buy a brand-new 2006 joint, but he could get something nice.

Cruze hopped off the bed and made a path to the closet, kicking out of his way Ramona's shoes that were strewn about, bags of dirty laundry, and an assortment of tote and duffle bags that she used for work.

Fuck her! He was sick of living in a pigsty, anyway. Strands of weave hair were all over the bathroom floor, and it clogged up the drain in *the sink and tub. Ramona's toiletries, hair products, and makeup were scattered all over the bathroom counter. In the kitchen, dishes were piled sky-high in the sink and a bunch of funky trash bags were stacked in a corner because they always managed to miss trash day.*

Cruze used to keep track of trash day, and also used to clean up behind Ramona, but ever since Moody had elevated his position, he didn't have the kind of time he used to have.

Cruze stopped dead in his tracks, grimacing as he thought about the bloody job he'd been assigned to handle tonight. Rolling through the streets, riding shotgun with Sameer and collecting Moody's money was a come-up, and he appreciated not having to hustle nickel and dime bags on the corner, anymore. But dumping bodies for that nigga, Moody had taken shit to a whole different level. Sameer had been excited about it and was looking forward to making more easy money, but Cruze doubted if he had the stomach to touch a dead body, ever again.

Even though he hadn't killed the muhfucka and therefore, didn't have any blood on his hands, his involvement still wasn't right. His mother was probably turning in her grave. He swallowed down a hard knot of guilt and shook his head. What he needed to do was get out of the game completely before something bad happened. It wasn't too late to enroll in a junior college and see about getting back into basketball. Shit, his jump shot was still nice—he hadn't lost his skills.

Needing luggage for his belongings, he angrily dumped all Ramona's stripper gear out of the duffle bags. Stilettos clunked to the floor and unwashed lingerie that held the scent of cigarette smoke, liquor, and musky pussy floated out of the bags, joining the rest of the mess that littered the floor in the cluttered bedroom.

Prepared to grab his clothes out the closet and stuff them in Ramona's bags, he opened the closet and gawked as he realized he'd need Sameer's car, after all, if he planned to transport the ridiculous amount of sneakers he'd accumulated.

Holding his cell phone and while his finger was poised to call his boy, he heard the familiar click of Ramona's heels against the wooden stairs that led to their third-floor apartment. Deciding he'd listen to what she had to say before he made a rash decision, he slid the phone back inside his pocket. He swung the door open and rushed down the stairs to meet her halfway.

Seeing his baby looking good in a tight, yellow dress and observing the way her curly, blonde ponytail bounced on her left shoulder, Cruze's pent-up anger instantly evaporated, and all he felt was intense love.

"Damn, babe, what took you so long to get home?" he inquired, relieving Ramona of the heavy duffle bag she was lugging. Even though she was dead wrong for staying out that late, Cruze didn't feel like arguing about it. She was home now, and that was all that mattered.

"There was a bachelor's party, and I had to stay," she said, looking weary.

It wasn't unusual for Ramona to whine and request a piggyback ride up the three flights whenever she wasn't in the mood to deal with all the steps, and so Cruze extended an olive branch. "I can tell you had a hard night, so come on…hop on my back."

"No, I'm good," she said, stomping up the stairs like she was upset with Cruze.

"What's wrong with you?" he growled, his irritation with her returning.

"Nothing," she said at first. Then she sighed and muttered, "We gottta talk, Cruze." Her voice was low and strained and she wouldn't look him in the eyes.

Eyebrows furrowed, he stopped in the middle of the stairs and studied her face. "Talk about what, Mo?"

"I'll tell you when we get in the house." She rushed ahead, impatiently. Baffled, Cruze stood for a moment, stroking his chin and trying to figure out why she was acting so cranky and weird when she was the one who'd fucked up, again—not him!

Maybe her period came on, he surmised, disappointed that he wouldn't be able to dig in that pussy tonight. He could tell by her pissy attitude that she wasn't in the mood to give up any head.

When Cruze entered the apartment, he slammed the door and dropped her bag in the middle of the living room. "What the fuck is your problem?" he demanded.

She gazed at him with pain evident in her eyes. "I can't keep lying to you. I'm sorry, Cruze, it's over."

He flinched, his features contorted in agony as if she'd kneed him in the groin. "What's over?"

"Us." She glanced down at the floor. "You can stay here; I'm leaving." She turned and moved hastily toward the bedroom.

Cruze raced behind her, grabbing her by the arm when she reached the threshold of the bedroom. "Hold up! How you just gon' bounce without telling me what I did wrong?"

"Don't put your fuckin' hands on me. I'm not dealing with that shit tonight." Ramona yanked her arm from his grasp and glared at him.

"What you gon' do?" he bellowed, pushing her inside their room, causing her to trip over the clutter on the floor. She jumped up and started swinging at him and he knocked her into the dresser. A few of the rubber-banded money stacks thumped to the floor.

Ramona wrinkled her forehead. "How'd you get all that?"

"Don't fuckin' worry about it, trick-ass bitch!" Eyes bulging and enraged, he picked up one of the fallen stacks and used it to smack Ramona across the face repeatedly, and then he commenced to beating her about the head and shoulders with the thick packet of bills. "I was gon' take you shopping for an engagement ring. And this is how you do me? I should have known better than to try to turn a hooker into a housewife."

"I'm not a hooker, and you know it," Ramona declared, crying.

"Yeah, whatever. Yo, you fuckin' want to leave? Then, what the fuck you waiting for? Get the fuck out, you dirty bitch."

"Stop it, Cruze. It's not even like you to be acting so ugly and calling me disrespectful names."

"Oh, no? Then, what should I be doing—begging you to stay and crying like a little bitch?"

"No."

"Then tell me what you expected?"

"I expected you to understand that with you only being eighteen and me being twenty-five, there's really no kind of future together for us."

Cruze made a sound of disgust. "You so full of shit, Mo," he snarled. "Age wasn't nothing but a number when I had my face between your legs and when my dick was up in those guts. But now my age is suddenly a problem."

"I met someone, Cruze," she said, taking steps away from him.

"Who?"

"It don't matter. But me and him…we're serious. He's gon' take care of me."

"What the fuck have I been doing?" Cruze jerked his head toward the money on the dresser. "How you think I got all that paper—by sitting on my ass? I did shit for you that I wouldn't even dream of doing for anybody else."

Cruze punched the wall, creating the sound of an explosion. Ramona jumped and then rushed to the closet and began snatching items of clothing off hangers and quickly stuffing them inside her bag.

She hurried to exit the bedroom, and then paused in the doorway. "I'm sorry it had to end like this, Cruze. I do still love you. I always will, but I have to do what's best for me."

"Fuck you!" He threw a stiletto, narrowly missing her head.

Looking shook, Ramona backed out the door. "I'll be back for the rest of my stuff tomorrow. And in case you plan on acting the ass, I'ma have five-oh with me," she threatened.

"Whatever, bitch!" He stalked across the room and grabbed her. As

Ramona thrashed and clawed, Cruze dragged her body down the hall-way and through the living room and then forcibly tossed her out the front door.

His mother had once cautioned him to hold his emotions inside and to never let anyone see his sensitive side, and so he stood stock-still and didn't make a sound as he listened to Ramona's clacking heels as she ran down the three flights of stairs. When he could no longer hear her foot-steps, he bit down on his bottom lip so hard, it bled. With the taste of blood in his mouth, he kicked the coffee table over, knocked the TV off the stand, and unable to hold back the tears any longer, he fell to his knees and bitterly cried.

Twenty-Nine

"I love you…"

Arabia cringed. The way he said *I love you* made her skin crawl. The whole time they'd been *seeing*—okay, *fucking*—each other he'd never used those words, not once.

Now, over the course of a week, he'd used those three words numerous times. Too many times to keep count. In fact, she'd stopped counting after he'd said it the thirty-eighth time. And here he was saying it again.

She sighed, wondering why he had to make this more complicated than it needed to be.

"Eric. You don't love me."

"I do, baby…"

Baby. She couldn't stand hearing him call her that. Not now. He disgusted her. One thing she couldn't stand was a begging-ass, whining man.

She shook her head. "Eric, stop. I'm not your baby. Okay?"

"No. That's where you're wrong. You'll always be *my* baby, Arabia. Always. Mine. And I still wanna be with you. *You*, Arabia; not Gwen, baby. *You*. I left her for you."

Oh, he sounded ridiculous. There was something seriously wrong with this man, and it had nothing to do with *her*. Well, that's what she needed to keep telling herself.

"Have you been drinking?"

Eric sniffled. "No. I'm hurting. Not drunk."

Oh. She didn't know what to say. So she said nothing.

Eric sighed heavily into the phone. "I walked away from everything to be with you, Arabia."

She frowned, quickly finding her voice. "And there lies the problem, Eric. You had no business leaving your wife and family for *me*; especially when I didn't ask you to."

"You didn't have to," he said. "I left her because my heart was with someone else—you. I couldn't keep living a lie. I was no longer in love with my wife. And you gave me a reason to want out."

"Then don't say you left her for me. You left because that's not where *you* wanted to be."

"You're right, baby…"

There was that word again, *baby*.

"Eric, look. You have to stop this. Stop calling me. Stop texting me. Please. We're not going to be together. Face it. Please. I don't want to sound callous. But I can't do this with you. It's over. And— after the way you threatened me in those text messages, then showed up here and embarrassed me down in my lobby, I'd never trust being anywhere alone with you."

"Please don't say that, baby," he said gently. "I didn't mean those things. I didn't mean to come to your place like that. I was just so fucking angry with you for abruptly ending things between us the way you did, then refusing my calls. It hurt me. You hurt me. Still, I know I was wrong. I had no right to speak to you like that." He took a breath. "I've never spoken to a woman like that before, and I had no right to do it to you, baby. I love you. I'd never do anything to hurt you, Arabia. Ever. You have to believe that."

Arabia didn't know what to believe. She really didn't think he would hurt her. Or do anything to try to ruin her life, although she had no clue what he could do to possibly ruin her. But okay. Still, she didn't want to believe that he'd come swinging through her door with a hacksaw or anything crazy like that, either. But she didn't know what he was capable of.

She'd purposefully over the years only involved herself with men who had a whole lot more to lose than she, for fear of something like this. Thus far, it had worked for her. But she hadn't considered the possibility of having a man willingly give up everything to be with her. Then what?

What happened when a man felt like he had nothing else to lose?

Arabia shook the question from her head. No. Eric had only spoken in anger like he'd said. He hadn't meant what he'd typed in his text to her that if he couldn't have her, no one else would. So its cryptic meaning held no real meaning. Did it?

For whatever reason, she felt the need to apologize to him again. In case he hadn't heard her the three other times. "I'm sorry, Eric. Really I am. I should have handled things differently."

"You've broken me, Arabia." His voice was low, slightly above a whisper.

She swallowed. "Eric, that wasn't my intention; to break you."

"Then why'd you do it, huh, baby? Why?"

Arabia massaged her left temple. She felt a headache pressing its way to the front of her head. She closed her eyes, and breathed through her nose. A part of her wanted to hang up on him. But the other part of her, the small piece of her that really did *like*—or care about—him wanted to hear him out. Didn't she at least owe him that much?

Maybe.

"Baby, are you there?"

She sighed. "Eric, you can't keep doing this. Calling me like this. What do you want?"

He sniffled again. "I want you to tell me what kind of woman comes into a man's life, then fucks him over, huh, baby?"

Arabia frowned. "I didn't fuck you over, Eric." *You did*.

"Why can't you be honest with me, huh? Just tell the truth for once. Can you do that, baby, huh?"

She ignored the question. "Eric, what have I ever lied to you about? Please tell me."

He snorted. "No. How about *you* tell *me*. You're the one who likes playing with motherfuckers' lives. Stringing them along, then dismissing them. I was good to you, Arabia."

She swallowed. He was right. He had been. "Yes. You were, Eric. And I'll never forget the times we shared to—"

"Fuck all that," he said, cutting her off. "Why'd you do it?"

Surprisingly, he wasn't yelling or screaming or cursing at her like he'd done in previous calls. In fact, he was eerily calm. Too calm. A nagging voice in the back of her mind told her to not continue this conversation. Hang up. Change her number. And move on.

But...

"Do what?" she asked.

"End it? And don't bullshit me. You owe me that, Arabia."

She sighed. Had he really thought all those times she tried to encourage him to stay with his wife that she'd done so out of some sense of duty to her? No. She'd encouraged that he stayed for her. She knew the truth was rather silly in the grand scheme of things. But, still, it was *her* truth. It didn't need to be his. So she told him, "Because you left your wife." There she'd said it.

She heard him sigh. "If you didn't want me, why did you string me along? For two fucking years, Arabia. You dangled that sweet pussy and all that wet dick sucking you did over my head, kept me coming back. For what? So you could turn around and fuck me in the end?"

Arabia felt her stomach lurch. He made it sound so damn dirty. She hadn't sought him out, though. He'd wanted *her*. He'd wanted to continue seeing *her*. He'd wanted to leave his wife for *her*. She hadn't asked him to. Hadn't pressured him to. He'd done it because that's what *he'd* wanted to do. So why was he blaming her?

He snorted. "Ain't this some shit. So you're telling me had I stayed with Gwen, you and I would still be together?"

Arabia took a deep breath, then blew it out slowly. "Yes. More than likely."

She heard him curse under his breath. "What a sick fuck," he muttered. "So you really never had any intentions of having a life with me, did you?"

She shook her head as if he could see her. "No," she said softly. "Well, yes. I mean, not one where we'd run off and get married. I'm sorry."

Eric grunted. "No. Fuck that sorry shit, Arabia." There was an edge to his tone, but he managed to keep his voice low and steady. *"Bit…"* He caught himself from calling her a *bitch*. He took a deep, steadying breath. "Do you have any idea what you've done, huh? Do you?"

There was a deafening silence over the phone. And then she heard it. Sniffling. Then sobbing.

Arabia blinked. *Is he crying?*

She groaned inwardly. Oh God, no! He *was* crying.

"I g-g-gave you my heart, A-arabia. And you took and twisted a knife in it."

She blinked again. Stunned that Eric had broken down in (or perhaps *resorted* to) tears. She didn't know if they were real or not. But they *sounded* real. And *he* sounded wounded.

She didn't need *this* today—a grown man crying on the phone.

"All y-you had to d-do w-was t-tell m-me the truth before I got all caught up in you." He sniffed, then blew his nose. "Unh, shit. I can't believe this shit. Crying over a fucking woman. All you had to do, Arabia, was tell me before I put a fucking ring on your finger that what we had wasn't going anywhere."

She swallowed. "I know, Eric. I should have. I tried."

"You *tried*," he repeated as if he hadn't heard her. "Well, obviously you didn't *try* hard enough. All it takes is opening your mouth and saying what's on your mind. Not once did you say, 'Hey Eric, I'm only with you for as long as you're married' or let's try this one: 'Hey, asshole, I'll keep fucking you for as long as you want as long as I'm your mistress.' *You* accepted my engagement ring, Arabia, as a promise to spend your life with me. Not play fucking games, then turn around and dump me."

But she hadn't been playing games with him.

Had she?

No, no, of course not.

She'd never told him anything other than what he wanted to hear. And most of it had been true. She *had* wanted to be with him, as long as he stayed married—okay, so she hadn't come out and told him *that* part.

Eric blew his nose again. "You're nothing but a user and a liar, Arabia; you know that, right?"

Several seconds ticked before she finally said, "Eric, I never used you. Ever."

He sniffled, then grunted. "Bullshit, baby. And you know it. I know I said I wouldn't call you out your name again. But face it. You're nothing but a heartless *bitch*. How many other men have you used, huh, Arabia? How many other lives have you fucking destroyed?"

Okay, so maybe she didn't respect men like him, but she wasn't *that* heartless.

Was she?

She didn't seek out to destroy men. And she resented him for saying that. She wasn't the malicious bitch he was trying to paint her out to be.

She bit into her bottom lip. She was trying desperately to remain empathetic to his misery, but she was slowly losing her patience. He was pushing her to the edge. And she didn't know how much more she was going to sit here and allow him to blame *her* for his mess. He and his marriage had both been broken long before he'd dragged (yes, *dragged* because she was minding her own damn business—thank you very much!) her into his world.

She let out a breath. "Again, I apologize. I don't know what more to say, Eric."

"Just say what a fucked-up human being you are, Arabia. Say it."

"Okay, Eric. I'm a 'fucked-up human being.' There I said it. Satisfied?"

He grunted. "Hell no. You fucked my life up, Arabia."

She sighed again. Clearly he believed what he believed and she needed to let him.

"Eric, why are you blaming *me* for this? I didn't do anything to you. Or take anything from you that you hadn't wanted me to have. Like I said before, I didn't use you. Ever. Nor have I used anyone else. You make it seem like I plotted on you. Like I pursued you. You're trying to make me out to be some predator who lies in wait to strike my next kill."

Well, she did—lie in wait when she had her sights on someone. But she hadn't with him, so he didn't need to know that he was right.

"Who else are you giving that pussy to, huh, Arabia? How many times were you whoring around on me, huh…?"

She blinked.

"For all the whoring you do, you're always so quick to judge me," her mother had said nastily.

"I don't judge you, Mother. I simply find what you do, bouncing from husband to husband for his money, disgusting."

Claudia snorted. "Ha! Arabia, get over yourself. And you think what you do, bouncing from married man to married man for his hard dick is any better? What's disgusting is you. Every man I've ever been with put a ring on my finger and made an honest woman out of me. Not parade me around as his dimwitted concubine." She stared at Arabia, and sneered. "*You're nothing but a reckless, heartless whore, my darling daughter. Then you have the nerve to want to justify why you sleep with another woman's husband. I didn't raise you to play second best to anyone, Arabia. Ever!*"

"No," Arabia snapped. "*You raised me to be a gold digger! Same difference!*"

"No," Claudia countered. "*The difference is, I raised you to always be a lady in the streets, but to know when to whore for your own damn husband! Not another woman's. And everything you hate about me is what you see in yourself. So do not think for one moment you can ever pass judgment on me without passing it on yourself. Remember that.*"

Arabia shook the memory from her thoughts. She was nothing like her mother. Nothing. And she refused to believe—

"Huh, Arabia? Tell me. I asked you a question," Eric said, bringing her back to their conversation.

She let out an aggravated sigh. "Tell you what, Eric?"

"Tell me how many other married motherfuckers you're fucking over?"

Arabia gasped. Her cheeks heated, and she felt herself suddenly shaking from the inside out with anger. "Whom I'm *fucking* is *none* of your business, Eric!" she snapped defensively. Her teeth clenched. "It's over between us. Now don't call me again, or you will leave me no other choice but to file for a restraining order against you."

And with that, she finally did what she should have done the minute she heard his voice on the other end of the line.

She disconnected the call.

Thirty

2006

"Moody's bugging," Cruze complained, and then bit into the messy cheesesteak he was holding in both hands.

Sameer had two sandwiches in front of him: a cheesesteak and a hoagie. He shook oregano over the Italian hoagie. "You eating free, ain't you? So stop complaining."

Cruze stretched out his legs and scowled. "Man, fuck a free sandwich. Ain't we got enough delis right there in New York? I don't see why we had to drive all the way to Philly to get that big-belly nigga something to eat. The way his gut's starting to stick out, he need to be thinking about getting a gym membership instead of constantly stuffing his face."

"Word," Sameer agreed, chomping into the hoagie. "Mmph! This shit bangin', though. You can't get a real Philly hoagie or cheesesteak nowhere in New York."

Frowning as he chewed, Cruze wiped his mouth with a napkin. "Why can't you? There's a place over on—"

"Man, don't tell me you can't tell the difference between those knock-off cheesesteaks and the real thing?" Sameer cut his eye at a chick in tight jeans standing at the counter of the steak shop. "Plus, look at the view. I ain't never had no Philly pussy before. 'Scuse me while I go holla at shawty." Sameer pushed his chair back.

Cruze checked the time on his phone. "Man, we on Moody's clock and *that nigga's timing us. So, you ain't got time to get a hotel and you ain't fucking the bitch in the car."*

Sameer looked offended. *"Why not? It's my ride."*

"Man, I put money into them wheels, too. I ain't tryna ride all the way back to New York smelling pussy fumes mixed with stinkin' fried onions. Fuck that, man. Get the bitch's number and then get with her on your own time."

"You ain't no fun no more, Cruze. Ever since shawty bounced, you been acting like a bitch on her period. Why you lettin' shawty stress you like that?"

"Ain't nobody stressed over no bitch. I'm fuckin' sick of Moody sending us on sucka missions, like we still corner boys. I thought he moved us up the ranks, but this here shit..." Rolling his eyes at the environment of the Philadelphia steak shop, Cruze let his voice trail off.

"I don't know about you, but I like being on Moody's payroll and getting a certain amount of paper that I can count on every week—plus bonuses. Niggas will be lining up to take your spot if you don't want it. So go on and hug the block again if that makes you feel like your own man." Sameer shook his head disgustedly.

Cruze let Sameer's words sink in. He pushed his unfinished cheesesteak to the side. *"I knew I shouldn't have ate this greasy bullshit. Now, my stomach starting to act up."*

"Damn. You startin' to sound like a lil' bitch, complaining about everything. I swear to God, if I had Ramona's number, I'd call her myself and beg her to please bring her stripper-ass back home." Sameer burst into his trademark stupid giggle.

Cruze stood up abruptly, nearly toppling the table. *"Ain't shit funny, muhfucka! Talk grimy about Ramona again, and I'ma fuck you up in this dip. I can't believe you took something I told you in confidence and threw it back in my face. Who else did you run your mouth to about Ramona strippin'?"*

Sameer reared back, looking disgusted. "I ain't have to tell nobody, 'cause everybody around the way already knew. Niggas been throwing dollars at that ho for years."

Cruze glared at Sameer. "She ain't a ho."

"I don't see why you taking up for her when she dipped on you."

"Whatever. Just keep her name outta ya mouth."

Thirty minutes later, Cruze carried the box that contained six cheese-steaks back to the car. Brooding, he walked ahead of Sameer.

The drive back to New York was tension-filled. Sameer had started off telling corny jokes, trying to get Cruze out of his funk, but Cruze didn't feel like talking or laughing. Staring out the window, he sat in defiant silence.

He missed Ramona so bad, the pain was palpable. Sleeping alone was the worst, and nights like this when the pain felt particular acute, he felt mad at the world. The thought of going back to his empty apartment made him feel like rolling his window down and retching. There were plenty of bitches he could get with, but fucking anyone other than Ramona made him miss her worse than he already did.

Love sucked. It was torture. His head hurt constantly and his heart beat erratically, like he had a cardiovascular condition. Every creak of the steps outside his apartment door was Ramona coming home, where she belonged. But when he swung his door open, he'd find one of the neighbors climbing the stairs, which would cause his heart to drop hard in disappointment.

Sometimes his heart hurt so bad, he felt like smoking some shit or sticking a needle in his arm. No wonder there were so many fiends in the world. Muhfuckas needed something to dull the excruciating pain of being lovesick.

Sameer's phone vibrated, pulling Cruze out of his dismal thoughts. Sameer peeked at the screen and put it on speaker. "We on our way, Moody."

"Y'all niggas should be halfway here by now," Moody grumbled.

"*Yeah, man. We close.*"

"*How close?*" Moody demanded.

"*Um...*"

Cruze sat up in his seat. "*Tell that bastard—*"

"*Shh!*" Sameer held a finger to his lips. His desperate eyes beseeched Cruze not to lose his temper and blow their cushy jobs. "*Uh, we in North Jersey right now, but we won't be long.*"

"*A'ight. Hurry the fuck up!*" Moody disconnected the call.

Cruze twisted his lips to the side and shook his head. "*Man, you one ass-kissing muhfucka, you know that?*"

"*Look who talkin',*" Sameer shot back. "*You should know all about it, the way you kiss that bitch's ass.*"

Cruze narrowed his eyes threateningly. "*I told you—*"

"*Fuck you, Cruze! You ain't gon' be talkin' shit about my manhood and think I'ma sit back and take it.*"

"*All I'm sayin' is you need to get off that nigga's dick.*"

Sameer gave Cruze the finger and they drove the rest of the way in silence. As they neared the elegant home that Moody was leasing, Cruze sighed, again. "*I'm sick of working for this black bastard. He living like a king and treating us like peons. We need to put our money together and go out on our own. For real, Sameer. Something about Moody don't rub me right. The shit he have us doin'... That nigga gon' fuck around and get us killed. My mom always told me—*"

Sameer gave Cruze the side-eye. "*I know you ain't go there—bringing up something your moms said. You need to chill, nigga, and play your position.*" Sameer got out of the car. "*Be patient. Moody got big plans for us.*"

"*I bet,*" Cruze said sarcastically. "*He got plans for us to keep picking up cheesesteaks for his greedy ass...and dumping bodies.*"

Cruze opened the passenger's door.

Sameer held up his hand. "*Nah, man. Stay in the car. The way you act-*"

ing, you might fuck around and say something to Moody that'll make him send our asses back to the block." Sameer slammed the door and strolled to Moody's doorstep with the box of cheesesteaks tucked under his arm.

Sameer was right and so Cruze stayed in the ride and leaned his seat back further. To pass time, he perused the CDs in the console of the car. Then, hearing a familiar voice, he sat up suddenly and craned his neck in the direction of Moody's front door, and his eyes nearly popped out of his head. Standing in the doorway, accepting the box of cheesesteaks from Sameer was none other than Ramona. What was his fuckin' girl—well, his ex-girl. Whatever the fuck she was—what was she doing at Moody's crib dressed in a sheer robe?

Before Cruze realized what he was doing, he was out the car, slipping on damp grass as he raced to get to the front door. He had no idea what he planned to do, but punching Ramona in the face and then wrapping his hands around her neck was at the top of the list. He'd stomp Moody's brains out after he strangled the life out of that no-good, cheating-ass, stripper-bitch whore!

Mid-rush toward the front door, Cruze suddenly felt like he'd run into a brick wall. He hit the ground hard. It took a moment to come to his senses and when he did, he discovered Sameer on top of him. He'd forgotten that fuckin' Sameer had played football in school and the muh-fucka had tackled the shit out of him, knocking the breath out of his body.

"Get it together, Cruze. You gon' get us killed over that bitch, and she ain't worth it, man."

"I'ma kill her," Cruze gasped, trying to catch his breath. "I can't believe she did me like this," he gurgled. "And that dirty nigga, Moody! Out of all the bitches he could have, why'd he have to take my girl?"

"I don't know, man. I had no idea about him and Ramona. But I ain't tryna lose my life over no stripper and you shouldn't, either. Come on. Get up and get the fuck back in the car before we both wind up at the bottom of the Hudson."

Sameer gave Cruze a hand and pulled him to his feet. The world spun fast and Cruze teetered, unable to keep his balance. Sameer helped hold him up as Cruze staggered and limped toward the car. With a hand over his chest, it appeared that he'd been shot in the heart and critically wounded.

Ramona ran her hand over the waves in Cruze's hair, and he closed his eyes blissfully, grateful that it wasn't a dream. She was really at the crib, taking care of him. When Sameer got word to her that Cruze was sick as a dog and hadn't been showing up for work, she came to their old apartment to see about him.

And after fucking him back to good health, she began putting on her clothes, ready to bounce.

Cruze squeezed his eyes closed, unable to watch her as she prepared to leave him all alone, again.

"Where's my other heel?" Ramona asked, peeking under the bed. Her voice and noisy movement around the bedroom were making it impossible for Cruze to gather the inner peace he was trying to find.

Agitated, his eyes popped open. "Just answer one question, Mo. Why dat ugly nigga?"

Ramona let out a sigh. "You know why. I already told you I'm only with him for what he can do for me. But my heart is still with you, Cruze. I promise I'm gonna make sure you move up the ranks in the organization. Moody's gon' personally groom you. Trust me, babe. One day me and you are gon' be running the show." She hovered over him and caressed his arm.

Cruze shrank from her touch and glowered at her. "Yeah, right—tell me anything."

"I'm serious. After you become second in command, we'll get rid of Moody...somehow. I haven't figured out all the details, but—"

Cruze sucked his teeth. "Man, get the fuck outta here with that Scarface bullshit. How we gon' get rid of Moody? You been watching too many gangster flicks."

"Look, we in a good position with me working from the inside. I'm working for us to have a better future, and I know what I'm doing." She sat on the bed and clenched his chin, forcing him to look in her eyes. "I got this. Do you hear me?"

Cruze yanked his head away, pulling his chin out of her grasp. "All I hear is that you left me for Moody. Out of all the bitches in the world, I can't understand why that bastard had to take my girl."

"He didn't know about us. I told him you were like a little brother to me."

Her words hit like a harsh slap and Cruze flinched from the impact. "A little brother, huh? Wow." Heart crashing against his ribcage, he reached for the half-blunt in the ashtray next to the bed and lit it. His throat burned and his eyes watered as he held the smoke in his lungs.

"You're making shit more difficult than it has to be. Be patient and trust me, okay?" Ramona took the blunt from Cruze's fingers and puffed on it.

Cruze blew out a thick cloud of smoke and glared at Ramona. "How could I ever trust you, again? This shit you doin' ain't right, Mo."

"Since when you got so many morals? As long as we get what we want, you shouldn't be worried about what's right or wrong," Ramona snapped.

"I'm talking about what you doin' to me!" he snapped. "That's the shit that ain't right."

Ramona abruptly stood up. "Grow up, Cruze. Can you please start looking at the big picture?"

"No! I'm not trying to get rich or die trying. All I need is you. I love you, girl. Why can't you understand that? I don't give a fuck about all that other shit you talkin'. I just want shit to be back like it's supposed to be—you and me, together. You ain't supposed to be with him!"

Exasperated, Ramona rolled her eyes toward the ceiling. "You don't get it. "I'd be a fool to give up Moody's money to live in this dump, again.

And I'll be damned if I'm ever going back to the club, swinging my ass from anybody's fuckin' pole—not in this life," she said adamantly.

"We don't have to stay here; we could move somewhere better, baby," Cruze said in a desperate voice. "I got some money stashed."

Ramona shook her head ruefully and audibly sighed. "You don't have the kind of long money that Moody has, and you never will as long as you doing grunt work for him. And that's where I come in. I'm gon' make sure my baby runs with the big dogs. But like I said, you have to be patient."

Cruze took in several long, deep breaths, trying to steady his racing pulse. "So, you expect me to fall back and wait around while you laying up with that muhfucka?"

Ramona lifted a shoulder and studied her lacquered nails.

Cruze stared at her, pain flooding his eyes. "Do you have any idea how hard it is to sleep at night when you ain't here?"

"I know, baby. I know," she soothed. "But it won't be forever."

"I'm not with this creepin' bullshit with my own girl. How long is it gonna take before we're back like we used to be?"

Ramona shrugged with both shoulders. "That depends on how long it takes for you to learn the business."

She was promising him something that was so far off in the distant future, he figured he might as well give up all hope of ever being happy, again. "This is so fucked up, Ramona. Really. Fucked. Up," he said, pounding the bed as he emphasized each word. He took a last puff on the blunt and then stubbed it out. Smoke wafted up to his eyes, burning them. "So, tell me something," he said, looking at her through eyes that were squinted from anger and the effects of the weed.

"Tell you, what?"

"Do you suck his dick like you suck mine?" The brusque, crude words were spoken with the intention of humiliating Ramona.

But she didn't flinch. "Moody's my man, now. Of course I suck his dick."

Hearing Ramona refer to Moody as her man made Cruze want to keel over and die, but he kept it together, leveling a look of disgust at her. He spat twice and fiercely wiped his lips with the back of his hand. "Ain't this some shit? I oughta fuck you up. I let you kiss me all over my mouth, never dreamin' you been slurpin' on that muhfucka's dick."

"Yes, Cruze. I suck Moody's dick," she said boldly, enunciating each word. "But…"

"But, what, you fuckin' ho?"

"But, I don't swallow his nut. I can't. I only swallow your creamy cum, baby."

Cruze threw his arm over his head and gave the headboard a backward punch. "That's supposed to make me feel better? I swear to God, Mo, I wish I never met your skanky ass."

Ramona took a seat on the side of the bed, again. She gently ran her fingers up Cruze's thigh that was covered by the sheet. "I'm sorry, boo. Let me make it up to you," she said in a sultry tone.

"Fuck, no!" Cruze grabbed a pillow and put it over his lap, concealing his dick before she inched her fingers up to it.

"Come on, let me taste that sweet meat," she crooned with a smile as she tugged on the pillow.

"No! Go on home to your man, and leave me alone." Cruze stubbornly kept the pillow in place.

"I miss that thick milkshake, baby. I know your young ass still gotta lot of cum left up in them balls. And I love the way it splashes in my mouth before it slides down my throat."

Cruze averted his gaze, wouldn't look at her.

"You came in my pussy twice tonight, but you forgot to feed me some of that sweet protein, so stop being stingy." Her eyes traveled from the pillow up to his face and she could tell by the way he was biting on his bottom lip that he couldn't ignore the offer much longer.

With his dick expanding beneath the covers and with blood rushing to his head, Cruze tossed the pillow aside and lifted the covers. Gripping his elongated dick at the base with one hand, he roughly pulled Ramona downward with the other. "Suck this shit, you dirty bitch."

"Yeah, but I'm your dirty bitch," she said, laughing. She kissed the head and licked the drippings that seeped from the slit. "Now, say it," she whispered with a smile in her voice.

"Say what?" Cruze groaned as Ramona softly fondled his balls.

"Call me a dirty bitch."

"Ain't no doubt about that. You know what you are," he responded gruffly.

"But I'm your dirty bitch, and I know you still love me. Am I right?"

"Yeah, you right. Now, stop talking and get on this," he said, hips thrusting in sexual need.

"I'll get on it after you say it. You know my mouth gets real juicy when you call me names."

All he could think about was how good it would feel to slide his dick back and forth over her moist tongue, and how much he missed shoving his cock down her fleshy throat. Writhing with need and motivated by hot lust, Cruze said in an agonized voice, "You my dirty bitch, and I love you."

"Aw, yeah, baby. Call me some more names," Ramona cooed.

"No! I already said that twisted shit. Now, what are you waitin' for— suck my dick," he bellowed as a nearly savage lust blazed through him. Every muscle in his body flexed as he thrust upward attempting to stick his dick between her lips. Furious with himself and with her, he clutched Ramona's hair in both hands. Pulling her downward, he pushed his lengthy pole inside her warm mouth. She gagged and struggled as he forced his dick deeper into her throat. Cruze held Ramona's head in place while he fed her measured thrusts of hot dick meat. The more she gagged, the slicker his dick became, gliding easily deep into her narrow neck.

There was no reason to be gentle with her. She wasn't his girl, anymore. She was Moody's bitch.

With each angry hip thrust, Cruze was growing closer to busting a nut. He curled his toes and let out a growl as a tingling sensation trav-eled from his nut sac and down the length of his dick. In a frenzy of lust, pain, and love, he called her a slut, a cum-sucking bitch, and a trifling whore. And he tried to rip Ramona's hair out from the roots when a blast of cum shot out of his dick.

The aftershock from the explosive orgasm caused Cruze's body to quake. Completely spent, he released Ramona's hair and collapsed against her, resting his head on her chest.

No longer angry, only weak and defeated, he murmured, "I love you, baby. Don't leave me, Mo. Take your clothes off, babe, and get back in the bed. Please, baby."

"I have to go," she said, easing away from him. "But I'll be back." She pondered briefly. "Not tomorrow and probably not Monday. But, maybe I can get away on—"

Cruze pressed his finger against her lips. With misery glistening in his eyes, he said, "Shh. I don't want to be sitting around here, waiting for you. It hurts too much. So, don't make promises you can't keep. Just call me the next time you're ready to see me, ai'ght?"

He hated how he sounded like a straight bitch. He needed to man-up and tell Ramona he wasn't no damn booty call. But instead he said, "I just want you back, Mo. And I'll take whatever I can get. You feel, me, girl?" He reached for her hand and squeezed it.

"I feel you," Ramona said, sliding her hand out of his. "Thank God we finally got some kind of understanding." Ramona smiled and sighed with relief as she extracted her car keys from her new Versace bag, a gift from Moody.

"See you soon, Cruze," she said, blowing Cruze a kiss before strutting out of the bedroom.

Sitting on the bed, alone and brokenhearted, Cruze rolled another blunt. He put on his headphones and listened to Jay-Z express his feelings perfectly as he rapped the lyrics to "Song Cry."

Thirty-One

"I met someone," Arabia confided to her sister, Maya. She was the only one of her sisters whom she told such things to; although she knew the minute they hung up, Maya would be on the phone with their other sisters blabbing her mouth, unless Arabia told her to keep it between them.

"Mmm. Oh, okay. So is he married?"

Arabia rolled her eyes. Her sister was being messy. "No."

"*Whaaaaat?*" she screeched sarcastically. "Girl, not married? And *you* like him?"

"I guess." She shrugged. "I find him interesting."

"Lord, Jesus," Maya exclaimed. "*You* find someone who *isn't* married interesting. Oh, I know we're in the last days now."

"Whatever, smart-ass. I can't stand you."

Maya laughed. "Lies. You know I'm your favorite big sis."

Arabia rolled her eyes, smiling. "Maybe."

"Maybe my ass. So tell me about this *someone* who you met who isn't married. Does he have a girlfriend?"

"No, he…" Wait. She had no idea if he did or not. Have one of those. A girlfriend. She frowned. Not that it really mattered. Truth was, he was a distraction. He was everything she craved and shouldn't want, and yet she allowed him to tempt her at every turn. And what disturbed her most was, she *liked* him tempting her.

They'd been talking and texting practically every day since her last date with him, but she hadn't thought to ask him that. She knew he had to be giving that long, black dick to someone. Still, a part of her didn't believe she had a right to ask considering her own situation.

Yes, she was single. But she was still involved, even if she didn't feel *attached* to any of them. Well—with Theodore dead and Eric now running around like a nut—there was *now* only Wellson, whom she adored, but…

"He what?" Maya asked, cutting off her train of thought.

"He doesn't. I don't think."

"You don't *think?* Well, don't you think you might want to *know?*"

Again, Arabia shrugged. "It's really not that important. It's not like I'm trying to marry the man. I simply said I met someone. I didn't say I was running off to elope."

Maya sucked in a breath. "Now wouldn't that be a treat. You married."

"Uh-huh. Good luck with that. You have a better chance at having another set of twins before that happens."

"Girl, shut your mouth. My name is Maya. Not Alexis. I'm not pushing out any more babies, not out of this cooch. I already told Chase if he even thinks it, I'll slice his dick off. And he knows how much I love that thing."

Arabia groaned. "Ugh. TMI. I don't need to know anything about your love for his *thing*, girl."

Maya sucked her teeth. "Whatever. So did you fuck him?"

Arabia blushed, feeling heat swirl through her body, remembering how her pussy had sloshed around his dick the night he'd picked her up and thrown her down on his bed, pinning her down and taking what he wanted.

Gone lightheaded, Arabia had cried out in delirious abandon, her nails raking his muscled, sweat-slicked back as he plummeted her over the edge of bliss with his deep, delicious strokes. His dick feverishly sliced into her cunt, filling her, stretching her, fucking into parts of her body she hadn't known existed. She'd been so wet. No. *Fucking* wet. So wet that her pussy juices sluiced out of her trembling body, and soaked the sheets beneath her.

She had always prided herself on having a juicy snatch, but the way Cruze's cock had slashed into her core, its thick shaft brushing against her quaking walls, stroking over her swollen spot, she was flooded with arousal, drowning in it, like never before.

If his cock had felt that delicious wrapped in latex, she only imagined what it'd feel like naked. Oh how she'd wanted to feel him raw inside her. Oh, God, what the hell had she been thinking? He'd fucked her senseless.

He'd fucked her so hard, so wet. His big dick had plundered all through her pussy, knocking at the opening of her cervix. Surely there had to be a wet stain and the scent of her cunt still lingering in his mattress.

She remembered slapping him for getting all caveman on her, manhandling her. But after that, the world had blurred around her as he pounded into her. He'd fucked her with a savage force, animalistic need and want overwhelming him—and her—as his dick slid in and out of her. She'd never been fucked breathless before.

When she finally blinked him back into focus, he was smirking at her, taking everything she was, everything she'd ever be, and he'd taken it all for himself, leaving nothing for anyone else. He'd fucked her as hard as needed, and she received him willfully. His mouth brushed her neck and then he'd sunk his teeth into the column of her silky skin, eliciting a mewling from her.

He'd marked her. Let whoever else she was fucking know that she'd whored herself out to another motherfucker.

Goddamn him.

Cruze Fontaine was everywhere he shouldn't be—in her head, her memories, all over her skin.

The thought alone made Arabia shiver with want.

When he'd finished with her, she'd limped her way to the bathroom to freshen up, hoping whomever else that manwhore was fucking sniffed her out the next time the arrogant fuck had that bitch's ass up, and her face pressed down into his mattress.

Would serve him right.

He was lucky she hadn't been messy enough to leave her panties tossed under his bed.

Ooh, he made her want to—

"Umm, hello?" Arabia heard Maya's bangles clanking as she clapped her hands together. "Are you there? Earth to Arabia."

Arabia's lids fluttered. "Yes."

Maya sighed. "Yes to what?"

"Yes, I'm here. And, *yes*, I fucked him."

"Ooh, you filthy *slut*," Maya hissed, and then they both burst out in laughter.

"Yes, girl. I'm slutty to the core."

"Bitch, I can't stand you. When I grow up, I want to be just like you. I love how sexually carefree you are."

"Life is too short not to be," she said unapologetically. "I refuse to be deprived." And, yet, Cruze had managed to deny her his tongue and somehow she was okay with it—for now.

There was something clearly wrong here.

Arabia walked into the kitchen and eyed her smartphone on the bar. She flinched when she saw the number of missed calls and texts. From Wellson. From a blocked number—Eric, she was certain. From her mother.

Ugh, her mother. Why couldn't that woman simply leave her

the hell alone? She added no value to her life. Never had, never would.

She needed to call Wellson, she thought. They needed to have a serious talk. She'd been avoiding him—sort of. Making excuses to not see him. Making herself unavailable to him over the last several weeks. He never pressured her, never made her give more than what she was willing to give. She never imagined ever contemplating ending things with him. She never *wanted* to end things with him. He'd been a constant in her life for the last three years. But now…

He wasn't enough.

He'd never been enough.

None of them ever were.

Yet she'd kept him around because she truly liked him. But she loved the trips and the gifts more.

But now she found herself liking Cruze more. They were only fucking. Well, had fucked. And, yet, she felt strangely connected to him. And, for some odd reason, a sliver of guilt surged over her for still being with Wellson, even though it'd been weeks since she'd been intimate with him. It wasn't like she owed Cruze, Wellson, or anyone else any explanations. And it damn sure wasn't either of their concern whom she gave her pussy to, either. But, crazily, she felt she needed, she *wanted*, to break things off with Wellson.

But why?

Cruze offered her no guarantees. She'd just met him, for Christ's sake. So why the hell was she considering abandoning what she knew, what was constant, for some fleeting fantasy with some big-dicked playboy who didn't kiss, or eat pussy?

She needed to stop this foolishness. And stop it now.

"I know that's right," Maya said, slicing into Arabia's thoughts.

"Do you. Live your life. Now back to this man who you've fucked. Was it good?"

Arabia closed her eyes and shuddered. His touch, his mere presence, alone made her wetter than a lake. The man made her want to crawl out of her skin. He made her come hard. Made her pussy hot. Made it spew her juices like an erupting volcano.

"Yes, girl. It was. Had *me* in *my* car driving down to Philly for it."

Maya laughed. "Ohmygod. *You* driving to a man for some dick? Oh yes, the world is definitely coming to an end."

Arabia rolled her eyes up in her head, but she laughed as well. "Whatever."

"So far, I like him."

Arabia's cell buzzed. She stared at the caller ID, and smiled. Thick Chocolate. The name she'd programmed into her phone for *him*. Her body flushed at the thought of him.

God, she had to get ahold of herself before she went up in flames. She pushed the phone aside in a feeble attempt at not answering. She didn't want to come off desperate. Thirsty. Hungry.

But, shit—she was *desperate*, for more of him. She was *thirsty*, for another taste of him. She was *hungry*, for more of his good fucking.

She smiled. "Yeah, I like him, too."

Maya chuckled.

"What's so funny?"

"Oh nothing. I was thinking, what if you've finally found someone you can love."

Arabia coughed. "Oh, no, bitch! Don't curse me. You know I'm severely allergic to *that*."

"Girl, bye. How would you know? You've never *been* in love."

"Well, I've been in *like*. Close enough."

Maya snorted. "Lies. But you keep telling yourself that. Then again, this is you we're talking about. Miss Heartless. So, yeah, you might be right."

"Ohmygod, Maya. Kiss my ass. I'm not *heartless*."

"Okay, Arabia. Whatever you say, boo."

Arabia's phone vibrated, and this time it was a call. Thick Chocolate.

Heat swept through her.

Oh, God…fate or omen?

The devil was trying to make her sin.

She wanted to answer. Wanted to hear his voice.

And she had to fight an inner battle to not want those things. She had to fight the urges, even as the sight of his name on her screen sent a flutter of butterflies twirling in her stomach.

The call went into voicemail.

"Anyway. Does this someone you *like* have a name?"

Arabia smiled. "Yes. Cruze."

"*Cruze?*" Maya repeated. "What kind of name is that? Is he black? Please tell me he isn't some white man, Arabia."

Arabia laughed. "No, Maya. Relax. He's not white. He's very much black." She licked her lips at the thought of suckling his dark berry to get to his sweet juices.

She yanked her phone from the counter, and texted. HEY

She was holding her cell, staring at it, when it buzzed in her hand. WYD? he texted back.

"Well, that's a relief. Is he mixed?"

Arabia shrugged, then shook her head. "I don't know. With his high cheekbones and smooth dark skin, he could have some West Indian in his blood. Or maybe he's…"

THINKING ABOUT U, she responded back in earnest. It was the truth.

"Or maybe he's what?"

Arabia shook her head. "Straight from the Motherland. No. He *is* from the Motherland. He's an African warrior." Mmm. Hung like a Zulu god.

AWW. DAMN. THINKIN ABOUT U 2

Arabia grinned, then bit into her bottom lip.

She wanted to see that man. Had to see him.

☺ I'LL CALL U. 5 MINS?

Seconds later, he sent another text. COOL

She set her phone down, her body overreacting and overheating to raw feelings of excitement, desire—and need. God, he made her feel so vulnerable and raw, like he was peeling her skin back and opening her up.

She couldn't wait another moment longer. "Maya, I love you, girl," she said abruptly. "But I gotta go. I'll call you one day next week."

"Well damn. Who said—"

Click.

She ended the call, before she could finish her sentence. Then she reached for her cell again.

And called *him*.

Thirty-Two

This shit felt too good to be true....

But he hadn't felt this happy—*this* relaxed, in years. Not since Ramona.

Fucking Ramona.

No matter what he did, somehow she always managed to find a way to creep up in his thoughts. She was poison. And he wasn't about to allow his infected thoughts of her to snatch what semblance of joy he was feeling.

He couldn't compare what he felt *now* to back *then*.

Yeah, Ramona had been his first love, and she'd been his first taste of heartache, too. Hell, she'd been his *first* everything.

But he had been a lil'-ass kid then. Now, he was a grown-ass man. He was more than a hard, horny dick. He knew more. Had grown more experienced with women. And he knew when a broad was playing him, or trying to catch a come-up.

That wasn't Arabia. Fuck no. She was different.

She was her own woman. And, yet, she knew how to play her position and let him be the man. Her man. Well, that wasn't what she called him.

But it was definitely moving in that direction.

Cruze smiled inside. Yeah, that's right. *Her man.* Though he hadn't officially come out and called her his girl. He'd been toying with the idea.

She was definitely *wifey* material.

She was more than he imagined she'd be. Yeah, she used her femininity to seduce him. But she'd somehow—with her sass and brash—found a way to pull him from out his shell. Darkness whirled around him, and, yet, she'd unknowingly become a bright light in his somewhat gloomy existence.

No, Cruze hadn't expected things between them to heat up the way they had, but they had. And, hell, he wasn't complaining. Things between them were popping hot and heavy. And they were quickly becoming an item. No lie. He was feeling her, hard. And he knew she was feeling him too.

Still, he didn't quite know what to do with these new feelings. He didn't know when it'd happened, when something inside of him shifted. But he was addicted to her. He craved every smooth, silky inch of her. However, he didn't want to play himself. So he held back. He held back from freely giving into the pleasure. He fought the urge to let go and simply go with the flow.

All he'd ever known was pain.

And loss.

And disappointment.

So this, this was foreign to him.

And, yet, he didn't want anything to ruin it. Happiness was always short-lived for a muhfucka like him. And…and he didn't know what he'd do if he lost this, this feeling.

He tried not to overthink it. Tried to stay in the present. Hell, that's where he wanted to be—in the moment…with *her*.

So he shook the ominous thought of something this good being a sign that something bad would soon follow from out of his mind.

His cell phone rang. It was Ramona. He shook his head. And Arabia eyed him from the corner of her eye as he frowned at the screen. Any other time he would answer on the spot. Drop whatever he was doing for her. Not today. He sent the call to voice-mail—surprising himself, then shutting off his phone.

He'd get at her later. Right at this very moment, his priority was sitting next to him. He was trying to chill with Arabia's fine ass with no interruptions.

Usher's "Can U Handle It" seeped out though the speakers, and he leaned his head back on the headrest as Arabia drove.

He inhaled.

Shit, it felt good to be chauffeured for a change.

She'd surprised him—and herself—when she'd called him and said she wanted to take *him* out. On a date. He couldn't help but smile. No female had ever offered to take him anywhere except to bed.

So when she pulled up to his crib in her Aston Martin, and kissed him lightly on the lips when he slid into the passenger seat, Cruze knew then…she was the *one*.

He still hadn't *kissed* her; not in the way two lovers would. But he'd come a long way with a peck on the lips. And Arabia seemed okay with that.

She didn't pressure him. Didn't try to take more than he was willing to give. And it hadn't gone unnoticed, or unappreciated.

He stole a glimpse at her through the corner of his eye.

Damn, my baby looks good driving this whip; her sexy ass.

She licked her lips as she maneuvered through the city traffic with ease, and he felt his dick stirring in his boxers. He opened and closed his legs, pressing them tightly together, then opening them wide again. He clasped his hands in his lap, and pressed down on the building pressure in his dick, fanning his legs.

Shit.

He wondered if she even knew the type of effect she had on him. How aroused she made him. She made him come undone every time he was around her.

Feeling Cruze eyeing her, she glanced over, and smiled.

He turned his head to her, his eyes coming to rest on her, and smiled back. And there went those dimples that she'd grown to love. She felt her heart flutter and her cunt clench, as his eyes grew dark and unexpectedly liquid as he looked at her.

Heat swooped around the cabin of the car, making her hot, wet.

God, what was happening to her?

The sight of him made her sizzle with desire.

She stayed wet for *him*.

Stayed hot for *him*.

Stayed ready for *him*.

Lord, help her. She wasn't *in love*. But she was beyond lusting him. She couldn't recall when it'd happened. When she became so, so, open to him.

But it had happened.

And he was slowly becoming the air she needed to breathe. Yes, the woman was wild for him. He made her hungry. Oh how she wished there was a way she could put her car on cruise control and lean over and suck his dick. She'd suck his balls dry right now in broad daylight in all this weekend traffic. She wanted to feel his warm nut coating her tongue and sliding down the back of her throat.

She swallowed back the greedy need that pooled in her mouth, and shifted in her seat.

Cruze made her dizzy. She hated admitting it. But she was obsessed. Bewildered. She wanted him—not just his body, his lips, his dick—but every part of him. He was so dark, so brooding, so badass, but beneath the mask, she saw glimpses of a compassionate, kind-hearted, passionate man.

And she yearned for him to bare his soul to her. She wanted him to unleash his burdens, to let her into the dark spaces of his heart and mind.

And that—those desires—frightened her.

Yet, he managed to make her smile. Managed to make her heart dance to the beat of something exciting. Made her think of possibilities that she'd never given thought to.

"Yo, you good?" Cruze asked in that deep, panty-wetting voice that made her shiver with want, snatching her from her thoughts as he reached over and gently squeezed her thigh.

Arabia looked over at him, every nerve ending in her body aflame with want. Her gaze caught the side of his thick neck. She swallowed. She wanted to lean over and suck on his Adam's apple. Instead, she nodded and said, "I'm more than good. I'm great."

Cruze's brown orbs darkened, and his lips shaped a coaxing smile. "Me, too, babe."

Babe.

He called her *babe*—the word sliding from his lips like warm honey, and Arabia felt her stomach heat.

It was a first—him calling her that. And she liked it. She liked it a lot. And his smile—God how she loved it when he smiled. It always felt sensual. Inviting. Even if it wasn't meant to be.

"You should do more of that," she said.

His brow raised, his eyes lighting with interest. "Do more of what?"

"Smile."

"Oh yeah?"

Arabia nodded. "Yeah."

"Why you say that?"

Arabia glanced at him and shrugged. "You always seem so deep in thought. I don't know. Distracted." She turned back to the road. "You have a beautiful smile, Cruze," she said huskily. "When you smile, you make me want to smile too."

His eyes went liquid again. And then his lips tipped upward, and those dimples flashed. "Maybe I have a reason, *now*, to smile more," he said earnestly, reaching over and running the back of his long, thick fingers down her cheek.

Arabia's skin heated and she blushed, glancing over at him again.

"I dig you," he said. "A lot."

"Me, too," she said, then smiled. God, why did this man make her spine tingle at the mere sight of him looking at her?

She turned back to the road, exhaling. He was more than she expected, more than she could have ever hoped he'd be. She wasn't sure where things were headed with them, but somehow she found herself dreaming of more, hoping for more.

Jason Derulo's "Kama Sutra" started playing and Arabia found herself bobbing her head to the beat with thoughts of tying Cruze up. The thought made her pussy heat.

She pressed a button on the stereo to lower the volume, then asked, "Would you let me tie you up?"

Cruze looked at her, barely managing to stifle the frown forming. "Tie me up, as in using a rope to tie me down?"

Her breath hitched at the imagery of him being stretched out naked, his arms and feet tethered to the bedposts. "Yes. Well, no. I'd use silk scarves."

He blinked. Then shook his head, but he was grinning. "*Helllll* no." He laughed. "Yo, you wilding. I ain't with that bondage shit."

"Well, would you let me blindfold you?"

What the fuck? She stayed trying to do the most. *Kinky-ass.* Cruze shook his head. "Nah. I'm good on that, too."

Arabia laughed. "What, you scared?"

"Never that, baby. But why you tryna tie a muhfucka up, anyway?"

Arabia looked over at him. "Maybe I want you naked and vulnerable."

Cruze shifted in his seat. "Yeah, a'ight. How 'bout I tie you up?"

Arabia moaned. "*Mmm.* Yes. Tie me up, daddy," she teased.

Cruze's dick thumped in his lap. He laughed, shaking his head. "Yo, you wild."

Again she looked at him, her eyes dark and hungry. "*You* make me wild, Cruze."

He swallowed, feeling his body heat from the inside out. He smiled again, his heart warming.

A few moments later, Cruze noticed they were on I-76 heading west. "Yo, hold up. Where we going?" he asked.

Arabia grinned. "It's a surprise."

Cruze shook his head. "Yeah, a'ight. Surprise me by telling me the *surprise*."

She laughed. "Then it wouldn't be a surprise, silly. Now sit back and relax."

Several moments later, she veered off on exit 342, then followed the signs toward her destination. When she'd called him to take him out, she'd decided she wanted to do something she hadn't done in years. Be silly, and have fun.

"I'm taking you to meet my relatives," she offered, holding back a snicker.

Eyebrow raised, Cruze eyed her suspiciously. "Your relatives? You have family out here?"

"Yes," she said, turning onto West Girard.

When Arabia finally turned into the entrance for the Philadelphia Zoo, Cruze gave her a confused look. "I thought you said we were meeting your peoples?"

"We are," she said calmly. "They're here on exhibit."

"On exhibit?" he questioned. "What, they performing *here* or something?"

"No, they're not performing." Arabia parked the car, then looked at him. "We're here to see my cousins. The spider monkeys."

Cruze burst out laughing.

Thirty-Three

Cruze was a habitual early riser, always waking up the same time every morning. 4:30 a.m. Most times, he'd awake earlier due to the nightmares that often plagued him, finding their way into the crevices of his mind, snatching him from any hopes of sleeping through the night. But last night, he'd slept peacefully, waking to the gentle caress of the sun streaming through his bedroom.

Instinctively, he reached for the space beside him, wanting to feel her heated skin beneath his fingertips. She'd stayed the night. A first. And he wanted to pull her into his body, and wrap her into his embrace.

But there was no Arabia.

He listened for any sound of movement—there was none. It was eerily silent. And empty. He frowned, coming more awake as he rose up on his elbow and stared at the indented pillow, then the empty spot where she'd lain beside him, her soft body curled into his side.

His chest tightened and he blinked, open to the possibility that she might have left. But...why would she?

Because...

He shook his head. Hadn't they fucked each other breathless through the night? Hadn't he given her a side of him he hadn't given any other female? Yeah, he did. So where the fuck had she gone? He didn't want to think the worst; still he cursed under his breath, feeling those old wounds of abandonment peeling open again. Maybe he shouldn't have asked her to stay the night, then he wouldn't be feeling like he'd just been punched in the gut.

He bit back another curse. He didn't want to admit that not waking up to her still in his bed had crushed him, making it almost impossible to breathe. He glanced around the room and clenched his fists. The fucking bitch didn't even have the decency to leave "a thanks for the good fuck" note.

Pissed, he yanked back the covers and threw his legs over the edge of the bed just as she came sauntering back in the room carrying a wooden tray with a bowl of fresh fruit and melted dark chocolate. Shit. Now he felt like a stupid-fuck for calling her out her name and for thinking the worst of her.

Damn. He was really bugging. Hard.

Still, he sighed inwardly, surprisingly relieved that she hadn't left. Him.

"Good morning," she greeted, a smile easing over her lush mouth.

"Mornin'," he said, leaning back on his elbow. "I thought you left," he admitted.

"Oh, no. You're not getting rid of me that easy," she said pointedly as she approached the bed. "You have me all to yourself, *allll* morning." She set the tray down on the bed, then tilted her head. "That's if you *want* me."

Hell yeah, he wanted her. His dark eyes swept over her body, from head to toe and back again, coming to rest on her swelling breasts, her thick nipples. Instantly, he felt himself becoming aroused. She was wet and ready, aching between her legs, her clit pulsing, and Cruze could sense her hunger for him as she could his for her. He was hard, now, at the sight of her, his dick bouncing up and down as his gaze caressed her body.

No woman had ever had this type of effect on him, his body. Not even Ramona. Shit. He had to stop this. Comparing *this*, to that—*her*.

She walked over toward his stereo, then turned on the CD player, her thick, juicy ass on display. Cruze eased back in bed, his stomach suddenly rumbling for more than mere food.

Seconds later, Jon Schuyler's "Space" started playing as she made her way back to the bed. "Hungry?" she asked huskily, innuendo thickly laced in her question.

She shot him a cheeky grin at her double entendre, and Cruze let out an audible sigh, the look in his eyes ravenous. "What you feeding me," he rasped, his heavy-lidded gaze heating over her skin.

"Something sweet," she answered back, her tone teasingly sensual.

She flicked her tongue at him, and Cruze groaned. Shit. She'd quickly become his dirty little plaything. His, and his alone, and that knowing sent him reeling over the edge. She hadn't even touched him yet, and he was ready to bust, pre-cum drizzling out of his dick.

Arabia licked her lips. Mmm, the sight of his beautiful erection made her want to flick her tongue over his dick and lick at his tip, then wetly slide her lips vigorously up and down his thick length. The walls of her cunt contracted with want, making her pussy surge with warm juices. Oh, God, yes. She wanted him bad.

Only him. And this, this was a startling revelation. She'd never wanted anyone as bad as she wanted him, now…and in the future, in *her* future. God. She never imagined ever thinking that, that she could see a future—a real one—with anyone.

Arabia looked at him—and it reminded her of how damn ruggedly beautiful he was, the sensation rippling through her soul, shocking her to her core.

Things between them were happening so fast that she hadn't

had a chance to fully comprehend, to completely absorb, the fact that she was becoming tangled up in him. And she hoped like hell she wasn't in this alone. The thought of giving herself wholly to a man—to *him*—frightened and, somehow, excited her.

She climbed up on the bed. Then instructed Cruze to rise to his knees. He gave her a questioning look, and she smiled lazily at him. "Trust me. Please."

He smirked. "Yeah, a'ight. Don't be trying to tie me up in here."

Arabia laughed, pulling him by the hand. "Dreams do come true, don't they?"

"Not today, they don't," Cruze shot back, a smile forming his lips. And with little prodding, he finally acquiesced. Then they were both on their knees in the center of the bed, facing each other— the breakfast tray and his protruding sex the only things between them.

She smiled, and then he smiled again.

"What you 'bout to do?" he asked huskily.

"Feed you," Arabia said seductively, just above a whisper.

Cruze flushed, then pulled in his bottom lip. "Oh, word?"

She nodded slowly as she dipped two fingers into the bowl of melted chocolate, swirling them until her digits were coated.

"And then what you gonna do?" Cruze probed, eyeing her. His stare piercing her so hotly that it set her cunt ablaze, made her clit ache.

"You'll have to wait and see," she said teasingly, trying desperately not to touch herself. "Just know. It might get messy."

"Maybe I want it messy," he teased back.

Heat flashed in her eyes as she coaxed him to open his mouth and pulled her hand from the bowl of warm chocolate, before sliding her silky soft fingers in. Cruze's mouth closed over her fingers, and he sucked; his tongue laving her sweet fingers, then sucking them again until her fingers were clean. Arabia's pussy clenched.

She moaned. "Mmm. You like that?"

Cruze licked his lips. "Yeah. I love that shit."

She scooped a finger back into the chocolate, then slowly swirled it over her right nipple. She scooped again, then coated her left nipple.

Cruze groaned, and Arabia smiled naughtily. "Eat me," she said, cupping her breasts as an offering.

"Damn," he muttered, his dick bobbing viciously, his balls tightening, swelling. He grabbed his dick, shook it, then stroked it. Arabia freed her breasts from her hands and reached beneath him and squeezed his balls.

"No. Let go. I'll take care of that."

"Fuck," he hissed. "When? I wanna fuck."

"Soon enough," she whispered. "Now eat."

He eyed her, smiling indulgently at her. Then lowered his head and flicked his tongue over her rigid chocolate-coated peak. Arabia let out a whimper, her head lolling back as he tongued her nipple until it became more rigid, more sensitive, aching and tight. Then he turned and gave the other nipple equal attention, his tongue swirling over the tip, then suckling it into his mouth.

Surprisingly, he took his time, his tongue moving unhurriedly over each nipple. Arabia let out what sounded like a purr, reaching for more melted chocolate, then grabbing his cock and coating its shaft until it was covered in chocolate, making his dick darker, sweeter, more mouthwatering.

Cruze moaned. "Yeah, baby. Stroke that dick." He caressed her breasts, then alternated between flicking his thumbs over each nipple or pinching them, intensifying her lust. And then he cupped her breasts and brought them together, moving his mouth back and forth from one nipple to the other until he sucked them clean.

He sucked them gently at first, and then harder with wet rhythmic pulls that made the room spin and had her seeing stars.

Arabia's nectar dripped from her slit and slowly slid down her inner thighs. She slid a peach slowly over Cruze's lips, then into his mouth. He grinned, his dick stretching as she stroked him, and the sweet fruit dissolved on his tongue, causing him to groan.

She leaned in and flicked her tongue over his lips, then sucked his bottom lip into her mouth, savoring the sweetness of his lips.

A fire blazed in his eyes, and Arabia knew she was bringing him a new kind of pleasure. One she hoped he'd never forget.

She plunked a strawberry into his mouth. Staring right into his eyes, she watched him chew, then swallow. And the heat in her gaze notched up, causing his body to light up. His desire for her was roiling out of control, like a wild brushfire.

Bryson Tiller's "Exchange" seeped through the speakers.

"Why you fucking with me?" Cruze murmured.

"What, what am I doing?" she asked coyly.

He cast his gaze down at the enormous, turgid erection in her hand slathered in chocolate, then looked back up at her, deeply in her eyes. "Yeah, a'ight. You know what you doing."

Her eyes flickered, and an unexpected heat singed his senses. He saw something in her eyes at that very moment—the way she looked at him, the way no other woman had ever looked at him. And it suddenly overwhelmed him. Cruze felt wanted. Arabia wanted him. And he *felt* it. Or had he imagined it.

Nah. He saw what he saw. He kept his gaze locked on hers. And there was that flicker again, of heat, of lust, of...*want*.

He swallowed. God, she was breaking him. Brick by brick, she was slowly uncovering a layer of him. And he didn't know what to make of it.

Arabia reached for another strawberry with her free hand and swirled it into the chocolate. She brought it to Cruze's lips, and he bit into it, its juices splashing out and trickling down his chin. She licked her lips, then leaned forward and licked his chin, then gently sucked it into her mouth, before licking down his neck, then over his shoulder, then trailing her tongue along the center of his chest. She pinched his nipples unexpectedly and he shuddered, emitting an animalistic growl that vibrated through his body.

"Shit, baby. *Fuck.*"

He wanted inside her. Now. So he reached for her pussy and cupped her there. His thumb sliding over her clit, before his fingers found her puffy cunt lips, slick and hot.

And there they were, heavy-lidded gazes locked on each other, stroking each other, teasing each other. Arabia moaned. He moaned.

He grunted. She grunted.

Arabia slowly twisted her hips and moved her pelvis, sucking a shuddering breath between her teeth. Cruze's finger slipped between her folds and she choked back a sob of pleasure, her sticky fingers cupping his balls, while her other hand rapidly stroked the length of him.

"Aaah, shit, yeah," he murmured. "You gonna make me nut."

"Mmm, yes," she breathed out. "Give it to me, daddy. Mmm. I want you to nut all over my hand." She reached for more chocolate and swirled her hand over and around the head of his dick. Cruze's body jerked. He thrust his hips, matching her strokes.

"C'mon, let me get some pussy."

"No," she whispered, her gaze burning into his. "Not yet."

Cruze hissed, cursed beneath his breath. He didn't know how much more of this sweet torture he could handle. She had his body overheating. He couldn't take it any longer. His face was etched in ecstasy, eyes closed, head thrown back.

"Oh, shit," he groaned. "I'm coming. I'm coming. Aaah, aah… aaaaaah! I'm getting ready to bust."

"Mmm. Yes, yes…give it to me. Give me that nut. Come for me. Mmm. Come for me…"

Another growl, and Cruze exploded, his body shaking as his climax ripped through him, his orgasm shooting out in thick white ropes of hot pleasure.

And then Arabia hunched over and sucked him into her mouth, her tongue swirling over the head of his sweet creamy dick, catching the remaining drips of his orgasm. He moaned as she pulled back, her wet mouth dragging over his shaft. She then licked her way back down his shaft, then back up his length, to the tip, where she used her tongue to swirl away the mixture of chocolate and nut. Her sultry lips slid up and down his shaft, up and down, making him wetter and wetter, sucking the remaining chocolate away until Cruze began to feel lightheaded.

She sucked him deeper into the recesses of her greedy mouth until her lips pressed into his groin; she swallowed him, then extended her tongue and lapped his balls as she hummed and gurgled. Oh, God—fuck yeah. She gurgled and hummed and sucked and licked until she coaxed another gut-wrenching nut out of him.

Then, satisfied, she eased back up on her knees and brought her nut-covered hand to her lips. Cruze eyed her lazily and spent as she slid her tongue over the back of her hand, then sucked her fingers into her mouth, tasting him, savoring him.

He could do nothing but flop back on the bed, pulling Arabia down with him. And they lay quiet and sticky and breathless in the aftershock of something Cruze had no words for.

"I want you to fuck me in my ass," Arabia said in Cruze's arms. Her voice came in a low, gentle rasp out of nowhere.

His chest tightened, and he fought to keep the frown from covering his face. He'd fucked lots of pussy. But ass? Nah. He'd never gone that route before, and he'd never thought about sliding his dick in any. He equated ass with shit. And shit on his dick wasn't a good look. So the idea of anal sex never appealed to him.

But now…

He rose up and looked down at her. "Yo, you see how big my dick is?"

Arabia looked up at him through her lashes, and smiled. "Uh, yeah. I see it. And?"

"And aren't you scared that shit's gonna hurt?"

"No." Arabia moaned and wrapped her arm over his chest. "It'll be a sweet burn. It'll hurt, but it'll be the kind of pain that brings me to pleasure. My ass is already clenching in anticipation."

Cruze laughed, shaking his head. "Yo, you a freak; you know that, right?"

She nodded, running a hand over his nipple. "Yeah. And now I'm your freak." Oops. She hadn't meant to say that. Had she? No, no. She really hadn't, even if she'd thought about it over the last few days. But there was no way to take it back. Still, she couldn't really be his. Could she? Oh, God, he and his dick had her so, so, damn confused. She had some loose ends in her life. There was Wellson. And lest she forget about that pesky-ass Eric still lurking in the shadows, trying to break her resolve to take him back.

She lightly pinched Cruze's nipple, and a quivery breath left him. "So what are you going to do about it?"

"I'ma handle it," he admitted, curiosity slowly spreading through him. If she wanted him to fuck her in her ass, then he'd have to man-up and fuck her shithole loose. "But, I'm sayin'…you gonna have to make sure that ass is cleaned out good if you want my dick in it."

Now it was Arabia's turn to laugh, and she looked up at him.

"Boy, stop. I stay clean. And I stay ready. And when you stay ready, you don't ever have to get ready. You just make sure *you're* ready when I put this ass up on you."

He arched his eyebrow at her and shook his head.

"Yeah, a'ight. We'll see."

Arabia ran her hand over his chest again, then kissed his shoulder. Her hand shamelessly glided down over the ripples of his abdomen, then brushed over the thick thatch of hair that framed the base of his dick, before settling over his shaft. Instantaneously, she felt him thicken beneath her touch.

Cruze closed his eyes for a moment. He'd come a long way from the last time she'd been in his bed, when he'd grabbed her wrist and told her he wasn't beat for broads touching him. But now he *liked* her touching him. *Wanted* her touching him.

He fucked. Hard. Making love wasn't his thing. So when had he become that dude who wanted, craved, to make love to a woman as badly as he wanted to make love to Arabia?

The shit was mind-boggling.

"Where did you learn to be so nasty?" Cruze asked.

A laugh burbled up from the back of her throat. "I'm not *that* nasty," she said, feigning insult. "I happen to be a woman who is very comfortable in her skin, in her sexuality. I love sex, and lots of it," she admitted. "And I take what I want. Is that a problem for you?" She slid her warm hand up and down over his abs and his chest. Her touch made him shiver, and his dick stretch.

He grunted in answer. Hell no. It wasn't a problem for him. He wanted sex with her—lots of it. And right now he wished she'd shut up this talking and take his dick. Take it and fuck it. Ride it. He wanted some pussy. More of it, to be exact, but for whatever reason, she was being stingy with it. What the fuck was up with that? He didn't want to be the one to take it—again, but fuck if he wouldn't—because he knew, at the end of the day, she wanted him to have it. Own it. Possess it.

"You ever been in a threesome?" he asked, unsure as to why he asked or if he really wanted to know the answer to that. But the question was asked, and now it hung in the air between them, dangling like a noose.

The Weeknd's "As You Are" began to play, and Arabia sighed. To tell, or not to tell…

She knew—and now he knew, she could be a wanton. Could be a sex-crazed slut. But she wasn't sure she wanted him to know her dirty secrets. Wasn't sure she wanted him to know her darker, dirtier self—the one who frequented sex clubs and fucked on the side of abandoned buildings.

No. He couldn't know. She didn't want him to know.

And, yet, she shifted her body, rolled on her side, then looked at him and admitted a part of her truth. "Yes," she whispered. And somehow, when she nodded her head, Cruze let out a breath—one he hadn't realized he was holding.

She propped up on one of his pillows and Cruze rolled toward her, too, as she continued, "I was fourteen."

Cruze's eyes went wide with surprise. Damn. She'd been giving out her pussy like that? His face was expressionless, but inside he was looking at her crazy. "Say what? You were fourteen?" *Fucking grown-ass lil' heifer.*

Arabia nodded again. "Yeah." She sighed, then closed her eyes and allowed herself to slip back in time. "My boyfriend at the time was nineteen. And—"

Cruze frowned. *"Nineteen?* Damn, he was old as hell."

Arabia agreed. "But I always liked older guys." She swiped a strand of hair from her face. "Anyway, Efrain and I were together for almost a year. And we'd been having sex for about three months, when one night I was at his house down in his basement. The lights were down low. He was between my legs, eating my pussy, fingering me, getting me ready for him…"

Cruze cringed inwardly. But said nothing.

Arabia pushed out a breath. "Then out of the corner of my eye, I saw movement. And when I looked over, it was one of Efrain's cousins and another guy coming toward us, their dicks out."

Cruze frowned. What the fuck?

Arabia pulled in her bottom lip, shaking her head. "They'd been in the room watching us."

"And you didn't know?"

She slowly shook her head. "No. They came from out of no-where. But later, I learned they'd been in the closet the whole time. But then, I didn't know. And when I asked Efrain why they were in there with us. He told me…"

"I wanna fuck you with my cousin and my boy," he murmured. "You gonna let us fuck you, baby?"

"No," she said, trying to get up. But Efrain held her down with his body weight, and crashed his mouth over hers, kissing her, tonguing her, his fingers in her pussy.

He nipped at her ear, then whispered, "Be daddy's slut for me. OK? Let me 'n' my boys get this good pussy."

Arabia tried to wriggle herself free, tried to push him off her. But then his cousin yanked her by the wrists and had her arms stretched out over her head, holding them there, his grip cutting into her flesh.

And then Efrain's friend leaned in and sucked on her nipple, while Efrain dipped his head back between her legs and sucked her clit into his mouth. Arabia wrenched and cried out in pain and unexplainable plea-sure. Frightened and disturbingly turned on, she stopped fighting and gave into the sensations, her legs spreading wider, her pussy growing wetter, welcoming.

"Yeah, that's it, baby. Take that big dick. You my freaky bitch…"

"And then they took turns fucking me," she whispered, looking directly into Cruze's eyes. Something stung her eyes. Tears. And she blinked them back. "They held me down and fucked me for what felt like hours. And—once they started, I didn't know how to stop them."

Cruze felt his nose flaring. His jaw twitched. "That's some fucked-up shit," he hissed. "Word is bond. If I ever ran up on them muh-fuckas, I'd…" He stopped himself, feeling his blood boil. He'd put a bullet in them fuck-boys. There was no way he could let that shit slide if he'd had known her back then. He despised pussy-ass niggas. He would have definitely dropped them.

"Yeah, it was," she said softly.

Cruze pulled her into his arms, and she nuzzled against him. He placed a kiss on her temple, surprising himself at this new show of affection.

"But what was even more fucked up," she said softly, swallowing back a knot of shameless heat. She took a deep breath and shook her head.

"What?" He had to know, needed to know. So he used one bent finger to lift her chin to make her look at him. "Tell me."

She took Cruze in; his brown eyes on hers. She bit her lip. She'd already told him more than he needed to know, but there was no stopping now.

"I liked it," she whispered.

Thirty-Four

Cruze had been thrown off completely by Arabia's confession. When she'd admitted that she enjoyed having a train pulled on her, his first reaction had been: *What kind of twisted shit is this?!* And he was about to kick her out of his bed, but after thinking about it, he had to admit that he was no angel, either. With the body count he had on his hands, who was he to judge her? Regardless of the fact that Arabia was a classy slut, he dug the shit out of her, anyway.

But those muhfuckas that had fucked her over... Mmph! They'd better hope Cruze never ran into any of their punk asses, 'cause they were guaranteed to get some hot lead straight to the dome if he ever did.

So far, Cruze had seen three sides of Arabia: classy slut, arrogant bitch, and playful woman-child. And keeping up with her different personas kept him on his toes.

Like tonight, for example. They were strolling along touristy South Street and approached an art gallery with a sign in the window, announcing that couples' painting would be held in a half hour. On a whim, Arabia wanted to try it and persuaded Cruze to join her.

He'd never heard of couples' painting, and not knowing what to expect, he made a quick dash into the Rite Aid and bought a pack of condoms. Knowing Arabia, there was probably something freaky involved.

In his mind, Cruze pictured him and Arabia in a private room inside the gallery. He envisioned himself holding a paintbrush and an artist's palette, and covering Arabia's beautiful, nude physique with body paint. He didn't have any artistic talent, but he was capable of drawing pictures of easy shit like the sun, a flower, or a heart. He'd decorate the shit out of her titties, her pussy, and her naked ass with his artistic creations.

Afterward, he'd fuck her good and hard, the way she liked it. But he wasn't too happy with the idea of accidentally getting paint on his clothes. Fuck it, though. For Arabia, he was willing to ruin his expensive ripped jeans and T-shirt.

It turned out Arabia didn't have anything kinky in mind. They shared a relaxing two hours together, painting and drinking vino. While Cruze was buying condoms, Arabia had gone to a liquor store and bought a bottle of red wine for the occasion.

Ever since Cruze had been old enough to drink, he'd been a cognac man, but Arabia enjoyed good wine and he'd shared the bottle with her. Along with six other couples, Cruze and Arabia were being instructed on how to work with acrylic paint on canvas.

Although Cruze's only artistic talent was in rolling breathtakingly beautiful blunts, after the two hours were over, he'd somehow completed a picture of a pair of lovebirds sitting together on the branch of a tree that had hearts and colorful circles for leaves.

Cruze's picture didn't look bad at all. But Arabia's finished canvas was amazing and looked like it had been created by a professional artist.

"You got skills, babe. Let me find out your artwork is hanging in galleries all over the world," Cruze teased as he and Arabia made their way down South Street with their canvases wrapped in plastic and tucked under their arms.

"Honestly, I've never painted anything before." Upbeat, Arabia gestured animatedly as she spoke, then she suddenly assumed a sour expression. "But I probably would have done a much better job if we hadn't gotten stuck with the instructor-bitch they assigned to us."

Cruze wrinkled his forehead. "Why she gotta be a bitch? I thought she did a good job, and she was extremely accommodating."

Arabia arched a brow. "Too accommodating, if you ask me. The way that big-titty ho kept flirting with you, it seemed to me she should be working for tips at Hooters instead of being an art instructor."

"I didn't peep anything. Trust, I know women, and I would have picked up on it if she was trying to hit on me. You got it wrong. She was only doing her job, and being helpful. Besides, I would have checked that bitch if I thought she was disrespecting my gir—" Cruze caught himself and rephrased his words. "I wouldn't sit there and allow any woman to disrespect you, Arabia."

"You couldn't see what she was doing because she was being sneaky about it, but I saw her."

Cruze came to a halt and clasped Arabia by the arm. "Now you got me curious. What exactly was she doing?"

Arabia's eyes wandered to Cruze's crotch and lingered there. "Exactly what I'm doing right now—scoping out your dick. Measuring it in her mind, salivating over it, and imagining herself sucking every drop of cum out of it."

Cruze was shocked. "Whaaaat?"

Arabia burst into sudden laughter. "I'm only kidding. But she was helping you a little too much for my taste."

"Man, you had me going. Why you bullshitting? I was about to turn around, go back to the spot, and go in on that bitch."

"What were you going to say?" Arabia asked, falling out laughing.

"I was gon' say, 'Yo, bitch, keep your eyeballs off my shit. My dick ain't up for public scrutiny. This is for my girl's eyes only.'" Cruze had slipped up, again and referred to Arabia as his girl, and this time it was too late to take back the words.

Laughing, Arabia didn't seem to notice. "Ooo, you're stupid, Cruze; I had no idea you were so silly."

It had been a long time since he'd genuinely laughed or had caused anyone else to laugh for that matter. And it felt good.

When Cruze and Arabia resumed walking, they both reached for the other's hand. An unconscious act, as natural as breathing. But after realizing they were holding hands, they both lapsed into an awkward silence, acutely aware that yet another shift had occurred in their relationship.

As they headed for Arabia's car that was parked in a lot a few blocks away, the pavements of South Street became more and more congested with hordes of people, many acting wild like college kids on spring break. Some were talking loud, singing, and drunkenly staggering around, while others argued and broke into fistfights. Yet with all the craziness transpiring on South Street, Cruze and Arabia felt like they were the only two people in the world.

"What's that smell?" Arabia inquired, sniffing the air.

"Onions. Jim's Steaks is at the end of the block," Cruze informed.

"I've heard so much about Philly cheesesteaks, but never had one. Have you?" Arabia asked, looking wide-eyed and adorable.

"Yeah, I've had my share. They're kind of greasy, though. Might be a lil' too messy for you."

"I don't care. I can get messy," Arabia said with a smirk.

"A'ight. Let's do it."

When they reached the restaurant, Cruze let go of Arabia's hand and opened the door. As she entered ahead of him, his palm went to the small of her back. He hadn't gone so far as to put his arm around her waist, but he was protectively touching her…keeping her close. All of his senses were on high alert. If any one of the South Street parade of fools even thought about bumping into her, stepping on her feet, or causing her any kind of harm, they'd have to get through him.

Seated at the table, Cruze took a couple of bites and pushed his plate away.

"You don't like it?" Arabia asked, chewing and talking at the same time.

Cruze couldn't help from smiling. He liked that she could get down and put her elbows on the table, plus, the way she was tearing into the cheesesteak was so cute. Even though he wasn't all that crazy about cheesesteaks, seeing Arabia so relaxed and carefree made him feel good. Shit, there was no point in bullshitting about it; whenever, he was in her company, he was happy as fuck.

Without realizing what he was doing, he picked up a napkin and wiped ketchup from the corner of her mouth.

Their eyes locked and Arabia gently grasped his wrist and brought his fingers to her lips, and kissed them.

It was a sweet and simple gesture, yet Cruze's heart sped up as if she were sucking his dick. "Arabia," he rasped in a deep voice.

"Yes?" She released his wrist and smiled at him, waiting for him to continue.

"I dig you." His voice came out tortured, like it was killing him to express any kind of emotion.

"You do?" Her smile widened. "Well, guess what? I dig you, too. A lot. And I'm gonna show you exactly how much when we get back to your place."

"Oh, word?" Cruze grinned back at her, but in the back of his mind, he was thinking that admitting that he dug her was only putting it mildly. His black ass had fucked around and fallen in love with Arabia. He was sure of it. But it was too soon to mention it. He couldn't risk scaring her off by confessing some corny shit like that.

The last time he'd given his heart too soon and too freely, it had been crushed and torn apart, changing him from a sweet, warm-hearted young man to the cold-blooded brother he later became.

Nah, he couldn't admit to Arabia what he was really feeling. He'd continue to let her set the pace, and simply go along for the ride. Whatever they were doing made them both happy. No need to fuck up what they had by placing labels on it.

Not yet, anyway.

Cruze cracked an eye open and looked over at Arabia's empty side of the bed. She'd kissed him goodbye about an hour ago, and he missed her already. Sitting on the side of the bed, he glimpsed a black silk scarf on the floor and shook his head. It was the scarf he'd allowed Arabia to bind his hands together with last night. Thank God, his leather headboard had prevented her from tying him to the bed. He wasn't ready for all that.

There had to be a certain amount of trust to allow someone to render you helpless, and for some reason, Cruze trusted Arabia completely. He smiled thinking back to their wild night. Getting his dick sucked and asshole licked while his hands were tied up was all kinds of freaky. Damn, Arabia was doing shit to him that had never been done. Tongue in the ass had a weird effect. Had him gritting his teeth and curling his toes. It took all his willpower not to whimper in pleasure like a lil' bitch.

But he was going to have a talk with Arabia about all this ass play. If he didn't lay down some ground rules, she was liable to show up with a strap-on, and try to make him her bitch. He laughed to himself and then immediately frowned when his phone rang and Ramona's name appeared on the screen.

She'd been calling nonstop for over a week now, and he couldn't avoid her any longer. It was time to deal with Ramona's ass, but he had to smoke a blunt, first.

He hit the ignore button, and then cut open a Dutch. As he emptied the cigar, his mind went back to the time period from age eighteen to twenty-one when Ramona had possessed his mind, body, and soul. He'd been young and dumb back when he'd allowed Ramona to make him her side dude while she was with Moody.

Through Ramona's influence, Cruze had moved up the ranks in the organization, and he soon became Moody's right-hand man. He was also one of the groomsmen at Ramona's and Moody's lavish wedding and became godfather of their firstborn child—Chancellor—the son he hadn't known he'd fathered.

It wasn't until after his twenty-first birthday that Cruze's feelings for Ramona finally changed. He was no longer a lovestruck teenager, and was able to look at her through the eyes of a grown man. And what he saw was a selfish and manipulative bitch that had preyed on his innocence and stolen his youth. He wanted to hate her, but for some unknown reason, he couldn't. He felt bound to Ramona as if she were blood.

No matter what, he always had her back. Comforting her over the years when Moody started treating her like shit, and not only started fucking a slew of other bitches, but also developed a penchant for bringing them to the house and fucking them while Ramona was in another part of their palatial home.

Cruze was the one who had accompanied Ramona and the kids to Disney World and other vacations while Moody was back in New York laid up with several of his bitches. Unbeknownst to Moody, Ramona had given Cruze his own set of keys to their crib, in case of emergency. There was nothing Cruze wouldn't do for Ramona, except give up the dick. That's where he drew the line, and up until the night of the shooting, Ramona had been desperately trying to find a way to get back into Cruze's heart—and back in his drawers.

But she sealed her fate at the kids' funeral when she confessed that Cruze had fathered Chancellor. All the love he'd ever felt turned to pure hatred. Then disgust. And finally, he was left with no emotions for her except pity.

Cruze dreaded making the call to Ramona, but it had to be done. Procrastinating, he went to the bathroom and peed, and before dialing her number, he took a swig of Henny straight from the bottle.

Ramona picked up on the first ring. "Why'd it take you so long to return my calls?"

"Been busy," Cruze responded dismissively, blowing out weed smoke.

"I guess you heard about Big Crockett."

"Yeah, I heard," he said dispassionately.

"Well, aren't you excited? You can come back to New York, now."

"Nah, I'm good where I'm at."

"But I need you here. Things are really getting bad with Moody. He's much worse since you came over, and the doctor is pushing me to put him in a nursing home. I can't make that kind of decision by myself, Cruze. That's the kind of thing we need to discuss together."

"You're a big girl, Mo. Handle your shit," he said coolly.

Hearing the coldness in his tone, Ramona was briefly quiet. Then she took an audible breath. "Are you gonna hold Chancellor against me for the rest of my life?"

"Yeah, I am. I despise you for what you did."

"I lost both my children; how do you think I feel?"

"Look, you know as well as I do that Moody brought all this shit down on himself, and it kills me that *my* son...and Niyah, too, had to pay for his mistakes." Cruze went silent, thinking about Chancellor—seeing the bullet hole in his forehead. Once again, all the breath left his body. "It's time for us to cut ties, Ramona," he muttered in a broken voice

"What?" Ramona said anxiously.

"You heard me," he said calmly, and then pulled on the blunt, holding the bitter smoke in his lungs.

"You can't be serious."

He blew smoke out through the side of his mouth. "I'm dead serious. Moody's health issues ain't none of my business, yo. I been carrying y'all niggas for long enough, and I don't want you calling me anymore about nothing. In fact, delete my number, 'cause I'm blocking yours."

Ramona gasped. "Cruze! This is not the time for you to be acting like this."

"You're right, I should have cut ties with you years ago."

"How you gon' turn your back on me, you ungrateful bastard?" Ramona exploded. "I made you! You wasn't shit before me! And you wouldn't know shit about the game and wouldn't have a dollar to your name if it wasn't for me."

"Man, whatever." Cruze's voice rose in anger. "You chose that muh-fucka over me, and now you stuck with him and all his problems. All I can say is make the best of it. I'm hanging up, now. Have a good life. Peace out!"

Ramona shouted something indistinct, but Cruze disconnected in the midst of her tirade.

And then he blocked her number. For the first time in his entire adult life, he truly felt free.

Thirty-Five

At fifteen minutes past seven, Arabia glanced at her watch, the heels of her Manolo Blahniks clicking impatiently against the gleaming marble floor as she paced the lobby of the Trump International Hotel and Tower in Midtown Manhattan. He was late. Fifteen minutes, to be exact. He was never late. And Arabia's first thought was, *he isn't going to show.*

She let out an irritated breath. She'd spoken to him two days ago to set up their dinner date—although her seeing him tonight was the furthest thing from a *date*. Still, he'd texted her late last night to confirm the time and the place. And they'd agreed on meeting at seven p.m. here, then have dinner and drinks at Jean-Georges, which was located inside the five-star hotel.

So why wasn't he already here?

She checked her phone for any missed calls or text messages. There were none. She frowned, smoothing a manicured hand up over the side of her sleek chignon.

She captured the attention of several patrons and hotel guests, as well as a few staffers, all mesmerized by her stunning looks. However, not one of them caught her eye, or piqued her interest. So she kept her eye trained on the front entrance of the hotel and ignored their glances.

She was about to call him when she spotted him coming through the door. When his gaze lighted on her, he smiled walking toward her. She smiled back. He was as handsome as ever in his navy blue custom-fit Brooks Brothers suit and Salvatore Ferragamo loafers.

"Hey, baby," he greeted smoothly as he wrapped her in his arms and leaned in for a kiss, his lips catching the corner of her mouth as she turned her head. "Sorry I'm late. Got stuck in traffic."

She cocked her head to the side. "I didn't think you were going to show."

"What, and stand up a beautiful woman? Never, baby."

Arabia smiled. "Well, I hadn't heard from you so I didn't know what to think. A text would have been nice," she said pointedly.

"You're right," he said sheepishly. "I apologize."

"Well, apology accepted. Now shall we eat? I'm famished."

"Ah, I like the sound of that." He took her arm, tucking it over his as he guided her toward the restaurant.

The moment they arrived at the restaurant, the maître d' immediately ushered them to the table she'd reserved for them. She loved dining here with its luxurious white leather seating and pristine table settings. It was sophisticated. And the stunning floor-to-ceiling windows offered magnificent views of the city.

He sat across from Arabia, taking her in as if he were trying to commit every detail of her to his memory, right down to the tiny beauty mole slightly above the right side of her lip. God—oh how he loved kissing those beautiful lips.

"It's good to see you, Wellson," she said as she reached across the table and touched his hand. She was going to miss him. But there was no time for sentiments. Their relationship had run its course, and she needed to end it. Let him go. And move on.

Wellson's gaze slid down to the hint of cleavage peeking out through the slits of her blouse. She smiled inwardly. She hadn't wanted to be over-the-top sexy, so she'd settled on wearing a sleeveless, pleated cocktail dress with a high-low hem which had a relaxed silhouette that showcased a modest amount of cleavage. She paired the dress with a pair of strappy six-inch heels, and allowed her bare silky legs do all the talking. Although it was over, she still wanted his last image of her to be "Damn, she's sexy as hell. I'm going to miss all that good loving."

She regretted the fact that she hadn't handled breaking things off with Eric in the most pragmatic way, but this time, she planned on doing things differently. Amicably.

She didn't want to hurt him, but it had to be done.

She didn't know what had gotten into her lately. But she wanted to cut all ties with her married lovers. No. Wait. She did know. *Cruze* had gotten to her, in her…and all over her. He was the root of her change. He hadn't changed her, per se. But he'd given her reason to *want* change.

Wellson laced his fingers with hers. "Good to see you, too. I've missed you."

His gaze skittered to her ring finger. It was bare. She hadn't worn his engagement ring. And he wondered why.

Arabia smiled.

"What would you like to drink tonight?" he asked when a waiter quickly appeared. "Wine? Or—?"

She shook her head. "No, water is fine for now. I'll have wine with dinner."

"Okay then. Make that two bottles of Fiji water," he murmured to the waiter. "And we'll have the wine pairing with our dinner."

The waiter took their orders and then quickly disappeared.

"So… I'm glad you wanted to see me," Wellson said. "Because I've wanted to see you, too."

Arabia swallowed back a sliver of what felt like…guilt.

"I have something I want to share with you," he continued. "Something that I didn't want to tell you over the phone. The last three years being with you have been incredible, baby. You've given me some of the—"

Oh God, oh God…she had to stop him.

"Wellson, wait," she interrupted. "I have something I want—"

He put a hand up, stopping her. "Let me finish, baby."

She cast her gaze downward, then slowly nodded, looking up at him through her lashes. She braced herself with a slow breath.

"As I was saying, you've given me some of the best years of my life, Arabia. And I don't know what I would have done had you not come into my life when you had…"

Arabia's pulse raced. She felt herself on the verge of throwing up the remaining contents of her shrimp salad from lunch. "Wellson…"

"Please, baby. Let me finish. Holding this in has been killing me."

She blinked. An eyebrow rose in question. "What's been killing you, Wellson?"

"Well…" This time he reached across the table and slid his hand over hers. "There's simply no other way to say this except to just say it. I've met someone else."

Arabia blinked. Wait, had she heard him right? He'd met someone else? As in someone else he was *fucking?* Or someone he…

She carefully drew back her hand. This was not what she'd expected to hear come out of his mouth. "You've met someone," she repeated, more as a statement than a question.

He flashed her a wry grin. "Yeah. Surprise, huh?"

Arabia shrank back in her seat. "When?" she asked, feeling surprisingly crushed by the news. He slashed her, deflating her ego as the waiter returned bearing their entrees. Wellson didn't answer her question until the plates had been served and the waiter retreated.

Then he cleared his voice. "I met her on one of my flights here to see you," he explained. "We talked most of the flight, then exchanged numbers once we landed."

"Oh," was the only thing she could manage to say. Suddenly her mouth had gone incredibly dry and she'd lost her appetite. She reached for her water, and took two long swallows. This was *not* how she pictured her night going.

"Tiffany's…"

She made a face. "Who?"

Wellson smiled. "Tiffany. The young woman I met. She's a flight attendant."

Arabia tilted her head, and stared at him. "And how long have you and this Tiffany been an item?"

He loosened his paisley tie. "Not long—about a month now. I didn't want to mention anything until I was sure where things were going."

She fixed him with a hard stare. "And now you're *sure?*" *Because bastard, once you leave, there's no coming back to this good pussy.*

He nodded. "As sure as I'll ever be. Tiffany and…" He paused, gauging Arabia's reaction. There was none. On the outside, she was as calm as could be, but her insides were churning. She wanted to toss her water in his face. Sling her plate of black sea bass crusted with seeds and nuts at him. "We're in love."

"In a matter of a *month?*" she asked incredulously. "Do you even know her?"

"I know all I need to know for now," he said, the beginnings of a smile glinting in his eyes. "Don't you believe in love at first sight?"

She cringed inwardly. Sadly, she'd never been in love to know whether or not it bloomed at first glance, or after the first night of good fucking. So she didn't believe in any of that happy-ever-after fairytale shit.

"I didn't want to hurt you," he gently said. "You're an amazingly incredible woman, Arabia. Passionate. Beautiful. Smart. Sensual. Any man would be honored to have you in his life." *And his bed,* she thought. *Don't forget that part.*

She blinked. Oh, the irony of it all. *He* was leaving *her* for some young flight attendant bitch. The gall of him! He could have told her this shit over the phone, instead of having her traipse over here in all of her finery.

Oh, what a damn hypocrite she was. She'd planned on doing the same thing to him. But he'd beaten her to it. And now she felt…oh, hell—she didn't know what to feel about this. Her cheating married lover had fallen for a younger woman. Probably some bitch with Daddy issues.

Arabia smiled at him. "I'm happy for you, Wellson. Really. I wish you and…"

"Tiffany," he offered.

"Yes. I wish you and Tiffany all the best."

"As I do you," he assured her, his tone filled with a sincerity that matched his gaze. "One day, Mr. Right will find his way to you, baby."

Arabia nodded. "I'm sure he will." She decided not to mention her own intentions for asking him out. What would be the point? He'd already made his.

But then another part of her wanted him to know.

So she told him, "I wanted to tell you, that I met someone too."

Wellson's brow shut up, surprise registering over his face. "Oh?"

"Yes. I met him by chance at a meeting in Philadelphia." *But I'd fucked him at a nightclub.*

"Oh. I see. Is he married?" *Like he of all people should be asking me some shit like that. Mmph.*

Arabia shook her head. "No, he isn't." She reached into her handbag and pulled out a small box. Placing it on the table between them, she slid it over to him. "I guess I won't be needing this anymore."

Oh, how her heart ached returning the expensive bauble to him.

He frowned. "What's this?"

She swallowed. Her throat slowly tightened. "Your ring."

He pushed it back to her. "I don't want it. It's yours."

Though she didn't want to show it, relief danced in the pupils of her eyes. She loved her ring. "I can't," she said, pushing the box back in his direction. "It wouldn't feel right."

He shook his head, his hand over her hand again. "Consider it a gift for the three years of good loving you've given me."

He managed to wring a laugh out of her. "*Good?* Is that what you're calling it?"

He chuckled. "Okay, okay. Stupendous. How's that?"

"Better," she said, a genuine smile curving her lips as she quickly curled her fingers over the box and slid it back toward her. She tossed the box back inside her handbag before he changed his mind.

And he threw his head back and laughed. "Arabia, baby. You're something else. I'll never forget the time we spent together."

"Neither will I," she admitted. And she meant it. There were truly no regrets. And, in a strange sort of way, she was relieved that he'd been the one to break things off.

"Good. Now can we eat?"

"Yes, by all means. I thought you'd—"

"So this is who you've been fucking now," interrupted a gruff voice.

Arabia whipped her head around. When her eyes landed on who stood at her table, shock and dread churned through her veins, her face a wreath of horror.

Oh God. No. This couldn't be happening. This wasn't happening. Not here. Not now. No, no, no. She had to be imagining his presence. But the murderous expression on his face confirmed her greatest fear.

"E-eric," Arabia croaked. She suddenly felt lightheaded. "What are *you* doing here?"

"I should be asking your whoring-ass the same thing," he snarled. "But the answer is already sitting across from you."

Wellson scowled, the muscles in his jaw twitching. "I'm going to need you to watch how you speak to her," he warned. "Is there a problem here?"

Eric held up his hands in mock surrender. "No, my brother. No problem here. But she is one sweet piece of ass, isn't she? How many times has she had them soft lips wrapped around your dick?"

Oh God, no!

Wellson leapt up from his seat. "If you say another disrespectful thing out of your mouth about her, I'll kick your ass."

Arabia's heart sank, embarrassment and shock flashing over her face. Her heart was pounding so fast and hard she thought she'd drop dead in any second. He was causing a scene. And Wellson was now caught up in the middle of it.

She swallowed hard. "Wellson, no, please." She stood. "I'll handle it."

His nostrils flared as he kept his stare locked on Eric.

Eric gave him a sardonic look. "You heard her. She'll take care of it. Like the way she used to take care of this dick; isn't that right, Arabia?"

And before she knew it, she whirled around and slapped his face, drawing more attention to her table. He didn't flinch.

"How dare you, disrespect me," she hissed, her fingers curling into claws, slashing her nails across his face. "I told you it was over, Eric. And now you've taken to *stalking* me. How much more pathetic can you be? Go back to your crippled-ass wife. And leave me the hell—"

She saw his fist coming at her. But before he could punch her face in, Wellson lashed out and blocked his fist, punching Eric on the side of his head, causing him to wobble before he hit the floor.

The whole place froze as staff and patrons took in the spectacle that she'd become.

Arabia shrieked as Eric dragged down with him the edge of the tablecloth, bringing dishes and glassware crashing to the floor around him.

"I told you to watch how you spoke to her," Wellson snarled, opening and closing the fist he'd used to knock Eric out as he looked down and stood over his limp body.

Then he turned his attention to Arabia, his eyes narrowing on her face. "Now do you mind telling me, what the *hell* that was all about?"

And suddenly her evening turned into a night of pure hell.

Thirty-Six

Cruze had been hesitant about venturing into the city. Even though Crockett's crew was probably too busy scrambling and reorganizing to be worried about him, one could never be too cautious. But since Crockett's henchmen rarely went outside of Brooklyn, Cruze accepted Arabia's invitation to dinner at a three-Michelin-star restaurant that had a two-year waiting list. The chef had announced on his Twitter account that there was an unexpected cancellation at five o'clock and Arabia snagged it. She was so proud of her accomplishment, Cruze couldn't turn her down.

The place was fancy, and the food looked like art. Really small portions, though. And it definitely didn't seem worth the five hundred bucks Arabia had forked over. But not wanting to burst her bubble, he kept his opinion to himself, thanked her, and told her that dinner was awesome.

The drive back to Arabia's place was very pleasant. Coming off the George Washington Bridge and onto the West Side Highway, with the river on the right, and the Fairway sign zipping past on the left, the whole city seemed to open up to Cruze and Arabia. Seeing New York from this perspective made Cruze realize how much he missed his hometown.

He looked over at Arabia and she looked good as fuck behind the wheel of her Aston Martin. But she was driving like Miss Daisy, though.

Cruze leaned forward and checked the speedometer. "You're only doing fifty, bae. A car like this wasn't built to creep; it was meant to go fast."

She poked out her lips. "I'm driving within the speed limit."

"Yeah, but the thrill of driving a fast, luxury whip like this is to see how quick it'll go from zero to sixty. If you're worried about the cops, we could take it to Lafayette Street, north of Houston and go for it. Actually, if you catch a string of green lights on Lexington or Madison Avenue, you could push it up to eighty without worrying about traffic," Cruze gushed excitedly.

"No, I'm good. This car is just for show; I don't need to find out how fast it'll go," Arabia said, slowing down a little as she took a curve.

Cruze's face creased into a frown. "You don't have to slow down. The Aston Martin has hard suspension—it's good for holding curves at high speed. You babying this car too much."

"Are you trying to get us killed? I'm not taking any curves at high speed. And damn right I'm babying my beautiful car."

"Mmph, I thought you were a dare devil," Cruze teased.

Arabia glanced at him and then quickly refocused her gaze on the road ahead. "And you know I am…when it comes to indulging my sensuality. But I'm not an adrenaline junkie who needs to jump out of planes or race cars to get a rush. Doing that kind of scary stuff isn't fun to me."

"That's right; I forgot…you're scared to ride on the roller coaster." Cruze laughed. "But you're gonna get over that fear when we go to Great Adventure next week."

She scrunched her brows together. "No, I'm not. No roller coasters for me. I'm serious, Cruze. I can do a Ferris wheel and the carousel, but that's about it."

Cruze laughed and shook his head. "I'm not trying to hear that.

You been picking out all the shit we do, and I've been going along with everything. Now, it's my turn and you gon' get on a roller coaster with your man. You dig, ma-ma?"

"Nooo, I do not dig," she said, mimicking his jargon and laughing.

He glanced at the speedometer, again. "Yo, Arabia, you gotta pick it up a little bit. I wanna hear how the motor sounds when you hit a hunnit."

"Are you nuts? I'm not hitting a hundred." A sudden look of enlightenment came over Arabia's face. "I think you've been hinting that you wanna get behind the wheel. You wanna drive my car, Cruze?"

Cruze's lips curved up into a big smile. "I thought you'd never ask. Pull over on the shoulder."

"No, that's dangerous. Wait until we get off the highway, okay?"

"Yeah, whatever makes you comfortable, baby." Grinning and rubbing his hands together gleefully, he leaned back in his seat.

Out of nowhere, a dark car with tinted windows swerved from the lane on the right, nearly colliding into the Aston Martin.

Cruze bolted upright as the car weaved back into its lane.

"Ohmygod, what the fuck—is that driver drunk or something?!" Arabia shouted.

Cruze glared out the window at the reckless driver. "I don't know what his problem is, but let's get away from this fool. Get all the way over to the far left."

"Okay," Arabia said, her voice trembling from nervousness. Slowly and carefully, she merged into the left lane. "What's that car doing, now?" she asked, gripping the steering wheel, her eyes darting from the side mirrors to the rearview mirror.

Peering out of the passenger's window, Cruze shook his head. "I don't know where that muhfucka went; I don't even see the car now."

"Good. As long as his drunk ass is nowhere near us, I'm good."

Visibly relaxing, Arabia loosened her grip on the steering wheel. "And where the hell are the damn police when you need them?"

"I know, right? That muhfucka skidded out of his lane and damn near sideswiped us."

"Oh, God, perish the thought! I would have died if that car would have scraped the paint off my pretty baby." She patted the steering wheel as if comforting her car, then lovingly ran her hand over the gleaming dashboard.

Cruze chuckled at Arabia and in the next instant, a bullet pierced the back window and lodged into the hood of the car. Arabia let out a shriek.

"Oh shit! Them muhfuckas shooting! Duck, bae," Cruze implored her.

"How the hell can I duck and drive at the same time?!" she screamed frantically. "Why are they shooting at us? What the hell's going on, Cruze?"

"Step on it, Arabia. You gotta drive this thing. No time for bull-shitting now," Cruze bellowed, reaching under his seat and pulling out a gun.

Shocked by what she saw, Arabia gawked at the gun in Cruze's hand. "Ohmygod! You have a gun? Have you lost your mind!" she shrieked incredulously. "What the hell is going on here? Why the hell is there a gun in my car, huh, Cruze? Ohmygod!"

"Baby, now is not the time for a buncha damn questions," he snapped irritated. He couldn't believe these crazy muhfuckas were trying to get at him in broad daylight. But fuck that. It was either kill or be killed. And he'd be goddamned if he was going for the latter. *These niggas gotta get got!* He shot a look over at Arabia. "I need you to drive this muhfucka, baby! I promise I'll explain every-thing later. Right now. DRIVE!"

The black car pulled up beside them again, and this time the driver lowered his window, revealing himself; another man was up front, and two in the back. Cruze recognized all four of them. They were Crockett's men.

"DRIVE!" Cruze yelled again, sliding down his window, pointing his weapon, and firing rapidly. "Press down on the muthafuckin' pedal, Arabia, and gas these niggas!"

"I c-c-can't," she stammered, her teeth chattering from fear.

"You can. You can do this, baby," Cruze urged forcibly as the driver in the dark sedan pulled back from his direct firing range. Then they quickly proceeded to return fire, riddling the back of the Aston Martin with bullets.

Arabia screamed. And then she felt it—something warm puddling inside her lacy La Perlas. Dear God—*no*. She pissed herself. No, no, no. This wasn't happening to her. This had to be some horrible nightmare she'd soon wake up from.

Pop! Pop! Pop!

More shots rang out. Hysterically, Arabia sideswiped another car, then repeatedly lost and regained control of her vehicle while screaming at the top of her lungs. "Cruze! Cruze! Crrrrrrru-uuuuuze!!!! WHAT THE FUCK IS HAPPENING?! OHMY-FUCKING GOD!" She was zigzagging all over the road and running into the metal pavement dividers. "I'm gonna die! Ohmygod, I don't wanna die! Please, God!"

Other motorists were slamming on their brakes, screeching tires, and honking their horns, as they tried to get out of harm's way by pulling onto the shoulder of the highway, all at the same time.

Cruze couldn't think straight with all of Arabia's histrionics. He knew she wasn't built for this life. But shit. He needed her to get focused and drive. "Arabia, I need you to shut the fuck up, baby!" he yelled over his shoulder, still firing his weapon at the wannabe henchmen. "And hit the fuckin' gas!" He hadn't meant to snap on her, but he'd smooth things over with her once they got to safety. But right now, he needed her to focus. And get them the hell to safety.

Pop! Pop! Pop!

Arabia screamed again, glass shattering in back of her, shards flying over her head. Her foot accidentally going down on the pedal caused her Aston Martin's twelve-cylinder engine to kick into high speed in a matter of seconds, unexpectedly surprising and shocking her.

Her vision blurred from tears, a burst of adrenaline surged through her veins causing her body to overheat. And before she knew what was happening, she gripped the steering wheel and accelerated.

Now unencumbered, Cruze was able to retaliate with gusto. No longer content to engage in the shootout by merely extending his arm, he lifted off the seat and stuck his entire torso out the window.

Arabia swerved, causing his body to swing, and he cursed, "Fuck!" Aiming his weapon at the assailants, he pulled the trigger, blasting out the sedan's windshield. Arabia swerved again and his body almost went out the window. "Hold the wheel steady," he yelled at her, then continued firing until the car behind him went into a tailspin and flipped over, then suddenly went up in flames.

"I got all them muhfuckas!" He flopped back into his seat, then gazed at Arabia with concern. "You a'ight?"

"Am I *all right?*" she asked incredulously. "Do I look fucking *all right* to you, huh, Cruze? Do I? I've just been fucking shot at! My so-called man had a fucking gun under his seat in my car! And you're asking me if I'm all right? Are you fucking *kidding* me? No. I'm not all right! I'll *never* be all right, ever again," she sobbed, her bottom lip trembling. Everything in her body shook.

"I'ma make it up to you, baby," Cruze promised, reaching over and placing a reassuring hand on her knee. "Pull over anywhere, so I can drive."

Arabia swung her vehicle off the next exit and ran up on a curb, her brakes screeching to a violent halt. Shaking and crying, she swung open her door, and jumped out. She gasped and heaved, noticing how her once beautiful car was now perforated with bullet holes and marred with scraped-off paint.

She leaned over and vomited, her stomach churning in knots. The sounds of police sirens and fire trucks could be heard in the near distance. And the only thing Arabia could think was, *I'm going to jail. I'm going to have to wear one of those God-awful jumpers. And some crazy butch bitch is going to try to fuck me with a plunger.*

She wailed. The sight of her exotic car all mangled made her knees buckle. The front bumper hung to the ground. The driver's side headlight was smashed out. The side-view mirror hung off the door. The passenger door was dented in so badly, Cruze could barely open it, and the back window was completely shattered. Arabia let out a piercing noise that sounded like a wounded animal howling.

The smell of burning rubber assaulted her nostrils and when she looked down at the tires, heavy smoke wafted from one of the rear tires that apparently had been shot out. Arabia had unknowingly been driving on a dinged-up rim.

Arabia cried out, her heart aching for her coveted vehicle. "Ohmygod! My car! My fucking car! You son of a bitch! It... it's deeeeeesttttttroyed!" She couldn't catch her breath; her lungs seemed to constrict as she fought for air.

Cruze winced as he pulled Arabia into his arms and held her tight, his heart still racing from his own adrenaline rush. He gently caressed her head, trying to calm her, his hand stroking over shards of glass that somehow tangled in her hair.

"Baby, we gotta get out of here," he said softly, feeling even worse about dragging her into his violent lifestyle. "The police are probably all over the place."

Seemingly stunned by shock, it was at that moment Arabia went eerily silent.

Cruze didn't know what he would have done if anything had happened to her...if he'd lost her to gunfire. He reached for his cell, pushed in a number, then spoke into the receiver. "I need a cleanup."

"Cool," the voice on the other end said. "Where?"

Cruze gave the location of Arabia's mangled car, then disconnected the call.

"I swear on my last breath, baby, I'ma fix this shit," he said, feeling her trembling in his arms. "Let me get you home."

He held her close and tight and one by one, tears escaped her eyes. Everything else became a haze.

"Arabia, baby..."

She heard his voice. Calling her. But he sounded far off. Sounded like he was calling her from another part of the world. Because the world she was in, was on fire, pierced with bullets. Gunfire rang out in her ears. She was moving through rooms of her loft aimlessly.

Dazed.

"Baby, I gotta get you outta these clothes..."

They were shooting at him, at me. *He was shooting back...*

Pop, pop, pop!

"Arabia, please, baby...can you hear me...?"

I was in a shootout...

She wasn't dead. She hadn't been shot. But her whole body burned. She couldn't wrap her mind around what she'd witnessed. Out of nowhere. Bullets flying. Glass shattering. Her life flashing before her eyes. Her head was spinning. How did this happen? *Why* did it happen? What kind of monster had she gotten herself involved with?

"Baby, please…say something…"

Cruze's voice faded in and out.

She smelled fire. A car. *Their* car.

Something was burning. Tires. *Her* tires.

Oh, God—*her* car. Gone.

She heard the screaming in her head.

More gunfire. *Pop, pop, pop…*

"Arabia, baby…c'mon, let me help you out of these…"

Unease crawled over Cruze's skin and coiled around his neck in what felt like a chokehold as he called Arabia's name. She had a blank look on her face, and her eyes were vacant. She was unresponsive. If only he would have kept his ass in Philly, none of this shit would have happened. It was all so goddamn fucked up now. And he hadn't wanted Arabia to know, see, this side of who he was trying to get away from. He tried to bury that part of him along with his demons, but he just couldn't catch a break. In the end, something or someone was always trying to pull him right back into that same dark place he'd fought so hard getting out of.

He had no one to blame for the fucked-up predicament he was now in, except himself. He was kicking himself for getting all wrapped up in Arabia, and letting his guard down. Now look what happened. He could have been killed, or worse…*her*.

"Arabia…"

Some of the numbness had worn off, but she was still in shock.

"Arabia, c'mon…you're scaring me, baby. Talk to me…"

She blinked. Confusion clouded her beautiful brown eyes as Cruze came into view. She blinked again.

Cruze's hand stroked her chin. "Baby, you had me worried for a minute…"

She stared. Then tears welled and a sob crept out of her throat.

Cruze tried to comfort her, but she pushed his arm away. Her nostrils flared and her eyes blazed. Then came the rage, like a wild-fire, its heat and flames engulfing Cruze, catching him completely off guard as she leapt up and attacked him; her fists swinging wildly as she punched and clawed at him.

"You motherfucker! You almost had me killed! You no-good piece of shit! You low-life thug! I should have never *fucked* you! I wish I had never met you!"

Cruze blinked. *Oh shit.* Her words pierced through him. "C'mon, baby. You don't mean any of that."

"Yes, the fuck I do!" she snarled as she launched herself at Cruze, her long nails aimed directly at his face. "I hate you for what you put me through!"

Cruze wasn't in the habit of putting his hands on females, but he couldn't let her fuck him up, either, so he curled his arm around her waist and tried to restrain her. But she let out a shriek of outrage and began kicking and thrashing like a wild woman.

"Get your fucking hands off me!" she demanded. And when he wouldn't let go, she bit his arm hard, her teeth sinking deep into his skin.

"Ow, *fuck*," he yelped, letting her go. He put his hands up in surrender. "Calm down, baby. Let me explain…"

"Let you *explain?*" she scoffed, her chest heaving in and out. The metallic taste of blood was now on her tongue, his blood. She'd broken the skin on his arm. "Calm down hell! You can't explain shit to me! Don't ever want to see your murderous face again! You murderer!"

He cringed. "C'mon, baby. You don't mean that."

"Don't call me that, you killer!" she yelled. "I'm not your baby. I'm not anything to your hoodlum-ass! Now get the fuck out of my home! Now!"

He blinked, stunned by her venomous words. He'd never seen this vicious side of her, and he didn't like it. He'd rather had taken two bullets to the chest than to endure her fury. And, still, he tried desperately to talk, to reason, to hold out from tossing in the towel.

But Arabia had become blinded by shock and rage. She cursed and screamed until her throat ached. "Fuck you, Cruze!" she spat. "I hate you!"

In her wild fit, she reached for a crystal ashtray, and slung it at him. He ducked out of the way, the sharp object missing him by mere inches.

"I want you out of my home! And out of my fucking life!"

Stunned at her aggressive behavior, he hung his head, somehow feeling as if he deserved everything she dished out. She'd hurt his pride, stabbed his ego, and crushed his spirit with her words. He felt the sting of tears in his eyes as he reached for the door.

Tears streaming down her face, she snatched off her heel, and hurled it at him. "Get out! Get out!" She snatched off her other heel, and threw it. "Get out! You fucking killer!"

Nothing more needed to be said. He opened the door, and walked out, shutting her world out from his. The last thing he heard as the door closed behind him was, "I fucking hate you, Cruze Fontaine!"

Arabia grabbed a crystal decanter. And then there was a smash against the door, the sound of glass crashing against the floor, cognac splattering everywhere.

And then she sank to the floor on her knees, the gurgling sound of gut-wrenching sobs clawing their way up her throat and out of her mouth, the sound of a broken heart.

Thirty-Seven

Three weeks. That's how long Arabia hadn't seen or spoken to Cruze. Three weeks, six days, and approximately thirteen hours and forty-three seconds.

This thing between them had never meant to be a love story, she kept reminding herself. It wasn't supposed to last. Ever. She knew this. And, still, she ached for him. Missed him. Everything in her burned raw. Her heart, her soul, the pit of her cunt, throbbed from the longing and emptiness. And she hated him for that.

She sat up in bed with a strangled cry just short of a scream. *3:35 a.m.* How could that no-good son-of-a-bitch do this to *her?!*

Hurt her like *this?*

Haunt her in her dreams like *this?*

She'd never trusted a man before. And she shouldn't have trusted him. Against the warnings that had flashed in her head like floodlights, she'd allowed him to come into her life—in spite of, and, somehow, he managed to rob her of her senses. She'd known from the beginning *not* to get involved with the likes of him, that he'd be trouble. He was only supposed to be a *fuck 'n' go.*

Not *this*—a lover she couldn't stop missing or thinking of.

He'd captured her heart. And that wasn't her.

No. She only loved one thing, herself. Men came and went. She'd proven that every time she'd dismissed one, and moved on to the next without a second thought. She'd always been in control, orchestrating her own life, compartmentalizing her feelings.

Now this.

She wasn't *this* woman.

Out of control.

Lost.

Lonely.

Confused.

Still wanting him, still missing him.

In the blink of an eye, she'd become a walking contradiction of emotions. Everything about not being with Cruze nauseated her, made her physically ill.

She'd given up her control, and handed it over to him. And he'd abandoned her. Walked away without another word. Okay, maybe she'd cursed him out horribly. Still, why hadn't he come back to her?

Arabia hated herself—more than she hated him—for that.

Nobody was perfect.

But Cruze—*that big-dicked bastard!*—had been perfect for her, so she'd sadly thought. Oh, how wrong she'd been.

Still, for the first time in her life, someone had come into her world and had opened her heart and mind to new possibilities. Cruze had done that. He'd pushed her, unknowingly, to dream of finally having a love of her own.

A killer! A thug!

Before the lies, *before* the gunshots, *before* the stray bullets…

She jammed the back of her fist into her mouth, and bit back a scream, her life flashing before her eyes.

Yes. She'd been the one to end it. She attacked him. Told him to never fucking call her again. Told him how badly she hated him. In that moment, she'd meant it. Oh how she meant it, every last word. Now those words burned the back of her throat like acid.

It was over. Sadly, it had to be—for her sake.

Still, she hadn't expected him to *not* call. And she hadn't expected—for weeks—to be foolishly holding on to hope that he would. Picking up her cell, checking for messages and missed calls that she knew hadn't been left.

It was torture.

And when the agony of not being with him, or hearing his voice had finally become too much for her, she deleted all of his contact info and changed her number—for *her*, more so than him. She couldn't trust she wouldn't try to call or text him, beg him, to come back to her.

But that heartless bastard hadn't called her. Nor had he attempted to come groveling back to her on his hands and knees to apologize, to win her back—*nothing!*

He hadn't stalked her to give him another chance, hadn't sent flowers, cards, or gifts—not one damn thing to overwhelm her, to beg her for forgiveness. He'd simply given up, moved on with his life.

Fuck her, right?

The fucking manwhore was probably somewhere laid up, pumping his dick into some other bitch, slicing into her cunt, giving her all the heated pleasure he'd once given her.

She swallowed, hard.

What kind of man was he?

A man who'd never given a damn, that's who.

And what kind of woman had she become because of him?

Weak.

Vulnerable.

Obsessed.

She felt like someone had taken a wrecking ball and smashed through her chest, knocking the wind out of her. She cried out. Slung the photo of the two of them—the one they'd taken while at the zoo, the one she'd been desperately clutching to her chest since the wee hours of the morning—across the room. The frame hit the wall, glass shattering everywhere.

Like her heart, her life was smashed into a thousand-and-one tiny pieces. Arabia felt herself starting to hyperventilate. She felt as if she would throw up at any moment. This, this pain was killing her. She could barely breathe. The sadness was strangling her.

She struggled with her tears.

She was helpless. Things that she had never wanted were now things she craved most for. She had never felt so, so…

Her cell phone buzzed madly. She sucked in deep breaths, and when her smartphone fell silent, the landline started to ring. She knew it had to be one of her sisters, most likely Maya out of the three. But she didn't have the energy for any of them. Not at this time of morning. They'd have to wait until she was ready to deal with their inquisitions. And the inquiries would surely come, along with their opinions.

She sighed, breathing in regret with every breath.

Finally, she closed her eyes, and all that she saw in those few silent moments was…*him*. His smoldering brown eyes, his lips, his dimpled smile, his sculpted shoulders, his chiseled chest, his rippled abs, his thick, veiny dick; his beautiful muscled ass—every part of him.

Her lids snapped open.

Oh, God!

He was everywhere she didn't want him to be—in her head, on her skin, on her tongue, on her breasts, on her clit, in her pussy, in every crevice of her soul.

Arabia despised weak women. Had snubbed them. And now she had become one. She was a slave to his memory, to his touch, to his thick black dick. This wasn't her. Losing sleep. Being this needy, crying, bed-ridden, lovesick bitch.

Shedding a tear over a man was *not* who she was.

And, yet, here she was.

Behind closed doors, a sniveling hot damn mess!

Fuck you, Cruze Fontaine!

He was a liar! A goddamn thief! A user!

Wait. Who was she kidding?

He hadn't *used* her for a damn thing. He hadn't taken from her anything she hadn't been willing to give. And she'd given of herself willingly. So, no, he hadn't stolen anything from her. He'd taken her, roamed her body freely, because she had wanted him to. However, she'd almost gotten killed, thanks to him, and she couldn't lose sight of that. *Ever.* The idea of being with him after what had happened frightened her. But the realization of *not* being with him scared her more.

And, now, a thousand questions raced through her mind: What if…what if she reacted hastily? Had she overreacted? Should she have given him a chance to explain? Was she wrong for her behavior?

After several painful moments of contemplation, Arabia shook her head, shaking loose the craziness of second-guessing herself.

No.

She'd done what she had to do. *Her* life meant more to her than having *him* in it. She had every right to be livid with him. He should have told her he had hit men out to do him in. He had no business dragging her into his deadly drama.

She knew better than to fall for a man like him. Men like him never changed. The streets were in them, stamped in their DNA, embedded in their brain. It flowed through their veins. Trouble followed them wherever they went. It was Karma. All the fucked up things they'd put out into the universe eventually came back to them. There was no escaping it. It always came back. No matter how far, or how fast they tried to flee from it, somehow, some way, that bitch Karma would find her way to them, and sink her teeth in.

And make them pay for their sins.

Arabia took a deep, burning breath. Her walls, her world, had come tumbling down because of him. She had been better off before she'd met him—*fucked* him. Before she knew him, touched him, smelled him, tasted him, felt him in every part of her soul. The realization made her blood boil. He'd ruined her. And, sadly, she'd let him.

Pull yourself together, Arabia! All a man like him would ever do is bring you down with his bullshit and drama. You're better than that, girl. So get over it. Goodbye and good riddance!

Yes. Goodbye. She had to let it go. Let *him* go—all of him. She had to pull herself out of this chasm of depression that consumed her, and held her hostage.

Yes. It had to end. All of it.

Now.

Arabia swiped her hands over her face, sweeping fresh tears from her flushed cheeks. Holding a hand to her quivering stomach, she inhaled, deeply. Steadied her racing heart. Her mind was made up.

These were the last tears she'd ever shed over the likes of him, or any other man.

Groaning in misery, Arabia swiped away a lone tear and flopped back onto her bed, the back of her head swallowed by the king-size pillow. Lying in his shirt, she brought its collar to her nose and inhaled the faint scent of him, for one last time.

It was over.

Yet, he was everything she knew she shouldn't want.

And, still—haunted by his eyes, and his touch, and by the last time they'd made love and every other time in between, she slid her hand between her legs, where she ached most.

Oh God, yes.

This would be the last time she told herself as her fingertips slowly brushed over her clit.

Oh God, oh God.

Her body arched up from the mattress, her fingers delving inside the empty space of wet heat, where she craved sexual healing most. This would be the last time she'd allow herself to feel anything for Cruze Fontaine, she promised herself as she felt herself quickly coming undone, melting under the sheets.

It just had to be.

Thirty-Eight

Hair matted. Face crusty. Everything in her body ached. Burned. She was raw and empty and broken-hearted.

And she hated *him* for making her feel this pain. *This* was what she'd spent her entire life avoiding. And now she was hurting…because of *him*. How dare he come into her life and disrupt her entire existence with gunshots and bloodshed?

Goddamn him!

And he *still* hadn't come to her, hadn't tried to beat down her door… nothing! Maybe he hadn't cared after all. Maybe all she'd ever been to him was a good piece of ass, another wet hole to dump himself in.

Served her right for all the years of whoring with married men.

This was her payback for all the hearts she'd broken over the years—unintentionally or not.

All they were ever supposed to be was a fuck-n-go. Nothing more.

She blamed Ashley for this shit. Had it not been for that bitch Peaches taking ill, Ashley would have had her ass in Philly that day instead of sitting around at some stinking-ass vet with a sick dog.

"Fuck you, Ashley!" Arabia snapped out loud. "The minute I'm out of this funk, pack your shit! You're gone, bitch!"

She let out a loud groan.

Who was she fooling? She'd never fire Ashley. If it weren't for her keeping things running smoothly, her advertising firm would probably be going under right now. No, Ashley and her team of execs were holding it down while she…while she recovered from her terrible…*accident*.

Yes, that was what she'd told them. That she'd been in an accident. That she'd been in the wrong place at the wrong time. That, that…three gunmen tried to carjack her at a red light. Then when she'd sped off, they started shooting at her. And she was too shaken up to return to the office. That was her lie for the first two weeks.

Now this week, she'd been stricken with the flu. Yes, that's right. She had the flu in the middle of June. The lie had rolled off her tongue before she even had a chance to realize it. So she'd run with it.

Truth was, she was *sick*.

Sick of still missing him.

Sick of still wanting him.

Sick of still aching for him.

Sick of breathing him in her dreams.

Sick.

Sick.

Sick.

And being sick with the flu paled in comparison to what she was feeling this very moment.

Lovesick.

She couldn't shake this burning hell she was now in.

She couldn't shake *him*.

She couldn't even say his name. It seared the back of her throat like acid.

She was such a pathetic bitch.

Over *him*.

A man!

This didn't happen to her. But it had. And now…

She swallowed back another sob.

Then closed her eyes and breathed in deeply until it burned her lungs. Her funk overpowered the smell of *him* still on her skin. But, no matter how bad she smelled, he was still here, lingering, hovering, in the air around her.

She exhaled.

She reached over from the bed, where she'd been lying for the last four days, and grabbed another Philly cheesesteak from off the plate on her nightstand. Cheesesteak deliveries were the only time she opened her door. She'd stay hidden behind the door and crack it open so her doorman could stick her sandwiches in. She'd snatch them from his hand, then hand him his tip, before slamming the door in his face.

She bit into her sandwich, and cheese and ketchup oozed out and dripped down her chin.

Using the back of her hand to swipe away the gooey cheese and ketchup mixture, she started crying again. She'd taken to eating the messy sandwich loaded with onions, because her life had become such a smelly mess, like this stupid-ass cheesesteak.

She hadn't bathed. Hadn't shaved. Hadn't brushed or scrubbed. Or bothered to change her panties.

Her life stunk. And so did she.

She just lay in bed and watched reruns of *Being Mary Jane*. What a sad bitch!

God, she hated Mary Jane. She was a weak bitch.

And she hated herself. Because so was she.

She choked back a sob, and reached for the remote to her stereo, turning on her CD player again. Jennifer Hudson's "Giving Myself" started playing—again. Arabia sat up in bed and rocked and cried and hummed along to the song. And then she looked up and called out to God.

"God, why'd you do me like this?" she cried out. "Why are you torturing me? Have I not been obedient?" She shook her head. "Okay, scratch that. Maybe I haven't been. But damn it, I've been loving and kind, haven't I?" She shook her head again. "Okay, okay. Maybe I haven't been that, either. But do you think…do you really think I deserve *this?* If this is my punishment for sleeping with married men, I swear to you, Lord, if you find it in your heart to forgive me, I'll never sleep with another married man. I swear. Cross my broken heart and hope to…well, I don't hope to die. But this pain is killing me."

Body and soul, she'd given herself to *him.*

Unexpectedly, she'd handed herself over to *him.*

And now she was left with nothing. Not him. Not her heart. Not her dignity.

Nothing.

She'd lost everything she was to *him.*

Some reformed thug who'd almost gotten her killed.

Her life flashing before her eyes, she reached for the box of tissue on the other side of her bed, and blew her nose.

And when she had enough of Beyoncé singing her version about how she'd rather go blind than to see her man walk away, Arabia was curled up in a ball bawling her eyes out.

Her cell buzzed.

She refused to look over at it. Refused to lift it up from the night-stand, where it laid face-down, to see who it was this time, calling her. So she took another bite of her sandwich, and savagely chewed, her stomach bubbling as she swallowed.

She had gas. Bad.

But she suffered through it, chomping away at her sandwich as a reminder that he'd introduced this sandwich to her, and this was her consequence for opening herself to him. A knotted stomach filled with gas.

She was dying inside. All she needed was a coffin and a gravesite. And she'd be ground ready.

Her cell buzzed again.

Then her landline.

Then her doorbell.

Then came the banging. Loud. Obnoxious banging.

And then—oh God, no...there were *voices*.

The blood in her face drained.

Not one, not two, but three very loud voices.

"Open up, Arabia! We know you're in there!" That was her sister Tamara.

Then Alexis: "If you don't come open this door, I'll call the police to have it knocked open! Try me!"

More banging.

"God, please don't tell me she's in there dead over some man," she heard Tamara say. More banging. "Open up this goddamn door, Arabia!"

Then came Maya's voice: "Arabia, open up, girl. Please. We're worried about you."

Arabia groaned. Then glanced around her room in horror. She couldn't let them see *her*. Not like *this*.

Then came the pounding again. "You have ten seconds to open this damn door, Arabia. Ten...nine...eight..."

Arabia threw off the covers, knocking over her sandwich, stepping over dirty dishes and old sandwich wrappers.

"Seven...six...five...four..."

She raced to the door. "All right, all right...I'm coming. Damn!"

She held her hand up to her face and blew out a breath. She made a face, her lips twisting. Her breath was wretched.

"Three...two...one..."

Arabia slid back her locks, then slowly opened the door.

"God, you're so ugly right now," Tamara hissed, pushing past her. "You're so fucking selfish, Arabia."

One by one, they barged in, jostling Arabia out the way.

"And you smell," Alexis chimed in, pinching her nose together.

"Yes," Tamara added, "your ass stinks. What the hell? Why are you moping around here letting your cat-juice marinate in your drawers? I smelled you all the way out in the hall."

"Will you bitches shut up," Maya snapped. "Can't you see our baby sis is hurting?" Maya pulled Arabia into her arms and hugged her tightly. Arabia couldn't hold back the tears. She sobbed on Maya's shoulder. She needed her sisters more than she realized.

She'd thought she could get through this alone. But she couldn't. And that knowing tore her up even more.

Maya coughed, then gagged. "Okay, okay. Girl, I love you," she said, prying herself out of Arabia's hold, "but you smell like sewer water. No offense, but I'm choking here."

Tamara rolled her eyes. "I told you this bitch stinks."

Arabia nearly bared her teeth. "I don't need your insults right now, Tamara. If you don't like the smell, then leave."

Tamara fixed her with a hard stare. "Bitch, I'm not going any-damn-where until *after* our intervention. Now go wash your ass, so we can nurse your grieving ass back to health."

Alexis and Maya took one look at Arabia and their hearts ached for her. The love bug had finally bitten their baby sister and it had torn her ass up real good.

"Yes, go clean yourself up," Alexis said, almost pleadingly.

"Please and thank you," Maya added.

Arabia sucked her teeth. "All right. Y'all sit," she said, relieved that her bedroom was the only place that looked as if it'd been turned into a war zone.

The three sisters eyed Arabia as she walked off.

Tamara scowled. "If I ever see the bastard who did this to her, I'm going to claw his damn face."

"Girl," Alexis said, "his dick must have been dipped in gold for him to turn Arabia's ass inside out like this."

Arabia cringed. "I don't need you bitches talking shit about me behind my back," she yelled over her shoulder. "I need your support. Not a bunch of ridicule."

"Girl, bye," Tamara said dismissively. "You're getting both—our support *and* ridicule. So, go. Wash. That. Ass. We'll be right here *still* talking about you when you get back."

Arabia shook her head. God, she loved her sisters. She truly did.

"Much better," Maya approved when Arabia finally emerged from her room forty minutes later, wearing a pair of pink lounge pants and matching top. Her still-damp hair was in a French twist. And she'd managed to slip on a pair of diamond-hoop earrings, a little bling to brighten her otherwise bleak existence. She felt somewhat better. Not as tense. It was amazing what a little—okay, *a lot*—of soap and hot water could do. The shower was nice. She even gave herself a facial. But she still needed a good soaking.

Maya handed her a mug of white tea. Then ushered her into the kitchen where Alexis and Tamara were, sitting at the breakfast bar.

"Okay," Tamara said as she stood and opened her arms. "Now you get a hug."

Arabia rolled her eyes, setting her mug on the counter for a sisterly hug. "Whatever," she said, stepping into her embrace. Moments later, Arabia stepped back and was then hugged by Alexis.

"We love you, girl," she whispered into Arabia's ear.

"I know," Arabia said.

"Awww," Maya teased. "Sister moments. So sweet."

"Okay, okay," Tamara snapped. "Enough of the Oprah moment shit. Tell us what in the hell happened. And don't you dare leave anything out. And I do mean *nothing*."

And so she did. Told them everything—well, except the part about fucking *him* on the dance floor. They needn't know *that*.

When she was done reliving every terrifying detail, it felt like a ton of weights lifted off her. She still felt empty, but she felt much lighter—if that made any sense.

"*OhmyfuckingGod!*" Tamara shrieked. "I can't believe this shit. You need Jesus, girl."

Arabia loved her sisters dearly, but the way Alexis and Tamara were scowling one minute, blinking their eyes the next minute, then muttering curses the next after that, she regretted confiding in them the humiliating truth of the events leading up to her breakup with Cruze. Her short-lived love affair.

She wished at this very moment that it was only Maya here with her.

"What an asshole," Alexis hissed. "Street thug trash! That bastard, Cruze, or whoever he is didn't deserve you."

Arabia cringed. Maybe it was true. But it wasn't what she wanted to hear. She felt like she was being sliced open, and slowly bleeding out.

"Exactly," Tamara said fervently.

"He isn't *trash*, Alexis," Arabia defended. "He showed me a side of him that I don't think he showed anyone else." He was beautifully flawed, and had been perfect enough for her. That's all that mattered to *her*.

"Yeah, that he's murderous," Tamara snapped. "That's the side he showed you."

Arabia sighed, then surprised herself when she said, "He was only trying to protect me. They started shooting at us, first."

Tamara gritted her teeth. "And he conveniently happened to have a gun tucked under the seat of your car, huh? Arabia, will you wake up! Listen to yourself."

"And it's a good thing he did," Arabia muttered. "Otherwise—"

"Oh, this has to be some new Stockholm syndrome shit I'm hearing," Alexis pushed out, "because this bitch is still in shock."

"I'm *not* in shock. I'm hurting, Alexis. You weren't the one there. He wouldn't have had to start shooting them if…" Her voice trailed off, and she shook her head. They'd never understand. And she didn't expect them to. She choked back a sob. He had no business putting her life in danger, but she wasn't about to give her sisters the satisfaction of hearing her say it.

Alexis rolled her eyes and Tamara just snorted. But it was Maya who reached for her hand and gave it a comforting squeeze. The gesture melted her heart.

Alexis twisted her lips. "Mmph. Well, maybe he isn't trash. But he's still a gun-toting thug. And he had *you* in some high-speed shootout, like you were starring in some damn drama series. Who does that?"

"My God, Arabia," Tamara hissed. "You could have been *killed*. What were you thinking?"

"I—"

"She *wasn't* thinking," Alexis interjected, before she could get the rest of her sentence out. "That's the problem. She never thinks. Just does. Tamara, you know how she's always been. Reckless."

Tamara grunted. "*Mmph*. Girl, preach. Even with her fucking married men. If that isn't reckless, I don't know what is."

Arabia frowned. "I beg your pardon? Um, hello! I am sitting right here. There's no need for you to be talking as if I'm not. And I *wasn't* being reckless. I'm never reckless, as you so eloquently put it. Everything I do I give thought to."

Tamara snorted. "Well, apparently not enough thought. Otherwise, you wouldn't be in this mess."

Arabia scowled. "My *mess*—as you call it, is mine. And mine alone. I didn't ask *you* here to clean up *my* mess. And I didn't call *you*"—then she pointed at Alexis—"or *you* for a shoulder to lean on. So why the fuck are you bitches coming down on me? Do you think I asked for this, huh? Do you?"

Maya reached over and touched her shoulder. "Arabia, none of us think you asked for what happened to you. It's horrible. And I can only imagine what it was like being in it. Ever since we heard the news, we've been worried sick about you."

Arabia relaxed at her sister's touch. "I know," she said softly. More tears streamed down her face. "I already feel bad enough. I don't need them two self-righteous bitches making me feel any worse than I already do."

Tamara shifted in her seat. "I don't mean to come down on you, hon." Her tone softened. "You know we love you and would do anything for you. Anything. But we haven't heard from you in *weeks*, Arabia. Then we have to find out from some stranger at your workplace that you were in some shootout. After not hearing from you all this time. How do you think that makes *us* feel?"

Arabia swallowed. "I'm sorry. I should have taken your calls. I was too embarrassed to say anything. I didn't want any of you to know what I'd gone through." She covered her face in her hands. "God, I feel so fucking stupid."

Maya rubbed her back. "It wasn't your fault," she said gently. "None of it."

"Well, maybe not," Alexis stated. "But she can help what she does about it. And we're here to help her. Have you blocked his numbers?"

Arabia shook her head slowly, biting the inside of her cheek. She wished she hadn't. She wanted to hear his voice, one more time. All she needed was one phone call to him.

But for what?

It wasn't like he really cared about her.

"No. I didn't block him. I changed my number."

"Good for you," Alexis said. "Wait. So he's the reason you changed your number?"

Arabia nodded, embarrassment washing over her all over again.

Tamara grunted again. "*Mmph*. You let that hoodlum disrupt your whole damn life. And why isn't his black ass in jail? You reported it to the police, didn't you?"

The look on Arabia's face said it all.

"Arabia!" Tamara and Alexis shouted.

"What the hell, girl?" Tamara questioned. "Are you serious?"

Alexis shook her head, utterly baffled.

"I did report it. I just didn't mention his name." Of course, there hadn't been any police called. How could she call them *without* implicating herself? She'd been the one driving—the shooter, no less—in *her* car. Oh God—her car. She wanted to scream. Her once beautiful luxury car destroyed, now a thing of the past, dragged off to some chop shop. Thanks to...*him*.

Tamara drained her tea. "Okay. Someone tell me why the hell we're sitting here drinking tea? I need me a bottle of wine. This bitch has officially lost her mind."

Maya gave her an icy glare. "Tamara, shut the hell up. Before I spill the *tea* on your ass. Okay? Because you and I both know some of the crazy shit you've done." She tilted her head. "Now don't we?"

Tamara shot her a scathing look of her own, a warning to keep her mouth shut.

"No. I'm not going to put your business out there like that," Maya assured her. She was the sister they all confided in, trusting her with their deepest, dirtiest secrets. "But don't go throwing stones at Arabia, either. Your glass house isn't all that perfect."

Arabia blinked. But before she could open her mouth to question, to probe further, Maya took her hand in hers, and said, "Look at me, Arabia." Arabia looked at her sister, her eyes brimming with tears. "I'm going to ask you something, and I want you to answer truthfully. But before you do. I want you to ignore Tamara and Alexis. Fuck them. This is you and I talking." Arabia nodded. And then Maya eyed Tamara and Alexis. "And you two don't say shit. Or I swear I will drag the both of you."

Tamara flinched, her stare glacial.

Alexis threw her hands up. "I'm done."

"Good. Now tell me, Arabia. Do you love him?"

Arabia choked back another sob. The question hit her hard. It hit her in the chest and nearly snatched her breath away.

She needed to see him, one last time. She didn't want to keep fantasizing about, yearning for, what could have been. But it was over. She knew it. But she couldn't go on lying to herself, even if he didn't love her back. She needed to be free to live in her own truth. And the truth was, she didn't want to breathe—without him.

"Yes," she whispered.

Maya stared at her, hard. Then a smile hovered on her lips. "Then go to him."

Arabia blinked, surprised, her tears falling heavy now.

"You heard me. Go get your man."

Thirty-Nine

The team lost.

By one fuckin' point!

It felt like a dark shadow was hovering over Cruze, fucking up everything good in his life. It was the first time the team had played white kids out in the suburbs, and the boys had expected an easy win. They were so shocked and upset about losing, they showed their natural asses when the buzzer went off. It was pandemonium on the floor, and Cruze couldn't wrangle the boys in as they threatened and cursed out the referee in the vilest language anyone had ever heard come out of the mouths of eight- and nine-year-olds.

And the moms on the team didn't help. In fact, many of them instigated and encouraged the chaos. Of course, numerous people recorded the meltdown, and for reasons that Cruze couldn't fathom, one of the ignorant-ass moms from his team posted the incriminating footage online, captioning it, *When you had enough of a racist ref!*

The video of Cruze's boys cursing and fighting and acting like heathens had gone viral, making it on WorldstarHipHop.com and other sites that promoted ratchetness. With a glass of Hennessy in hand, Cruze groaned as he sank into a chair in his living room.

The ref hadn't shown any partiality. The boys lost fair and square to the white kids, who probably had personal trainers and went to expensive basketball camps two or three times a year. So, in that sense, the other team did have some advantages. But Cruze's team had natural abilities in addition to having a good coach and two former NBA players giving them pointers.

His best player, Barack, had shocked him the most. The boy behaved like a feral little animal, snarling, throwing punches, and head-butting one of the players from the opposing team. That kid ended up with a busted lip that required stitches.

Now Cruze's team was suspended for two weeks. In a matter of minutes, he and the boys had lost their stellar reputation and had become pariahs in the youth league basketball circuit.

Bret was beyond livid and ordered Cruze to take the boys to a five-hour conflict resolution seminar on Saturday.

And that's why Cruze was drinking. He didn't feel like sitting up in a boring seminar with those wild, unhinged, ADHD little knuckleheads.

Cruze was so infuriated at his team, he was tempted to listen to the advice Marquan had given him. Marquan's alcoholic-ass had called with an idea that he said was much better than Bret's method of whipping the team back into shape. Marquan suggested that he and Cruze take the boys out into the wilderness somewhere, upstate and make them fend for themselves after he and Cruze had beaten the shit out of them with bats covered with barbed wire.

Cruze shook his head. The drunken muhfucka had been dead serious.

Practicing with the boys every day had helped keep his mind off of Arabia. But now that they were suspended, he was forced to confront his pain.

His hand tightened around the glass of Henny. He brought it to his lips and took a big gulp. He grimaced as the bitter taste burned his tongue.

Arabia. Damn. I fucked up, big time, bae!

He'd waited a week, giving her a chance to calm down a little before trying to plead his case again, and when he'd finally gotten the courage to call her, he discovered she'd changed her number. That was a kick in the gut like no other, and she couldn't have made it any clearer that she wanted nothing to do with him.

A lowlife thug! That's what she'd called him before kicking him out of her apartment and her life, and he supposed she was right.

Everyone he loved had always left him: first, his mom, then Ramona, Chance, and now Arabia. He'd been foolish to think he could ever have even a small slice of happiness. That shit only happened in the movies. Cats like him, if they had any sense, fucked every pussy in his path, and stuck his dick in every open mouth, and never caught feelings. He'd known better, yet he'd stupidly allowed Arabia to draw him in.

It wasn't only her extraordinary good looks that had captivated him, nor was it merely her sense of style, or her erotic sensuality. His feelings for her went beyond all the surface stuff. Arabia was like a twin soul. Loving her had made him able to finally love himself, something he'd struggled with since the age of thirteen.

The short time they were together had been heaven. Arabia was something special. Truly one of a kind. Waking up in the morning to the sensation of her soft body curled next to his had been the closest thing to nirvana he'd ever known. Inhaling the intoxicating scent she left in his sheets long after she'd gone used to give him so much pleasure, and now her fading fragrance was a taunting reminder that he'd allowed a living goddess to slip through his fingers, and he was devastated.

Yes, he was back in his old stomping grounds—hell on Earth. And no amount of luxury items, or being successful in real estate, and having money to burn could make purgatory a comfortable place to dwell. Engulfed by regret, he simply burned in his own misery.

For the last three weeks, he'd tried to ignore the pain in his heart, but now it was too much to bear. Cruze stood up, ready to appeal to the Lord for help. But he couldn't stand tall. His shoulders slumped and his stance became shaky in the knowledge that he'd done so much wrong in his life that it wasn't likely that God would be merciful toward him.

"Ma!" he cried out in anguish. She'd always been there for him, while she was alive…and he suspected she assisted him in the after-life. There was no other way to explain him escaping numerous brushes with death other than divine intervention. But she'd really come through this last time.

Looking back, it seemed impossible that both he and Arabia had come out of the highway shootout without as much as a flesh wound. Cruze was convinced that his mother's undying love had surrounded him and the woman he loved, acting as a protective shield against a hail of bullets that no mortal man should have survived.

Eyes misty, he looked heavenward.

Ma, I've done so much dirt in my life that I'm ashamed to even talk to you. I apologize for not sticking to the promise that I made on your death-bed. Please forgive me. Ever since you left me, I've been so lost. I keep getting into dangerous situations and I keep making stupid decisions and bad choices. I don't want to continue down this road. I need redemption, and I was wondering if you'd put in a good word for me…with the Man. I don't have the heart to appeal to Him, myself.

Although I love Arabia with every breath in my body, I realize it's over for me and her. But if there's any way the Lord sees fit to influence her moves and help guide her back to me, I promise to be a better man. If that's too much to ask, then it's all good; I understand. After the way I endangered her life, it makes sense that she hates me and wants nothing to do with me. So, on second thought, all I'm asking of God is that he gives me some peace of mind. No one should have to live a life of constant misery. If He is a forgiving God, then maybe I'll get a little relief from this terrible suffering.

That's it; that's all I want. Thanks for listening, Ma.

Cruze ambled to the kitchen with the glass of Hennessy and poured the remaining liquor down the drain. There was no point in getting drunk. Accompanying the boys to the seminar tomorrow with a hangover wouldn't be a good look.

From this point on, all he could do was put one foot in front of the other and try to get through each day and focus on being a better human being than he'd been thus far. The first thing on his list was to turn things around with the team, and show the boys that it wasn't always about winning. It was about being your best self. He had to teach them that if they went through life reacting violently every time things didn't go their way, they were headed for self-destruction. And Cruze loved those kids too much to stand by and allow them to make the kinds of life-altering mistakes that he'd made.

He'd been robbed of the opportunity to raise Chancellor, but in the memory of his son, he would guide his young charges to manhood to the best of his ability. Although he'd only be coaching his current team for a few more years before they moved on to the teen league, Cruze had plans for them that included college tuition, summer basketball camps that promoted diversity, and intense counseling for their emotional well-being. Living in the 'hood exposed those kids to so much crime and violence, it wasn't any wonder that they behaved like heathens, unable to control their impulses when they got embarrassed on the court by a team of little white boys whom they felt they had an edge on.

Cruze cringed thinking about the video of his team that was circulating on the Internet. But even he had to admit that seeing those little rascals cursing out the ref and threatening to fuck him up was funny as shit. It wasn't right, but he started chuckling when he recalled how swiftly Barack had head-butted that little curly blond-headed boy who'd shot the winning point for their team from the free-throw line.

It dawned on Cruze that he was actually laughing out loud, and he lifted a thick brow in wonderment. They said that laughter was good for the soul.

His doorbell suddenly rang and his good mood instantly turned to aggravation. No one came to his apartment uninvited and un-announced except that uppity, entitled Valentina.

Okay, I've had it. Enough is enough! I'ma grab that broad by the collar and drag her back to her apartment. Then, I'ma demand that her husband either put his bitch-in-heat on a leash or start doling out enough dick to keep her horny-ass satisfied enough to stop sniffing around my fuckin' door.

With a deep scowl on his face and his dark eyes filled with fire, Cruze stomped to the living room and yanked open the door. He took a hostile step forward, and then came to an abrupt halt.

He gasped. His legs felt unstable as he stared in shock at the angelic vision standing before him dressed in powder-pink lounge pants and matching top.

Arabia!

With her hair pulled back in a French twist, her face was un-obstructed, allowing Cruze a clear view of her stunning bone structure. The twinkling diamonds in her ears radiated an ethereal glow, giving her an almost unearthly beauty. Cruze could have stood in the doorway staring at her for the rest of eternity. His prayer had been answered, that quick.

He looked up, and silently thanked his mom, then brought his gaze back to the woman who stole his breath and made his heart race.

Arabia's lips quivered as they both stood staring at the other, their eyes soaking in everything they'd missed. "I-I'm so s-sorry," she stammered. "I-I can't take this pain of being without you any longer."

Cruze's heart flooded with emotion. He opened his arms, and she fell into his embrace, burying her face in the space between his neck and shoulder. And wept.

Cruze closed his eyes.

Then exhaled.

Epilogue

Fire.

It was all around them. The candles. The fireplace. Flames danced everywhere. They were in the middle of Vermont in a cabin overlooking Lake Morey, snowed in from last night's blizzard. The lake was frozen. Snow and biting subzero temperatures besieged them. But inside they were cozy, surrounded by heat.

Heat from the crackling fire.

Heat from their bone-melting sex.

And they were catching their breaths, heavy-lidded and satiated, shivers of pleasure still wracking their bodies. Now they were stretched out on a white mink rug—naked beneath an expensive fur-like coverlet, basking in the glow of firelight. The heat between them was so palpable that they could both feel the sizzle, hot and electric.

The nearby fire crackled. And Arabia closed her eyes as she nestled deeper in Cruze's arms. So much had happened between them in the last six months. Cruze's nightmares still seized him, but they came less and less. And he was thankful for that.

Ramona…she was a major part of his past, but she was now far removed from his future. That part of his life was over.

Cruze continued to dedicate himself to HYPE. After the fiasco with his team being suspended, he'd decided to turn lemons into lemonade. No longer needing to hide from publicity, he called a press conference. With Bret and Marquan at his side, he appealed to the public to not label the children as young thugs, but to view their actions as a cry for help. They were victims of their environment, but they could be saved from the bleak future that seemed inevitable if the community pooled their resources and helped to increase the programs at the center.

Although the community didn't contribute much, the media exposure gave Cruze a national platform, and the cameras loved him. Three major corporations came forward with funding for the center and Vitaminwater became a sponsor for the team, which helped to change their status from a local team to a travel team that competed statewide.

In addition to continuing his work with the center and maintaining his real estate holdings, Cruze now held corporate board seats with two prestigious companies. He sometimes found it hard to believe that he'd gone from drug-dealer to becoming a suit-and-tie-wearing, briefcase-carrying businessman.

"If my mother could see me now," he often thought, and then quickly reminded himself that she was always with him in spirit, helping to shine the light on his path that had led him out of the darkness. She was always there, nudging him with gentle whispers, encouraging him to make wiser choices.

And Arabia?

She was officially down to one man in her life. And she was more than happy with that. One man was all she needed. She had to finally get an order of protection against Eric. And she and her mother were still at odds. That would never change between them. She despised her. In her heart, she knew Claudia killed her father. She'd never falter from that belief. The woman was capable of murder, just as she'd been capable—many years ago—of locking Arabia in a dark, windowless room for hours, just as she'd been capable of calling her *worthless. Whore. Unlovable.* Things she'd never shared with anyone—not even her sisters because they'd never believe her, no matter how close they were. So those horrors she'd kept bottled up inside, her dark secrets possessing her.

But Claudia was wrong. Arabia was worthy. And she was loveable. She'd always been.

Cruze had proven that.

She was wanted and cherished by him.

And, yes, she still whored—for *him*, the man of her dreams, her dark, dreamy lover. He'd found his way into her heart, and vowed to spend the rest of his life loving her, protecting her, and—of course—fucking her whenever, wherever, she wanted him.

"I'm all yours, this dick is all yours," he'd told her. No, *promised* her. And, with everything in her, she'd believed him as he'd caught her wrist and dragged her hand to his hard dick. Then he'd pulled her hand away and brought it up to his chest and pressed it flat over his beating heart. "My heart is yours, baby."

She'd lost it. And together they'd cried tears of joy, tears of pain, tears of regret, tears of loss, tears of forgiveness, tears full of promise.

That night, they'd clung to each other, vowing to never let go of what they had almost given up, almost lost. Each other.

The weeks that they'd been a part from one another after that horrible shootout had been torturous for her, for him. In the midst of it all, they'd both realized that they were damaged. Flawed. Two tortured souls. But, somehow, still a perfect fit for each other. And that was all either cared about.

Still, she hadn't told him about her past penchant for sex clubs—occasionally. And he hadn't found the words to tell her about everything in his other life, the murders, and the number of bodies by his own hands.

Did it really matter?

It was all in the past. Maybe some secrets were best kept buried, for now. As far as either was concerned, they had a lifetime to uncover untold stories, and share each other's deep, dark secrets. For now, all that mattered was this very moment.

The present.

Arabia inhaled. Breathed Cruze in. She smelled him all around her. His musk. His manliness. His love. His desire.

Heat.

It swept through her in a rushing wave causing her pussy to flutter and clench. She needed him. Wanted him. Craved him.

She slowly opened her eyes, a slow grin unfurling on her face as she extended her hand and admired the five-carat, emerald-cut engagement ring he'd wowed her with. His proposal had both shocked her, and brought her to unrelenting tears.

She'd gotten the man. The ring. And a love of her own.

Maybe happily-ever-after did exist.

She reached over and pinched Cruze's nipple.

"Ow, baby," he groaned, stretching lazily. "Why'd you do that?"

She rolled onto her side to face him. "I wanted to make sure this—*you*—were real."

His mouth twitched with amusement. "I'm all real, baby. *This* is all real. Me and you, and that big-ass rock on your hand."

She grinned. "Isn't it beautiful. I love it almost as much as I love you; maybe, even a little more," she teased.

He laughed. "Oh word?"

"Maybe."

"Yeah a'ight. I got your maybe," he shot back, pulling her into his arms, his dick brushing against her thigh. She grinned happily, like a child. And then his smile matched hers, his dimples deep. God help her—she couldn't get enough of him.

Cruze leaned forward so that his lips brushed her ear. "I'm all yours, Arabia. And I'm not going anywhere." His voice was low, sensual—and it was making her wetter than she'd already been. He pulled back so that his gaze was locked on hers, and the desire she saw there matched hers, and almost drowned her.

Many times—in the past, she had thought, could have sworn, she'd seen love glinting in his eyes, but he'd never confirmed it, and she hadn't wanted to assume.

Maybe she'd been imagining it. Maybe she'd seen what she thought she wanted to see at the time. But, tonight, she didn't have to second-guess, or wonder. She knew. He loved her—all of her. And she felt it.

Cruze pressed his lips to her forehead, then ran the tip of his finger down the bridge of her nose and his dimples flashed again. He gazed at her, his eyes glowing with unfettered desire. "You're never getting rid of me, baby."

Arabia smiled and caressed his jaw. "And I never want to."

"Good."

Even though she saw the kiss coming, it still made her heart flutter and her cunt clench with want as his lips brushed hers. A log popped in the fire as Cruze kissed her mouth, sucking on her bottom lip, then nipping at her top lip, before his tongue slid in to taste her and he leisurely explored her mouth, savoring her, wanting more of her.

He groaned into her mouth, lapping at her lips, then sliding his tongue back inside the plush warmth of mouth. Oh God—yes. She was melting, melting, melting. Every part of her was drowning in a pool of desire so deep, so intense, that she felt herself cry out. He literally snatched her breath away, sucking it into his kiss with sensual flicks of his tongue over hers as he slid his fingers through the folds of her pussy. He stroked her walls. She was wet, soaking wet. And it was all for him, all because of him.

Slowly, he pulled his fingers from her body and broke their kiss, leaving her with an empty ache that made her mewl out with need.

Her gaze flashed wide, then narrowed to burning slits of arousal as he took his fingers and slid them into his mouth, tasting her essence, her passion. The intimate act caused a fresh burst of liquid desire to flood her pussy.

The sight rendered her speechless.

"*Mmm*, baby," he murmured. "Damn. You taste so sweet." He kissed her lips again, then trailed his lips down her neck. "Can't wait to taste your pussy."

Arabia blinked. No, no… this wasn't happening. Him. There. His mouth, his lips, his tongue…*there*—between her thighs.

He slid down her body, spreading her legs open. Yes, yes—oh sweet God, yes. It was happening. He was trailing down her body, his tongue tracing the contour of her hip, then glazing over her abdomen. Goose bumps rose to the surface of her flesh as soft wet strokes of his warm tongue slid to her navel, dipping inside.

"Oh, Cruze," she moaned.

His mouth and tongue journeyed lower. And then, right there— oh, yes…she felt his heated breaths against her slick folds as he visually drank her in, memorizing her sex, his fingers spreading her swollen lips, so wet and ready.

"Damn…so fuckin' beautiful."

And there went his tongue—against her clit, licking and laving. He'd never gone down on her, ever. Oh how she'd prayed for the day. *Sweet bliss.*

He tongued her entrance. He circled her slit, licking and gently sucking, then slid his tongue inward, licking her, tasting her, from the inside out. He ate her. Drank from her. Then licked her all over again.

"I've fucked you many times," he rasped, looking up at her through a haze of lust. "But now…" He licked over her cunt lips, then slid his tongue along her slit.

She gasped, clutching the rug, her body arching to him.

"Tonight," he murmured huskily, lifting up over her and blanketing her with his body. "I'm gonna make love to you."

She trembled. "*Mmm.* Yes, yes, yes…"

She spread her legs wider, inviting him into the space she'd now reserved for him, and only him. "Take me, Cruze," she whimpered. "*Please.*"

And he did.

Took her like never before. His dick slid ravenously into her body—raw, the width of him devouring her wetness, the length of him claiming her core. He stroked her deep and slow, relishing in the clutch of her silky walls until they were both vibrating with need. The slick sounds of her cunt mingled with her hitched breaths, along with the *pop-pop* of the crackling fire.

Arabia moaned, her entire body tightening around him.

"Aah, shit," he muttered. "You feel so good, baby…"

A savage blaze burned in his eyes when he looked at her. He loved her. He was *in* love with her. She completed him. Made him want to be loved again, and to love back. She made his heart full, and his soul fuller.

He found all that in her—his future wife, the future mother of his kids.

He moaned, rocking against her, his gaze latched on to hers.

"Mmm, Cruze…"

God, hearing his name slip from her lips—*fuck.* Lust pounded at him. She was pulling him in, drawing him closer to orgasm.

Her cunt clutched him. "I love you," she whispered, tears slowly rolling out of her eyes. "I love, I love, I love you," she murmured repeatedly over and over.

"I love you, too," he rasped, his dick slowly, rhythmically, sloshing in and out of her warm juices. They were both almost there. Nearing nirvana.

"Come for me, baby," he urged, his voice above a whisper. And then his mouth was back on her hers again, making love to her mouth, kissing her, teasing her, tasting every part of her tongue, snatching her breath again, then giving her his. Languorous. Sweet. Their breaths slowly became one.

She rocked.

He pushed.

She moaned.

He groaned.

The air around them exploded in heat, in passion, in raw hunger. A mass of erotic tension gathered, like a brewing storm, building, building. Desire and lust overwhelming, every stroke brought them closer to a sexual healing neither knew, or imagined, existed.

She was full…of love, of dick, of him.

Slick.

Hot.

He pumped slowly, lazily, into her cunt, the head of his dick brushing over her G-spot, then nudging her womb. Oh God, oh God, ohhhhh-fucking God! She tightened and swelled. Then arched up to him—sobbing as she wrapped her arms around his broad shoulders and stroked his sweat-slick back, caressing the hard muscles as he filled her soul with everything he was, with everything he'd ever be.

"I love you, baby," he growled low, his words vibrating over her skin, before his lips met hers and they sank into an endless kiss.

And then he came, spilling his love inside her body, bathing her pussy with his seed, flooding her with his hopes and dreams…and deepest desires.

He, too, had finally found a love of his own.

ABOUT THE AUTHORS

A prolific writer, Allison Hobbs is the national bestselling author of twenty-seven novels and novellas of multiple genres, including paranormal and fantasy. Allison received a Bachelor of Science degree from Temple University.

Cairo is the author of *The Pleasure Zone*; *Dirty Heat*; *Between the Sheets*; *Ruthless: Deep Throat Diva 3*; *Retribution: Deep Throat Diva 2*; *Slippery When Wet*; *The Stud Palace*; *Big Booty*; *Man Swappers*; *Kitty-Kitty, Bang-Bang*; *Deep Throat Diva*; *Daddy Long Stroke*; *The Man Handler*; and *The Kat Trap*. His travels to Egypt are what inspired his pen name.

IF YOU ENJOYED "SEXUAL HEALING," BE SURE TO CHECK OUT

by ALLISON HOBBS
AVAILABLE FROM STREBOR BOOKS

CHAPTER 1

Maverick and I were not ready to become parents. But after ten years of marriage, the pressure was on us, not only from our families, but also from the media and our fans.

While Maverick was in Los Angeles filming a Lexus commercial, I had the task of interviewing potential candidates that the surrogacy agency considered good matches for us. We'd both agree on the final candidate, but I wanted to get the ball rolling and at least start vetting the women.

There was no medical reason that prevented me from carrying a baby full term; I simply didn't want to put my body through that kind of trauma. Also, my husband and I were still building our brand and there was no way for me to fit a pregnancy into my hectic schedule.

God forbid if I suffered a bout of morning sickness and vomited while tasting some of the disgusting food the contestants prepared on *Cookin' with Cori*, my food-based reality show.

Unlike other celebrities, I decided not to fake my pregnancy by wearing prosthetics. I was going to be fully transparent, documenting and sharing my journey every step of the way.

If the blogosphere exploded with accusations that I was buying my way out of morning sickness, labor pains, stretch marks, hanging boobs, and postpartum depression, then they were right. Why should I suffer through any of the inconveniences of pregnancy when I didn't have to?

There would be controversy over our decision, but I was certain my husband and I would stand together, hand-in-hand, and face the critics. We'd argue that Maverick's career wouldn't have to be interrupted by a pregnancy, so why should mine? People could say and think what they wanted, but I felt it was empowering for a woman to keep her career intact—like a man—and still bring a child into the world.

Though the haters would probably say: Cori Brown is so selfish! So shallow! So unwomanly! I had so much influence over women in the age range of twenty-one through forty, I was certain that many out them would agree with me and come to my defense.

Nonetheless, controversy sold and I was looking forward to all the free publicity my husband and I would receive once the news got out that we were using a surrogate and were proud of it!

The media had dubbed us, "Mavcor," a blending of our first names, Maverick and Cori. Maverick earned the lion's share of our income, but I was no slouch. Though we were already worth tens of millions, our goal was to become billionaires. The way things were going, it was entirely possible that we'd reach that goal within the next five years.

Maverick Brown and I had been inseparable since college when he was the star quarterback of the school's football team, and I was his devoted girlfriend who'd won her way to his heart with superb cooking skills.

Maverick received the Heisman Trophy and of course, various NFL teams were pursuing him. I wasn't about to let him leave me behind, and so I persuaded him to marry me a few weeks before graduation. Although I would have preferred a big, dream wedding, I agreed to a simple ceremony before he ran off to training camp. Unfortunately, his newly hired agent butted in our business and convinced Maverick to hit me with a prenup. It was the worst pre-nup in history with nothing in it that benefited me, but I signed it, anyway. I had to if I wanted to marry Maverick Brown. From the day I signed that horrible prenuptial agreement, I made a decision that Maverick and I would be permanently joined at the hip. No separation, ever. And absolutely no divorce. We were going to stay together, forever—no matter what it took.

Before being sidelined by a knee injury, Maverick had a stellar nine-year professional football career that included two Super Bowl wins and numerous lucrative endorsement deals. With Maverick's money, I opened a soul food restaurant in Harlem called Bay Leaf, made it a success, and then made a hefty profit by selling it. The rest of my story became history: three bestselling cookbooks and a series of instructional DVDs. I also had my own reality TV show where I whipped up Southern cuisine while blindfolded contestants, who were not told any of the ingredients, had to rely on their palates and sense of smell to duplicate the dish I'd prepared.

The contestants on my show were mainly untalented assholes with huge egos, but their obnoxious personalities combined with my sassiness, killer wardrobe, sexy apron, and stilettos had helped make my show a smashing success during the first season. I was set to begin taping season two in a few days.

Back in the early years of our relationship, I used to keep Maverick happy with the soul food recipes passed down by my grandmother, Eula Mae Barber, a former madam from back in the forties. After her brothel was shuttered, she opened a restaurant and a hotel ıs able to earn a good living. Though she was considered ...ssful, she didn't want her twin daughters to ever have to ...tle the way she had, and she sent them off to college to find ...ood husbands—preferably doctors. Grandma Eula Mae had a thing about doctors. Even before she became senile, she spoke of doctors as if they were gods and the only men worth marrying.

She was sorely disappointed when both her girls became college professors and married businessmen. She was even more disappointed when they put their careers first, allowing their marriages to crumble.

Out of all of Eula Mae's descendants, I was the only one who had an interest in cooking. I was the only one in the family who was interested in braising short ribs or frying catfish to perfection. For me, standing next to Grandma Eula Mae while she eyeballed the measurements for banana-blueberry pancakes was fascinating, like watching a scientist at work. Everyone else sat at the table and gobbled up her food, but couldn't care less about the masterful skill it took to prepare the meal. While my cousins ran out of the house, holding their noses and complaining about the stench of chitterlings, I had my hands immersed in water, helping my grandmother clean those pig guts.

I was raised on soul food, but rarely touched the stuff, anymore. Maverick and I were extremely picky about what we put into our bodies. We practiced a healthy lifestyle, and neither of us would dream of stuffing ourselves with the high-fat food that had made me famous. But we didn't share that information with the public.

With maturity, my husband had become even more smoking hot than he'd been back in college. At age thirty-three, Maverick Brown was increasingly sought after to promote not only the usual sports gear and custom brews but also luxuries that most viewers could only imagine. Currently an analyst for a major sports network,

Maverick was in negotiations for his own Sunday evening show.

Recently, a Hollywood casting director had offered him a juicy role in an action movie. That deal hadn't been finalized yet, but it was only a matter of time before my hubby was showing off his ripped body on the big screen.

We were indeed a power couple, living our dream, and the idea of me slowing down for a pregnancy was unthinkable.

ONE

Desirous.

Hedonistic.

Orgasmic.

Drenched in exotic beauty, Nairobia Jansen was all of those things, then some. She was Kama Sutra. A dangerous combination of… seduction and sin.

She was good pussy.

Good fucking.

She was sweet surrender.

And the gray-eyed, half-Dutch, half-Nigerian beauty knew it. After all, she was every man's wet dream. And over the years she'd become the forbidden fantasy of her share of women as well. No. She wasn't a lesbian. But she didn't consider herself heterosexual, either. In fact, she hated labeling her sexuality. She found it constricting, and goddamn boring. She refused to live her life confined to someone else's definition of who she should or shouldn't be. She fucked whom she wanted, when she wanted, however she wanted, with abandon.

But it was no secret she loved the taste of pussy. Hell, most of the world had probably seen her with her face pressed between the thighs of a slew of women during her porn-star days. She was Pleasure back then. It was unbelievable how that time in her life felt like a lifetime ago. Still her reputation followed her. She was a legend in the porn industry. And she was certain many men had jacked off watching her get fucked from the back, her ass bouncing up and down on a long dick making it disappear, while she tongue-fucked another woman. Pussy was heavenly. She loved licking into its wet folds, sucking on its plump golden lips. She loved the way its scent stained her tongue. Loved the heat of another woman's cunt melding into her own, grinding clit-to-clit, creaming out an orgasm.

However, make no mistake. She loved the wet, juicy, slosh-slosh sound her pussy made every time it was being deep-stroked by a long, hard, throbbing cock more. So—hell no, she could never be a lesbian. She loved dick too much.

Nairobia drew in a deep breath, and resisted the urge to wince at not having had some good pussy since the death of her...well, the only woman who she'd once ever considered sucking and fuck-ing exclusively. Marika. The thought of her being gone was still too much to give thought to. And tonight wasn't the time for gloom.

No. It was a celebration. The grand opening of her latest adven-ture, a club—nestled inside what used to be a lesbian club—in the midtown section of New York. Its sole purpose was to cater to the carnal desires of wealthy men and women who stepped foot through its doors. She'd bought the space a little over a year ago as an invest-ment to add to her already impressive portfolio. And now her dream of opening the doors to one of the world's most erotic sex clubs would become a reality.

Tonight.

Nairobia stared at the wall of water cascading behind the sleek, curved bar before her eyes locked on the bartender. She was scandalously dressed, as always, in a form-fitting, sheer linen gown, a front and back slit crawling up to the crack of her luscious bare ass, and golden sweet pussy.

A Chopard diamond necklace, with over a 140-carats of teardrop-shaped diamonds, cascaded around her neck and dripped down into her cleavage. Her shoulder-length hair was pulled up in what she liked to call a naughty girl chignon. Her hair pulled back, twisted into a loose bun, then loose strands of hair pulled out, framing her face for that freshly "just-fucked" look.

The messier the better, that's how she liked it. Like sex, she liked it wild.

"What's your poison, Mademoiselle?" the bartender asked over the music. Silk's "More" melted out through the world-class sound system.

She glanced around the club.

Chic.

Sophisticated.

Heated marbled floors.

Swathes of billowy ivory silk covered the walls on the first floor.

Candles of enormous sizes flickered about the expansive space.

Gas-lit torches lined the walls.

Draped candlelit booths.

Oversized white leather sofas and armless chairs.

Massive floral arrangements perfumed the air.

She looked up at the vaulted ceiling, then fluttered her gaze back to the milk chocolate Adonis in front of her, his eyes dancing over her body. Every muscle in his sleek torso bunched, and her pussy clenched.

Goapele purred out of the speakers about being ready to play. And Nairobia was more than ready. She stayed ready. Always wet, always ready. She thrust her pelvis to its beat, then reached over the bar, positioned in the center of the floor, and pulled him into her by his spiked collar. She kissed him on the mouth. Sunk her teeth into his plump bottom lip. Then nipped at the small diamond hoop earring in his left ear. There was a panther's head tattooed on the back of his neck. And her mouth watered to bite it. She resisted the urge.

For now…

Save for his collar, the six-foot-four bartender's sculpted body was naked, dusted in gold as was every other wait staff, server, and bartender. He grinned as Nairobia leaned further over the bar and her hungry gaze slid down his body and fastened on the meaty dick hanging between his muscular thighs.

Mmm.

Josiah.

Josiah.

Josiah.

He was drool inducing as was everyone else who would work the club, including the deejays and the bouncers. It was a mandatory requirement—to be beautiful, to be sexy, to be…fuckable, whether you were dressed or undressed. And, oh how he was so, so very fuckable.

Nairobia knew she would feed the staff her pussy and she'd feast on their hard dicks, and weeping cunts. But rule number one: she would not, ever, indulge the patrons' libidos. No, no, no. Sexing the clientele would make for bad business. And fucking over good coin was not how she'd managed to brand her name, and her delectable talents. No matter how many thousands of dollars would pour into her club tonight—or on any other night, no matter how many loins would ache for her loving touch, she wouldn't cross the axiomatic line. Not with the patrons.

She fixed her gaze on the sight before her. The swells of Josiah's biceps made her clit tingle, but fucking him right this very moment was the farthest thing from her mind. She wanted his long tongue on her clit, in her pussy.

She whispered in his ear, "My poison tonight is, *een natte tong op mijn kut.*" A wet tongue on my pussy.

He smiled, then replied huskily, "Your every wish is my command, Mademoiselle." His bulging chest muscles and abs rippled. Even the sight of his thick forearms, lined with wide veins, made her pussy churn in delight. She imagined him using her naked body as his human bench-press, lifting her up over his head the way one would a set of one hundred-pound barbells.

Nairobia inhaled deeply and held it. She rubbed a smooth hand over his rock-hard pectorals, right before pushing out a warm gush of cinnamon-scented breath, slipping her tongue into his ear and telling him how her pussy whispered from beneath her gown, how it longed for his long, thick tongue. *"Mijn poes verlangt naar uw tong."*

He understood nothing she said, which made it that more alluring. *He will submit to me,* she told herself. *As they all will, offering me his tongue…and his big, thick cock, if I so desire it.*

Josiah disappeared from sight as a rich, sexy ballad filled the air. Nairobia blinked. Then a sly grin eased over her lips as she prowled around the bar. There he was. Lying on the tiled floor behind the bar on his back, his hands behind his head, his dick lying languidly across his rippled belly…

Mmm.